ALLIED FLAMES

THE KNOCKNASHEE STORY - BOOK 6

BY JEAN GRAINGER

Copyright © 2025 by By Jean Grainger

All rights reserved.

No part of this book may be reproduced in any form or by any electronic or mechanical means, including information storage and retrieval systems, without written permission from the author, except for the use of brief quotations in a book review.

NO AI TRAINING: Without in any way limiting the author's [and publisher's] exclusive rights under copyright, any use of this publication to train generative artificial intelligence (AI) technologies to generate text is expressly prohibited. The author reserves all rights to licence uses of this work for generative AI training and development of machine learning language models.

I dedicate this book to Mac and Mary, very special people whose real life friendship is an ongoing inspiration to me.

CHAPTER 1

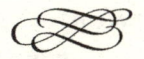

KNOCKNASHEE, COUNTY KERRY, IRELAND

APRIL 1943

My dearest Richard,
    I can call you 'my dearest' now, but...now that I can write, my heart breaks at the thought you will never read this letter. I can't believe you are gone. I know all the evidence suggests you are, but I just can't accept it. Deep in my heart, I can feel you around me and believe you are still with me. I hope so. I long for it to be true. Well, not really that, to be honest. What I really long for is for you to not be dead. But if that can't be, then at least you floating around me is better than you just being gone. And if you are here with me in spirit, I hope you can feel how much I miss you and can see me writing to you.
    It's strange to think I wrote my very first letter to you into the ether as well – and look how that worked out. I know it wasn't actually to you but to poor old St Jude, the patron saint of hopeless cases. I'm sure the unfortunate man is inundated with requests. And I bet all the other saints heaved a sigh of

relief when he got that job and were relieved to be asked only to find lost things, like Saint Anthony, or look after cats, like Saint Gertude. As Pádraig Ó Sé might say, 'Hopeless cases seems like a wicked-tough job.' And yet I pray every day to St Jude and St Anthony and any other saint who will listen, begging them to bring you back to me, even though I know that's an impossible task. A hopeless case. Like me and my sad hopeless grief that doesn't want to let you go, even though I know I must.

Life here in Knocknashee is trudging along, and I'm trying to be stoic and not look like one of those medieval paintings of women with long faces and sad eyes. Honestly, though, I don't think I'm making much of a job of it. Everyone is so kind to me, but I feel like I'm always mourning someone. People must think I'm a right Jonah – they're probably afraid to be near me in case they meet their end as well. But while they're all being so good, the trouble is, they don't really know you and they can't understand the connection we have. Richard, I can't bring myself to say 'had' – not yet. Not yet. They think I'll get over you quickly because we had so little time together. But I know the truth. I will never get over losing you. When I lost you, I lost me too. Every time something funny happens, or I have a bit of news, I make a mental note to include it in my next letter. Then it hits me all over again – you won't be there to read it.

And here's the worst thing. I didn't miss Declan the same way. I hate admitting it, even in a letter nobody will ever read, but it's true. I loved Declan. I truly did. But it wasn't like this. Not like it is with us.

I lie in bed at night and fantasise about our wedding. I imagine my dress, and what it would be like coming to the church here, with Father Iggy at the top of the altar and you standing there beside him, so tall and handsome. And I'd walk up on Maurice's arm – he'd give me away – with a bunch of flowers in my hands, and I wouldn't limp even a tiny bit (so this is not a very realistic dream, but that's the great thing about dreams, isn't it?). And you'd smile when you saw me, and everyone would turn to look and think 'doesn't poor little Grace Fitzgerald with the bad leg scrub up nicely?'

And everyone would be in the church, all our friends here, and your parents, and Sarah and Jacob and Nathan and Rebecca and their girls, and Mrs McHale.

And we'd say our vows.

Tilly would be beside me as my bridesmaid, in a pair of trousers, scandalising the parish, not for the first time of course. And there would be a wonderful wedding breakfast, but we'd just be wishing it to end so we could be alone.

And then we'd sneak away, up to my bedroom, and we'd lock the door and... Well, you know me, I can't write the next bit, but you can guess, I'm sure, what comes next.

Our long awaited day can't happen now. And knowing it gives me a physical pain in my heart. Because that's what it feels like, Richard. My heart is truly broken in half. I can mend it, and stick it back together in time, but it will never be the same. I'll never be the same. The Grace who fell in love with you all those years ago is gone, and the shell that's left will just have to carry on without you somehow.

And yet... No, my dearest darling, I know I shouldn't let my mind go to this. I can't give in to the terrible feeling in my soul that tempts me to hope you are not gone and will come back to me some day. I cannot afford to hope, Richard, because when reality sets in for good, I will lose you twice. And losing you once is already breaking me.

The children in the village have been so thoughtful. They all made cards and sent them to me. Everyone I meet sympathises, but they're just words. And I know they are genuine, and words are all anyone has, but they mean nothing. I have to bite my lip when people say God only takes the good ones young, or how brave you were, or how you are with my parents now, because I'm afraid of snapping and that wouldn't be right. People are doing their best.

Eleanor and Maurice are running the school, which is a relief. I don't think I can face the classroom just yet. Eleanor's husband, Douglas, has been moved to Gibraltar, apparently, but that's all she knows – the RAF are scant on details.

Tilly is staying down here in Knocknashee, though I know she'd much prefer to be in Dublin with Eloise. But she's afraid to leave me out of her sight in case I walk into the sea. Eloise went back last week. I think they thought it was too hard for me seeing them happy together, but it's not at all hard. Even if their relationship will always have to be covert, I'm glad they love each other. Same with Charlie and Dymphna, and Maurice and Patricia. They've all had their fair share of troubles and loss and deserve to be *happy. Other people being miserable won't make my heart less broken, but it feels like they don't want to flaunt their happiness under my nose. Everyone is worried about me. I wish they wouldn't.*

I'll sign off now, but I love you, my darling Richard, forever. You will always be with me, no matter what.

Your darling Grace xxx

Grace folded the letter and placed it in an envelope and then added it to the biscuit tin she used to store Richard's letters to her. She had stuffed her letters to him in it as well. His sister, Sarah, had brought them with her when she came to tell Grace the awful news.

It was probably silly, writing to a dead person, but she didn't care. Richard Lewis from Savannah, Georgia, began as her pen pal, then became her closest ally and eventually the man she loved. He loved her in return and would have been her second husband. A part of her wanted so hard to believe Richard wasn't dead, but she wouldn't give in to foolish false hope. Instead she'd deal with her grief in her own way. And if that meant writing letters to him, even if he would never read them, then so be it.

She strapped on her calliper and went downstairs.

'Prime Minister Churchill today, to celebrate twenty-five years of the Royal Air Force, was given his honorary wings. Here's a report from our London correspondent, John Mitchell.'

The gravelly lisping voice of Churchill coming from the big Pye radio on the windowsill of the empty kitchen was unmistakable. The cherry tree, in bloom another season, swayed in the gentle breeze in the back yard. Spring was bringing the peninsula to life again, and the idyllic finger of land that jutted into the Atlantic on Ireland's southwest coast looked fresh and clean and innocent once more, the whipping winds and raging tides of the winter forgotten.

The British prime minister went on. 'I am honoured to be accorded a place, albeit out of kindness, in that comradeship of the air which guards the life of our island and carries doom to tyrants, whether they flaunt themselves or burrow deep.'

Grace switched off the radio.

The wonderful RAF was not what she wanted to hear about today.

Because the truth was, for whatever doom and havoc they were wreaking on the Germans, Hitler's forces were doing the exact same thing in return. And Richard was one of their victims. The news never told you about the countless women just like her, in England, in Germany, in America and Italy and Australia and everywhere, whose hearts were just as broken as hers. The way they reported the news, it was as if all Allies did was kill Germans, with no casualties at all on their side, but she knew better.

'I'm sorry, Grace.' Patricia Fitzgerald, Grace's sister-in-law – a woman she barely knew – stood in the doorway. She was married to Grace's only brother, Maurice. The very brother who had left Knocknashee decades ago as an ordained priest, and somehow in the intervening years became laicised, got married to the girl he fell in love with when he was a seminarian in Cork, had two children and then landed himself and the whole family up on Grace's doorstep from the Philippines just last month.

The problem was that he'd chosen to share none of these life-changing developments with his only living sister. Grace had been angry with Maurice for excluding and abandoning her for so many years, but the news that Richard was dead had eclipsed everything else in the past weeks.

Patricia turned to leave. 'You're busy, Grace, I'll come back...'

'Patricia.' She knew she sounded weary, but she had no energy for soft-soaping anyone any more. 'I don't know how many more ways to say this, but this is your home now. I know you are trying to be considerate, but please, it doesn't help me to see you walking on eggshells around me and apologising for even existing. And the girls can play and make noise and leave their things around. I know you're trying to quieten them, but there's no need.'

'Well, I was just going to make Maurice and the girls some soup for lunch...'

Patricia had short dark hair – shorter than was usual for women her age – kind eyes and a slim, almost boyish figure. She was tiny compared to Maurice, who looked exactly like their father, tall and brawny, with red-gold hair and green eyes.

'Then go ahead and do that. I'll get out of your way.'

'Or you could stay and we could talk?'

Grace could see Patricia hesitate. The other woman was clearly nervous. *Oh, for goodness' sake.* Was she now the kind of person who made people nervous?

'Or if you'd rather be alone, I understand,' Patricia continued.

A wave of guilt hit Grace. Patricia must think her an awful person. She'd barely said a civil word to her sister-in-law in weeks. But nonetheless her instinct was to leave. She hadn't the energy for conversation. And anyway, words didn't help. If she stayed to chat, it might seem as though she wasn't going through this alone, but the reality was that she was very much on her own. This was not her first experience of sudden, tragic death. She had become a widow at just twenty-one. No indeed, she thought ruefully, she was a seasoned mourner. Despite this, Richard's death had been such a terrible shock.

'I could make an herbal tea?' Patricia offered. She and Maurice had spent years in the Philippines, which meant they had some odd ideas about things. One of these was making tea from anything other than black tea leaves.

Grace smiled at a memory. When Richard arrived in London to work as a war correspondent, he couldn't stand tea. But as the war wore on, with coffee no longer available and ground chicory root offered as the disgusting alternative, he had turned to tea. In the end he became quite a lover of it.

Sometimes Grace forgot Richard was American. But then, every so often, something would come up between them. Like how he thought her brother's name was pronounced like the French name Maurice. He'd wondered why Eddie and Kathy Fitzgerald, her late parents, had chosen a French name for their son. Grace had to explain that in Ireland the name was a translation of Muiris and pronounced more like Morris.

'Grace?' Patricia's voice startled her. This happened a lot – she would go off on a thought, a memory, and time around her stood still.

'I'm sorry. I was miles away. Yes, please, tea would be nice.' Grace forced a smile. It felt unnatural to smile now, like those muscles were as stiff and sore as her gammy leg.

Patricia brewed tea with some chamomile flowers and a clump of mint that she kept in a tin jar. To Grace's surprise, it was very nice.

Grace got a pang of conscience. Her sister-in-law was trying her best to help, to get to know her, to make herself useful. 'How about we chop the vegetables for the soup after this?' she suggested. 'You do the spuds, and I'll do the carrots and parsnips. I think we've an onion too. And we have a shin bone in the larder, so we could boil it for broth to give it a bit of flavour?'

'That would be ideal.' The other woman seemed relieved.

'So how is it being back? Has it changed much here, do you think?' Grace asked as they sipped their tea.

Patricia pursed her lips in thought. 'Honestly, it's hard to say. I was only sixteen when I was sent to England in disgrace.' She gave a rueful chuckle.

'Do you want to tell me the whole story?' Grace said, glad to be off the subject of her own grief. 'I heard something, but not everything.'

'Are you sure? I don't mind telling you, but you've enough to be –'

'I'd like to hear about someone else for a change.' She smiled. 'Please, tell me.'

'Well, all right then. You know we lived in the seminary? Mam was the cook and my dad was the caretaker, and they relied on the order for their living. When the priest in charge of the seminary found out Maurice and I had become close, they had to ship me out, on pain of losing their jobs and their home. Fraternising with the seminarians was a mortal sin as far as they were concerned. We were just kids, innocent really, but they didn't see it like that. I was treated like some kind of conniving temptress, and Maurice was like a lamb to the slaughter in the face of my womanly wiles.' She sighed a little sadly.

'Where did you go?' Grace felt a wave of sympathy for Patricia's poor sixteen-year-old self, exiled from her home and country for the crime of falling in love with a boy.

'I was lucky, to be honest. There was talk of sending me to a laundry for "fallen" women. But my mam pleaded against that, and I was sent to my Auntie Bea in England. She had lots of little ones, so I helped her and finished school.'

'And stayed in touch with Maurice?'

Patricia blushed slightly. 'Well, I had no way of keeping in touch with him – they made sure of that, and my mother and father would never have given him my address. I'd caused enough of a ruckus by being friends with him in the first place. But I wrote to a friend of his – he told me his friend Johnny Clafferty lived in Cahir, County Tipperary. So I wrote to Johnny and gave him my aunt's address, asking him to pass it on to Maurice.'

'And did he?' Grace found she was fascinated. There had been no opportunity to ask the details of her brother's romance with his wife given everything that had happened since they arrived.

'He had a terrible crisis of conscience, the poor lad. He knew all the trouble that was caused, and Maurice had decided he was going to take his final vows by then, so he didn't send it on. Not for years.'

'Really? That's awful.'

'Sure, he was only trying to do the right thing.' Patricia paused as if contemplating whether she should go on. 'Grace, I know Maurice should have told you about us. He could have written, but he was sure you'd be just like your sister and –' She looked flustered, as if she shouldn't have said anything. 'I just mean…not that Agnes was –'

'No. I know. Agnes was the reason Maurice went back to the seminary that time he came home to tell Mammy and Daddy he hadn't a vocation. I knew he never wanted to take his vows. My father didn't want it for him either, although I only found that out recently.'

'Well, then you know all the upset it caused. Not just to Maurice, but to me and my family also.'

Grace heard a sharpness in Patricia's tone that unsettled her. Patricia clearly blamed Agnes for much of their troubles. Did she also blame Grace by association?

'So how did you and Maurice finally meet again?' she asked gently.

Patricia sighed. 'Johnny Clafferty's mother died, and Maurice heard and wrote to his old friend to offer his condolences. He'd been sent to Manila by then, and Johnny was a curate in Dublin – this was a few years after they were ordained.' She took a sip of her tea. 'Johnny wrote back, asking Maurice how he was getting on, and Maurice replied with the truth, that he hated it, he wasn't cut out for it and he really regretted letting them bully him into the clergy.'

'And Johnny decided then to give him your address?'

'Yes. He said he was warned at the time not to do or say anything to encourage his friend in his foolishness. That it would be bad for both of them if he did. But he went against them, albeit later, and told Maurice where I was.'

'And so Maurice wrote to you?'

'He did. By then I was nursing in Bristol. I was doing a line with a chap from there – it was assumed we'd marry. My aunt got the letter, and she decided not to tell me – partly out of loyalty to my mother and partly because she thought it would only throw a spanner into the works and it was best left alone.'

Grace found herself curious despite everything. 'So what happened?'

Patricia smiled. 'One of my cousins I looked after – Bea's son Conal – always had a soft spot for me. He was younger than me, but by this time I was in my early twenties and he was seventeen. He found the letter and confronted my aunt, said she had no right to keep a letter from me, that I was a grown adult and it was my own business.'

'And she gave in?'

Her sister-in-law chuckled. 'You don't know the women in my family – they don't do as they're told by anyone.'

'So how did you manage to make contact again?' Grace wondered at how she'd never known any of this. Did Agnes have any inkling? Surely not, but then with Agnes it was hard to know. If she had any idea, she would never have mentioned it, for fear of scandal.

'Conal knew that my Auntie Bea would never give me the letter, and she'd know if he took it, so he waited till she was at Mass, found it and copied out the address and the gist of the letter for me.'

'And what did it say?'

Patricia blushed. 'Well, just along the lines that Maurice had never forgotten me, that he was leaving the priesthood – he was not right for it, as he'd always known he wasn't – and that if I wanted to contact him, that was the address.'

'And you did?' Grace watched as a robin landed on the cherry tree – to her, always a sign that loved ones were near.

Patricia pursed her lips again, something Grace realised she did when she was considering something. 'I thought long and hard, to be honest with you. Jonathan, the lad I was going out with, was really nice, and I knew he'd probably produce the ring by that Christmas, and if I hadn't heard from Maurice, I would have said yes. I flip-flopped between writing and not – I can't tell you how many attempts wound up in the bin – but in the finish, I posted one. Just saying how it was good to hear from him and I hoped he was all right, and that I was doing fine over in England. I didn't mention Jonathan, and I gave Maurice the address I was staying at. I was living in nurses' halls of residence at the hospital.'

'Then what happened?'

'Well, then we began writing. And there's something about writing letters – it kind of allows you to say things you might not say face to face? I don't know...'

Grace did know. She understood exactly. She and Richard had only met in person a handful of times, but they had built up such a strong bond through letters over the five years they had written to each other that it was as if they knew each other inside out.

'After a few months, he asked if I'd consider moving there, to the Philippines. He could get me a job in the hospital in Manila. Despite being in the process of laicisation, he was on very good terms with the hierarchy there. They understood him and accepted his decision.'

'But you couldn't be together?'

'No, not until everything was done. But he told the bishop – a lovely man who was a great mentor to Maurice – and he gave his blessing for me to go over. On the proviso, of course, that we didn't begin a relationship until he was free to do so.'

'So how did that go down with Jonathan and your family?'

A shadow of pain crossed the other woman's thin face. She was not beautiful in any conventional sense, but there were kindness and empathy in her eyes. She was clearly also resilient. 'Jonathan was very sad, but he understood when I explained. My parents never spoke to me again.'

'Oh, Patricia, I'm so sorry...' Grace felt her pain.

Patricia nodded, her lips pursed. 'Mam died last year. Dad two years before her. My sister wrote, said it killed them, what I did. That they were so ashamed, mortified that I would take an ordained priest from the Church. They were let go from their jobs in the seminary and lost their house too – it was part of the job, you see. I tried to explain. I wrote so many times but never got a reply. I don't know if they ever read them.'

Grace instinctively reached across and took Patricia's hand in hers.

'Neither of us felt we had any support,' Patricia continued. 'Your sister made her feelings on the matter very clear to Maurice when he said he wanted to leave, and he knew him being a priest meant the world to your mother. My family shunned me. So we just thought it was best for us to stay away, start our own family in Manila and let the past be in the past.'

Patricia's story hit Grace hard. She had never considered how the scandal might have affected Patricia's family, or how her family, like Agnes, might have rejected the couple's decision. She had a better understanding now why her brother had made no contact as long as Agnes was alive. Judging by his wife's family's reaction, they must have felt nobody here would accept them. Grace was sure that wouldn't have been the case with the Fitzgeralds. She was certain her father would have welcomed them. Mammy was not a hard-hearted woman, and though it would have been a shock, and to a certain degree a disappointment, Grace was sure she would have come around to the idea in the end too. But Agnes would never have forgiven him, and Maurice had excluded Grace because he had lumped her in with Agnes. He didn't know her, to be fair, so perhaps his assumption was reasonable, but Grace still found herself getting angry at the thought that he'd imagined her solely as a younger version of Agnes. He could have checked.

'Well, I understand now a bit better how things were for you,' she said to Patricia, 'and I appreciate you trusting me. It's a hard story to tell.'

Patricia gave her a sad, pale smile. 'And I understand too why you're upset,' she said. 'You've a right to be angry with Maurice for lying to you all these years, Grace. Besides, you've had so much to be sad and angry about yourself. All we can do now is go forward and try not to get bitter.'

'I know, and you're right, but it's hard, isn't it?' She heard the wobble in her own voice.

'Very,' her sister-in-law said, and gave Grace's hand a gentle squeeze.

CHAPTER 2

Grace and Patricia worked companionably alongside each other, a new warmth between them as they chopped vegetables for the soup and chatted about Patricia and Maurice's two girls. Molly and Kathleen – now going by her Irish name, Cáit – had started in Knocknashee National School. Maurice too was doing fine. He had been a teacher in Manila at a large boys' school there, so he was qualified, and though he was rusty on the Irish curriculum, Eleanor Worth, the other teacher, was very helpful.

The clatter of something falling into the letterbox cut through their conversation.

'I'll go,' Patricia said.

Grace decided she would finish the soup and then soak in the bath. Her polio was much better these days, but if she skimped on her hot baths and exercises, within a few days, she would feel the ache again.

'It's for you.' Patricia offered Grace the heavy cream envelope with her name typed on the front and three American stamps in the corner, so neatly aligned it looked as though they had been placed with a set square.

Grace put down the peeling knife and the carrot she was holding and wiped her hands on a tea towel before taking the envelope from

Patricia. Her heart raced. What was this? Richard was the only American she knew who would be writing to her. Unless it was Sarah, his sister? But she wouldn't type Grace's name – she would handwrite it. All Grace's instincts screamed that Richard was still alive, and as she held the cream envelope, she felt a small but powerful flutter of hope in her heart. Had there been some mistake? Perhaps Richard was not dead? Maybe he never went up with the US Air Force to witness a bomber mission over Germany that night? Maybe he got injured only and was in a hospital somewhere? Maybe he was captured? Maybe he'd parachuted out of the plane as it crashed, and they'd had word he was still alive? The mere thought of such a possibility made her feel dizzy with anticipation.

Stop! She slumped into a chair by the kitchen table.

Richard and Jacob Nunez, his brother-in-law, were both dead. They were flying in a B17 over Germany, and a Luftwaffe plane strafed them; the fuel caught fire and the plane crashed and burnt. There were no survivors. To think otherwise was foolish and, ultimately, the road to even more heartbreak. Richard, like all the others she had loved, was gone. She had to accept it. Why could her stupid, stubborn heart not agree?

She focused herself and opened the envelope. It contained a black-rimmed card and a note, which Grace scanned quickly.

Dear Grace,

I hope I can call you Grace, though we've never met. My name is Arthur Lewis, and I'm Richard's father. We are holding a memorial service for Richard and Jacob, Sarah's husband, here in Savannah in June, and I would be very happy if you could attend. I know how much you meant to my son and how you two were planning your wedding. I won't offer you my condolences, because to do so would suggest I sympathize more than empathize. So instead I offer you the opportunity to grieve here at his childhood home with us, his parents and his siblings.

If you can come, I will arrange and pay for passage for you and anyone you would like to bring for support and will arrange all of your accommodations. There will be no expense to you. Please just telegram to the above address with your response. (Apologies if this is crass—I'm not familiar with how things are done over there. We tend to be straight-talkers here in Georgia.)

Kind regards,

Arthur Lewis

She put the note down and picked up the card. It was embossed, with a photograph of Richard, smiling, his hair blowing slightly in the breeze.

In loving memory was written in gold letters above the photograph, and below in the same gold lettering:

Arthur and Caroline Lewis request your presence at the memorial service for their son Richard, shot down by enemy fire over Germany.
23rd June 1943
Christ Church Savannah.

Tears flowed down Grace's cheeks. Somehow this was worse, more final, than any official notification of Richard's death. His own family were acknowledging he was gone. So why did she find it so difficult to do?

'What is it?' Patricia asked tentatively.

Grace handed her the invitation and the letter, which Patricia read before giving it back to Grace with a sad smile.

'That's nice, I suppose. It's important to have some...well, an event...something to mark his death.'

Grace had found Patricia's manner a little off-putting at the beginning. Patricia was a very forthright person. She spoke without guile or preamble; she said things as she saw them, no euphemisms. She used the words 'dead' and 'death', not 'passed on' or 'with God' or 'in heaven' the way other people did, and Grace found she appreciated it. Other people were trying to be gentle, she knew, but it was as if nobody could say the words, and for it to be real, it needed to be verbalised.

'It's nice of them to ask me, certainly...'

'Will you go?' The other woman was as forthright as usual.

'Ah no, I don't know them. I only met his sister, Sarah, once, and I was in no fit state to talk to her then.' She sighed and put the card and letter back in the envelope. 'But it was kind of them to include me. I'm sure it was just a formality on their part, but I appreciate it.'

Patricia looked unconvinced. 'I think he sounded sincere, like he really wanted you to go. And if he's going to pay…? You said Richard's family were well-off, didn't you?'

Grace nodded. 'They are, but I couldn't take advantage like that. Anyway, I don't think I could… I'll telegram and gratefully decline.'

Patricia stared at her intently. It made her uncomfortable. It was as if the woman could sense the vain flutter of hope still beating in Grace's heart that would not allow her to accept Richard's death.

'Maybe take a few days to think about it?' Patricia said at last. 'Maurice can manage the school with Mrs Worth's help. And you could take someone with you. Tilly maybe?'

'No.' She pulled herself up from the kitchen chair to face her sister-in-law. 'I know you mean well, Patricia, but I just couldn't face it. Thank you, but I won't be going to Savannah.'

'All right.' Patricia went back to the soup. 'It's your choice, of course, but maybe just sleep on it.'

Grace didn't reply. She had no intention of crossing the ocean again. She couldn't think of anything worse than being around Richard's family without him, having to share their grief, having them look at her withered leg and wonder what on earth handsome, rich, wonderful Richard saw in a girl like her. It would be too hard to bear. No, if Richard was dead, she would grieve for him here in Knocknashee for the rest of her life.

CHAPTER 3

TWENTY MILES SOUTH OF STRASBOURG, FRANCE

APRIL 1943

'I didn't believe it when they told me, but here you are, like a pair of bad pennies.'

The bearded man, who looked like he had a year's worth of grime on him, chuckled. His jacket and moleskin trousers were dark, shiny with dirt, and he wore an open-necked collarless shirt that may have been white at some point in the far distant past.

'Sorry it took me so long to get here. I wasn't in the area, and shall we say, communication and travel are a bit tricky these days. But our people are looking after you all right, I'm sure.'

Richard sat up from his makeshift bed. He and Jacob were being hidden in a barn filled with bales of hay, and a little room had been built into the middle, so even if someone came to inspect, hundreds of bales would have to be removed to get to them. The secret space was accessed by a narrow passageway, but only the family hiding them, the Ducrots, knew which bales to move to access it. Richard had had to fight feelings of claustrophobia at first, but he was increasingly grateful for the safety, and their hideout was surprisingly comfortable. Day and night were the same, the murky gloom keeping them in a state of eerie twilight. The sweet smell of hay and the squeaking of burrowing rodents were his constant companions. They had made two beds of more bales, and the farmer's wife, Madame Ducrot, had given them some sacking to use as blankets. They had a bucket to relieve themselves, and once a week, she gave them a bucket of water for washing. Richard had a full beard now, and his hair was long enough to tie in a ponytail. He'd lost weight, he knew; the flight suit the air force had given him, his only clothing, hung off him. The daily ration of bread, some milk and a piece of cheese was not enough, but the Germans took almost everything the Ducrot farm produced so the old couple were feeding them from their own miserable rations.

He had at first wondered how the Nazis allowed them to keep such a huge store of animal feed and bedding, until the young woman who'd delivered them here, who spoke good English, explained that the milk, cheese and cream the farm produced were all confiscated to feed the Germans stationed nearby. Up until the invasion, the Ducrots had never seen a machine for baling hay, but apparently the Germans provided one, complete with a lecture on the superiority of German engineering, all with a view to increasing production. They came every week with a truck to collect, leaving only the meagre leftovers for the Ducrots.

Since he and Jacob had crash-landed three weeks ago, they'd been moved from place to place, but now they were here with the Ducrots for the foreseeable future. It was safer to sleep by day and be awake by night. During the day, it was critical never to make a sound. Madame Ducrot, the farmer's wife who had almost as much of a beard as Richard had himself, insisted on total silence by day, despite the wall of bales. To add to the terror for the elderly Ducrots, a German officer was billeted in their house, so having Richard and Jacob in the barn was so courageous. They were an older couple, and they had a son who was mentally impaired. So under no circumstances must he, their son, Antoine, see them either.

'Alfie?' Richard gasped. Was he imagining it? Surely not? The Irish accent was the only thing that identified the man. His hair was an indistinguishable colour, long and straggly, and his beard was flame-red. Gone was the good-looking athletic man they'd known in Paris; this guy looked like the hobos who rode the railroads back home. Richard looked closer. He had the same dark-grey eyes, though, and when he smiled, he showed his crooked front tooth. It was Alfie O'Hare all right.

'Well, it's not the king of England.' Alfie laughed.

'How did you...?' Richard was breathless; the exertion of talking took a lot out of him. The injuries he'd sustained when he parachuted out should have killed him – he broke so many bones and lost a lot of blood – but mercifully the local maquisards brought him and Jacob to a safe house and patched them up. This farm was their seventh move. Or maybe their eighth.

'Well, Richard, apparently you asked about me, and you mentioned Didier Georges too.' He raised a disapproving eyebrow, clearly this was not something he was happy about. 'You were delirious, and you're a lucky boy that Gilles who found you isn't trigger-happy, because that's dangerous talk. But they knew you were Americans, and word went out that someone was looking for me. I was a hundred miles away give or take, but two big, thick Yanks parachuting into occupied Germany who knew me by name? Well, I decided it could only be you two.'

Alfie pulled up a bale of hay and sat on it. Jacob was sleeping. Richard nudged him with his good foot; the other one had a broken ankle and hurt like hell.

Alfie took a packet of cigarettes from the breast pocket of his filthy jacket, but to Richard's relief, he didn't light up, just left it hanging between his lips. Smoking in a hay barn was inadvisable.

'So, you got my attention.' Alfie sucked on the untipped cigarette, and Richard noticed he had no fingernails on his right hand. The blood had congealed and scabbed over, but his hands looked malformed now. He shuddered to think how that happened. 'What the hell are you two doing here?'

Jacob stirred and groaned as he turned. Like Richard, he was in a bad way physically, not helped by the constant moves from one safe house to the next. They never knew what was happening, but they did exactly as they were told, when they were told to do it, because there was no doubt in their minds that these people were all that stood between them and the Germans. A pair of Americans would be a nice prize, and judging by the scars on Alfie's hands, and the evidence of the Germans' heinous handiwork on others who had helped them as well, death would be the preferred option if they were caught.

Alfie cocked his head at Jacob and raised a questioning eyebrow.

'His leg is broken. So is his wrist and probably some ribs. It was set after we crash-landed, but not by anyone who knew what they were doing. Some guy came last night to reset it. We had to chloroform him to keep him still, so he's still out of it.'

Alfie seemed unperturbed; this was just how life was now. 'Are you all right?'

'I don't know. Everything hurts, but' – Richard shrugged – 'I'm alive, I guess.'

'For now.' Alfie chuckled. 'How come there's just the two of you?'

'We were sent up with a crew of ten. We were supposed to write eye-witness accounts of a bombing mission. There were some journalists on each of the planes that night. Jacob and I were the only non–air force people on ours. Well, normally there would be ten – pilot, copilot, navigator, bombardier and gunners. So two gunners were left off to put me and Jacob up. We were flying in formation with six other planes.'

'And Jerry shot you down?' Alfie exhaled again. The heat and the smell of their unwashed bodies, mingling with the even more pungent body odour coming from Alfie, in the confined space were making Richard feel nauseous.

'Yes. I don't know if anyone survived from the other planes. We got the order to bail out and we did. Two gunners and the navigator died before we could get out, same for the pilot and copilot, being in the cockpit – the bomber was in flames – but the bombardier and two other gunners parachuted out as well. I think one is dead and two survived, but I'm not sure. I think that's what the people who picked us up said. You remember how terrible my French is.'

Alfie laughed.

'But once they figured out we were both Americans, they decided to keep us together, I guess. The other guys, I don't know where they are. I think Jacob landed a few miles from me. I thought he was gone when I was picked up. A few days later, I was staying in a convent and he showed up with some girls, barely teenagers, and the nuns did their best to patch us up.'

'Yeah, the two gunners made it. The bombardier died of his burns a few hours after he was picked up. Pity.' Alfie shrugged like the man had missed the bus, not lost his life, but Richard guessed there wasn't much room for sentimentality in Alfie's business these days. 'Tell me, how are things in Knocknashee?' Richard thought he detected a touch of softness in the other man's voice.

'Good. Odile is thriving. She's so funny and cute, speaks English and French as well as Irish. Tilly speaks Irish to her, Grace in English, and Eloise in French.'

'Who's Eloise?' Alfie asked, his brow furrowed.

'Ah…Tilly's friend…' Richard didn't know how much Alfie understood about his sister, and it wasn't his place to say. He coloured a bit and cursed his blundering. He needn't have worried.

'So she finally found herself a woman, did she? Fair play to her. And my mother? Is she all right?'

Richard nodded. 'Worried sick about you, but she keeps saying that if you died, she'd know. She has a sense for these things, so she knows you're not dead. Oh, and she got a note from some pal of yours, Nico Gomez, who said you were seen and were alive.'

'By God, eh? Nico and I are old mates from the Franco days. I thought that fascist gobshite was the worst the world had to offer, but no, it seems not. I never thought that Dutchman I gave the note to would do it, didn't think he'd make it across the mountains to be honest. He was in a right state, but he must have been tougher than he looked.'

Jacob moaned and looked like he might sit up, but the effort proved too much and he lay back down again.

'What about you? And Constance and Bernadette?'

'Well, as you can see, I'm still standing, though how, I've no idea, to be truthful with you. Didi told you we busted out of jail in Paris?'

Richard nodded, moving his aching ankle. Apart from that, he was on the mend, he thought. Bruised and battered, but he'd be OK. He wasn't so sure about Jacob.

'Well, I've been here and there since, trying to stay out of trouble.' Alfie winked, and Richard knew he was doing nothing of the kind. He had the distinct impression that once he'd mentioned Alfie's and Didier's names, they were treated as much more important patients than previously. He didn't know for sure, but he'd bet his shirt on the fact that Alfie wasn't just laying low waiting for the war to end.

'Constance is OK. She was arrested a few months ago. They treated her fairly badly, and she won't ever be the same again, but she's OK. She and I are still together.' His voice took on hardness then, the avuncular, cheeky way he had gone. 'We had something fairly damning on the arresting commandant, so she was released.'

'And Bernadette?'

Alfie shook his head. 'Nothing, a few possible sightings, but it came to nothing.'

'We always hoped, for Odile...' Richard remembered Bernadette as a short, blond, curvy, cheerful new mother. She'd looked at her husband, Paul, with such adoration, and Richard remembered wondering if anyone would ever look at him like that.

Alfie shrugged. 'After Paris, Constance and I joined with a group, lived in the Bois de Boulogne for a while, caused a bit of havoc. But I got picked up, Didi and myself and a few others. Once we busted out, we had to go south. We went down by Biarritz, met up with some people there, got involved with moving people' – he took the cigarette from his mouth and returned it to its packet – 'into neutral Spain. I know that territory a bit, since the war in '36. But then I was needed over here, so we've been in Lyon for a while, making a bit of trouble for Klaus Barbie. He's the head of Gestapo in Lyon since last November. A sadist. He's another one that will get his comeuppance, just you wait and see.'

Though Richard liked Alfie enormously, something about the way he spoke now gave him a chill. Gone was the happy-go-lucky Irishman; this person before him was every bit as ruthless as the enemy he faced.

CHAPTER 4

'So what do we do now?' Richard asked.

Alfie snorted. 'Do?' He cast a disparaging glance in Jacob's direction.

'Well, can we get out? Can your people help us to get to Spain or…?'

Alfie raised a quizzical eyebrow. 'Richard, we're old friends. So that's the reason you two weren't left for the Nazi dogs to chew on. But let's just face reality here for a second. You have a smashed ankle and are battered head to toe. Your man Jacob here is touch and go as to whether he's going to make it at all. Neither of you is in a position to go anywhere. Getting out of occupied France nowadays, even in the whole of your health, is close to impossible. The border crossings are heavily guarded. You might be Americans, and that might have helped your cause last time you were here, but you are the enemy now, so like the rest of us, you are just rats in a barrel. And he's a Jew, to add another layer of excitement. So even if I could consider trying to get you out now – which I won't be doing – it's not just a matter of taking a few sandwiches and heading off up into the mountains, whistling as you go.'

Richard swallowed his shame and frustration. He knew it would be difficult, but he had to get out of here. All he'd been able to think about since he woke up after crashing was how Grace must think he was dead, and after all she'd been through, he couldn't bear to think of her grieving again. 'I know that, but I need to get back...we need to get back. I'm engaged to Grace Fitzgerald...'

'Are you now? Well, isn't that a turn up for the books? She's sound, Grace. I always liked her when she was knocking around with our Tilly. Better than that sour lemon of a sister of hers, that's for sure.'

'She's dead,' Richard said.

Alfie grimaced, and sucked on his unlit cigarette.

'Well, I'll shed no tears for her. She was a cranky auld bat. But now to more pressing matters.' Alfie indicated towards Jacob. 'He's in no shape to go anywhere, and you're not much better by the looks of you, so for now anyway, you'll stay put here for as long as Madame Ducrot will have you and be grateful for it. They're taking a huge risk with you two here. Your man they have staying is all right, as they go. But he's not going to hesitate to blow the whistle if he gets even a whisper of you. The Ducrots will be shot if they're caught, and poor Antoine, God knows what would happen to him...'

He stopped talking and raised a finger. The very faint hum of an engine could be heard. Silently Alfie put his finger to his lips. The bales that formed the door to the little secret room had been replaced by Monsieur Ducrot when Alfie arrived, so they were sealed in, which meant all sound was muffled.

They could hear voices, though, shouting. The car engine stopped. Dogs barked. It might be the Ducrot dogs; they had two Border collies, one ancient, one sprightly. Antoine adored them both and they him; Richard could sometimes hear him playing with them, him laughing and them barking. But it could also be the German Shepherd dogs that accompanied so many Nazis. The voices came closer, still too hard to distinguish, and even if Richard could make out the words, he wouldn't understand them. The Ducrots were peasant people who spoke with the Alsatian intonation in their French.

Slowly Alfie pulled a pistol from inside his trousers. He lifted one foot and placed it on a bale, then slid a knife from a sheath attached to his lower leg and handed it to Richard. He leant his back against the wall of hay, facing the entrance that would be created if the bales blocking the access were removed. He gestured for Richard to get behind him. There was an old sack on the floor that Alfie threw over Jacob, covering his head and body.

The dogs barked manically, and the raised higher voice of Madame Ducrot could be heard. This was not a routine call to collect provisions; something was wrong. Richard's heart thumped in his chest. Surely this wasn't the end, after surviving so much?

The sounds became louder – they were in the barn, the dogs still barking. And Richard could make out a German giving some loud instructions. Monsieur Ducrot spoke, and Alfie nodded silently; he must have thought the old Frenchman said the right thing. A gunshot, followed by a scream. Richard met Alfie's eyes. What was happening? No way to know.

The exchanges outside seemed to go on for long minutes. First Madame Ducrot, then they could make out Monsieur Ducrot speaking, the tone suggesting he was trying to calm things down. And howling – which could have been Antoine. Then the voices receded, and so did the barking. They heard an engine firing up and a vehicle driving away.

Richard went to move, but Alfie shook his head, raising a single finger, the gun still cocked. They stood still for what seemed like fifteen or twenty minutes. Richard had no watch, so it was hard to know; his had been lost somewhere along the way.

The bales were moved, the only sounds a scurrying from the furry inhabitants and the grunting of Monsieur Ducrot at the exertion of lifting them.

Then he was there, small, sweating, his face white. He looked like a boy more than a man, skin and bone, no taller than five feet, with a bald head and soft, gentle eyes. He had a slight stoop, but his arms were wiry and sinewed. He and Alfie exchanged words in rapid French.

Alfie's face expressed sadness, and then he turned to Richard. 'They shot the old dog of Antoine's. He's inconsolable. It was a routine call apparently. That's what they said anyway, but the Germans never do anything off the cuff. Everything is planned, a reason for everything. This was a muscle-flexing exercise, a shot across the bow to the Ducrots to do as they're told or next time it won't just be a dog.'

'Should we move?' Richard asked, but Alfie shook his head.

'Too risky. No, stay here, a month or so, see how he is...' He nodded at Jacob, who had hardly moved. 'Exercise that ankle once you think it's healed. Push-ups, lift bales, lift each other, run on the spot, every exercise you can think of. Whatever you do, don't just lie down all day. You'll be weak as water if you do, and there's no chance I'll try to get you out if you're not physically strong enough for it.'

Richard tried not to gasp in horror. A month in here? No books, no paper, nothing to do, barely enough to eat, no natural light? But he forced himself to calm down. He was safe and stood at least a chance of getting back to Grace. And Alfie was right – the Ducrots were taking an unfathomable risk in helping them. He should be grateful. And he was. But a whole month? And what if Jacob didn't improve? What then?

Alfie seemed able to read his mind, and as the old man turned and left back through the passageway, he said, 'I know. It's not easy. But believe me, the alternative is a hell of a lot worse.'

'Could I get some paper, maybe, and a pencil?' Richard asked.

Alfie shook his head. 'Too dangerous, no way to dispose of it if you're found. You can't risk burning anything here – the whole place would go up like a tinderbox. I'll see if I can get you a French book and maybe a dictionary – bury them in a bale when you're not using them. You should teach yourself the language, it would help.'

This was far from ideal, but he knew it was the best Alfie could do.

'Thanks. Once Jacob comes around, we'll exercise and try to learn a bit more French.' He shook Alfie's hand. 'I mean it, Alfie, I'm very grateful. I know we're a problem you don't need.'

'Well, I can't face Grace Fitzgerald if I let you die, and your mate there is a good lad too. I liked him in Paris – he's committed. And Didi told me about all the work you were doing in London with refugees, and writing articles to encourage Americans into the war, so it's quid pro quo.' He made to leave, and Richard hated the bereft feeling.

'I'll see if we can get some books to you, but promise me you'll find a way to hide them in case you are found.' He paused and fixed Richard with a look that spoke volumes. Sympathy, kindness, but also grit and sheer bloody-mindedness. 'If you are, for the love of God, don't say a word. It's hard, I won't lie. They have ways of getting information out of people.' He held up his mangled fingers. 'Nobody here knows my real name. They call me Felix, and I'd prefer to keep it that way. Richard, if they find you, they *will* torture you.' Alfie's eyes burnt with something Richard couldn't identify. Rage? Fear? Exhaustion? Probably all three. 'And they'll promise it will stop if you tell them, but once you do, they'll just shoot you. They won't even bother deporting you, so nothing will be gained for you by talking, but you'd be sentencing a lot of good, brave people to death. So, try your best not to.'

His insides twisted in fear, Richard could only nod as Alfie O'Hare left the hay bunker and the bales were pushed back into place.

CHAPTER 5

SAVANNAH, GEORGIA

Sarah Lewis was only half listening as her mother droned on about flowers for the memorial they were organising. As if any of it mattered. Jacob and Richard were dead, and Caroline Lewis was focused on trivia. She never mentioned Richard at all; it was as if nothing had happened. To listen to her, you'd think she was organising a wedding, not a memorial for her dead son and son-in-law. Sarah knew her mother was bad at the emotional side of things, but this was beyond contempt. That said, Caroline had paid scant attention to Richard when he was alive, so perhaps it was not unexpected that she seemed incapable of acknowledging him in death. And she had detested Sarah's husband, Jacob.

Sarah was just back from New York, where she'd visited Samuel, Jacob's favourite uncle, who was a jeweller in Manhattan. It had been a strange meeting. Uncle Samuel had the thickest New York accent Sarah had ever heard. Jacob had never brought her when he had visited his uncle, and she'd wondered if it was because she was a gentile. But it was not as if she could ask Samuel about it, so she would never know. Then he offered her a string of pearls as a gift, which she felt obliged to take. He'd gone on and on about his son, Chaim, who was worse than useless apparently, and would never take over the business. He had planned to give it all to Jacob, but now he couldn't. This seemed to cause him more distress than the loss of his nephew, but Sarah knew that Uncle Samuel was, in Jacob's words, 'emotionally constipated', and gave him the benefit of the doubt that he was sad at Jacob's death.

'He's a schmuck, that kid,' the old man had said as he pottered around his shop, his white hair sticking out in all directions, the bags under his eyes giving him the look of a bloodhound. 'I told him! Going over there, getting his ass shot off for nothin'. My old man got outta that dump, came over here, and he'd turn in his grave if he knew his grandson was volunteerin' to get back there. His ma, my sister Deborah, all day long kvetchin' and cryin', tellin' me to talk him out of it. But you know what Jacob was like – nobody could tell him nothin'. And now look at him – dead.'

Sarah had fought back the tears. She'd been expecting something else. She didn't know what…but something. A way to feel connected to Jacob, to be part of his world, even if he couldn't be part of hers any more.

'Sarah, honestly, you're miles away. Is the pink too…festive? Black ribbons on gardenias feels wrong…' Caroline was making a list for the florist and stood before her daughter in the drawing room of their Savannah house, waiting expectantly for an answer.

Sarah looked at her mother – *really* looked – trying to find a trace of grief, a telltale puff around the eyes from crying, a smudge in her perfectly applied make-up, but there was nothing. Her dark hair was in a chignon at the nape of her neck, and she wore a grey day dress, fitted to the waist, knee-length, square-necked, dark-grey linen buttons, expertly tailored, and patent black shoes, short heels. At her neck and throat, perfect pearls. Not cultured, she pointed out over breakfast this morning; they were natural pearls from Western Australia. The pearl was formed by a natural irritant, not an injected one as with cultured pearls.

Sarah had muttered something to her mother about knowing all about irritants. She knew it was childish of her, and her father had shot her a warning glance across the table, but she felt like she wanted to lash out. Her mother was driving her crazy.

Caroline constantly criticised Sarah's clothes, her hair, everything about her, how she cared nothing for grooming. Three times her mother made her appointments at the salon. Three times Sarah didn't show up. Instead she wore an old, battered US Air Force khaki-green combat shirt of Jacob's every day. Jacob was a journalist, so Sarah had no idea where he had gotten the combat shirt. The tape sewn over the right breast pocket, where the name would be, was ripped off, but she had found the name STILLER written in pen on the inside collar. Sarah wondered who Stiller was. Had he caused the big ink stain on the bottom of one of the pockets where someone put a pen in and it leaked, or was that Jacob?

Knowing Jacob, she reckoned he had found it in a dumpster or picked it up leaving a party. In all the time she had known him, he had never once bought new clothes. Even the suit he – grudgingly – wore for their wedding was borrowed from a friend of Nathan's, who was slight like he was. The men in Sarah's family towered over Jacob, so nothing they had would fit him, and he would never waste the money on something like a suit. The shirt still smelled vaguely of him. Caroline had begged her to throw it out, but she never would.

Coming back home, although she'd promised Richard she would, was a massive mistake. Her father was kind and doing his best, but he was devastated about Richard and had no experience with showing his emotions. He tried to sympathise with her about Jacob, but every time he did, it sounded awkward and forced, and eventually, to the relief of both of them, he stopped.

'Maybe grey?' Sarah suggested, not caring one bit what her mother did with ribbons or flowers or any of it, but she knew from experience you had to play along. It was funny because initially Caroline Lewis was totally against the idea of a memorial. She said there was no body, and until such time as someone brought her son's body home, she would not behave as if he was dead. She said they should wait, that he might not be dead at all. That night, the screaming and crying from her parents' room rang out all over the house. But the next day, her mother had gone about as if on autopilot. She spoke of Richard in the present tense – he likes this, he doesn't like that – but simultaneously she arranged his memorial. It was very strange. When people called to sympathise, she looked glassy; she accepted their condolences but never reacted.

'Grey? Hmm. Maybe a dove grey could work. Or what about ivory? That's probably better –'

'I'm going out.' Sarah cut across her mother, and before Caroline had time to ask fifty questions or look offended, she grabbed Jacob's shirt from the hallstand and went outside to the porch.

She had no idea where she was going. Her life here, or what had been her life here, seemed alien to her now. It made no sense to her; she was like someone outside looking in. Girls she had been friendly with before she went to London with Jacob and Richard had called and made plans to meet, but to Sarah, it was as if she was visiting a zoo, looking at the exhibitions of animals that were sentient and had limbs and everything else but were different from her, nothing like her at all. Her friends all said how sorry they were, but they didn't know Jacob. Of course they'd all heard of the scandal – how Sarah Lewis had married a penniless Jew. So they said the right things and made the right gestures, but then once that was done, they talked about dresses, and dances, and weddings and babies, and their husbands or boyfriends…and Sarah had never felt so alone or missed Jacob more. She longed to tell him all about them. He was a serious person, he took the problems of the world onto his own shoulders, and their frivolity would have amused and frustrated him.

The only person in her life who understood what Jacob meant to her was Richard. He was the only one she could talk to about him. He knew both of them; he'd lived with them. Her brother understood. But he was gone too. And the guilt she felt at not putting the loss of her brother before that of her husband was hard to bear as well. She missed them both on a visceral level, but she knew life had to go on. She was trying, but nothing and nobody helped.

She walked across to Forsyth Park, looking at the flowers in bloom. A big fat bumblebee sat in a bougainvillea flower on a porch; the beds were a riot of pinks and blues and greens. Savannah in early summer was such a delight. Even with the war on, it felt untouched by it all. Savannah was a grand old lady who was putting on her finery regardless of what everyone else thought. Just meandering around her home city was soothing to Sarah's battered soul.

Sarah really hoped Grace would come to the memorial. She'd reminded her father to invite her, but he said he'd already done it. Grace would know what she was going through. She desperately wanted to be around someone who understood.

As she walked, she offered a silent prayer of thanks to Oglethorpe for his plans to make this city exceptional. Beauty in all its forms calmed her now in a way it had never done before, and the squares of Savannah, one leading to the other, street after street, with their public buildings on each corner, the willow trees, the live oaks, the magnolias and myrtles, all combined to calm her.

She remembered going out to Wormsloe with Jacob one time – he couldn't believe she'd never been – to see the Spanish moss that hung down from the oaks, forming a tunnel of trees and giving them a fairy tale look.

She had seen all of this her entire life, but it had never impacted her like this. She made her way all the way to River Street, past the allegedly haunted houses, the bars and restaurants steeped in folklore and legends. The ships that came up the Savannah River seemed to almost touch the quays either side because it was so narrow, but the pilots, generations of the same families, ensured that everything went in and out smoothly. She sat on the wall behind the markets that had traded on the banks of the river since the 1800s and gazed at the flowing water.

Jacob loved this city, and though he said it was packed full of monuments to the American Revolution, he always reminded her how it was a deeply Jewish city. The cobbled streets of this old place had Jews walking on them, thriving here since the early days of the settlement, and he felt so at home here. He would tell the story proudly at dinner parties in London, how in 1733, yellow fever started killing off Oglethorpe's settlers, one of the first casualties being the only doctor in the colony. Luckily for Oglethorpe, a ship carrying Sephardic Jews, one of whom was a doctor – an ancestor of Jacob's – arrived and the Jews were permitted to disembark, despite a rule that no Jews or Catholics inhabit the new colony. The Jews landed and thrived, and at one point, they made up thirty-five percent of the population of the city, founding the Congregation Mickve Israel with a beautiful synagogue on Monterey Square that held the oldest Torah in North America.

Sarah's heart burnt with despair. Jacob would never tell that story again. His dedication to his people, his outrage at their treatment at the hands of the Nazis flamed like a fire in him – how could that fire just be snuffed out? Just like the Jews of Europe, sent to camps, shot dead, rounded up like cattle – to them he was just another dead Jew. But he wasn't just another Jew; he was Jacob Nunez, and he was the love of Sarah's life.

She wanted to go and see his mother, who was also a widow. Jacob hadn't mentioned her much. Sarah had asked about her, but he just said his mother kvetched all the time, wanting him to live a small life when he was straining to get loose. 'Kvetch' was one of his favourite words – it meant to whine and complain. He had two sisters, married with kids, who he dropped an occasional postcard to, but any time she tried to talk to him about his family, he just said, 'You're my family now. You're all I care about. Everything else is the past. We are the future, Sarah. We're the future.' His dark eyes had smouldered with intensity, his floppy curls falling over his glasses because he was always too busy to get a haircut. He was like a ball of energy, so focused, so driven, so principled, so passionate.

She knew her family and friends didn't understand why she had, in their eyes, thrown everything away for Jacob – a chance of a good marriage, a fine house, all of that. But like her husband, she had a desperate longing to be free, to experience life, to see it all, do it all, on her own terms. That spark was always in her, but Jacob had fanned it to a flame and now... Well, now what? She could not go back to that old life, that was for sure. Marriage to some wealthy man, a genteel life here in Savannah. No. Whatever else the future might hold, it wasn't going to be that.

'Mind if we join you?'

Sarah looked up from the low wall on which she was sitting to see a couple standing beside her. The guy was around her own age and wore dark trousers and a white shirt. He was average height and build, slightly balding, and had big, kind brown eyes. The woman with him was dark and lithe, with a mop of chestnut curls.

'Ah...I was just going.' She didn't know these people, and she was in no mood for small talk.

'You look a little down in the mouth, ma'am,' the man said, and the woman smiled at her gently. 'We thought you could use a friend.' His accent was pure Savannah, slow and drawling, and he said this as if it was the most natural thing in the world, but Sarah was nonplussed. 'You don't know me,' the man continued, 'but I think I know you, or at least who you are.'

'I'm sorry, I...' She stood and made to walk off. The last thing she wanted today was someone trying to sell her something or get her to join their church or whatever they wanted.

'You're Sarah Nunez, right?' the man said as she tried to move away. 'Jacob Nunez was your husband?'

She turned to stare at the man. 'Who are you?' she asked, not caring if it sounded rude.

'I used to live in a house...well, I call it a house...' He smiled. 'It was more of a hovel. I lived there with Jacob and some other people before the war. I think we never met because he always said you refused to come there – wise move, by the way.'

'Very wise, believe me.' The young woman winked conspiratorially at Sarah.

The man laughed good-naturedly at this. 'I was invited to your weddin',' he explained, 'but I was in the Pacific. I'm just home on leave for a week.'

'Oh, right, I see... I'm a bit... I...' She was mortified to realise there were tears in her eyes again. Nobody in her life apart from Richard really knew Jacob, and meeting this man... 'But how did you know who I was?'

'That's my shirt,' he said, nodding at her outfit. Then he chuckled. 'I'm David Stiller. I'm with the 159th out of Jacksonville.'

Sarah blushed with embarrassment. 'Oh...David. Of course, I'm sorry. Jacob often mentioned you, but I never got to meet you. He always spoke very highly of you.'

Stiller chuckled again. 'I doubt that. But yeah, Jacob was a good guy. I liked him a lot. I was gonna call by your house, but I wasn't sure if that was a good idea or not, so I'm sure glad I ran into you.'

'Me too. Do you want your shirt back?' she asked, praying he'd say no.

'Nah, keep it. We had a party one night and Jacob got soaked with a beer keg that exploded, so I gave him that.'

'Thanks. I don't have much of him left. You know he died?' The words were like razor blades in her mouth.

'I heard. I'm real sorry. He was one of a kind, that's for sure.'

Sarah wiped her eyes with the sleeve of the shirt, then sat back down on the low wall, suddenly tired from the weight of her grief.

The woman nudged David, and he grinned. 'I'm so sorry. I never introduced you. This is Rachel, my fiancée. Rach is a naval nurse, but we're just lucky to have wrangled a week's shore leave together.'

Rachel held out her hand in welcome. 'I'm pleased to meet you, Sarah. I didn't know Jacob well, but I'm so very sorry for your loss.'

'Thank you,' Sarah said, and the tears flowed again.

David and Rachel sat beside her on the wall as she wept. Despite everything, there was something comforting about being with these people who actually knew Jacob.

'He was shot down over Germany,' she explained through her tears. 'He was going with a bomber squadron to photograph the raids. My younger brother was with him – he was a reporter too. They're both dead now.' She swallowed, the words forming hard lumps in her throat.

'Oh, that's rough. You poor thing,' Rachel said.

David nodded grimly. 'This damned war. Feels like it ain't never gonna be over.'

Sarah exhaled. 'I promised them both I'd come home if anything happened to them. We were living in London, but…'

'I hear ya,' David said. 'It's hard to come back to everythin' the same, everyone carryin' on like nothin' is happening, when for us the world feels like it's on fire. My mama is talkin' about the neighbours and church group on Sunday, and collard greens and gumbo potluck lunches, and I know she can't do nothin' about the Japanese or the Germans, but on and on she goes, and I wanna scream. You know, this stuff don't matter jack sh –' He stopped himself from swearing, but Sarah knew how he felt.

'I know exactly what you mean,' she said. 'My father is arranging a memorial for my brother and Jacob, and all my mother can do is ask me about ribbons and flowers. I can't bear it. I feel like I should go back to London. At least I was doing some good there. But I can't stand to be there without…' She swallowed as the tears came again. Rachel pulled her into a comforting hug.

'I know what you mean, Sarah,' David said. 'Can't be there, can't be here… It plays with your mind.'

'David's right, Sarah.' Rachel gave her shoulders a squeeze. 'Give it time.'

'Yep,' he said sadly. 'Ain't no other way.'

Sarah turned to him. 'You sound like you know what you're talking about?'

The two exchanged glances, and Sarah saw that Rachel was now tearing up too.

'Yeah,' David replied. 'It comes to everyone sooner or later. It's the price of war. And the price of love.'

CHAPTER 6

KNOCKNASHEE, COUNTY KERRY

APRIL 1943

'Auntie Grace, we're home!'

From her bedroom upstairs, Grace heard the back door close as Cáit and Molly returned home from school.

She scrambled to put away the letters she had been reading, Richard's letters to her and hers to him. Those letters were the alpha and the omega of their love story. It was torture to read them – especially the ones he'd written since they finally got engaged – but she was compelled to do it every single day. Like people who bit their nails till they bled or pulled out tufts of their own hair or picked at scabs – they knew it was hurting them, they knew the wounds would never heal unless they let them alone, but they couldn't stop. And neither could she.

But the letters were her private things, not to be shared, and much as she loved her little nieces, she didn't want them intruding on those secret moments that were all that were left to her of her life with Richard.

The tin of letters safely stowed in her bedside locker, she opened the bedroom and called down to them. 'I'm up here, girls.'

They were already on the stairs, running up to meet her, their little faces aglow. Grace was amused to see that Kate O'Connell, Charlie McKenna's stepdaughter, was with them. Kate was two years older than Cáit, and Grace had asked her to keep an eye on her nieces as they adapted to living in Knocknashee. Grace had never been to Manila and had no idea what it was like to live there, but she was sure it was very different to living in Ireland on the Dingle Peninsula. Kate had taken to her big-sister role with relish, and the two Fitzgerald girls clearly adored her.

'Hello, Kate,' Grace said. 'And look at the two of you all full of the joys of spring today. Did you have a good day at school?'

The two younger girls answered both at the same time, and Grace threw a conspiratorial wink at Kate, who giggled.

'Are you all right, Auntie Grace?' Molly asked. 'Were you lying down?'

'You're not sick, are you?' Cáit said, with obvious concern.

She laughed. 'No, not at all, Cáit,' she said. 'But it's very good of you to ask. I was doing a bit of reading while you were all at school.' *And I had a bit of peace and quiet to myself*, she thought, but didn't say.

Molly threw her skinny arms around Grace and gave her a hug. 'I'm glad you're not sick, Auntie Grace. Because that would be awful.'

'You're very good, Molly.' She kissed her head. 'So what are you up to now? Have you homework to do? Or are you ladies of leisure?'

The three girls giggled.

'We've got homework. But only a little, so we should be finished soon,' Cáit replied.

'Then we're going to play,' Molly declared confidently, 'until Daddy and Mammy come home, and then we'll have tea. At least I hope we will,' she added with less certainty, which made the others smile.

Patricia had recently taken a part-time job with Dr Ryan, who was managing his practice alone since the old nurse and midwife for the peninsula had retired some while ago. He was delighted to find someone qualified who was willing to help. It meant that while Patricia was at work and Maurice and the girls were at school, Grace had the house to herself. Truth be told, she didn't mind sharing with them; it was good to have so much life in the house these days. But it was also nice to have some time to herself, and she treasured those moments alone, now more than ever.

The girls scampered into their bedroom – which had previously belonged to Grace – and she could hear all three of them chatting happily together as she went downstairs to make herself a cup of tea. She winced as she tackled the stairs without her calliper. Her leg was aching today because she'd walked to the cemetery and back yesterday and it was too much. She needed to go to see Hugh Warrington; maybe her calliper needed adjusting. But she couldn't summon the energy to go and visit her old doctor and his wife, Lizzie, who had always been so kind to her.

She put the kettle on to boil on the stove and had just sat wearily at the kitchen table when she heard a gentle knock followed by the front door opening.

'Grace, are you there?'

It was Charlie McKenna on his post round. Normally he just left the post on the hall table, so Grace wondered what he wanted. She loved Charlie – he was the closest thing to a father she had left – but she just wasn't in the mood to talk to anyone. That was one of the surprising things about grief, how exhausting it was. She was tired all the time, and sleeping didn't help. But she couldn't be rude either, so a chat it would have to be.

'I'm in the kitchen, Charlie,' she called out. She heard his tread in the hallway before he popped his head around the kitchen door.

'Hi, Gracie. How are you, pet?' he asked gently.

'I'm all right, Charlie. You know, one day at a time.' It was a lie – she wasn't all right and she knew it – but there was nothing anyone could do, so there was no point going on about it.

He pulled up a chair and sat opposite her at the kitchen table, his hazel eyes fixed on hers. 'And the truth?'

Charlie had been one of her father's closest friends, but when Eddie and Kathy Fitzgerald died, leaving eleven-year-old Grace in her sister's care, Agnes, who didn't approve of Charlie, insisted on cutting all but the most cursory of contact with him. It wasn't until Grace started getting letters from Richard that her friendship with Charlie had rekindled. Poor Charlie had had his own fair share of troubles: his wife, Maggie, dying young, and his two children, Declan and baby Siobhán, taken from him by the machinations of Canon Rafferty, the former parish priest. Charlie was in a bad way for a few years, but he was better now. He'd married Dymphna O'Connell, a widow with two young children, Paudie and Kate, and the couple had a baby together – little Séamus, who was the light of their lives.

Grace swallowed and fought the tears. But they flowed freely in a torrent of grief and a little guilt. Because, of course, Charlie was Grace's father-in-law through her first marriage to his son, Declan.

'I know, love, I really do,' Charlie said gently. 'When Maggie died, I thought I'd go mad with the pain of it. It's like nothing else. So I do know.' He sighed. 'And I know you loved my Declan. We all did. But this is different, isn't it?'

Grace could only nod. It was true. A nicer, kinder, funnier, cleverer man than Declan McKenna you could not find, and she had loved him very much, but Charlie was right. She'd been heartbroken when Declan died, but this wasn't the same. This felt like the bottom had fallen out of her world and she was at the end of a deep, dark well and nobody could reach her. She was alone and cold, and she knew if she could ever truly accept that Richard Lewis was gone, she would never get over it.

'You know, we all go up every week to the church and say our prayers, and Father Iggy tells us all about the saints and what have you,' Charlie said. 'And for a long, long time, I would go, and I'd sit there and feel a whole load of different things. Profound loneliness, fury, jealousy of people who had their wife, bitterness, hatred, a pain in my chest that made me think I might be having a heart attack, and glad to have it just to end this horrible torture.

'I never got any comfort from it. Not a shred. And I was vexed because I was a good enough Catholic. I worked hard. I did the right thing most of the time. So then, when something awful happened, wasn't I supposed to take solace in the words of priests and friends and neighbours about how Maggie was in heaven and she was at peace and all the rest of that old claptrap?'

Grace was shocked. Charlie wasn't overtly devout, but she'd always thought he had a strong faith. 'But you didn't?' she asked.

'Nah, not a bit. I was just angry and bitter, and the only relief for me was at the bottom of a glass.' He gave a wry smile. 'And we know how that worked out for me, so I don't suggest you take to the drink.'

'How did you get over it?'

Charlie cocked his head to one side as if trying to form the correct words. 'I...' He paused. 'I was plastered one night – absolutely out of my mind with drink. Maggie was dead, Declan was gone, Siobhán was gone. The canon had it in for me, and I'd no money. I didn't see any point to going on, so I went out to Cuan Pier. I was going to throw myself off it...'

She might have been shocked at that thought at one time, but now she understood. 'And what stopped you?' Charlie would never lie to her, and she needed to know there was light somehow after all this loss.

'I was up on the cliff, the ocean crashing hard below, and Maggie came to me.' He spoke quietly now. 'I heard her voice – I didn't see her – but she said, "You didn't lose me, I'm here all the time, sure where else would I be?" I sat down on the grass – it must have been two or three in the morning, wintertime – and I heard her talking to me. I don't remember what she said after that, but we talked for a long time, and her voice was so soothing. I woke the next morning, soaking and freezing and hungover, but I knew then she never really left me, and I was able to go on.'

He smiled. 'I do remember asking her where the key for my good bicycle lock was. It was missing for ages, and it was a really good one, so I was vexed that I couldn't open it. I went back to the house that morning and washed myself and put on dry clothes. And wouldn't you know, the key for the lock was in the pocket of the trousers I put on.'

Grace reached over and took his hand. 'Do you really believe the dead are somewhere around us?'

'I do. And not because of Father Iggy, and he's a good man, but because of that night. I think when people we love die, it's a way for us to connect to that other world – a way in, if you like. I feel Declan around me all the time, especially if I'm fixing something and it's not going my way. I stop and ask him to help, and it seems to work out all right.'

'I go to the grave, and I talk to Mammy and Daddy and Agnes,' she admitted. 'And I say prayers for Declan. But Charlie, I don't have a sense of them around me.'

'I think you have to ask them to be. I think if you talk to them, your parents, Declan, Richard, even Agnes, and tell them you're struggling, that you need help, they won't let you down.'

'Did Maggie ever come to you again?'

'One other time,' he said. 'That time I had no drink taken, so there's no explaining it away. I was lying in bed, the night before Dymphna and I got married. I had that photograph of Maggie – one we got taken on the street in Killarney. A photographer took it, and Maggie went to collect it, and I thought it was a mad waste of money but she wanted it, and I'm so glad she did. You know the one? I keep it on the mantelpiece now, but it used to be beside my bed.'

'I do.' Grace smiled.

'Well, I had it in bed, looking at the two of us. She was linking my arm, and she was looking up at me and laughing. I remember putting it on the bedside locker and facing it towards me. I was sleeping on my side, and that photograph was the last thing I saw before I fell asleep. I was so sad because I knew it wouldn't be right for Dymphna to have to look at that picture every night, but much as I love Dymphna, I didn't want to put the photograph of Maggie away.'

'So what happened?'

'I dreamt of Maggie. She was with Declan and Siobhán – they were walking in a field of buttercups. Then there were bees buzzing and butterflies and the sun was warm. She came to me in the dream, and she kissed me, and she said that she would always be with me but it was time for me to go on.'

'That's lovely.'

'The next morning, the photograph was face down on the bedside table. I don't remember doing that. But anyway, I took it downstairs, put it on the sideboard, in at the back. It was like she was saying "I'm still here, but this is going to be Dymphna's house now so time for me to take a back seat." That's what I took from it anyway.' He shrugged.

Grace found she was warmed by the story. Charlie was not one for tall tales. He was like Declan that way, very practical and factual. 'I wish I could sense anyone, but I can't,' she said sadly. 'I remember when I was small, being so scared at the idea of having a guardian angel...'

'That is frightening, Gracie. I know what you mean. But these are your people. They love you, they'll want to help you...'

Well, maybe Mammy, Daddy and Declan, Grace thought. *They loved me.* Agnes, she wasn't so sure. But perhaps that's why she couldn't sense them in the way Charlie was describing. She might be blocking them out because she didn't want to let Agnes in. In many ways she had forgiven her sister for the terrible things she had done over the years, but she wasn't certain she could forgive her for the part she had played in destroying the lives of others.

A thought struck her. 'Charlie, you said Siobhán was in the dream with Maggie and Declan before you married Dymphna. But Lily – I mean, Siobhán – isn't dead.'

'No, she's not. But she might as well be as far as I am concerned.'

She stared at him. 'But you know she is well and happy and cared for. I thought that's what you wanted.'

Charlie stared at her glumly. 'That's what I thought, Gracie. But it turns out I was wrong. I want to meet her, to know her. I know it could be so disruptive, though. Does that make me a bad person?'

She blinked, unsure of how to respond. 'Of course not, Charlie.

How could it? She's still your daughter – and Maggie's. And we lost Declan so young and in tragic circumstances. But…'

'But…?'

'It's just that Declan told her that they were related, but he didn't tell her how. As far as I am aware, she had no idea when she met him that she was his little sister. I don't know if she knows now. But it'd likely be a great shock to her. And she's very young, Charlie – we have no way of knowing how she would react to that news.'

Charlie shook his head sadly. 'You're right, Gracie,' he said at last. 'It's a foolish hope of mine. But I can't help thinking that I'd just love to see her, even just the once, so I can tell Maggie I've seen her and everything is fine. I know Declan will tell Maggie, but I'd like her to hear it from me as well. Because she was our baby. Our little girl.'

Grace could feel the wave of pain as he spoke. It shocked her. She had never thought that he could be this upset about not being in touch with Lily Maheady, the name given to baby Siobhán McKenna by her adoptive parents, Sylvia and Joey Maheady, in the United States.

'She wrote to Declan,' Charlie explained. 'And we got a lovely letter from the family when he died, but nothing since.'

'She doesn't know you, Charlie,' she said softly.

'I know. That's just it. I'm her father and she doesn't know me.'

She sighed. She thought that she might regret this, but she would do it anyway. Charlie had been there for her when she needed help; it was the least she could do. 'Would you like me to write to the Maheadys and ask them how she is, maybe try to get the lie of the land as regards how much she knows? It might be less, well, disruptive, coming from me?'

His face lit up. 'Would you, Gracie? Would you do that for me?'

She smiled. 'Of course I would, Charlie. But you mustn't build your hopes up. They may not be happy about it, and if they object, then that'll have to be the end of it. Promise?'

He nodded. 'Promise. But if you could do that, Grace, I'd be so grateful to you.'

'I'll let you know as soon as I hear from them – one way or the other.'

There was a small cough from the hallway, and both Grace and Charlie turned to see young Kate standing in the doorway.

'Hello, Daddy,' she said to Charlie. 'I heard your voice. Are you finished with your rounds yet?'

He smiled at the child. 'I am indeed, love. So we can be off home to Mammy, if you're finished playing.'

Kate beamed at him. 'I'll get my stuff and say goodbye to the girls.'

'Take your time, love. Sure aren't Grace and I having a good old natter here while we're waiting for you.'

'She's such a sweet girl,' Grace said as Kate disappeared up the stairs to fetch her schoolbag. 'She's been so kind to Cáit and Molly. It's really helped them settle in.'

He nodded. 'She's a pet, all right, is our Kate. And Paudie too. He's a grand lad. They both take such care of little Séamus. And I have my wonderful Dymphna too. I'm a very lucky man, all said.'

She smiled. Charlie had gone through such hardship for so many years, but his life had now turned around. She would never love again, she knew that, but maybe there was some peace for her too in the far distant future.

Kate, Cáit and Molly bounced happily into the room, and Charlie stood to leave. He pulled something from his jacket pocket and handed it to Grace. 'I almost forgot. The reason I'm here is because you got a telegram, and I know who it's from. I took it off the machine because Nancy's varicose veins are playing up something wicked. And I know what it's about.'

Grace. My father said you are not coming to the memorial in June. Please change your mind. PLEASE. We really need to see you. I need to see you. You are the only one who understands. Sarah.

'So, are you going?' Charlie asked.

Grace shook her head. 'Sarah's so kind, and Mr Lewis offered to pay and arrange it and everything. He even said I could bring someone with me. But I just can't, Charlie. I find getting out of bed a hardship. I haven't it in me to go to a funeral for Richard so far away, in his world of people who don't know me and don't know what we meant to each other…'

'I know you don't want to, Gracie, but I think you should. That poor girl has lost her brother and her husband, and the only person she feels she can share her pain with is you. Do it for Richard, Grace. His family want you there. You were about to be his wife – he'd want you to go.'

She knew he was right. She'd replied to Richard's father, declining the offer to travel to Savannah for the memorial in mid-June. He'd responded that he was very sorry to hear it, and that if she changed her mind, all she had to do was let him know. They seemed genuine about the invitation, and perhaps being around people who missed him as much as she did might be helpful. Certainly she knew Sarah would not have sent a telegram like this if the invitation had just been for the sake of form.

And yet she couldn't agree to go. Because if she put her mind to it, she could imagine her parents, Agnes and Declan together in Charlie's heavenly field of buzzing bees and butterflies. Maggie McKenna was there with them too. But no matter how hard she tried, there was one person she could not – would not – imagine there. And how could she grieve at a memorial for Richard Lewis when her stubborn heart would not even acknowledge that he was gone?

CHAPTER 7

Grace wrote that same day to Sylvia Maheady to ask about Lily. She was mindful as she did so that she and Declan had not been fully truthful with the Maheadys when they first visited them back in 1940. It was such a complicated situation, and she and Declan had tried hard not to upset Joey and Sylvia Maheady or step on anyone's toes; it seemed the right thing not to tell them at the time. But she had to admit she felt a little ashamed of their lack of candour now. It took her a while to write the letter to Sylvia to her satisfaction. She kept it general, told Sylvia that she had been thinking of her lately and missed hearing from Lily since Declan died. She wondered if she should tell Sylvia about Richard but decided against it in the end. She wasn't prepared to put it down on paper like that just yet. Instead she told her that the family had been asking how Lily was doing. She also told her Declan's father had remarried and that he and his new wife had a lovely baby boy. She thought that might be important; maybe it would give Sylvia some reassurance about Grace writing to her. Finally Grace told Sylvia that if she or Lily had a mind to write to her, she'd love to hear from them.

Grace sealed the envelope and walked down to Nancy O'Flaherty's post office to post it.

'How are you doing, Grace?' the postmistress asked. 'It's good to see you. You haven't really been out and about much lately.'

'I'm fine, thank you, Nancy,' Grace replied, wishing she was fine.

Nancy gave her a sad smile. 'I'm sure you're not, pet,' she said softly, 'but that's allowed. Take care of yourself, do you hear.'

Grace could feel the tears welling at Nancy's kindness. All she could do was nod as Nancy took the envelope from her and put it into the postbag for the outgoing mail.

She felt a sense of relief that she'd handed the letter over to Nancy's care. She had done her duty to Charlie, and now it was just a waiting game. She didn't know exactly what she was expecting from the Maheadys or how she felt about Sylvia or Lily answering; she had other troubles to deal with, and those were concerns for another time.

The days were passing for her with little sense or meaning. She supposed she should really go back to work, but she couldn't bring herself to do it just yet. It was true she was moping about at home most of the time, but to be honest, that was all she felt able for right now.

* * *

DAYS TURNED INTO WEEKS. The weak spring sunshine warmed up, and the children became impatient for summer freedom. The rhododendron bloomed, and so did the fuchsia and primroses, lambs were growing in the fields, and everywhere seemed abundant with life, but still Grace's heart was heavy and cold and she fought to find even the tiniest spark of joy in each day. The news of the war was unbearable for her to listen to, so she had switched off the wireless and never read the papers any more. More destruction, blood, death and tears, day after day – that was all they had to offer. She read and reread her letters, as she couldn't focus on a book or anything else. She'd tried to bake a loaf two days ago and forgot the baking soda, so it never rose. She had a memory like a sieve, and hours seemed to slide by as she just sat on her bed, staring into space.

Tilly had tried to get her to go to Dublin, just for a change of scenery, but she refused, then Tilly tried to get her to go to the pictures, but Grace didn't want to. She tried to explain she didn't want to be distracted, have her mind taken off it. She wanted to live in the world of memories, to spend her waking hours in reveries of her and Richard together, to spend her nights dreaming of him. It hurt, but it was all she could do.

Charlie had been grateful and cheerful when Grace told him she had sent the letter to the Maheadys, but as the weeks went on, she could see his impatience grow. He didn't have to ask if there had been any post, of course. He was the postman, so he knew exactly what letters Grace was, or wasn't, receiving. But she was both saddened and, it must be said, also a little irritated by his glum looks when nothing arrived for her from America. Charlie had so many other things going for him, Grace thought. It was true that he had lost Maggie, but he had also found Dymphna, and she had brought Paudie and Kate with her, and now they had little Séamus. Grace had lost Declan and found Richard, but Richard had been taken from her before they had a chance for any kind of a future, never mind a baby. Grace had to admit she was feeling very sorry for herself these days.

She was a little dismayed to find that her irritation also stretched to her brother, Maurice, at times. It was a strange situation for them to be in. He and his family were used to their own home and so was Grace. So having to share wasn't always as easy as she wished it would be, although Patricia and Maurice did everything in their power not to step on Grace's toes, and she knew that.

The bone of contention between the siblings at present was Grace's refusal to go to Richard's memorial.

'I never met Richard,' Maurice said, 'but I am sure he was a fine fellow. And his family seem to have taken you to their hearts, Grace. So I have to admit that I am a little puzzled as to why you wouldn't want to go? Do you not think Richard would want you to go – for his family, if for no other reason?'

She wanted to sob again. She knew it was unreasonable, irrational even, but she hated hearing Maurice talk about Richard like that. Even though Maurice admitted he didn't know him, he then talked as if he knew what Richard wanted and she didn't.

Then again, maybe Maurice was right. Maybe she was being unfair to Sarah and all the Lewis family. But for once she wanted to do what was fair for her, and that didn't involve going to Savannah to mourn Richard just yet. She couldn't explain why she was having such a hard time accepting it. It wasn't hope – at least not in the way she had understood it previously.

Some days she felt as if there was a connection there between them that just didn't feel broken or disconnected yet. An instinct, telling her to wait and see. Then, on other days, the full realisation of his loss would hit her and she would be paralysed by the depth of her grief. Alone, she would sob until she could cry no more. But when she went looking for the connection, she would find it again, and her heart would feel some small *smidirín* of peace for a few minutes at least. A tiny oasis in a world that seemed otherwise so bereft of hope and joy for her right now.

May arrived, and with no sign of a letter from the Maheadys, Charlie McKenna was positively morose every time Grace saw him. And his behaviour wasn't just irritating Grace, it seemed.

She was home alone one morning when there was a soft knock on the back door. She struggled to her feet to open it and saw Dymphna McKenna standing outside with little Séamus in his pram.

'We came to say hello to Auntie Grace,' Dymphna said. 'Because we haven't seen her in a while and we were worried that she was all right, weren't we, Séamus?'

The little boy gurgled happily at the sound of his mother's voice, making Grace smile.

'Come in, Dymphna,' she said. 'I'll make a pot of tea.'

'That would be lovely.' Dymphna manoeuvred the pram into the kitchen, accompanied by squeals and laughter from the baby inside.

'Séamus is in great form.' Grace peered in at her little visitor, who treated her to a broad baby smile and held out his chubby arms to her. 'And he's got so big!'

'Sure, he's a pet,' Dymphna said proudly. 'And he'd eat for Ireland.

Nothing fussy about him at all. Paudie when he was his age had my heart broken with all the refusing of food, but this fella is a dream. So, how are you doing?' she asked as Grace made tea.

'I'm all right,' Grace said, trotting out her standard reply.

'I doubt that. Don't forget, you're talking to someone who's been through it herself here.' She placed her hand on Grace's arm. 'It will get easier, Grace, but it'll take some time. A lot of time.'

Grace felt a fat tear trickle down her cheek. 'I don't think I will ever get over him, Dymphna.'

Her friend gave her a sympathetic smile. 'Maybe you won't, *a chroí*. And maybe you shouldn't. But it will get easier.'

The women sat together for a full half hour, chatting over a cup of tea. Grace was grateful for Dymphna's support, and baby Séamus was a lovely distraction for her. She was sad when Dymphna stood to leave and returned the baby to his pram.

'Still no word from the Maheadys in America, I suppose?' her friend said as she wrangled the pram out of the kitchen into the yard outside.

'No,' Grace replied, surprised that Dymphna had mentioned it.

'Do you think they will reply to you?'

'I don't know. But the post would be very slow because of the war.'

'Yes, I suppose so.'

'Is it a problem, Dymphna?' she asked, suddenly anxious that Charlie's wife was upset with her for writing.

'Ah, sure, not really. But I'm worried Charlie is putting too much store into this young girl wanting to contact him. After all, she doesn't know him at all, does she?' She smiled at Grace. 'I'm sorry. There's me being as miserable as Charlie about it now. To be honest, I do understand him wanting to know she is all right. Wanting to see her even. But not to the point where it's all he talks about. On and on he goes about Siobhán this and Siobhán that. And I'm trying to be understanding, but 'twould wear you out. And it has Kate upset too.' She sighed. 'Kate was a toddler when her own father died, so she doesn't remember him in the way Paudie does. Charlie is the only father she's really known. And she likes being the only girl with the two boys.'

At this, Séamus gave a small, aggrieved whimper to get his mother's attention, his little face twisting into a petulant frown as he rubbed his eyes with his plump little hands. 'Here we go,' Dymphna said. 'This lad's getting tired and hungry now, Grace, so we'd better head for home.'

'What would you do if Lily wanted to meet Charlie?' The question surprised both Dymphna and Grace herself. She hadn't meant to just come straight out and ask it.

Her friend didn't answer for a moment. Then she gave Grace a wry smile. 'To be honest, Grace, I have a husband and three children to look after and a house to run. I don't have the energy for any tantrums from either Kate or Charlie about a young girl living her life on the other side of the world. But if I thought it would get this obsession about her out of his head, so he could stop moping about the house and pay the rest of us some proper attention, then, sure, I'd pack him off to America myself.'

Grace smiled and waved as Dymphna left the yard, heading for home. But she couldn't help feeling that trouble was brewing in the McKenna household and that she might be partly responsible for it.

CHAPTER 8

The response Charlie McKenna had been so anxiously waiting for arrived in early May.

Sylvia Maheady's letter made it clear that she and Joey had figured out a while ago that Declan and Lily were more than just the distantly related cousins that he and Grace had claimed they were.

They were so alike in looks, Sylvia wrote. I know you said that a lot of people on the west coast of Ireland have that look—dark hair, pale skin, and very blue eyes. But the family resemblance was still uncanny and unmistakable. It all seemed just too much of a coincidence, so after you left, it wasn't hard for Joey and me to put two and two together. That's why we didn't object to Lily writing to Declan, but it's also the reason I asked—well, pleaded with you, really—for you to do nothing to disrupt our daughter's life. I was so happy when you gave me the assurance I needed. And you can in turn be assured that Joey and I love both our girls the same way. It doesn't matter to us that Lily is adopted and that Ivy is our own child. We love them both dearly. We didn't want anything to happen that would cause upset to either of them.

But Lily is eighteen years old now and a young woman capable of making her own decisions. Joey and I had already been talking about telling her she was adopted. We felt she had a right to know. She's a very bright girl, so we thought she might have some inkling anyway. When your letter arrived, it seemed timely. So we plucked up the courage and told her. She wasn't shocked at all. She said she had guessed all along but was glad that we had finally told her the truth. And the first thing she asked after we told her was whether Declan was her brother. We told her that we didn't know for sure—which is true—but she could ask you. She was so full of questions we couldn't answer. She said she would write to you, hoping that you might be able to give her the information she is looking for.

There was a hint of sadness in Sylvia's letter. Grace could feel the conflict in the woman – loving her daughter and wanting to keep her and protect her but also understanding that she had to let her go to make her own way in the world. She admired the woman's courage. She was not sure she would be able to do the same in her shoes.

Enclosed with Sylvia's letter was an excited letter from Lily Maheady. Lily explained that she had met lots of people in her young life, but nobody ever had the impact Declan did. It was like she knew – *like my soul knew his or something.*

We had an instant connection, Lily wrote. *I love art, and I remember Declan was a really good artist too. We used to send each other little sketches. I was so sorry when he died, Grace. I missed writing to him, but I didn't know if you wanted to hear from me after your awful tragedy. It's terrible now to know that I will never get to know him properly as a brother, but you were his wife and that must be even worse. I really hope you find someone else to make you happy, but I am sure it will be very difficult after Declan. He was such a great guy.*

Grace felt a lump in her throat as she read Lily's letter. The young woman was so full of self-confidence and energy, but also so very young. Grace had indeed found someone to replace Declan, and he had also been snatched away from her. She couldn't help wondering if it was God's way of punishing her for not loving Declan in the way she had loved Richard Lewis.

But Sylvia's and Lily's letters brought some distraction, and she knew Charlie would be over the moon about the response. The Maheadys would know about him from the little news Grace had given them in her letter, but she felt there was still a long way to go before the two families were ready for direct contact.

Charlie, of course, disagreed. He wanted to write to Lily immediately. Or have Grace ask her to write to him. But Grace, mindful of her earlier conversation with Dymphna – and her own instincts – refused outright to do either.

'It's too soon, Charlie,' she explained. 'It's all still very delicate for the Maheadys, and even Lily herself. She's excited now, but who knows how long that will last? The shock of the situation might hit her later, and she could be very upset about it after all. We need to go slowly, give her time.'

Charlie nodded, but she could see he was upset by her refusal. However, after a short pause, he sighed and said, 'I'll be guided by you, Gracie. You met Lily and the family, so you know better than I do.'

But there was a bitterness in his voice that he couldn't disguise. Grace had seen the baby daughter he had lost all those years ago and he hadn't. That rankled with him.

'I do understand, Charlie,' she said softly. 'But we need to go easy with this. And you need to talk to Dymphna about it too.'

He threw her a pale smile. 'Of course, Grace,' he said. 'I don't suppose I could have Lily's letter to show her, could I?'

Grace wasn't at all sure that giving Charlie the letter was a good idea, but she handed it over, making him promise to talk to his wife about the whole affair before he did anything else.

He beamed at her as he took the letter. 'I promise, Gracie,' he said. 'And you're the best, you know that, don't you?'

* * *

IF GRACE WAS HOPING for some respite from aggravation now that Charlie had his letter from Lily, she was badly mistaken. A few days after the letters arrived, she had another conversation with Maurice one evening after dinner about Richard's memorial. He meant well probably, but she had fended for herself since she was a child and she was not going to have her older brother dictate what she was to do or how she was to feel.

In particular she did not need to hear from her brother that her refusal to go to Savannah was hard on Richard's family and that she should, perhaps, give them a chance. Well, maybe it *was* unfair. But she wasn't the only one being unfair. She knew God worked in mysterious ways, but why did those ways have to always involve Grace getting hurt and losing the people she loved? Also it was a bit late for Maurice to be showing such concern. Where was he when their parents died? Grace was only eleven years old, and Maurice had left her alone with their sister, Agnes. It's not like he didn't know what Agnes was like. Why did he think she would be any more approving of her crippled sister than she was of her spoiled priest brother? Grace had needed him then, and he wasn't there. And all because he was afraid that Agnes and Grace and others would think badly of him. So what if they did? Was that any reason to turn his back on his eleven-year-old sister who was stricken with polio and had just been orphaned?

Grace thought she had made it clear that she didn't want to discuss it any more, and she noticed Patricia had hushed him a few times when he tried to broach the subject earlier. But Maurice persisted, and when Patricia left the room to put the girls to bed, he started up again.

Grace finally lost patience. 'Maurice,' she said as firmly as she could without raising her voice, 'I'm glad to have you and Patricia and the girls back here with me. Of course I am. But you have to understand that I have had to look after myself for very many years now, and I've made my decision, so please stop badgering me. I just want some peace in my own home. Yes, mine,' she said, responding to a raised eyebrow from her brother. 'The house comes with the headmistress position, and I am the school headmistress. You have made your opinion clear on the subject of the memorial, and I don't need to hear it again.'

Maurice stared at her in surprise. 'Oh, Grace, I'm only trying to help you. I know you're so sad and lonely, and maybe not thinking as straight as you normally would. I don't want you to make a mistake you might regret later on. You are my little sister after all.'

'Yes,' Grace said slowly. 'I am.'

She knew she was risking her relationship with her brother and his family, but the need to say her piece got the better of her and she blurted it out – all the resentment that had been building up inside of her since she got that first letter from her sister-in-law begging for sanctuary bubbling forth unchecked. 'And I was your little sister when our parents died in 1932, and you abandoned me at the very time I needed you most. Why, Maurice? Why did you do that? Why couldn't you understand that I needed you back then? And if you did understand, why did you not write to me or contact me? I know you said it was because you were fearful I'd react like Agnes would have, but surely that was a chance you could have taken?'

Maurice stared at her in astonishment and hurt. 'I... I know, Grace,' he said at last. 'You are right. I should have contacted you, but I just thought that I'd make things worse for you.'

She could feel the blood pumping in her ears now, the pent-up fury at last finding voice. 'That sounds like an excuse, Maurice, if you don't mind me saying so. Maybe you were more concerned about making things worse for yourself.'

'I can see how you'd think like that, but I was just trying to do the best –'

'Seriously? Best for whom? The best thing for you maybe. Please don't say it was the best for me, because it wasn't. Our parents died, Maurice, both of them, and I was only a child. You knew better than anyone what Agnes was like, but you left me at her mercy, knowing how life would be for me. Do you know she never once visited me in hospital? My only relative in Ireland, my own sister, never came to see me – not even once in four long years. I was so embarrassed on the days visitors came, I would hide, because I couldn't bear the looks of pity from the staff and other patients. I never had one visitor. Can you imagine what that was like?'

'I can't, Grace, I'm sorry...' Maurice looked wretched, but she carried on.

'Then, when I came back here, she put me working but took all my wages. She said it was for my care when I'm old because I'll have to pay someone to mind me on account of being crippled. That I'd never have a husband or children. That I was destined to always be a burden. She isolated me from everyone. From Tilly, from Charlie, from anyone who could offer me a hand of friendship or a bit of kindness – she kept them from me. I had nobody, Maurice, and all we ever got from you was a flimsy Mass card saying you'd pray for us.'

'Didn't you have the Warringtons at least?' he asked tentatively.

'While I was in hospital, yes. But when I came home, Agnes told me I was nothing to them, just another patient, and I shouldn't bother them. She stole the letters they wrote. She lied about my Leaving Certificate, saying I failed when I got great marks. She was determined to keep me away from everyone, and the only one who could have helped me was you, but you never came...' Tears ran down her cheeks, the lonely child she'd been finally having her say.

Maurice stared, clearly upset at how hurt Grace was. 'Grace, I'm so sorry,' he began, 'but Patricia and I just thought –'

'Oh, don't bring me into this, Maurice Fitzgerald.' Patricia stood in the kitchen doorway, looking annoyed. 'For what it's worth, Grace, I told him exactly what you just said. Agnes or no Agnes, he should have at least tried to write to you and tell you about us. So I'm sorry, Maurice, but I won't let you make me complicit in this. I told you repeatedly you should write to Grace, I said it wasn't right, but you said it was best to leave well enough alone. So you need to sort this out with Grace, please, because I'm not being part of this.'

'I-I-I...' Maurice gawped at his wife and Grace like a fish out of water.

But Grace had had enough. She fled the room, choking back the huge sobs that threatened to overwhelm her before she could make it safely into her bedroom. Behind her she could hear Patricia scolding Maurice for upsetting his sister.

'I asked you not to push her,' Grace heard her say. 'Grace is grieving and fragile, Maurice. For goodness' sake, you of all people understand that. You shouldn't have persisted. I know you thought it was for the best, but she's a grown woman and she's made her decision – you should respect it. And now the poor girl is beside herself.'

Grace lay on her back, tears leaking from her eyes. She could still hear raised voices from downstairs as Maurice and Patricia argued. Despite everything, Grace was unhappy about that. She wanted Maurice to know how she felt about being abandoned as a child, but she had no wish whatsoever to cause any problems between him and Patricia.

She sat up as she heard a timid knock on her bedroom door. She was about to tell Maurice or Patricia to please leave her alone when she heard four-year-old Molly calling her.

'Auntie Grace, Auntie Grace, I'm frightened.'

Grace got up and limped to the bedroom door; her bad leg was acting up today into the bargain. She opened it to find both her nieces outside. Her heart melted at the sight of their fearful and anxious faces. This wasn't right. She would have to make it good with Maurice as soon as she could. But for now she needed to reassure the two little girls.

She ushered them into her room, and they all sat on the bed.

'I don't like when Mammy and Daddy fight,' Cáit said.

'Do they often fight?' Grace asked, surprised.

Molly shook her head, and Cáit added, 'Only that once before we left Manila to come to you, Auntie Grace. Otherwise they always get along.'

'Well, you've no need to worry,' she told them. 'Mammy and Daddy are just fine, and they'll be getting along again in a few minutes, just you wait and see. It's the same as when you two sometimes fight, or Kate and Paudie. When you love someone, sometimes they can annoy you and you get mad, even adults, but we always patch it up when we love each other. It's just part of life.'

'Are you sad, Auntie Grace?' little Molly asked.

She nodded. 'Yes, Molly, I am a little sad because I lost someone I loved very much. But I'll be fine soon too. Don't you worry about me.'

Reassured, the girls allowed her to bring them back to their room and tuck them into bed. She kissed them both and told them to sleep tight.

'Don't let the bedbugs bite,' Cáit said, and Molly giggled.

As she crossed the landing to her own room, Grace could hear Patricia on her way up the stairs and Maurice moving about in the kitchen. She hurried into her bedroom again and closed the door softly. She couldn't face either of them just yet, but she promised herself she would make it up to them tomorrow.

The next morning, however, she was up and out before the rest of the house stirred. She'd had time to think the night before, and there was someone she needed to see, someone she needed to talk to.

Mary O'Hare welcomed her with a great hug. She was alone because Tilly and Odile were staying up in Dublin for the week with Tilly's sister, Marion, and her family so Tilly and Eloise could spend some time together.

'It's good to see you, girl,' Mary said. 'But what gets you up so early today? You're not sick, are you?'

The funny thing about Mary O'Hare was she looked the same now as when Grace was a child. Bent over from rheumatism, with dark hair she cut herself. She could be intimidating, but Grace knew that beneath the gruff exterior was a heart of pure kindness.

She smiled. 'No, I'm fine, thanks, Mary.'

'You expect me to believe that, do you?'

'You are the third person who has said that to me recently.'

'That's Knocknashee for you, Gracie. A village of truth-sayers.' Mary laughed raucously at this. When she had finished enjoying her own joke, she asked, 'So what is it you want to ask me?' Mary somehow knew Grace had a question on her mind.

'I was wondering about Alfie,' Grace said. 'Is he…?'

'Oh, he's still alive and kicking, that lad, thanks be to God.'

'How do you know?'

Mary shrugged. 'I just do.'

'What does it feel like?'

'Just a feeling. Well, more of a connection. Like there's a thread that's not broke but would be if anything happened to him.'

'Sounds like the fates in Greek mythology.'

'I don't know about that.' Mary laughed again. 'But our lives and our fate are as delicate as spun thread, that I can believe. Once that thread is broken... But Alfie's thread is strong for now. Why do you ask, Grace?'

'I...'

'Do you think your Richard is still alive?' Her bright-blue eyes, buried in that wrinkled face, latched onto Grace's.

Grace shook her head.

'Are you sure?' Mary eyed her curiously.

She shook her head again. 'Truth is, I'm not sure of anything any more, Mary. But I just...'

'Have this feeling?'

Grace nodded miserably. 'I don't want to feel that way. I want to be sure he is gone so that I can grieve for him. This way is far worse. Not knowing, hoping, not wanting to hope.'

'Trust your instincts, girl,' Mary said. 'They'll see you true.'

'I hope so.'

'Are you going to Savannah, so?' her friend asked.

Grace shook her head for a third time. 'I don't want to, Mary. I can't.'

'Or won't?'

'Isn't that the same thing?'

'No, not really.'

She sighed. She had come to Mary because she thought this woman of all people wouldn't judge her. But now even Mary seemed disapproving of her. She couldn't please anyone these days. 'Do you think I should go? Even if I don't believe...or don't want to believe that he is gone?'

'Well, now, I think you should go,' Mary said. 'If not for yourself, then for the others.'

Grace grimaced. 'That's what Maurice said. And I was angry with him for it – we fought.'

'Ach, *cailín*, I wouldn't worry about that. Maurice is a good man, but he's easy to argue with all the same.'

She had to smile in spite of herself. Mary had hit the nail on the head as usual. Maurice was a good, decent man, but he could be annoying, especially when he was playing master of Grace's own house.

'Besides,' the other woman continued, with a mischievous twinkle in her eye, 'even a stopped clock is right twice a day.'

'So you think I should go?'

'I think, *a stór*, that you should follow your instinct.'

'Do you think he's dead, Mary?' Grace's voice was barely a whisper now.

'I can't tell you that, girleen, because I have no connection to that lad, but you do. The good people, the fairies and druids and the people long ago who knew things, they'd say he's part of your soul family – you knew him before this life, and you'll know him again. It's why some people stick in our lives while others just pass through. You are bound through the ages. So only you know the answer to that.'

Grace took the long way home, thinking about what Mary O'Hare had said. *I will do it*, she told herself. *I'll listen to my instinct and trust it won't do me wrong.*

By the time she reached home, she had made a decision. She would write to Arthur Lewis and tell him she would come to the memorial for Richard in June. If he didn't mind, she would take the opportunity to spend a few days in New York before travelling to Savannah. And she would ask Charlie McKenna to come with her.

CHAPTER 9

TWENTY MILES SOUTH OF STRASBOURG

'The cat is brown with a black tail and lives behind the opera house in a shoebox.'

Jacob's brow furrowed. He was easily worse than Richard at French. Alfie had been true to his word and had supplied them with a French novel, a romance from the eighteenth century with a convoluted plot about a woman who was to marry some rich guy but ran away with a poor guy; the poor guy was actually a rich guy too, but he was evil or something. They didn't grasp it completely, but they were using it alongside a small dog-eared dictionary to teach themselves the language. It was tedious and they got sick of it, but it was necessary, and besides, something had to fill the hours.

'*La chat...*' Jacob began.

Richard corrected him. '*Le chat.*'

His friend rolled his eyes. '*Le chat est brun avec une...*' He shrugged. 'I don't know what tail is.'

Richard looked it up. '*Queue*, it says here.'

'OK. *Le chat est brun avec une queue noire, et il habite –*'

'*Il vit…*'

'*Il vit dans une boîte de chaussures.*'

'*Boîte à chaussures,*' Richard corrected.

'*Boîte à chaussures.*' Jacob sighed in exasperation. '*Derrière l'opéra.* And if we ever need to explain where the cat has gone, this is sure gonna be useful.' He snorted.

Richard laughed. 'And the Georgia accent won't give us away at all.'

They were on the third week since Alfie's visit, and each day was the same monotony. They added a strand of straw to a cup for every day they were there, so they had some idea of how much time had passed.

'How are you now?' Richard asked. Jacob had been constipated, probably from lying still for so long and a diet of white bread with a few beans in a stew every few days. They were given water to drink, sometimes milk, and the Ducrots emptied the bucket of their waste every day, something that made Richard cringe with embarrassment.

They were both thin, but they exercised as much as they could in the small space. They remembered a routine the drill sergeant had put them through when they were in training for the bomber mission. The journalists had been groaning and moaning at the physical exertion they were unused to. Someone asked why it was necessary, and the sergeant replied, 'Because it is.' There was no further explanation. And now Richard and Jacob did a full workout each day, using the weight of their own and each other's bodies to prevent muscle wastage.

Monsieur Ducrot had gone up to the roof of the barn and removed two of the terracotta tiles to allow some air and light in. It was high above their heads, but at least it meant when they lay down at night, they could look up through the tunnel of bales that stretched almost to the roof and see the stars, and during the day, they could see the blue sky.

They longed to get out. But they didn't even talk about how hard it was being cooped up like this. It wouldn't help, and they knew they both felt the same way. So instead, they slept, exercised and learned French.

Occasionally they heard cars and voices in the yard. They slept a lot of the day, though now it was unbearably hot, so it was difficult. They both wore just underwear, the flight suits they were wearing when they were dropped were too heavy in this oppressive heat.

'Let's do something else,' Jacob suggested. 'Tell me what is so wonderful about Grace, and I'll do the same about Sarah.'

Richard raised an eyebrow. There was an unwritten rule that, though Sarah was Jacob's wife, she was Richard's sister, so he didn't want to hear any details of their private life.

'We can keep it clean,' his friend added with a smile.

Richard knew Jacob's leg was mending slowly; it still hurt like hell, he said, but his temperature was stable now, so there was no infection. One night, not long after Alfie left, Jacob was raving and burning up. Richard had had to wait for the Ducrots to come; it felt like hours. The wound on Jacob's leg was infected. Mrs Ducrot returned with a glass jar full of maggots that she put on the gash. Richard had to suppress a wave of vomit at the sight, but it worked. His friend's torso was a mass of purple and yellow bruises, and he'd lost two teeth on the top left of his mouth in the fall as well. But he, like Richard, was on the mend.

Sometimes Richard thought he would never not feel the ache in his ankle. At night, especially if he'd been exercising hard, it hurt so bad he could cry. But he pictured Grace and kept going. They punched a bale and bounced from foot to foot for hours, Richard gritting his teeth through the pain. But when it threatened to overwhelm him, he brought her into sharp focus in his mind, her beautiful face, her smile, the sound of her laugh, the curve of her hips, the swell of her bust, and he got through it by picturing how he was one day closer to being reunited with her. If he could just get strong, he could try to get out of France. Alfie had no reason to lie about how it was almost impossible, but people still did it. He and Jacob had met them when they came to London, so some people made it. A voice in the back of his head whispered, *For every one that makes it, thousands do not,* but he silenced it. He would be one of the lucky ones. He had to be – for Grace.

'You go first,' Jacob said as he lifted a bale of hay over his head and back down to his chest over and over, the muscles rippling in his sinewy arms. He grunted at the effort, the strain on his back and shoulders immense. Richard knew once Jacob was finished with the bale, it was his turn. In the meantime, he did squats, his arms outstretched as he went down as low as he could and pushed himself back up with the strength of his thighs.

'OK, here we go… Grace *est belle.*'

'Grace is beautiful,' Jacob translated.

'*Elle est gentille et drôle.*'

'She is gentle?'

'*Gentille* means kind, I think.' He panted as he rose from a deep squat.

'OK…she is kind and funny,' Jacob responded.

'*Elle voit le bon côté des gens, même les plus affreux.*' He groaned.

'Not a clue.' Jacob put the bale down and stretched.

'Try. Come on, you do know it…' He repeated the line.

His friend sighed as he thought. 'She…sees a good side?'

'She sees the good in everyone, even the awful people.'

'Oh yeah. OK…I can do the last part. Say it again.'

Richard repeated the last line.

'She makes me laugh and she is unique.'

'Good job.'

'If you were thinking of betting on us getting out of here, what odds are we getting?'

Richard lay down on his bale bed, his muscles aching, gazing up at the clear dark sky. 'Honestly? Not great. What do you think?'

'I'm the same as you. But I try not to let myself go down that road. I just think about Sarah, getting back to her, going home…' Jacob sat on his bed. 'I do know this, though. Either I'm going home or I'll die trying.'

Richard agreed. Alfie had said a month; that was one more week. When he came back – they had to hope he'd come back – they were going to insist they be given the opportunity to escape. Sitting out the war here in this barn, not knowing what was happening, was not an option.

CHAPTER 10

THE ATLANTIC OCEAN

7 JUNE 1943

The *SS Maya* was a troop ship, and men and wounded soldiers were segregated from the small number of women and children on board. It was uncomfortable and cold, and the rations were meagre and tasteless, but nobody complained. Grace shared a cabin with a woman called Cheryl, who had two young children; her husband was a civil servant who worked at the American embassy, and they'd been stationed in England before the war. He'd been trying to get Cheryl to go home since the war began, but she had refused. Now one of their children, a six-year-old boy called Teddy, had some kind of lung disease, so she agreed to go back to America to have him treated. Hospitals in England were overrun with wounded servicemen, and he couldn't get the care he needed there.

There were a few other women as well, but mostly people kept to themselves. Meals were served in their cabins.

Little Teddy coughed incessantly. Cheryl apologised repeatedly until Grace begged her to stop. She tried to help, telling Teddy and his four-year-old sister, Martha, stories, making puppets out of socks and doing funny shows with them.

Grace didn't see Charlie for the duration of the crossing. The journey took longer than usual because of U-boat activity in the Atlantic – the troop ship captain had to zig-zag to avoid them – but everyone aboard was glad to be getting home. Securing passage was very difficult, but Arthur Lewis had managed it, so Grace was just grateful to be on the ship at all. They wore life vests day and night and were on high alert at all times to make for the lifeboats. Grace wondered often if taking such a huge risk for the sake of a memorial service was worth it.

A merchant ship, the *SS Irish Oak*, sailing from Florida to Dublin last month, had been torpedoed and sunk; thankfully survivors were picked up. But another ship bearing grain coming from Lisbon to Ireland had suffered the same fate, and those passengers and crew weren't so lucky.

To almost palpable relief, the voyage across the Atlantic went without incident, and they docked in New York on the fourteenth of June. The passengers were ushered into a bus and driven a few blocks to a processing hall in Manhattan; the arrivals hall at Ellis Island was no longer in use, Grace was informed by the ship's purser. Because it was a military ship and the number of civilians was small, they were checked and allowed on their way in less than an hour.

Grace stood outside the Works Projects Administration Building on Columbus Avenue waiting for Charlie. Richard's father had booked them into a hotel in the city centre and had telegrammed to tell her that someone would be sent to meet them from the boat. This was so different to the last time she was here with Declan. They had very little money and had stayed at a cheap boarding house.

Declan. How Grace longed for his reassuring presence now. He'd been nervous, given the reason for the voyage – to see with his own eyes that his little sister, Siobhán, adopted against his father's will when their mother died, was safe and well. It all felt like a lifetime ago.

She guessed that Charlie must be feeling that same anxiety now.

She saw Charlie walk out into the hot New York summer and squint as he looked for her. Grace felt a wave of affection for him. He looked older and unsure of himself out of his environment.

'Charlie, over here,' she called.

He spotted her and waved. "Tis hot, isn't it?' he said, wiping his neck with his handkerchief. He was wearing a suit, shirt and tie, an outfit Grace had never seen him in before, apart from the day he married Dymphna.

'It sure is,' she replied in English, mimicking an American accent, and he smiled.

'How are you feeling?' he asked in Irish. 'Is it like you remembered?'

'A bit strange in the legs,' she replied. 'I thought we'd never get off that boat, but now that I'm here...' She looked up at the enormous buildings and the street signs for Central Park, where she'd once taken a boat trip with Brendan McGinty, a police officer from New York. 'Yes, this is how it was, busy, noisy, but very exciting.'

'Look at that.' Charlie pointed upwards to a sign for Broadway and Times Square. 'We're really here, in New York City... I can't believe it, Gracie.'

'I know, it's amazing, isn't it?' She smiled.

A couple walked by, dark-skinned and with black curly hair. Charlie was trying not to stare, she knew, but it was unlikely he'd ever seen a Black person before. Everyone at home was white and Irish. The couple glanced at her and Charlie when they heard the two of them speak in Irish. Charlie had fairly good English, and it would improve if they spoke it.

'Right, English from now on,' Grace said. 'We need you to be able to communicate with Lily, don't we?'

Charlie inhaled, looked around him and exhaled raggedly. She could sense his trepidation.

'Trust me, Charlie, it's going to be all right. Lily's a lovely girl, and she's anxious to know more about her Irish family. Sylvia was kind and understanding when I wrote. It's going to be all right, I promise.'

Before Charlie had time to answer, a sleek, pearl-coloured motorcar pulled up to the kerb and a uniformed driver got out.

'Mrs McKenna?' he asked as he approached.

'Yes?' Grace answered with a smile. *This must be Arthur Lewis's driver.*

'My name is Edward. I'm here to take you to the St Regis. Let me take your bags.' He took Grace's suitcase, but Charlie said he was fine carrying his own, and the three of them walked to the vehicle. Edward opened the back door, and Grace got in. The seats were pale-ivory leather, and the trim inside the car was dark wood, like mahogany. Charlie sat in beside Grace and cast her a glance of incredulity. Dr Ryan had a Ford motorcar, and the canon had even had a Bentley, but this car was not like anything either of them had ever seen before.

Edward placed their suitcases in the boot, then slipped into the driver's seat. 'It's only a short trip, but the traffic in this city…' he said, turning back to them as he slid their car out into the stream of other motor vehicles. 'I think we'll go Broadway and East 55th rather than West 59th and Central Park onto 5th Avenue. If that's OK with you?'

'We have no idea. We trust you, Edward,' Grace said.

'Carnegie Hall.' Edward pointed to a terracotta brick building that took up one whole corner of a crossroads. 'Famous concert hall. You know how you get there, huh?'

Grace didn't realise he was asking her a question, and she didn't really understand it. She looked blankly at him and then at Charlie.

'How do you get to Carnegie Hall?' Edward repeated. He grinned to reveal a gold front tooth. 'Practice!'

She laughed and explained the joke in Irish to Charlie, who was having trouble adjusting to the strong New York accent. He laughed, and Edward seemed to enjoy that.

'Wanna hear about the hotel?' he asked as someone cut him off with much honking of horns.

'We'd love to,' Grace replied. Charlie seemed too awestruck by everything he was seeing to answer.

'Well, it was built by Colonel Jacob Astor in 1904. He went down with the *Titanic* in 1912, but when he built this one, he wanted a hotel to rival the finest in Europe. And, boy, he sure did that. You see that little copper room?' The car pulled up outside the hotel, and Edward pointed up to a small building under the canopy that went all around the ground floor, made of copper and glass, with curtains in the windows. He laughed. 'That's for the doorman. So if the St Regis is that kind to the doorman, imagine how you're gonna feel.'

As if on cue, a liveried doorman in top hat and tails came to place their cases on a red and gold trolley, and Edward bade them farewell as they were led up the red-carpeted steps, holding brass handrails that shone, up to a gilded entrance with a revolving door. Each door handle was decorated with an ornate S and R, and everything exuded opulence.

'Grace, are you sure we should be here?' Charlie whispered.

'Richard's father insisted we stay here,' she whispered back. 'It's incredible, isn't it?'

The lobby was made of marble, gilded decoration everywhere, with crystal chandeliers and hand-painted ceilings. An incredible gold postbox, with a golden eagle on it, stood in the lobby alongside a stunning grandfather clock. Every alcove and corner held antiques and curiosities, and Grace felt she could spend hours just exploring this place alone. Enormous vases, some as tall as she was, filled with fresh flowers, were on every table.

'This way please, ma'am.' The doorman led them to a large mahogany desk, behind which was a perfectly coiffed young blond woman with alabaster skin and bright eyes.

'Good morning, are you checking in with us at the St Regis today?' She beamed, showing a mouthful of sparkling white teeth.

'Ah, yes, Grace McKenna and my father-in-law, Charlie – Charles McKenna. I think the booking was made by Mr Arthur Lewis?' Grace tried to sound confident and not intimidated, which is what she was.

'Yes, Mrs McKenna, we've been expecting you. I understand you travelled from Europe?'

'Ireland, yes...' she replied. If the woman had noticed that Grace's and Charlie's clothes were not the finest couture, like everyone else in this hotel wore, she gave no indication of it.

'We're very happy to welcome you to the St Regis, Mrs McKenna and Mr McKenna, and we wish you a very pleasant stay. Cyril will show you to your suite and answer any questions you might have.'

A freckle-faced boy of around sixteen appeared in the livery of the hotel.

'And our suitcases?' Grace wondered if she should have taken them from someone.

'Are on the way to your suite already, ma'am. If there's anything we can help you with, please let us know, and welcome to New York. Your personal butler, Schmitt, will meet you there shortly.'

Wordlessly, Charlie and Grace followed the porter to the glass and gold elevator. Grace had never been in one before and was sure neither had Charlie, so she gripped his hand as the doors closed and the boy pressed the number eighteen. They were staying on the top floor. She realised she was holding her breath and allowed herself to exhale. They emerged from the elevator and walked down a deep-pile carpet corridor to the end, where two enormous doors were opened by yet another member of staff, this time a distinguished-looking gentleman with a snow-white moustache, neatly clipped, and a full head of silver hair, combed so precisely that not a hair was astray. He reminded Grace of the king on a pack of playing cards. His dark suit was trimmed with scarlet velvet, and he looked like a child's toy.

'Good day, Mr McKenna and Mrs McKenna. Welcome to the St Regis.' His accent had a trace of something – not American, but Grace had no idea what.

'Hello.' She smiled.

The man turned to the right, down another corridor, into an enormous living room overlooking the tallest buildings she had ever seen. The room had easy chairs and tables, sofas, a huge basket of fruit, a bottle of wine on ice and classical music coming from somewhere.

Charlie whispered, 'I hope he doesn't think we're married.'

She grinned. 'I don't think so.'

'This is your lounge, Mrs McKenna. Here are drinks and snacks. Please help yourself. If you are too warm or too cool, the air flow in the room can be adjusted using this lever...' He showed

Charlie a brass handle attached to an ornate gauge. 'The air comes through these vents.' He pointed to several gold grilles along the walls.

'Your bedroom is here, ma'am.' The man opened a door with a flourish to reveal two double beds dressed in ivory silk and damask, with an arrangement of pink and white roses, at least three feet across, on the side table. Grace's suitcase was on the special stand for the purpose. The man indicated towards a door on the left-hand side of the room. 'That is your bathroom.'

He then pointed to a button on the living room wall. 'This is to summon me should you need anything. And the other room' – he crossed the lounge again – 'is here.' This second room was decorated similarly but with some bronze and gold accent colours, which gave it a more masculine feel. Charlie's bag was on a matching stand in that room.

'Thank you, Mr Schmitt,' Grace managed.

'Just Schmitt, ma'am.' He smiled.

'Oh, I'm sorry…' She felt awkward.

'No need to apologise, Mrs McKenna. You may call me whatever you wish, but I just go by Schmitt.'

'Thank you, Schmitt.'

'I am at your disposal should you have any questions,' the butler added. 'Just press the bell and I will be here presently, day or night.' With a brief nod, he was gone.

They stood and marvelled for a moment or two, then Charlie spoke. 'Gracie, I think I better wake up now, because that back tyre on the bike has a slow puncture and I'll need to patch that up before I lug Weeshie Kelleher's box of whatever he does be ordering from Limerick up the windy gap.'

Grace laughed. 'It is like a dream, isn't it, that places like this even exist? I saw something like this in a film one time, but I thought it was made up for that. How can people need so much?'

'They don't need it, that's for sure. But it's just amazing. I mean, how they can change the temperature in the room with just a lever… If Declan were here now, he'd be itching to take it apart.'

'I know he would.' Grace allowed the wave of grief to pass over her. Tears sprang to her eyes, and Charlie drew her into a hug.

'What would he make of the two of us in here?' He chuckled. 'A postman and a schoolteacher. We could barely afford one of those apples, let alone to sleep here.'

'Richard played down how wealthy his family were, but I knew from things he said. Well, I guessed anyway…'

'It was very generous of his father.' Charlie looked out the window at the Manhattan skyline. 'That's for sure.'

CHAPTER 11

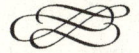

NEW YORK CITY, NEW YORK

'So, how do you feel?' Grace asked Charlie as they sat down the next morning to the most sumptuous breakfast either of them had ever seen. The dining room downstairs was spectacular, but Schmitt had offered them the opportunity to have breakfast in the suite, so they took it. It was as if the war wasn't happening at all. Charlie had kippers and poached eggs, after fresh fruit and juice and tea, and Grace had pancakes with bacon and maple syrup – a substance she had never even heard of until she came here the last time.

'Terrified,' Charlie answered.

'There's no need to be. Sylvia and Joey Maheady are really nice, and Lily and Ivy are lovely girls too.'

When Grace had made the decision to come to the United States for Richard's memorial, she had written to Sylvia Maheady to tell her about Richard and that she was travelling to Savannah for his memorial and stopping in New York City for a few days before leaving for Georgia. She also told Sylvia that she was bringing Declan's father,

Charlie, with her. She had written to them again when their journey dates had been fixed and given the name of the hotel where they were staying. Cyril, the young porter, had brought a telegram to her the previous evening. It was from the Maheadys to say they would travel into the city from their home in Rockaway Beach to meet Grace and Charlie the following afternoon. They said nothing about Lily.

'I'm very grateful to them,' Charlie said. 'I hope they know that. That I don't resent them or anything. They've given my daughter a good life by the sounds of it, and she has opportunities here that I couldn't have given her. The last thing I want to do is cause those people any pain at all.'

'Well, you can tell them all of that yourself later today,' she said kindly. 'Would you prefer to meet them alone or do you want me there? I'm happy to do either.'

'Can you come?' he asked. 'I'd feel better if you were with me. And Gracie, I want to say thank you, properly. If it wasn't for you, I wouldn't be here. I wouldn't even have the chance to meet my child again...' His voice was husky with emotion.

'Well, it's all down to Richard really.' Her eyes filled with tears at the very mention of him. 'He found Mrs McHale and Father Dempsey. Without those parts of the puzzle, we would never have known where to even start looking.'

Charlie reached over the table and placed his hand on hers. 'I know you're trying to help me while inside your heart is breaking. I know it is, because I know how that feels. And you only came here, to America, for me – you didn't want to go to the memorial service. And I'm more grateful than you'll ever know.'

Grace didn't trust herself to speak. Although she'd never been here with Richard, everything about this country – the accents, the cars, the people, the buildings – reminded her of him. How could life just go on? How was she supposed to do that? She had no idea.

She forced her mind back to Charlie and the meeting with the Maheadys. They had suggested meeting at a diner on 7th Avenue at to talk.

'Let's go for a walk in Central Park first and get some fresh air?' she suggested.

'Good idea. How's your leg now after resting? Better?'

She nodded. It had been aching after the voyage, but a bath in the deepest, widest tub she'd ever seen, with bubbles up to her neck, had soothed her. She remembered that first time Richard invited her over. She was supposed to go to a place called Hot Springs in Georgia, where President Roosevelt himself went for treatment for his polio.

Charlie picked up the complimentary newspaper and read the headlines. Earlier in the month a British Overseas Airways flight was shot down over the Bay of Biscay by the Germans, killing all seventeen people on board. The story was still running, not because deaths in this way were unusual – far from it, it was a daily occurrence – but because actor Leslie Howard had been one of the casualties.

'Richard met him once, you know,' Grace said, admiring the photograph of the handsome actor who had charmed the world as Ashley Wilkes in *Gone with the Wind*.

'Did he really?' Charlie shook his head in amazement.

'Yes, as well as being an actor, he wrote articles in London for the *New York Times* and other papers and magazines, and he would sometimes hang around the Associated Press office, or the bar there at least.' She gave a small smile. 'Richard said Mr Howard was always very nice, very down to earth.'

'Poor man, and poor Richard too. Good God, how many more people have to die before that madman is stopped? I know why we have to be neutral, God knows enough water has passed under the bridge between us and the British, but honest to God, it's brutal.' Charlie shook his head sadly. He never talked about the recent past in Ireland, nobody at home did, but Grace knew Charlie had been involved with the IRA, which opposed the partition of Ireland after the War of Independence. But despite that, he was a pacifist, in as much as anyone could be.

'They seem to think it was a plot to kill Churchill. The Germans might have thought he was on the airplane,' Charlie said, folding the paper.

'The purser told me as I was waiting yesterday that they are targeting and hitting U-boats at a great rate in the Atlantic. Which he joked was reassuring once we were docked. Until I reminded him that, unlike most others on the ship, we were going back and had to do it all again in a few weeks' time.'

'Yerra, we'll worry about that then, Gracie. And I think if your time is up, your time is up, so it doesn't really matter...'

'I sometimes think that too, but then if this war had never started, would Declan still be here? Or Richard? Or any of the hundreds of thousands of people who have died because of it?'

Her father-in-law shrugged. 'We'll never know the answer to that.'

Grace stood as Schmitt came to clear the breakfast table. 'We're going to walk in the park, Schmitt.' She wasn't sure if she needed to tell him what they were doing, but he didn't seem surprised.

'Very good, madam. Would you like a parasol?'

She knew what a parasol was but had only ever seen women in paintings use them. 'No thank you, Schmitt. I enjoy the sun on my face. We don't get too much of it in Ireland.'

He didn't smile; in fact she'd never seen him do so. He was very sincere and helpful but extremely serious. Grace had to admit that despite his politeness, she found herself on edge around him.

'Will you be requiring luncheon?'

She looked at Charlie, who shook his head. He let her do the talking because he wasn't as confident in his English, though she constantly reassured him that his command of the language was fine.

'No thank you, Schmitt. We are meeting friends for lunch, and we might get a small snack later, but we won't need a big dinner either.' Neither she nor Charlie was used to the huge portions, particularly after years of rationing at home, so they were full enough now for the entire day.

'Very good, madam. Enjoy your day.' Schmitt withdrew through the large double doors of the suite.

Grace exhaled again. She was more relaxed, even in these sumptuous surroundings, when it was just her and Charlie. 'Right, I'm going to get myself ready, and we'll go in a quarter of an hour. Is that all right with you, Charlie?'

'Fine by me.'

She went to her room and selected the red dress Eloise had insisted she buy when she was in Dublin after Richard left that last time. She'd been so happy then. She and Richard had finally declared their love for each other and planned to marry, and while they knew the war and everything that was going on in the world would mean it couldn't happen right away, it would happen and that was enough.

She would never have chosen red. Agnes always said she was better in dull shades because her copper curly hair was so violently carrot-coloured. Those were the words her sister had used – 'violent carrot'. But Eloise had insisted she try on the dress. It had a square neck and short sleeves and was fitted to the waist, with a flared skirt. When she emerged from the changing room, Tilly and Eloise had gasped, and even two other women shopping stopped and said it would be a sin if she didn't buy it, that it was perfect.

She slipped it on, and she did feel nice. Eloise had shown her a way to pin her hair up while leaving a few tendrils out to frame her face. The Swiss woman had also made Grace promise that she would never wear the dress without a slick of matching lipstick that Tilly had bought her as a birthday present to go with the dress. As she slid the last hairpin in place, Grace looked at her reflection. All she could see was pain.

She looked nice, she supposed. Not awful, anyway. But she'd lost weight, and the dark circles under her eyes were visible beneath her translucent skin. Her green eyes that once sparkled with joy were dull with grief. It was a familiar sensation, like pulling on an old coat. The day Agnes told her that Mammy and Daddy were dead, she was only eleven years old. Agnes said she would have to be brave and not cry, because it wouldn't bring them back, and Grace just had to be a good girl and do as she was told and stay out of the way while the adults managed everything. She'd experienced this then. And years later, as she waited for news of Declan, praying and begging and pleading with God to send him back to her, she'd climbed into her bed – the same one she'd had since she was a child – and felt it again. Panic, emptiness, numbness, a physical pain in her chest, fury, sobbing, silent tears with no sound, a sense of bereft, crushing loneliness, fear for the future...all on rotation. Sometimes the feelings came all at once, resulting in a constriction in her airways. Or in quick succession. But mostly it was one overwhelming emotion at a time.

Logically, and from experience, she knew well that it didn't stay this way. The grief never left you, but you sort of grew around it. Life went on, whether you wanted it to or not, and all you had to really do was hang on. But she wondered – this time, would she ever recover? It didn't feel like she would.

Nobody, not even her closest people, knew what Richard meant to her. She didn't explain. It was a private world, with just the two of them in it; they didn't need anyone else. She knew his people through him; he knew hers through her. But theirs was such a special place, a world where she could say anything, where she could reveal her true self, something she never did with anyone else. Nobody ever did really; everyone just wore different masks. Maybe if she'd met him in real life, and they connected as two physical beings in the world, she might have been more guarded, but they poured their hearts out to each other in letters, said things they might never have said even to each other face to face. There was no need for pretence or showing off. They saw each other as they really were. And she loved him. Oh, how she loved him. And now, like almost everyone she'd ever loved, he was gone, and the loss was nothing short of devastating.

She shook herself out of that train of thought; wallowing didn't help. Charlie was meeting the people who'd raised his daughter today, and after all he'd done for her, holding his hand through it all was something she could do for him.

She stood and smoothed her dress over her hips. She used to be curvier. Richard said he loved how her body looked – something she never envisaged happening to her. But she'd been loved and desired by two men. Three, if you counted Brendan, the New York policeman. She wondered if he was still here in this city. She imagined he was. Should she look him up? She had his address. Maybe it would be nice to see him, but then again, maybe he'd ask, 'Grace who?' She might just have been another in a long string of girls he'd charmed.

She had better finish getting ready, she thought.

It was a pity about the shoes, of course. She would love to be one of those women who could slip her foot into a dainty sandal, or a heel, but that was never going to be. She would be walking a lot; she remembered that from her last visit to this city. So she strapped on her calliper and clicked the steel into the heel of her built-up, tan leather shoe.

Fifteen minutes later, Schmitt called the elevator for them, and she and Charlie descended through the magnificent St Regis hotel.

CHAPTER 12

TWENTY MILES SOUTH OF STRASBOURG

'*Vite, vite...*' Monsieur Ducrot ushered them along the passageway through the bales. It was the furthest walk they'd done in weeks.

'What's happening, monsieur?' Richard whispered in French.

'Our neighbours, they were raided two hours ago, their barns searched, every inch of the farm turned over. They are looking for someone. We have to move you,' Ducrot hissed back, his rapid accented French difficult but not impossible to understand.

'Where is' – he almost said 'Alfie' – 'Felix?'

The old Frenchman shrugged, placed a hand on Richard's chest and gestured with his other hand that they should get behind him. The faint sound of a vehicle, maybe several, hung on the early morning air.

'*Merde,*' Ducrot swore. 'Go into the woods, behind. Dig in. Try to find cover.'

The elderly man shoved them to the right, around the back of the barn. It was dazzling to be in bright sunlight, and Richard's eyes hurt. He blinked and tried to focus.

'Run, fast... Go now!'

Jacob was slower than Richard, his injuries far more extensive, but they both did as Ducrot bid them and ran for the wooden fence that formed the boundary of the farm. They clambered over it, with Jacob half-running, half-limping behind Richard.

The hill behind the farm was covered in dense forest. They didn't dare look back to see if the cars had arrived at the farmyard. They just ran and ran, keeping low. The Ducrots had supplied them with clothes, and they'd pulled on trousers and shirts. So while they weren't in underwear like they'd been when the Japanese captured them in Sumatra, they might not be immediately identifiable as American airmen if caught.

They crossed a meadow, marshy and wet, with ducks and ducklings all around, and several ditches, but the forest was further away than it looked. Richard's chest heaved and he felt nauseous, his lungs burning from the exertion of running after being sedentary for so long. On they ran. Behind them came the sound of barking dogs. It was the Germans all right.

Eventually, hearts pounding, their bodies drenched in sweat and in unbearable pain, they reached the edge of the forest. The trees were in full foliage, so they entered the woods, glad of the sensation of being safe, even if they both knew they were anything but.

The forest floor was dry, the roots of trees criss-crossing a path. Up ahead was a small doe, who stopped and stared, her soft eyes frightened. How she'd made it this far without becoming someone's lunch, Richard had no idea. People were starving, he knew from before he even came here, due to the Germans commandeering the fruits of the abundant French farmland for themselves.

He'd heard a story back when they were in London, how the vignobles of the famous Champagne region, just a hundred or so miles east of where they were now, had taken to relabelling their wine, marking the cheap old plonk as Grand Cru and putting no markings at all on the premium champagne. Any Frenchman worthy of the name would know the difference, but the uncultured swine of the Third Reich had no idea.

They hid wine behind cellar walls, and the cellar networks under the vineyards, there since medieval times and before, became safe places for the Resistance. Didi Georges had once told Richard that the Resistance monitored where the big orders of wine were being sent, as it indicated there would be a large military presence. For all their intelligence, the Germans gave themselves away with stupidity like this all the time.

Farmers like the Ducrots didn't have the luxury of an underground network of tunnels and cellars, though, and so the Boche just stole every single thing, leaving the population to starve.

They slowed a little, just to catch their breath, and wondered what to do next.

'We should find a way of hiding. They could be here any minute if anyone saw us,' Jacob whispered.

Richard agreed, but how? All they could see were trees, and the land was steep, no undulations or hollows to use as a den. Richard still had the knife Alfie had given him that time he had visited. He'd strapped it to his leg as Alfie had done. 'Let's start cutting the lower branches.'

They worked using the knife, taking turns with it, and managed to cut a small number of branches. Jacob took them and placed them around the base of a tree, but Richard shook his head. It was laughably obvious as a hiding place. No, this was not going to work.

'Let's just keep going. There might be another farm or an outhouse or something,' Jacob gasped, the exertion after injury followed by weeks of rest causing his body to rebel.

'All right...'

They walked on. From the bottom of the hill, the forest looked dense, but now that they were here, the trees were very spaced apart; it was a planted rather than a natural forest. Not ideal as a hiding place.

Jacob stopped and pointed upwards. On one of the trees, between three sturdy branches, was a platform, probably built by kids as a type of tree house. 'What do you think?'

'I don't know. If they do come and we're up there and they see us, then it's all over.'

'We could drag the branches we cut up and cover ourselves?'

Richard looked down at the farmyard from the forest. The German vehicles were clearly visible in the Ducrots' yard now, and the same landscape of uniformly planted trees stretched in every direction. No matter which way they went, they'd be seen for a hundred yards.

'It's the best idea we've got, I suppose,' Richard said, going back for the branches they'd cut. Jacob climbed up, not complaining, but Richard could see the agony on his face. Richard shoved the branches up to him before clambering up himself. Helpfully, whoever had put the platform here had cut notches into the bark to give the climber a foothold.

He was halfway up when he heard the voices and saw the Germans making their way across the marshy ground towards the forest. His heart threatening to beat out of his chest, Richard half scrambled and was half dragged up by Jacob. Side by side, they lay flat, partially covered by the branches. Richard felt hopelessly exposed. One glance upwards and they'd be caught. He forced himself to picture Grace and offered up a prayer that he would survive. They'd been in scrapes before; maybe they'd get out of this one too.

There were four Germans – and two dogs. The dogs would surely pick up their scent. They'd had only the most cursory of washes in the last few weeks, and they stank. Jacob's eyes were closed. They never discussed how the fact that he was a Jew would mean his fate, if captured, could be considerably worse than Richard's. They spoke not a word, just lay there, face down, branches on their backs, and Richard watched four German soldiers steadily getting closer.

CHAPTER 13

NEW YORK CITY

Charlie twisted the napkin nervously and looked like he might be sick. They were in a booth in an Italian restaurant called Toffenetti's on the corner of 43rd St and 7th Avenue. They were early; the Maheadys were not due for another twenty minutes.

To distract him, Grace told him the story of the restaurant as it was written on the menu. 'This place opened in 1940 by an Italian man called Dario Toffenetti. He'd already had six successful restaurants in Chicago.'

They gazed in admiration at the thousand-seater place, complete with sleek glass, an escalator, and a stainless-steel kitchen visible from the dining room. Grace had been impressed by the ladies' room too; the décor was so lavish. There were also telephone booths, though she wondered who went to a restaurant and then needed to make a telephone call?

'This air conditioning is amazing, isn't it?' Charlie marvelled. 'I never even knew something like this existed. We'd have no use for it, but they need it here for sure, don't they?' They were speaking in

Irish, and Grace knew she should probably insist they use English so he'd be practiced by the time the Maheadys arrived. But the poor man was in such a state of trepidation, she didn't mention it.

'It's incredible. It's like a different world over here,' she agreed. Even the paintings on the walls were not like any she'd ever seen. According to the menu, they were surrealist and done by an artist called Hugh Troy. That could well be someone famous, but she had never heard of him.

'What do you think you'd like to eat, Charlie?' she asked, thinking it might be better to decide now rather than have him embarrassed when put on the spot by the friendly but busy staff.

'I'm not a bit hungry, to tell you the truth, Gracie, but I better order something or it would look very rude.'

'How about this?' She grinned as she read from the menu. '"Idaho potatoes, bulging beauties grown in the ashes of extinct volcanoes, scrubbed and washed, then baked in a whirlwind of tempestuous fire until the shell crackles with brittleness."'

'That's a lot of words for just a spud,' he said, giving her a ghost of a smile.

'Or what about sugar-cured ham? "These hams are cut from healthy young hogs grown in the sunshine on beautifully rolling Wisconsin farms, where corn, barley, milk and acorns are unstintingly fed to them, producing that silken meat so rich in wonderful flavour."'

Now Charlie grinned; he'd never heard food described in such flowery language.

'Or spaghetti – whatever that is – "one hundred yards of happiness."' Grace laughed.

'And this must be the man himself.' He turned the menu to show her a drawing of Toffenetti himself, with his bald head, under which was the motto 'Your satisfaction is our constant inspiration.'

'I think I'll try spaghetti. I don't know if I want a hundred yards of anything, but I can have spuds at home,' Grace decided.

'I'll have the spuds,' Charlie said. 'There's enough excitement in my life at the moment. I might as well eat something I can recognise anyway.'

Grace knew, being America, it would not be simply a matter of potatoes, and she was right. 'Well, you need to decide what topping you want.' She read from the list. 'Eggs and ham, sour cream and green onions, Monterey Jack, hot mustard and pickle, black-eyed peas, smoky beans...'

'Honestly, I've no idea in the wide earthly world what any of that is,' her father-in-law said. 'At home the only thing people put on spuds is butter. Well, at least I know what eggs and ham are, so I better go with that?' He didn't look sure.

Before Grace had time to answer, she looked up and saw Sylvia and Joey Maheady at the door, looking every bit as uncomfortable as Charlie. She waved to them, giving her broadest smile. They saw her and waved back, making their way towards where she and Charlie sat.

The Maheadys hadn't changed a bit. Almost as tall as her husband, with dark hair and eyes and the olive complexion of her Italian heritage, Sylvia Maheady was in her mid-fifties now, and while she wasn't glamorous in the sense that her clothes were sensible and not flashy, she did exude a certain style. Joey was of Irish descent, tall, thin, and balding, with pale-blue eyes. He was a fire chief now in the Rockaway Beach station.

'Grace, it's lovely to see you again. Welcome back to New York.' Sylvia was warm and effusive, shaking Grace's hand. Joey did the same, but with a nervous smile on his face.

'And you both look marvellous. It's so nice to be back in your wonderful city,' Grace replied. 'Now, this is Charlie McKenna.' She turned to Charlie, who was staring anxiously at the couple, as pale as a sheet. 'Charlie,' she said gently, 'these are Joey and Sylvia Maheady.'

'Mr McKenna,' Joey said, 'it's a pleasure to meet you. Please accept our deepest condolences on the death of your son.'

Sylvia looked over at Grace with sadness in her eyes. 'And condolences to you too, dear Grace,' she said.

Joey nodded in agreement. 'Of course, Grace. It is a terrible loss for both of you. Declan was a wonderful young man, and we loved spending time with him when you and he visited last time. Lily and

Ivy were so very, very sad when we told them. He had a big impact on them, and on Lily especially.'

'Thank you, Mr Maheady,' Charlie said gallantly in his best English. 'I know I can speak for Grace when I say we miss Declan terribly, but all over this world, families are facing the same thing. We can just pray it will end soon.'

They all sat down at the table. Joey sat beside Charlie and Sylvia beside Grace.

'Please call me Joey,' the American man said. 'And to be honest with you, I've been very nervous about today.'

'And please call me Charlie. I doubt you were as nervous as I am. If it wasn't for Grace here, I wouldn't have even considered it, but I always had a hope that one day I might meet...and I'm sorry, my English isn't as good as it could be...'

There was a short, awkward silence, until Sylvia Maheady spoke. 'Why don't you tell us the story, Charlie,' she said kindly. 'We only know it from the point where we adopted Lily – Siobhán, as you called her.' She threw a small smile of encouragement at her husband, who said nothing but nodded his agreement.

Grace exhaled and she could feel Charlie relax too; this was going to be all right.

Charlie told the sorry tale of how his wife Maggie died, and how Canon Rafferty decided that a man alone couldn't raise two children. Declan was only a small boy and Siobhán a new baby. He described how he'd tried everything he could, but it was no good – the canon had the power and he lost his children. He searched, he wrote letters to everyone he could think of, but to no avail.

When he finished speaking, Sylvia wiped a tear from her eye. Joey reached over and squeezed her hand.

'We're so very sorry, Charlie,' Joey said sincerely. 'It seems so crazy that the event that brought Sylvia and me so much joy is the same one that broke your heart.'

'You must know we would never have agreed if we'd known,' Sylvia added hastily.

'Of course not,' Joey said. 'We were told she was an orphan.'

Charlie turned and stared at the couple, his eyes filling with tears. Grace willed him on, she knew he'd been practising the English phrases he wanted to use. 'You both owe me no apology,' he said. 'You have my thanks for the care and love you've given my daughter. I wish that it had not been necessary, but Grace and Declan assured me that Lily is a happy, well-loved girl, and that gave me peace of mind I'd not known since the day they took her from me.'

Grace was surprised when Joey Maheady said, 'So what do you want to do now?'

However, before Charlie could reply, a middle-aged waiter with oiled dark hair swept back from his forehead and big brown eyes appeared with a notepad and pen. He spoke in the same accent as Brendan McGinty – real New York City. It made Grace smile.

'What can I get you folks? We got a ravioli today that you'd do time in jail for. It comes slathered in a rich tomato' – Americans, Grace noticed, called it 'tom-ay-to' not 'tom-ah-to' as they did – 'ragu with *parmigiano*, and chef just pulled a tray of lasagna from the oven that's taking every ounce of willpower I got not to go face down into it and die a happy man.'

The flowery language was not just reserved for the menu, it would seem.

Sylvia perused the menu. 'I'll have the ravioli, but can I get some olives too and some focaccia?'

'Coming right up. And for you, ma'am?' The waiter turned to Grace.

'Well, I think I have to have the lasagna.' She hoped she was saying it right. 'I've never had it before, but you make it sound wonderful.' She handed him the menu.

The waiter winked. 'You won't regret it.'

Joey ordered spaghetti with clams, and then the waiter turned to Charlie.

'What would you recommend?' Charlie asked. 'I'm new to this.'

'How about bolognaise? Ground beef with garlic and onions in a rich tomato sauce, served with pasta and a grating of *parmigiano*? Comes from Bologna, like my folks.'

'If you recommend it, I'll try it. Thank you.'

CHAPTER 14

*L*unch was a friendly and chatty affair, and the four of them discussed at length what would be the best thing to do. It was soon clear that neither party was a threat in any way to the other; Charlie and the Maheadys loved Lily and were all thinking of her best interests.

The food was delicious, if not like anything they'd ever eaten before. Charlie finished his plate of pasta in record time, and Grace thoroughly enjoyed the layers of meat and pasta and a creamy sauce, all smothered with melted cheese, that lasagna turned out to be.

Sylvia insisted she try an olive, a first for both Grace and Charlie, and both pronounced them very nice; although Grace didn't like it at all, she didn't want to offend them.

'What did Siobh – Lily say when you told her she was adopted?' Charlie asked, all reticence or nervousness gone now.

Joey confirmed what Grace and Charlie already knew from Lily's letter to Grace. 'She said she had guessed pretty early on after Declan and Grace visited. She said it was strange that everyone comments on how much Ivy looks like her Aunt Delores – my sister. Which she does – Ivy is the image of Delores when she was young. But nobody had ever said Lily looks like anyone in either my family or Sylvia's.'

Sylvia added, 'Both girls are dark-haired, but honestly, when we met Declan, we knew, even if we couldn't admit it – even to each other – at the start. And we were terrified he was going to claim her, try to take her from us.'

'All Declan wanted was to make sure she was safe,' Charlie said softly, the pain of the loss of his son as plain as day.

'We know that now, of course. And we know now that while you have lost a son, and Grace a husband, Lily has also lost a brother who loved her.' Sylvia was so sincere, so genuine, Grace could feel her empathy radiating towards them.

'Does she know about me? Being here, I mean?' Charlie asked nervously.

Joey shook his head.

'Not yet,' Sylvia said, throwing an anxious glance at her husband.

'I guess we just wanted a chance to meet you first,' Joey added. 'You understand that, don't you?'

'Of course, I do,' Charlie replied. 'Sure, I'd have done the same myself. It's a sign of what conscientious parents you are, not letting any Tom, Dick or Harry barge into her life without checking him out first.'

The two Maheadys looked relieved at this.

'She does know a little about you,' Sylvia said, 'from Grace's letter.' She turned to Grace with a sad smile. 'She was so excited to receive it, you know.'

Grace had answered Lily's letter at the same time as she had written to Sylvia telling her about the New York trip. She'd told Lily that her mother had died when she was a baby and that she and Declan had been unjustly taken away from their father. Declan had come back home later, but baby Siobhán – Lily – had vanished. Only years later had she and Declan been able to trace her. Grace apologised to Lily for not telling her the truth when they first met, but they had done this to protect her and her parents and Ivy, and Grace hoped she would forgive them for this. She had told Lily about Charlie and Dymphna and the children too.

'But your letter raised even more questions than it answered. For us too – because we didn't know the truth ourselves.'

'Which is why we jumped at the opportunity for…this,' Joey said.

'It seemed like the right thing to do,' Sylvia added.

'And now? Will you tell her about me being here in New York?' Charlie asked.

There was a moment's silence, then Charlie inhaled a deep breath. It was a trait of his that people who knew him were used to. Charlie always paused for a moment before speaking. It could be disconcerting sometimes, but he thought about what he said, and he was measured in his responses to everything. 'I know how difficult this is for you both, but I would very much like Lily to know I'm her father, to know about her mother, my late wife, Maggie, and her brother, Declan. I'd like her to know we never forgot her, that she was always loved and much wanted.' He exhaled, pausing again. 'But I also will be guided by you, her parents, as to what would be the best thing for Lily. You know her best, and I would never want to cause her, or you, hurt or pain.'

It was one of the longest speeches Grace had ever heard Charlie McKenna make – and in English too.

Sylvia and Joey looked at each other. Grace's heart went out to them. She could see the fear and anxiety in their eyes as they considered what was best to do.

Then Joey nodded and Sylvia said simply, 'Yes.'

'Lily's an adult now,' Joey said. 'She has the right to make her own decisions. So Sylvia and I will tell her you're here and let her decide what she wants to do next. Is that OK with you?'

Charlie swallowed, and Grace met his eye, giving him an encouraging smile.

'Thank you. Thank you very much. That would be very good,' was all he could manage.

'We'll talk to her tonight,' Sylvia said, 'and let you know in the morning how it went.'

'We'll be here for another two days, then we go down to Savannah,' Grace explained.

'For Mr Lewis's memorial. Oh, Grace...' Sylvia looked at her with such compassion, Grace felt her heart might burst. 'You've had to endure so much. I just pray your suffering is over now and that you find peace.'

Grace just nodded. She knew it was hard for people to find the right words; she also knew they meant well. But if Richard was truly gone, she didn't believe her suffering would ever be over. It couldn't be, because the rest of her life would stretch before her without him – and that to her was inconceivable.

Charlie insisted on paying the bill, carefully counting out the unfamiliar dollars. Irish money was a different colour, shape and size for each coin and note, but in America the notes all looked so similar, it was hard for him to navigate.

The Maheadys left the restaurant with the promise to call the hotel the next day, and Grace and Charlie found themselves out on the streets of New York City. Grace knew she should probably suggest some sightseeing, but her heart was breaking and she just didn't have the energy for it.

'I was thinking, Gracie,' Charlie said, 'maybe we should pay a visit to Mrs McHale? She was very fond of Richard, and maybe she doesn't even know he died. And I'd like to thank her for all she did to find Lily for us.'

Grace found to her surprise that was exactly what she wanted to do. She wanted to be with someone who knew Richard, who was fond of him, someone she could talk to about him. 'Let's do it, Charlie. Richard said she worked at St Patrick's Cathedral, I went there last time I was here with Declan, we lit a candle at the shrine to St Patrick. I don't know if the Lewises wrote to her or not. I doubt they would have, although she did meet them when Richard and Jacob got that award last year. Either way, you're right. We should pay our respects.'

'I made her a little thing,' Charlie said bashfully. 'Well, it's just a small thing, but I carved a St Brigid's cross out of a piece of bog oak for her. It's back in the hotel.'

Grace smiled at him. It was just like Charlie to do something like that. Declan hadn't got his kindness and ability to make things from nowhere.

'I'm sure she'll love it, Charlie,' she said. 'The hotel is on the way to St Patrick's Cathedral, I think. We just walk along the side of the park again and then turn down 5th Avenue. The hotel is there, and the church is a little bit beyond. I looked it up on the map Schmitt put in our room. So we can go back and collect the cross, then walk over to the cathedral afterwards.'

The heat of the day was oppressive, and they were both anxious to get out of the direct sunlight. The air conditioning in the hotel was so welcome, and they marvelled that everywhere here had electricity, a luxury that had yet to come to Knocknashee.

There was a wireless in the room, and Charlie switched it on to hear the news as the clock struck four. The American radio announcer's voice was so polished compared to the newsreaders at home. Everyone in Knocknashee had a battery-operated radio, where the wet battery would have to be taken to O'Donoghues to be charged. The wall of the back of the shop was lined with wet batteries being charged in turn. It was one of the services Charlie offered – to take a person's battery to be charged and delivered back to them. So many people on the peninsula never even ventured into Knocknashee, let alone Dingle or – God forbid – Tralee. They were almost self-sufficient, maybe buying a bag of flour twice a year, a bit of salt bacon now and again, tea, sugar and salt. They wouldn't believe their eyes if they saw the way life was lived here in New York.

There was a lot of conversation about coal strikes and whether FDR would seek a fourth term. An American submarine had sunk off the coast of Florida, killing everyone aboard, and Grace felt that kinship with others when hearing such things. Families, wives, mothers and children were getting the awful news, and from this day forward, their lives would never be the same. It was a ten-second snippet on the news, but earth-shattering for those left behind.

There was some kind of rioting in a town called Beaumont, Texas, white people attacking the homes and businesses of the coloured people, and Grace remembered Richard trying to explain how things were over here on that subject. Grace felt very weary of it all. Misery and loss, violence and hatred at every turn, and all that was left was grief. She remembered reading something in a book Father Iggy had given her, about revenge. That people who sought revenge and retribution ultimately had to dig two graves, one for the enemy and one for themselves. What was wrong with people?

The news was over, and Benny Goodman's orchestra struck up 'Take a Chance on Love.' She had taken a chance on love.

She mentally shook herself. This wallowing would have to stop. All over the world, people were losing those they loved. She had a strong faith, and she knew that Declan and her parents were in heaven with God. She hoped Agnes was there too. They were looking down on her now and wishing she wasn't such an old misery guts, no doubt. Richard too.

She knew Richard wouldn't want her to mope about like this. On their way back to the hotel, they'd passed a huge cinema, with red ropes on gold stands and a deep-red carpet leading up the steps to the movie theatre foyer, and Grace saw they were showing a film called *Hit the Ice*, starring the comedy duo Abbott and Costello. Maybe she and Charlie could go before they left for Savannah.

When Charlie arrived with the small black cross, exquisitely carved to represent the traditional rushes used to make the St Brigid's cross every February, she took it from him and admired it.

'It's absolutely beautiful, Charlie,' she told him. 'I've never met Mrs McHale, but I know she has great affection for our part of the world. She had relations in Dingle, I think. So I'm sure she's going to love it.' She handed it back to him, and he wrapped it in a piece of silver tissue paper he must have bought specially.

'I hope she does,' he replied. 'If it wasn't for her, we'd never have found them, and I'd be living out my days with Declan gone and not knowing what happened to my little girl.' He shook his head sadly.

'You can call her Siobhán with me, if you prefer,' Grace suggested. 'I know you call her Lily with the Maheadys, but if she's Siobhán in your heart, then we can call her that name among ourselves.'

Charlie paused in that way of his, and then said, 'You know,

Gracie, I thought it would jar with me, especially since it was Maggie who chose the name. Her mother was Jeannie, and she had an Aunt Jean as well, so she said another Jean was too much. But Siobhán being the Irish for Jean, it was the perfect choice. But she's Lily now, and I find I think of her as Lily as well. And sure that's a beautiful name, and God knows the poor girl would confuse the whole country over here if she was called Siobhán.' He chuckled. 'Remember the Cotter girls that came over to their aunt in Chicago last summer, Aoife, Éadaoin and Sadhbh?'

'I do,' she answered. They'd left together because their father's sister had a convalescent home in Chicago, and their aunt was happy to take her three nieces and train them up as nurses, but it nearly killed their mother to let them go.

'Well, I was delivering a letter from them to their parents, and Cáit was telling me they changed their names to Anna, Emma and Susan because nobody could figure out how they pronounced their names. They got tired of explaining, and for a finish, they just picked easier names.'

Grace felt a wave of sadness at that, but trying to explain over and over again that Aoife was pronounced 'Eee-fah', Éadaoin was 'Ay-deen' and Sadhbh sounded more like 'Sive' would get exhausting, she supposed.

'So at least Lily is straightforward anyway.'

'Well, you can tell her her original name when you meet her,' she reassured him.

'If she wants to meet me,' he said with a heavy sigh. 'She might not, Gracie, and I'll have to accept it if she doesn't.'

'She will,' Grace replied with conviction, gazing out the window at the Manhattan skyline. 'I know she will.'

'Well, we'll just have to wait and see, I suppose.' He paused and exhaled again. 'Now…will we go to Mrs McHale, do you think?'

'Yes, let's.' She smiled and took his arm as they left their suite.

CHAPTER 15

SOMEWHERE SOUTH OF STRASBOURG

Dearest darling Grace,
Oh, my darling girl, what I'd give for a piece of paper or a pencil or anything to use to communicate with you. Instead, all I can do is compose letters in my head and hope that somehow the sheer force of my love and willpower will transmit to you and you will know I haven't left you.

To explain where I am and what's been happening...well, it defies explanation, honestly, but I'll try. After we crash-landed in France, through the kindness of strangers and sheer dumb luck, Jacob and I were taken into the care of the local people. And after a few weeks of a battered and broken recovery, we were visited by none other than Alfie O'Hare, who is alive and well and somehow managing to evade the Gestapo. You would never recognise him—he looks completely different—but it's the same old Alfie under it all.

We were being cared for while we regained our strength in the barn of a farmyard; the old couple who owned it took care of us. But they were caught, and we had to make our escape. I don't know what became of them, but I fear it was not good.

Jacob and I ran for a forest behind the house and sought shelter there, but it was not like any forest I've ever been in. The trees were about twelve feet apart and planted in perfect order, with no coverage in between. So we ran but could hear the Germans in the farmyard below us and knew it was only a matter of time.

Jacob saw a platform high up in one of the trees, probably built by kids— or Jacob thought maybe game hunters? Anyway, we cut some branches as camouflage and climbed up, covering ourselves with the branches. The Germans made their way up the hill and into the forest, and within a few minutes, they were so close we could make out their features through the foliage. I was sure the sound of my heart beating would alert them, but they shouted back and forth to each other. They were definitely looking for someone, and they had two German shepherds on chains with them, who were straining to be let go.

They passed us, and we were just about to exhale when one of the damned dogs must have picked up our scent and began barking like crazy at the base of the tree where we were hiding. The officer in charge, an ugly brute with a broken nose and mean eyes, came back and looked up. Once he did, we knew it was all over.

"Come down or we'll shoot," he ordered, as his subordinates trained their weapons on the platform. We were dead either way now, so we did as he told us, and we climbed down and were immediately arrested.

We are now in a barracks somewhere south of Strasbourg—or at least I am. I haven't seen Jacob since we arrived. He was dragged one way and I another, so I don't know where he is or if he's alive. Jacob is Jewish, as you know. He's circumcised, and in his own words, he has a shayna punim, which is, I think, Yiddish for a pretty face, that is, in his mind, distinctly Jewish-looking. I'm scared he'll shout his Jewishness from the rooftops, even if they don't guess anyway. And if he does that, well...

Richard paused his mental letter. Writing to Grace was all that kept him sane in here. The cell was from medieval times, cold stone with only one slit high up on the wall providing natural light, and all he had was a stained pallet on the floor – he tried not to think what the stains might be – a bucket for his waste and a tray of some kind of slop pushed through the door once a day.

If Jacob was dead, and it was a distinct possibility that he was, then Richard had never been so alone. It was hard to stay mentally aware and alert. He found himself wondering sometimes if he even existed, if Savannah and his family and London and Sarah and Jacob were all just a mirage. But Grace – she was the one real thing. She was real, and human, and flesh and blood, not nebulous or a whimsy. She was out there in the world, somewhere far from here, somewhere relatively safe, and all he had to do was stay alive and find his way back to her. In the meantime, he communicated with her through letters in his mind. He'd tried to conjure up replies from her, but that was not possible; his mind went blank. So he had to just write letters to her over and over, telling her of his life. Although nothing ever happened here, apart from the daily interrogations. So the letter was the same most of the time, but it stopped him from going crazy.

I'm hoping Jacob is alive. He's a smart man and a good negotiator, so all I can do is hope. If I had your faith, I'd be praying now. But while I try it sometimes, it all feels a bit ridiculous. How can there be a God if all of this is happening?

You are the only tangible person I can latch onto, Grace; not another person on this earth can anchor me the way you can. And not just because I love you so much, you know that. People fall in love every day, and it's not what we have. We are twin souls.

I met a woman in a field in England months ago. She was a gypsy—Jacob was doing a story on the gypsies. I didn't tell you at the time, because I hadn't yet managed to tell you the truth about how I felt, but she said I had a twin soul and that she had red hair and green eyes. We knew each other before this life, she said. That was you, Grace; you are my twin soul.

Remember I told you about the ugly German officer who arrested me— the one who looks a bit like the farmer in the Looney Tunes *cartoons? Do you know them? His face is all puffy, and his nose is like a squashed tomato. I try to imagine him chasing the coyote with his musket as he shouts at me.*

He paused again. Today's interrogation had been a bit different from the previous ones. It wasn't the usual officer this time. Not the ugly one, but one of his superiors.

Sometimes when he composed his letters, he would tell Grace

what his life in German captivity was like: the beatings, the threats, the way they pulled out clumps of his hair, how his lip was split and how they seemed to wait until it had scabbed over before opening the wound again. He would tell of how, some nights, when he was flung back in his cell, bleeding and confused, all he could hear was a ringing in his ears, and how he feared he'd never hear properly again. Or how his eyes would swell up, so he couldn't see. Tonight, though, he wouldn't tell her that. Tonight, he'd lie to protect her, because that's all he could do for her now.

They wanted him to give them Alfie's name. They wanted him to tell them where Alfie was. Where Didier Georges was. Where some woman named Juliette was. He'd never heard of a Juliette, and he told them that, that he didn't know who they were talking about. He said he was an American journalist for the *Capital* newspaper in New York, that his boss was Guy Falkirk and that he didn't know one single person in France. He gave them Kirky's details in the hope that maybe someone would contact him, through some means, and word would get back that Richard was not dead. And in this fantasy, Kirky would tell Sarah, who would tell Grace, who could then relax, knowing he was still alive.

Today's interrogation was more civilised than usual. The officer offered me a cigarette, but I said I don't smoke. Then he sent one of his underlings out to get me a cup of coffee. I was afraid at first, but he said in really cultured English, "There's no catch, Mr. Lewis. Drink your coffee."

He asked me if I knew anyone in Switzerland, and I said I didn't. Had I ever been to Montreux? There something rang a bell. But why did Montreux mean something to me? I've never been there. Maybe I have—my brain is a bit fuzzy. The only thing I remember clearly is you. I wondered then if Tilly's friend Eloise was from there; she is Swiss. Maybe she mentioned it, or you did, but no...I don't think it was her.

After the coffee a medic came into the interrogation room and started cleaning my wounds. He never spoke, but he stitched my face. I have no mirror, so I don't know what I look like, but I'd imagine it's not great. Esme used to say, "He's so ugly, I'd hire him to haunt a house," which is just about how I feel right now. Then another soldier came in with a leather pouch, and

I was sure this was it—they were just going to inject me with something or do something real bad. But he shaved me and gave me a haircut. I hadn't had that done in what feels like months, and judging by the amount of hair on the floor when he got done, I must have been one hairy man.

He never mentioned anything about Alfie, or Didier, or anything the other guy was obsessed with. I didn't get roughed up at all. I asked where Jacob was, and the officer said he was fine. I don't know if that's true or not—I don't believe a word they say—but maybe he is alive.

I was given a plate of meat tonight and some potatoes; up to now it's just been a watery kind of stew. So something has changed, but I've no idea what.

Well, that's my news, my dearest...

Richard could feel himself getting sleepy now.

I hope you are all right, my darling Grace. I can't wait to see you, and hold you in my arms, and marry you. And we'll live wherever you want—I don't care, so long as it's with you.

Always and forever,

Your Richard

Then he turned on his side, facing the wall, and drifted off to sleep.

CHAPTER 16

SAVANNAH, GEORGIA

Sarah Lewis was in another world as her mother's voice cut through her dream. She had been in a deep sleep, but Caroline had barged into her bedroom and flung up the blinds to let in the bright sunshine, making Sarah's eyes smart. The room was decorated entirely in white, so the overall effect was dazzling.

Sarah didn't need to concentrate on what her mother was saying – it was always the same.

'I understand you are sad about your young man, Sarah, but time and tide wait for no man or woman. And while the first blush of youth is gone, you are still a fine-looking woman. Of course being a widow isn't ideal, but at least you don't have any children. So you could find someone else fairly quickly.'

Caroline hardly stopped for breath when she was on a roll like this. She opened the wardrobe and ran her hands through the various new items hanging there. 'Waiting around like some kind of forgotten old spinster and dressing in that eccentric way you imagine is interesting or bohemian or something isn't going to do you any good. I know you think I'm being harsh, but Porter Bragg is a fine man, and the Bragg place in Raleigh is a beautiful property. And Porter only has sisters, so... They have the most impressive aviary, so many species of birds brought in from all over the world. Randolf Bragg, the grandfather, was an ornithologist, as well as making a fortune in tobacco. And Porter's first wife died, so he's been married and widowed as well. And he is a nice man.'

Caroline stood at the end of the bed, arms folded. As usual, her dark hair was coiffed to perfection, and today she wore a lemon day dress with a white collar and cuffs, cinched at the waist, silk stockings and black patent shoes, diamonds at her throat and ears.

'I know you and I haven't always seen eye to eye, Sarah,' she continued, 'but you're my daughter, and I only want what's best for you. So please, will you get up and get dressed and go to the salon and get your hair fixed. Then take yourself to Jolie Femme and Darlene will do a nice facial, and you can put on that moss-green dress I had delivered yesterday. It's so difficult to find dresses for you, seeing as you are so unnaturally tall for a woman. And you must come down to dinner tonight with Daddy and me and at least meet the man.'

'No,' Sarah said quietly as she sat up. She had no energy for a fight, but she would not be paraded in front of this man like a cow at an auction. Besides, she had decided what she was going to do.

Speaking to David Stiller and his fiancée, Rachel, a few days ago had solidified things for her. They had told her they would marry once the war was over, but until then, it needed to be won, and if not by them, then who? That's why David was fighting and why Rachel had volunteered and was currently serving on a naval hospital ship. Of course David and Rachel were also Jewish, so for them this war was very personal.

Over coffee they'd asked Sarah what her plans were. She'd said she had no idea but knew she couldn't stay here. She explained about the situation with her parents and the promise she'd made to Richard.

'I get it, and I'm sure he just wanted to keep you safe. But if you can't stay here, then don't,' Rachel said simply. 'You're a different person now. We all are. There's no going back.'

'You speak languages,' David added. 'You have contacts. You could be useful. Go to New York, talk to that guy you mentioned – Kirky, was it? Tell him you can't stay here and you want to do something.'

When David said it like that, it all felt so doable. And it was. Daddy would be upset, of course he would. And her mother had grand designs to get her up the aisle with some rich Southern gentleman, which Sarah had absolutely no intention whatsoever of even entertaining for a moment. No, she'd do as David and Rachel had suggested. Wait till the memorial was over, see Grace and then go to New York and take it from there. Poor Porter Bragg would have to find someone else to admire his exotic birds.

Caroline had ignored her refusal and was still talking. 'You need to do something with yourself before the memorial anyway, though if it were up to me, we wouldn't even be having it, but your father is insisting, so you may as well do it today. I have a meeting with Monsieur Delor at ten thirty to finalise the catering. He's saying *fois gras* is too expensive, and the smoked salmon canapes are going to be difficult to source – apparently he doesn't feel comfortable serving it in these straitened times, whatever that means. Honestly, I know he's the best chef in the city, but these people do seem to put on airs, telling me what's appropriate or not.' She sniffed with indignation. 'And he's being paid handsomely, so really –'

'He's right.' Sarah's voice was flat and toneless, but she didn't care. 'It is too much when people are struggling to feed their families. And Richard, of all people, had no time for airs and graces.'

'Oh, for goodness' sake, Sarah, not this communist nonsense again. I know one shouldn't speak ill –' Caroline stopped herself as Sarah threw her a dagger look. 'Well... But honestly, that boy turned your head in some very strange ways. This is how it is – wealthy people of a certain social standing employ the lower orders. Without us, they would have no income. So pretending like we're the villains is very naive and foolish.'

'Jacob was not a boy. He was my husband and the love of my life. He was a man of high morals and believed in equality for all people. And nothing about him was foolish.' Sarah was trying to control her temper; she and her mother had barely had a civil conversation since she got back, but the woman was infuriating. The only reason Sarah was still here at all was because she'd promised Richard and because her father did need her.

'Yes, well, we have very different ideas about that. But let's put it aside for now and put our energies instead into making sure that this memorial is what your father wants and' – Caroline hesitated – 'an appropriate reflection of Richard's life.'

'A wonderful day – that's what you were going to say, isn't it?' Sarah raged at her mother. 'This is just another party to you. A chance to show off your house and your clothes, and to show everyone in Savannah that Daddy isn't divorcing you. You don't even want to have this memorial, I know – you're only doing it for Daddy. You don't even care enough about Richard after he died, isn't that the truth?' Sarah knew what she said was mean, but her mother's callousness had driven her to it.

'I...' Caroline composed herself, smoothing her dress over her slim hips and looking wounded. 'I do not want a memorial because I have no evidence that my son is *actually* dead. But regardless, I will not be spoken to like this in my own home.'

'You won't have to put up with me for much longer, Mother. I'm leaving after the memorial.' The words were out before Sarah had time to think about it.

'Leaving? Where are you going?' her mother demanded.

'To New York.'

'What on earth for?'

'To live, Mother. To work. To help with the war effort. To live my life and maybe travel back to Europe. I might go to Ireland to see Grace. I –'

Caroline snorted, an unladylike sound Sarah had never heard her make before. 'Ireland? Grace? That little crippled girl that became obsessed with Richard? Oh, honestly, Sarah, where do you get these ideas?'

Sarah threw back the covers and stood, moving towards her mother. If they were men or this was a film, she'd slap her now. But this was real life. 'First, Grace is not some little crippled girl – she's Richard's fiancée. She has polio but is perfectly capable. She was not "obsessed" as you call it. She loved him deeply, and in a way that I don't think anyone ever loved him.' She fixed her mother with a steely stare, the implication clear. 'And Richard adored her. If you knew anything about your son, you would know that.'

'Well, last I heard he had some other girl – an English one – so how true he was to the Irish girl, I don't know…' Derision dripped from every word her mother spoke. 'I think your father was wrong to invite her and some other person from Ireland to this event. It will be awkward for everyone, and they won't be comfortable either, mixing with us. Your father doesn't see things like that, because I organise everything. If it was up to him, Esme would be at the top table and Clay the gardener would be drinking champagne with the Smythes. He's got his head in the clouds, just as you do. You get that from him, but someone has to keep a grip on reality.'

'Grace was the love of Richard's life, and he hers!' Sarah shouted. 'And all of your stupid ideas of class and standing meant nothing to him. Just as they meant nothing to Jacob.' She lowered her voice, mirroring the intensity of her feelings. 'I'll leave after the memorial, but I swear to you this, Mother. If you say or do one thing, anything at all, to make Grace feel uncomfortable here – or her friend Charlie – then on my brother's life and on the life of the man I loved, I swear that I will never ever cross the threshold of this house again and you will be dead to me.'

Caroline sighed, sounding bored. 'Goodness, Sarah, must you always be quite so dramatic, my dear? It's really very childish and wearing. Now get up, get ready and be at the salon by ten.'

With that, her mother swept out of the room, leaving Sarah shaking with rage.

This was unbearable. She waited until her mother was called to the telephone and slipped out.

Clay was watering the blooms for the service, the fear of God put in him by Caroline that they would be in anything but tip-top condition.

'Clay, could I ask you for a ride to River Street, please? I know you're probably busy, but I'd appreciate it.' Sarah glanced about anxiously. She did not want her mother to arrive; she'd seen quite enough of her for one day, and she desperately needed to get away. 'Or I could take your truck, and maybe you could pick it up downtown later?'

Clay's truck was his pride and joy and always spotless. 'I sure can, Miss Sarah, but wasn't I s'posed to take you to the salon this mornin'?' he replied.

'I'm not going,' she said firmly.

A ghost of a smile played on the old man's lips. Sarah knew the help secretly hated her mother, so any defying of her was a good thing in their eyes.

'I need to get some more manure for the roses anyhow, so it's on my way... Hop in.'

Gratefully, Sarah slid into the passenger seat – something else that would send her mother into apoplexy. Her daughter riding in a truck with the coloured help? Sarah couldn't care less.

CHAPTER 17

NEW YORK CITY

Mrs McHale beamed at the sight of the visitors from Ireland and ushered them in as Grace explained who they were.

'Well, isn't it just wonderful to meet you now at long last. Richard told me all about you, and I was regaling him with stories of me going out by Knocknashee on my summer holidays as a girl. I used to stay on my uncle's farm in Dingle, and on days off, we'd cycle out to Knocknashee to swim and lie on the strand. Oh, we'd take picnics, and it was grand entirely.'

'And this is Charlie McKenna, the postman of Knocknashee, so he knows everyone.' Grace smiled as she introduced Charlie.

'Come in, come in. It's so hot today, I can't bear to be outside.' The old lady looked exactly as Grace had imagined her: small and round, with rosy cheeks and bright, intelligent eyes. Richard always called her an American Miss Marple, and Grace thought Mrs McHale would be cast perfectly if there was ever a film of the Agatha Christie sleuth.

Her iron-grey hair was cut in a utilitarian way, no fancy waves for her, and she moved slowly. Richard had mentioned she had arthritis. 'They say the heat is supposed to be good for the joints, but 'tisn't any good for mine, and poor Father Orliotto has some kind of desperate thing altogether – he can't stop sweating, the poor man. He do be in a pure puddle altogether by the time he has Mass said. I told him he should put his vestments on over his underpants and don't mind with the shirt and trousers, but he was horrified.' She chuckled and her whole body shook. 'Some priests do be very proper, and more of them, well, you'd be shocked. Father Mack – he's from Tennessee – has some songs that would make a sailor blush.'

The parlour was a small room, with four easy chairs and a table. They took a seat each, and Mrs McHale fussed around. She poured them each a glass of cold lemonade from a jug without even asking. It was tart and so welcome after the short walk from the St Regis. New York summers were punishing, Grace had to admit. The relentless heat and lack of breeze, combined with car fumes and so many people, made the city stultifying.

'Well isn't this a lovely surprise now...and aren't ye brave venturing out in this heat?' Mrs McHale's accent was still Irish, though she'd been in America for decades. 'I'll tell you what, didn't Marjorie Burns keel over in Mass earlier with the heat, and she's fond of the cookies is old Marjorie, so we nearly needed a crane to get her back up, so I'm not long home. Her son was to collect her, but sure he's neither use nor ornament, so I had to wait for fear she'd pass away in the sacristy, and we're flat to the mat with funerals this week already. Anyway, there's no sign of my man – he's obsessed with bears, would you believe? All he can talk about, brown bears and grizzly bears and polar bears. I'll tell you for nothing, I'd rather put down a night with a bear than listen to him going on and on and on...' She shook her head.

Grace smiled as she remembered Richard telling her how funny Mrs McHale was and how she went off on conversational tangents all the time about people nobody knew.

'Now, tell me all about Richard. How's he getting on? I didn't hear from him in a while, but sure the post is atrocious, and I know he's fierce busy with the writing. The night he invited me to see him get his award, well, I've been talking about it since. And his sister, Sarah, and his father too. Such lovely people. But sure, of course they are, because Richard is such a...'

The old woman stopped her chattering when she saw Grace's face. Her hand went to her mouth, and she sat back in her chair. 'Ah, no... please...no. Don't say it.'

Charlie glanced at Grace, then said, 'I'm so sorry. Richard was flying over Germany. He was reporting for the newspaper, and they were shot down. Nobody survived.'

'Oh dear... Oh, dear me. Oh...oh no. Poor Richard. Oh, God rest his gentle soul. Oh, dear me...' She was so shaken by the news that she wasn't making much sense. 'I had nobody to write to, you know,' she said. 'I never had a child, and my husband died long ago, so Richard became... Oh my God. I can't believe it. He was such a beautiful boy, such a kind heart, and oh...' She burst into tears, and Charlie gave her his clean handkerchief, which she took gratefully.

'It's a terrible tragedy,' Charlie said, trying to soothe her.

Grace couldn't say anything; it was all still too raw. She could just about pretend things were all right if she forced herself to. But seeing this old lady, who was so fond of him – and he of her – dissolve before her eyes was too much.

'He was getting married. You two were going to get married, and he wrote to me and said I'd have to come to the wedding. And I was thinking to myself, maybe I could. I haven't been home in forty-five years, there's not many back there would know me now, but I would love to have a reason to go. And I was thinking to myself I could afford the fare, once the war was over, of course. And I could go back and see all the places one last time before I die...'

'You could come anyway,' Grace heard herself say. 'I think Richard would love that, if you did. You could stay with me, and we could go to all the places you used to visit, and we could remember him together.'

Mrs McHale looked at Grace. 'He told me you were the kindest person he'd ever met, and he was right.'

'I mean it,' she said. 'Richard and I knew each other mainly through letters. Even my friends only met him once or twice. So I'd really like to be around people who knew him, who loved him.'

'Well, if you're sure, then I would absolutely love to do that.'

The conversation flowed, and though it was interspersed with tears from both Grace and Mrs McHale, it was a wonderful afternoon in the end. Charlie explained who he was, and thanked her for all the digging she'd done to unite Richard with Father Dempsey and ultimately with the Maheadys.

'Oh, poor Father Dempsey. He did nothing wrong, you know. 'Twas that other fella, Rafferty. He was a terrible man, may God forgive me for saying it about a man of the cloth, but really and truly.' She shook her head, incredulous that a priest could behave in such a way.

Nothing about the canon surprised Grace.

'And your little girl wasn't the only one, you know. I spoke to a man a while back – I told Richard about him – he got a baby from Rafferty too, and he was going to tell the bishop the truth but his wife talked him out of it. She was worried, I suppose, and who could blame her? But once I went searching, I found three more at least.'

'Do you know what became of them? Are they well and happy?' Charlie asked.

Mrs McHale sighed. 'Two of them were adopted by people who moved out of state. One went out to California, I believe, and the other to somewhere in the Midwest. And another little one was adopted, but I think her parents died, so I don't know what became of her. I visit Father Dempsey now and again – he's not well himself these days. He won't have long. Cancer.'

'Ah, the poor man,' Charlie said. 'We'll have a Mass said for him, and please pass on my thanks when you see him. I'm so grateful to you, Mrs McHale. I tried all the years to put it to the back of my mind once I knew there was no way I'd find Siobhán – Lily, as she is now. But when Declan came back and told me that she was happy and well loved, it was such a weight off my mind, I can't tell you. And now I might get to see her again...'

His voice cracked at the emotion of it all, and Grace prayed the Maheadys would send a message to say Lily wanted to see him. If she didn't, it would break Charlie's heart all over again. She had assured him that it was all going to be fine, that of course she would want to meet him, but what if she didn't?

The old lady reached over and patted Charlie's hand. 'You're welcome, Mr McKenna. Sure, to be truthful, I enjoyed it. I should be retired long ago, but they keep me around here out of pity. They know I'd only be rattling around my house on my own if they gave me the sack, so they let me stay on. But they have younger, fitter people to keep track of everything nowadays.'

'I doubt that very much, Mrs McHale.' He laughed. 'I'd say you are fairly vital to the whole operation.'

The bells rang for evening Mass.

'Now, I'm very sorry, but I have to go and play the organ for the choir. Our usual organist, Mr Delancy, is a much more competent player than me, I should say. But he broke his finger. He was cleaning his gutters, and didn't he feel something furry, and he's scared stiff of mice. But sure 'twas only a hairnet in the end, but 'twas enough to send him flying off the ladder and into his neighbour's yard, and he crushed her violets so she nearly made him eat the hairnet, so I'm the stand-in. Will I see you both again before you leave?'

'Would you like to join us for lunch tomorrow?' Grace said. 'We leave for Savannah the following day, but if you are free, we'd love to treat you? We're staying at the St Regis.'

'Well, now, isn't that one for the books!' The old lady chuckled. 'The St Regis. Do you know I never set foot inside the door of that place in all the years...'

'Well, we wouldn't be either, I can assure you, but Richard's father insisted on putting us up there.' Charlie looked a bit embarrassed.

'He's a right character, so he is, that older Mr Lewis. Danced the legs off me the night of the awards. And handsome too. Oh, you'd stand up to look at him, so you would.' She winked at Grace. 'So 'twasn't from a stone that Richard licked his good looks. And his father's not short of a bob or two, that's for sure, but a genuine man for all that.'

'So will you come tomorrow for lunch?' Grace asked. 'Charlie may not be there if he's meeting his daughter, but I will.'

Grace saw a look of panic cross Charlie's face at the thought of her leaving him alone to meet Lily, but she thought it would be for the best. Besides, she wasn't emotionally stable enough to go to that; she'd probably dissolve into tears and ruin it for everyone.

'I'd absolutely love to,' Mrs McHale said. 'Thank you very much. We can raise a glass to our boy. May the Lord keep and protect him.'

She showed them out, and to their dismay, the wall of heat in the city had not abated even slightly, although the sun was setting. They joined workers as they hurried home, jostling each other as they made their way along the streets and down into the subway.

'It's like another world, isn't it, Gracie?' Charlie commented as they walked along 5th Avenue. The shops were so glamorous and expensive-looking, and though there was a war on, you'd never know it here. Everyone was much better dressed and seemed in such a terrible rush all the time. Fabric was in short supply, and like in Ireland, dresses had got shorter and tighter, and it was quite common to see a dress made with two different fabrics. But while in Ireland it always seemed to Grace to look a bit haphazard, here it looked as if it was done on purpose. The mannequins in the window of the beautiful Saks store showed dresses with cinched waists, wide belts, soft necklines and beautifully cut skirts.

'Could you live here, do you think?' Charlie asked.

She thought about it. 'I often wondered where Richard and I would live. I could never picture him in Knocknashee, and London was only where he was for the war. His mother and him didn't get along, so I don't think he'd want to live in Savannah. I did wonder if here in New York would be a compromise…but it feels so ridiculous now.'

'I don't know. If I was a young fella again, with no responsibilities, I might have tried my hand to this place.'

She smiled. 'Don't let Dymphna hear you say that. She told me when we were leaving not to let you get any mad notions of dragging them all over here.'

He laughed. 'No, those days are behind me now, but it's some place, though. And no matter what happens, Grace, I'll always be so grateful to you for the opportunity to come here, even if Lily doesn't want to see me.' He sidestepped and held her arm as a man in a business suit nearly bowled them over.

'I'm sure she will, Charlie...' Grace tried to reassure him.

'Ah, sure, if she doesn't, I won't blame her. To her, I'm nobody, just some old Irishman. She couldn't remember anything – she was only tiny when she was taken – so maybe she won't want that in her life. I don't have much to offer her, especially compared to everything they have over here. Even if she does want to meet me, what am I supposed to say, Grace?'

She could tell that though he longed to see her, a part of him was terrified, and she didn't blame him. Of course it was daunting. 'Let's worry about that when we need to, all right?' she said, linking his arm as they passed a store called Russeks selling fur coats. No prices were in the window, but Grace could only imagine. Also the idea that it would ever be cold enough here to need a fur coat seemed unbelievable as the sweat ran in rivulets between her shoulder blades.

As they entered the mercifully cool hotel, Grace and Charlie both stopped in their tracks.

Charlie stopped as if rooted to the spot. Joey and Sylvia Maheady waited awkwardly, feeling as out of place as he and Grace did in these lavish surroundings, but the tall, athletic girl with sleek, long, nut-brown hair and piercing blue eyes seemed not to notice the expensive fittings and furniture, the air of money and grandeur. She had eyes for only one person. He was there, gazing at her, and she at him, and it felt like time stood still. All around people milled, but Grace and Charlie faced the Maheadys square on, fifteen feet of polished marble between them.

Lily Maheady glanced nervously at her mother, whose hand was on her back. Sylvia gave her a small nod and Lily swallowed. Slowly she walked forward, leaving her parents, and moved towards him, her eyes never leaving his. Without saying a single word, Charlie McKenna opened his arms, and as tears rolled down his cheeks, he welcomed his daughter into his embrace at long last.

CHAPTER 18

'I think I knew – not really knew, but something – when I met Declan. Something about him... I was only fifteen, but there was something familiar about him, and Mom and Dad were being weird every time I asked anything, but they were happy for me to write, and when he wrote back...' Lily was sitting on the sofa in the suite, one leg curled under her, as she faced Charlie.

'We just needed to know you were all right. We never forgot you. I tried so hard to get you back – I went to everyone. And your parents had no idea that I was alive. The person who arranged it, he told them a lie, that both your parents were dead, when in fact I was not.'

'Tell me about my mother,' she said, her gaze never leaving his face. It was as if she couldn't stop looking at him.

Lily was a self-assured eighteen-year-old and the one who seemed least fazed by the situation.

The Maheadys drew Grace aside. 'We're going to take a walk,' Joey murmured, 'maybe grab some ice cream, give those two some time to talk and not feel like they're goldfish in a bowl.'

He smiled, and Grace could see the tiny hint of sadness in his eyes. He was glad for Lily to know her father, of course he was, but a job that had been all his was now shared and would be forever more, and that was hard for him. Grace admired him so much; he was a wonderful father, and Lily and Ivy were lucky to have him.

'I think they want you, though...' Sylvia said a little hesitantly, not wanting to appear like she was issuing instructions. Everyone was trying so hard to be aware of others' feelings, it was touching. And so at odds with what was going on in the world. She wondered how individual people seemed so kind for the most part and yet this chaos of violence and destruction threatened everything they loved.

'I'll stay for a bit, but if they're getting on fine, I'll let them at it too,' Grace murmured.

Sylvia left, and as Joey was going through the door, she took his hand and leant in to whisper in his ear. 'This is a wonderful thing you are doing, both of you, but you especially. And I'm so glad for Charlie and Lily, but I hope you know that no matter what relationship they develop, you will always be her daddy.'

Joey squeezed her hand and nodded, his eyes bright.

Grace returned to the room to find Charlie laughing at Lily's impression of her teacher, who was Irish. They were getting on beautifully, and she wasn't sure she was needed at all.

'Grace, Lily is telling me how she wants to go to university to study medicine, if you don't mind. It's very expensive, but she's been selected for a swimming scholarship.' Charlie was bursting with pride.

'Oh, that's really exciting. Which university will you go to?'

'Vassar,' Lily said proudly.

'Oh my.' Grace was impressed. 'I've heard of that one. It's very prestigious, isn't it? Well done, Lily. You must have worked very hard to get in there.'

'I really did. I spent the last two years studying. Well, studying and swimming. Mom and Dad couldn't afford to send me there, and I really wanted to go, so a scholarship was the only way. I was lucky, though. The competition for the scholarships all over the country has lessened since all the men are being drafted. No doubt when the war is over and they all come back, us girls will get shoved aside again, but we may as well get some good out of this awful war.'

'I'm sure you'd have got it anyway, war or not.' Charlie beamed proudly.

'Did my mother like literature, or science or sports?' Lily asked.

Charlie's face softened as their daughter spoke about Maggie. 'Well, Lily, things were very different for us, and they still are really. Maggie grew up on a small farm not far from me. Her father died of tuberculosis when she was only eight years old, and her mother had to work very hard to keep the family going without him. Maggie had three sisters, all of whom emigrated, two to England and one to Australia. Maggie was due to go too. She'd had to leave school and get a job from the time she was thirteen, so her education was limited. But a funny thing – when you'd write to Declan and send him the little drawings you did, it always reminded me of Maggie. She was wonderful at drawing. I have a book at home with some of her sketches in it. She never had any training or anything – it just came naturally to her. She could draw the dog or a cat or a person, no bother at all to her. If she'd been given a chance, she might have been able to make a living at it, but things were different then.'

Lily's eyes softened with sadness at the unimaginable hardship Maggie had endured.

'She could read, of course,' Charlie continued. 'And she loved books. When she and I started courting – well, I hadn't any more money than her. My parents were poor too. My dad had a fishing boat, and I got a job labouring for a local farmer. When Maggie and I met, we had no idea how we could ever marry – even renting a house was beyond us. But we saved up every penny we had. Luckily, the farmer I was working for was a nice old man. He saw we were doing our best, so he gave me a ruined old cottage on the farm and said I could have it if I'd do it up.'

'Gee, that sounds so tough.' Lily's brow furrowed.

'It was, but we didn't know any better. Nobody had much back then. We were delighted with ourselves. We thought we were in Buckingham Palace, and we set about making the cottage habitable. We had to reroof it, so Grace's father, Eddie Fitzgerald, who was my friend, and a few other strong men around the place helped, and we fixed it up so it was fine and cosy. Maggie made everything inside the house. She used orange boxes to make the bit of furniture we had. She was working in the local convent – cleaning and cooking and that – so they gave her an old bed and two armchairs that had seen a great many better days. But it was like gold for us. We married and thought we had a palace.'

Lily smiled at the description. 'And then Declan was born?'

'He was indeed, and poor Maggie had a very hard time having him. There were no doctors much at that time – or we couldn't afford to be calling one anyway – but she survived it, and so did he.'

Grace had never heard this story in depth, so she was as fascinated as Lily.

'After that, poor Maggie had a lot of miscarriages. Three. I remember them all. I wanted to stop trying – it was too hard on her...' Charlie looked uncomfortable speaking of such matters, but the need to have Lily understand Maggie's situation overcame his shyness. 'But she refused to consider it.'

'Did you have to use some kind of birth control?' Lily asked baldly. 'I did a project this year on Margaret Sanger, the pioneering woman in the area of female reproduction and contraception. She got herself into some very difficult battles, but it is so fascinating.'

Charlie caught Grace's eye. Lily was a product of her world and didn't realise that even discussing matters like that were totally taboo in Ireland. For one thing, not much in the way of birth control was available, and for another, it was strictly forbidden by the Church, so no doctor would prescribe a woman any way of controlling her fertility. Abstinence was the only guaranteed way.

'No, that wasn't an option,' Charlie said with a wry smile.

'Why not?' Lily asked. 'I know the Church is against it. It's the same here. But you don't have families of nine and ten kids here, so someone is doing something.' She smiled knowingly.

'Well, that's as may be, but Ireland is very different. There, what the priest says goes. If he says no birth control, then that's the law and no more about it.' His voice had a hardness to it that Grace remembered from any time he spoke about the power of the Church. Lily picked up on it, Grace could tell.

'The priest isn't having to feed and clothe and educate these kids, though, is he?' Lily was indignant on her parents' behalf.

'Indeed.' Charlie nodded. 'But anyway, imagine our delight and amazement when five years after Declan was born, you were on the way.' He smiled and swallowed. 'Your mammy was so happy – she cried when she told me. She said she just knew you were going to survive to full term and be strong and healthy. She was very careful, no lifting anything, and little Declan was such a good lad – he was a great help to her. Slowly we started to dream that you might be born.'

'Tell me about my birth…' Lily hung on Charlie's every word.

CHAPTER 19

The searing New York heat outside created a haze over the city, but the air conditioning in the suite made sure they were comfortable. They sipped fruit drinks that had a kind of fizz to them that Lily called soda, big lumps of ice floating in the glasses. Grace took a seat on an upholstered chair near the window, near enough to hear but far enough away not to intrude.

'It was a beautiful spring day,' Charlie began. 'The clock had gone forward that day – I remember that. And there was a lovely smell of sweet furze on the air – the tiniest bit of heat from the sun releases the fragrance from the furze bush.'

'What is that?' Lily asked.

Grace settled herself, content just to sit and listen.

''Tis a bush we have, hard spiky leaves, but the flower – oh, it's lovely, so it is. It flowers twice in the year – once with a smell and once without. That bright-yellow velvety flower with a sweet honey scent is the one that tells us we've survived another winter and spring is on the way. It's a sign of hardship over, and we can turn our faces to the sun and look forward to the future. And that's what you were like for Maggie and me. And for Declan too. He was so excited to be a big brother.'

'Was it night or day?'

'It was mid-morning. I was just coming back after doing the milking and the various other jobs on the farm when Declan came running up the boreen to meet me. "Daidí, come quick. Mammy is making a strange noise and she's holding onto the table," says he.'

Lily smiled at the description.

'I knew Maggie was over her time – the poor girl was very uncomfortable those last weeks – so I sent Declan up to the farmhouse to have them summon Dr Ryan or Nurse Casey. I knew the farmer's wife, Kitty, would mind Declan, because 'twas arranged that she'd take him when the time came.'

At this point, the butler, Schmitt, made a discreet appearance, asking if they wanted anything. Grace ordered some more cold soda because even with the air conditioning, it was still so very hot. The man nodded and left.

Lily settled herself in the couch to get more comfortable. 'Go on… please,' she said, once the butler was gone.

'Well, I arrived at the cottage, and, sure enough, you were on the way all right. So I helped Maggie to the bed, and together we waited for the nurse or the doctor. It was getting on in the day now, and poor Maggie was in terrible pain, but there was nothing to do but wait. I knew someone would be out to us as soon as they could, but it's a very big peninsula we live on, and they could have been anywhere. I didn't dare leave Maggie alone, so I had no choice but wait.'

'Were you there when Declan was born too?' Lily asked, and Charlie chuckled.

'Indeed I was not. Her mother and the nurse were, and they hunted me out. I was told to go off and do a day's work and I'd be told in due course.'

'And where was my grandma this time?' Lily asked, and Charlie smiled at how she'd claimed the family already.

'She was crippled with rheumatism, the poor woman. She used to cycle a bike, but she wasn't able any more by that time. So she had to be collected, and I had no car or even a trap. And anyway, as I said, I couldn't leave Maggie.'

Charlie stopped as Schmitt arrived back with a tall silver jug of soda, ice clinking on top, and three cut-glass tumblers with slices of fresh lemon in them. He poured them each a glass and retreated once more. It was as if he had wheels instead of feet, his movement was so fluid.

'So what happened?'

'Maggie said to me that you were coming, and I had a look, and sure enough, you were. She nearly broke the fingers in my hand, and I thought I was going to have a heart attack into the bargain, but together, we helped you come into the world.'

'You delivered me? On your own?' Lily gasped.

'Well, Maggie was doing the work, but I helped, I suppose.' Charlie beamed at the memory. 'She held you, and I waited while she delivered the afterbirth. Then we scalded the scissors with boiling water and cut the cord.'

'With no medical help at all?' Lily's blue eyes were wide with amazement.

'The nurse arrived soon after, and I was shooed out of course. Men have no business in that situation generally. But I was very proud to have been there to help. And oh, you were such a beautiful little thing. And you would look up at me and grip my finger with your little fist and...' Charlie's voice wavered, and Grace knew that the next part of the story was going to be so painful for him.

'You don't have to tell me if it's too hard,' Lily said quietly.

Charlie shook his head. 'She was your mother, you should know.'

Lily reached across the sofa and took his hand in hers, wrapping all of her fingers around one of his. Charlie looked down, then looked up at her and blinked back tears.

'A few hours after you were born, Maggie was struggling to breathe. We thought maybe just the exertion of giving birth, she said she was grand, she thought she had pulled a muscle in her leg, and it was aching. She was nursing you on and off and I gave Declan his tea. You were settled in the crib beside our bed, and when I got Declan to bed I went back into the bedroom and I tried to talk to her, I couldn't. She couldn't speak and kept pushing me away. I was so worried. You and Declan were asleep, so I jumped on my bike up to the farm to get Kitty to come down while I went for Dr Ryan.'

Charlie swallowed. 'The doctor came. He brought me back in his car, but I knew by Kitty's face, it was too late. Maggie was gone. Just like that.'

'Oh, Charlie... I... What was it?' Lily was crying now too.

Charlie sniffed and took his handkerchief from his pocket, blowing his nose and wiping his eyes.

'A clot, most likely. The pain in her leg was the clot, and it went to her lungs and...' He swallowed. 'It's not uncommon. Her grandmother collapsed and died of the same complaint two years before, so there might have been something in her family.'

'It was quick, I guess. At least that,' Lily said, trying to find something to say. Grace's heart went out to her; there was no right thing.

'I drive myself mad, even now, wondering did she know? Did she feel alone? I wasn't there, and while she was waiting for me to come back, you woke up, so Kitty left Maggie and was trying to soothe you. Then Declan woke, so she was busy with you two, and when she went back up to the bedroom, Maggie was gone...'

The three of them sat in silence. Any platitude such as 'I'm sure she didn't' or 'she wouldn't have known' was trite and meaningless and disrespectful. The truth was they would never know the last thoughts that went through the mind of poor Maggie McKenna.

'So what did you do?' Lily asked eventually.

Charlie stood, walked to the window and looked out over the Manhattan skyline, his hands in his pockets, his back to them. Lily caught Grace's eye, looking worried she'd pushed too far.

Grace nodded reassuringly and mouthed, 'It's all right.'

Charlie spoke again but didn't turn back to them. 'I won't make any excuses. I should have been strong. I should have shown that I could cope. But I was devastated. I couldn't imagine my life without her. Dr Ryan arranged for a woman who'd been nursing her own child to feed you, and Kitty took care of Declan. I was numb – incapable of anything. It was like I was underwater. I could hear people talking to me, but I couldn't understand what they were saying, and anyway, I didn't care what they were saying.'

Grace and Lily sat silently and still, listening to every word.

'My friend Eddie, his wife Kathy, Maggie's relations, Mary O'Hare, Nancy O'Flaherty, everyone who cared about me and Maggie and our children, tried to reach me, but I...I... Lord knows, I tried. I did try, but I was consumed by the pain.

'Then one night Nancy came to the house, and she said if I didn't buck up and pull myself together, the canon was going to take you and Declan, have you placed with families that could care properly for you. She said I was clearly unfit to look after you. And if that was what I wanted, then I was going the right way about it.'

Grace was shocked; she could never imagine the gentle postmistress being so harsh to a friend in such pain.

'We argued, but you know, it shook me. I couldn't lose you too. So the next morning I got up, washed and dressed and shaved and went to the house of the woman who was caring for you. Mrs Maguire was her name – a grand woman, she was – and she lived just outside the village. My plan was to get you – or at least work something out with her where she could feed you but I'd care for you. I hadn't really thought about it beyond getting my children back. Then I was going to collect Declan from Kitty. I even stopped in O'Donoghue's and got him a few sweets, just to say sorry for being so useless and to reassure him that he was going to be all right.'

The distant sound of the New York traffic, the hum of activity, was all that could be heard in the sumptuous room. Charlie's voice was low and his delivery slow, each word causing pain, but all three knew it was necessary.

'I arrived at Mrs Maguire's house, and she told me that Canon Rafferty had come that morning and taken you away. I didn't wait for any further explanation and cycled as fast as I could to the parochial house. But Kit Gallagher, his housekeeper, said he wasn't there and didn't know when he'd be back. She shut the door in my face.'

Grace remembered the late housekeeper and could well imagine her doing something so cruel.

'I went to the farm where I was working to get Declan, only to be told the same thing. The canon had taken him.' Here, Charlie exhaled loudly through his nose, trying to steady himself.

'Eddie and Kathy Fitzgerald, Grace's parents, tried to help. Everyone did. But the canon was missing, and nobody knew where he was. Next thing I knew, I was summoned to a sitting of the district court in Tralee, only to find myself accused by a solicitor for the Church of being an unfit parent. They claimed I was a heavy and habitual drinker – which I wasn't, not at that time anyway – and it didn't matter how much I or Eddie Fitzgerald, who spoke up for me, told the judge that just wasn't true. He'd already made his mind up. Within about two seconds flat, he ordered that Declan and Siobhán McKenna be formally taken into care. Which meant the canon could effectively do what he liked with you.'

Charlie's voice was almost robotic now, dull and mechanical, but Grace knew it was masking deep trauma at the harrowing memory.

'I tried so hard to find you both,' he continued. 'I begged. I cried. I wrote letters. I scraped enough money together to get a solicitor, but to no avail. You were gone, and that was all there was to it. For years after, I tried. I wrote hundreds of letters, but it never amounted to anything. They wouldn't even tell me where you were.'

He turned to face them, his face craggy and a mask of pain. 'Canon Rafferty called the guards on me for setting foot on his property, said I'd find myself in jail if I harassed him any more. He had nothing more to say except that you and Declan were much better off, and I knew if I had a record of any kind, I could wave goodbye to ever seeing you again, so I had to accept it.'

'I'm so sorry,' Lily said, her eyes welling up with soft tears.

Charlie pursed his lips. 'I started drinking that night after Sergeant Keane left, telling me I'd have to let it go or he'd have to arrest me. And I didn't stop...for a long time.'

'But you did stop, Charlie,' Lily said gently. 'And Declan came back. He knew you loved him. And you found me...'

She stood, crossed the room and put her arms around him, resting her cheek on his chest as his arms went around her in return. 'It's OK. It's all OK.'

She soothed him as slow, silent tears rolled down his face.

CHAPTER 20

SOMEWHERE SOUTH OF STRASBOURG

As Richard walked around the exercise yard, the warm sun felt good on his face. He had panicked when the guard had come in and said simply, 'Out.' Another interrogation? He'd been left alone for over a week, fed every day and even given water to wash, but still no word about what was going to happen to him, or where Jacob was.

His muscles ached. He'd tried to stay physically fit in the cell, but it was so small and dark, it was difficult. There were a few other prisoners in the yard too, all of whom eyed him with suspicion. He was surprised to be led to this yard, and the guard nodded as if to say 'Well, go on then' as Richard lingered at the gate.

He walked in a circle, his face tilted upwards, and inhaled. Maybe he would survive, maybe he'd see Grace again, maybe there was cause for a tiny glimmer of hope.

The other prisoners were smoking, standing in a corner together, while he walked alone.

As he was on his second circuit, he saw a barrel of water in the corner of the yard, a metal cup on a string attached to it. He approached it and dunked the mug, as he'd seen another man do a few minutes earlier, and drank deeply.

The other men were then barked at to leave, and he went to follow, but the guard put his hand on his chest, impeding his progress. 'Halt.'

Richard felt worried and squirmed as the others walked past him, followed by the guard, the prisoners looking even more hostile than before. He assumed they were French, but since speaking was forbidden, he couldn't be sure. Who did they think he was?

The gate to the exercise yard clanged closed behind the men, and he was alone. He had no idea what would happen now. It was all so confusing. Beating him up almost daily for weeks, then the cordiality and totally different line of questioning, then nothing, but better food and no beatings. And now this. Were they playing games with him? And if so, why?

When he and Jacob were arrested, they had no identification on them. But their French was so poor, despite all the work with the romance book and the dictionary, they had to admit to being Americans, never sure if that was a help or a hindrance to their cause.

As far as Richard was aware – some of the interrogations were a bit of a blur – he was fairly sure he just kept saying the same thing over and over. He stuck to the truth in as much as he could – he was a journalist for the *Capital*, he was American, his name was Richard Lewis, he parachuted out of a plane that had been on a reconnaissance mission over Germany.

He told them he didn't know any of the others aboard except for Jacob. Who, of course, was not a Jew. Richard said he'd known him all his life, that they were school friends from Savannah, that Jacob was Episcopalian just like he was. Their families were friends, their mothers in the same church group, their fathers played golf together. He'd prepared that story with Jacob in the barn, going over it again and again. While Jacob was not happy about denouncing his faith, he did agree it was his best chance of getting back to Sarah. They even concocted a reason for him being circumcised – it was because he'd had balanitis as a child, and it had been done for medical reasons. His name was Jake, not Jacob, and his surname Nunez was of Spanish origin. With his slight frame and dark features, he could easily be Hispanic.

All Richard could do now was hope Jacob stuck to the story and that they believed him. He prayed the Nazis had fallen for it.

Richard was now so unused to exercise that his legs ached from walking. He longed to sit down but didn't dare. He thought about Grace, wondered where she was now. He allowed his mind to wander to Knocknashee. He pictured her coming out of her house, wearing her green dress, with her copper curls loose down her back. She would cross the street to Charlie and Dymphna's house, maybe call in for a cup of tea. It was mid-morning, so Charlie would be out on his post round, but Grace would have a cuddle with baby Séamus, the world's smiliest baby, who had no idea of the level of chaos going on in the world around him – he was safe and loved, so all was well.

Maybe she would go to the beach and meet Tilly and Odile for a picnic. Eloise might be there too, and all four would go paddling in the cold, clear water of the Atlantic, running from the waves and giggling if they got caught by the icy water. Three young women and a little French girl, who had no idea she was French, or that her mother was missing, or that her father was dead at the hands of the most evil regime the world had ever seen.

Richard was startled out of his daydream by the scrape of the prison yard gate opening, its hinges badly in need of some oil. The bright sunlight blurred the silhouette of the person entering, and Richard shielded his eyes to see better, but he could only make out a man in a suit, not a military uniform.

The man walked purposefully towards Richard, both hands loose at his sides. As he came closer, Richard could see he was young, maybe mid-twenties, and good-looking. His fair hair was longer than regulation military allowed, and his suit was well cut. The man smiled.

'Good afternoon, Mr Lewis. Beautiful day, is it not?' His accent was hard to place. European for sure, but exactly where, Richard couldn't say.

'It is,' he replied.

'Hard to imagine the world is so...' The man shook his head, at a loss to find an adequate adjective. 'But hopefully this will all be over soon and everything will be well once more.'

Richard had no idea how he should respond, so he said nothing.

'How are you feeling? Recovering, I hope?' the young man asked, the pleasant smile still on his face. They could be meeting at a yacht club in Savannah, Richard thought. That was the general tone anyway.

'Yes, much improved,' he replied.

'Good. Good. Yes. This is what we want, for you to be well.' The man smiled again. 'Are you married, Mr Lewis?'

Richard shook his head. 'No.'

'Sweetheart? I'm sure a handsome man such as yourself has plenty of girlfriends.' He gave Richard a conspiratorial wink as if they were buddies having a beer. Richard had no idea who this man was or what he wanted, but he was damned if he'd say anything about Grace to him.

'No. My life doesn't really lend itself to relationships,' he replied.

'I can see that. Lots of travel. But there is always time for a little diversion, is there not?'

Richard looked quizzically at him. 'Who are you?'

'Ah, a friend, just a friend.' The young man sighed. 'In these uncertain times, it is important to have friends. I was in America twice. Oh, what a country. I loved it there. I went to Boston to see the Red Sox. Well, that was not the reason I was in Boston, but my hosts took me to a game, as you call it, and what a wonderful spectacle it was. Then a year later I was in Washington, DC. A powerful place. So much of what happens for every man, woman and child on this planet is somehow connected to decisions made there. I walked along the Mall, visited the Lincoln Memorial, and when I was there, some people were doing a reenactment of the Gettysburg Address. Fascinating, really fascinating.'

What is this guy on about? Richard thought. *Is he trying to flatter me? Who is he and what does he want?*

'I'm sure you miss it – America, your family and friends. You parachuted in here, yes?'

'I did.'

The man began to sing. '"Comin' in on a wing and a prayer, with our one motor gone, we can still carry on, comin' in on a wing and a prayer..." That's number one on the Billboard charts at the moment, did you know that?'

'No, I didn't.'

'Your father is a banker, is he not? What you call over there a "hot shot"?' The man grinned at his use of the phrase.

'He's in finance, yes.' The piece in the *New York Times* about him when he won the Bustemer Award last year had given a biography of him. It gave a biography of Jacob too, but Kirky refused to have any mention of his Jewishness in the piece, and it was written before they even got back to the States. Jacob had been furious, but Richard was glad of it now.

The man smiled again. 'An American in our midst. But alas, the United States and Mr Roosevelt are not on the best of terms with the Führer so that's tricky for you.' He rolled his eyes. 'Always in a bad temper, that man. He'll give himself ulcers.'

'What do you want with me?' Richard asked, sick of this mysterious chat.

'Ah, that American directness. I like it. It's a bit disconcerting to us initially. We are the Old World, bound by the old protocols of behaviour. But our American cousins...just get right to the point. It's refreshing, if a little jarring.'

Silence hung between them for a moment.

'As I said,' the man continued at last, 'I'm a friend. I can help you to get home.'

'How?'

The man shrugged. 'Oh, it is not easy, as you can imagine. The borders are sealed tight. The Jews, you see, they are running away – whatever of them are left. And Eichmann has full authority to root out any remaining Jews in Europe. So unnecessary. So... Anyway.' He brushed away whatever thought he was about to express. 'Yes, getting out is difficult, but not impossible – if you know the right people and have the right connections.'

'Are you working for the Germans?' Richard asked, and the man chuckled by way of reply.

'I am working for myself, which is what any sensible person would be doing at this juncture.' He paused for a moment and regarded Richard shrewdly. 'Do you know when a rat is most dangerous, Mr Lewis?'

He shook his head, unable to make this man out.

'When he is cornered, when there is no clear way out. That is when you need to fear him. And the same is true of the Nazis. They are in trouble in Russia, and their allies...pah! Mussolini is a moron, so...' He gave a distinctly Gallic shrug, and Richard decided he was, in fact, French. 'Now all that remains is to see how this all plays out.'

'And what do you want with me?'

'To help, as I said.'

'Why? Do you know some of my friends?'

'Monsieur O'Hare? Or Felix, as he is known?'

Richard refused to confirm or deny and prayed his expression remained neutral.

The man shook his head. 'We don't...eh' – he smiled then – 'move in the same circles.'

'So why help me?'

The mysterious stranger smiled and shrugged again. 'Why do anything? Why bother? Maybe I'm trying to save my soul, or my hide? Or maybe I'm just a nice guy, as you Americans say. It really doesn't matter. But I...might be able to help get you out of here. To Switzerland. You will be safe there, *if* you manage to make it across the border. There are ways, if you have the right...resources.'

'Money? Is that what you want?'

The man laughed, a genuine hearty sound. 'Money? No. I have enough money and access to as much as I want. I don't need your money.'

'So what do you want, because you sure as hell didn't come here to get me released from a German prison out of the goodness of your heart. So I'd be grateful if you just told me the truth.'

The man put his hands in his suit pockets and kicked a stray pebble with his highly polished shoe. For a second he looked younger, more boyish. 'I believe in the cyclical nature of life – everything comes back around if you just have patience. The good *and* the bad. I will help you if you want it, and in time, sometime in the future, someone will help me.'

'To do what?'

His brow furrowed. 'About that I cannot be sure, not yet... It depends on so many factors. But I feel like something will emerge – I know it, in fact.'

'Do you know anything about my friend? We were arrested at the same time.'

The man shook his head and looked straight at Richard, his cool grey eyes unreadable. 'The Jew?'

'He's not Jewish,' Richard said, never breaking eye contact.

The man jerked his head to the prison building. 'They thought he was.'

Richard's heart sank. *Was*. Past tense.

'He only lasted an hour in there. It's all over for him now.' He straightened. 'So, Mr Lewis, do you want my help or not?'

'Can I at least know your name?'

'Just call me Gabriel, like the angel.' He winked.

'And you can get me out of here?'

'I can try.'

'And get me to Switzerland, in return for some unnamed favour I, or someone else, will do for you in the future?'

'Maybe...Mr Lewis. That is a distinct possibility. But also maybe not. But as I say, there are lots of variables. We live in uncertain times, you see. So, are you interested?'

Richard thought of Grace. He had a bad feeling about this. If this guy wasn't working for the Germans, how did he even get in here? Maybe it was a test, but even so, it was the best and only option right now.

'Yes.'

'All right, I'll be in touch.' Gabriel patted Richard's shoulder as if he was a benevolent uncle and strolled back in the direction of the gate, leaving Richard confused but cautiously optimistic. Maybe he wouldn't die here after all.

After taking a few steps, the man turned back. 'Try to stay strong, exercise, maintain your muscle. You will need it.'

A mirror of the advice Alfie had given him and Jacob, except this man had nothing of the reassuring presence of Alfie O'Hare.

CHAPTER 21

SAVANNAH, GEORGIA

23 JUNE 1943

*G*race stole a glance across the pew of Christ Church in Savannah. Richard's father had insisted that Grace take a front-row seat. His mother and father were first in the pew, then Sarah and Nathan and then her. Sitting in the row behind were Rebecca and her three daughters, Mrs McHale and Esme.

Finally putting faces to the names would have been interesting, but being here, in his place, with his people but without him, was tearing the heart from her.

She, Charlie and Mrs McHale had arrived in Savannah five days earlier, having taken the train from New York. Grace had mentioned Mrs McHale to Arthur Lewis when he telephoned the St Regis on the evening of their meeting with the old lady to check that everything was in order for their journey south. He had insisted that Mrs McHale join them for Richard's memorial. She had wept noisily when Grace and Charlie told her the news at their lunch the following day.

Grace had to admit that Richard's mother was not as she had expected. She thought she was going to meet an ice queen, but Caroline was very polite to her at their first meeting. She said she was delighted Grace made the journey, and that she knew how much she meant to her son. Grace wasn't sure Richard's mother was being honest, but it was nice to hear it anyway. It was a little more disconcerting to hear Caroline refer to Richard in the present tense – Grace had had to stop herself doing that in the past weeks, and each small reprimand was a stab to her aching heart. Even more unsettling were the conspiratorial looks Caroline threw her each time she did it – as if the other woman sensed that part of Grace clung to the vain and futile hope that somewhere, somehow, Richard was out there, alive and well, and would return to them both.

After their initial meeting, however, Caroline showed only a cursory interest in her guests, and Grace was fascinated to observe the Lewis family dynamics, which Richard had told her about, in action. While Sarah and her mother clearly didn't hit it off at all, Nathan seemed closer to her.

Seeing Nathan in the flesh took Grace's breath away. He looked so like Richard. Not as good-looking, but with the same physique: tall and broad, with short blond hair and dark-blue eyes. He was kind and welcoming, and she never doubted his sincerity. His wife was beautiful but in an intimidating way. She was polished and coiffed, her teeth were pearly white, and not a hair was astray.

The minister read from scripture, some Old Testament, some New. Then he read from the Book of Common Prayer; each person found a copy on their padded seat. Grace didn't recognise any of the prayers as ones she'd ever heard before, but they were on the theme of Richard being welcomed into the kingdom of Jesus.

Then, to her surprise, there was a hymn, and everyone sang with gusto. Following that, the minister spoke about Richard, the loss to his family and how he was now with God.

It was the first non-Catholic ceremony Grace had ever been to, and she found the proceedings strange. The building itself was not like any church she'd been in before. The pews were not dark wood as they were in most Catholic churches but painted white with ornate end pieces lining the aisle. There were two balconies running along the length of the church; one of which was where the uniformly dressed choir sat. The only colour, apart from white and some natural wood, was a stained-glass depiction of the Lord behind the altar. No statues, paintings, icons, relics or any other decoration like those she was used to. It was a restful place, she thought, plain and beautiful, and she wondered if Richard had sat here on Sundays as a little boy.

She didn't know the hymn, but it was beautiful. Nathan showed her where it was written in the prayer book as they sang.

We sing the praise of him who died,
Of him who died upon the cross,
The sinner's hope let men deride,
For this we count the word but loss,
Inscribed upon the cross we see,
In shining letters, God is Love,
He bears our sins upon the tree,
And brings us mercy from above.

Grace did her best to sing along, following the words in the book as the voices of the choir soared in several part harmonies.

The balm of life, the cure of woe,
The measure and the pledge of love,
The sinner's refuge here below,
The angels theme in heaven above.

How she wished those lofty words were true, that her faith would cure her woe, be a balm for the pain in her heart, but it wasn't. Nothing was. Richard Lewis, the man she loved with every fibre of her being, body and soul, was gone – at least that was what she had to believe, even if part of her didn't – or didn't *want* to – believe that it was true. Above all, sitting in this hot church – what Richard had told her about the heat in Savannah being like a hot, wet blanket over your face in the summer was true – surrounded by people who, until now, were only names on a page for her, she'd never felt more genuinely alone.

She wished Charlie was beside her, but he was seated further down the church, beside Kirky and all of Jacob and Sarah's friends – arty bohemian types that Grace was sure would have Caroline Lewis wrinkling her nose – old school friends and neighbours, and lots of the residents of St Simons Island. Grace had been introduced to so many people since she got here, she could hardly remember most of them.

The minister said the Lord's Prayer, and Grace struggled to remember it in English. Though she spoke the language fluently, she'd never had occasion to recite Ár nAthair in English before.

Then Arthur Lewis stood and approached the lectern. He stood tall and strong, and Grace wondered if that was how Richard would look when – *if* – he'd lived to be the age his father was now. Arthur was handsome, in an older man distinguished way, and his complexion spoke of a lifetime outdoors, more than behind a desk. His dark suit was undoubtedly tailored for him, and his white shirt was dazzling.

He pulled out a set of cards and glanced over them, then looked up, seeming to make eye contact with everyone in the full-to-capacity church.

'My son Richard has been honoured for his bravery, for his skill with the pen and for his ability to have people open up to him. All of those things are true. And to my shame, I tried my darnedest to get him to follow a different route. But Richard was his own man and said that banking didn't interest him the way it does me. And so he followed his own path, with no help or use of family connections. Everything my son achieved in his tragically short life, including winning the prestigious Bustemer Award for journalism last year, he did by himself.

'All over this country, indeed, all over the world, families are grieving their loved ones taken too soon by this war. Ours is just one more. Richard never wavered in his support for the Allied cause. When we met in New York recently, he told me the harrowing stories of refugees fleeing Hitler and the Nazis, about the jaw-dropping inhumanity of that regime. He spoke of the resilience of the British in the face of their cities being bombed to oblivion. And I know there are many people here today who doubt the sense of America fighting over there again, but as a man who has lost a precious son to this conflict, let me speak for him. We must press on. We have to. Because if we don't, the future is unthinkable.

'Richard was only twenty-five years old, so young, with so much to live for, but he made the most of those twenty-five years. He was a wonderful child, bright and funny, and his mother and I loved him very much. His biggest fan, however, was not either of us, but Mrs Esme Carter, who loved him since the day he was born, and he loved her right back. Esme meant the world to Richard, and she did me the great honour of showing me a letter he wrote to her before he went on the mission that would end his life. He closed the letter with that old Southern phrase "I love you a bushel and a peck and a hug around the neck" that Esme said to him every night before he went to bed.'

Grace stole a glance at Richard's mother who was surely not going to like this, but it was true. Richard always said Esme was more of a mother to him than his actual mother ever was, but to have his father more or less spell that out was brave. Grace didn't understand the situation between the races here fully, but it seemed that these coloured women raised white babies and the babies' mothers rarely saw them, or at least, in the case of the Lewis children, that was how it was. Richard would have been happy to see Esme honoured in this way and proud of his father for disregarding the rules by doing so.

Grace had noticed that Esme was the only coloured person in the church. Sarah had explained it would normally not be allowed – everything was strictly segregated and Esme's church was on the other side of town. But Arthur insisted that she come, that she would sit with the family, and in this town, it would seem, what Arthur Lewis said, went.

She gazed at Richard's father, mesmerised by the prepossessing power of the man. Having now met him, Grace finally realised how hard it would have been for Richard to refuse to do his bidding, and it raised him even further in her estimation.

'I didn't truly know my son until these last few years,' Arthur continued. 'It is not a nice truth to admit, but it's how it was. I was working a lot and rarely saw my children. When I did, I was not the kind of father who played or read stories. I regret that now.

'But when Richard left Savannah, taking Sarah with him, I might add' – a wry smile led to a ripple of laughter – 'I was none too pleased. He refused to join the bank with me, and Sarah refused to do as we wanted and marry a suitable man. Our older son, Nathan, also rejected finance in favour of medicine, and I'm very proud to say that though Caroline and I have managed to raise three very stubborn and pig-headed children, they were all right and I was wrong.

'Richard wrote to me regularly from the time he left, and I replied. I think the first personal letter I ever wrote was to my son in London. But through those letters, almost weekly, we got to know each other, and I found out what a fine man my boy had become.

'We mourn his loss today, and I know you all feel as I do, that he was too young. But I want you to know this. Richard lived more in his short life than many men three times his age, and he did so by following his own path. He did a job he loved, he cared deeply about right and wrong, and most importantly, he fell in love.

'The girl he was due to marry is here with us today. She made the journey across the Atlantic from her native Ireland with a family friend, Mr Charlie McKenna, and we warmly welcome them both and thank them most sincerely for being with us as we say farewell to our boy.

'Richard wrote to me often about Grace and what a remarkable young woman she was. He was absolutely right. I wish they could have married – it would have been the happiest day of his life. But I know that Grace is part of our family now, in every way.

'It feels wrong to be saying goodbye, especially without a body to bury. But I'm trying to find consolation in knowing that my son gave his life in the cause of freedom, in fighting totalitarianism and doing something he loved.

'Rest in peace, Richard. We love you.'

His voice choked on that last line, and Grace knew it was not something that Arthur Lewis said easily, but she was in no doubt that he meant every word.

'No. No, no, no, no, no.'

All heads in the church swivelled in the direction of Caroline Lewis, who had risen to her feet and was glaring at her husband. He, in turn, stared at her in surprise and alarm.

'Caro –'

'No! I'm sorry, but no. I'm just not having this. I'm not going along with this charade any longer.'

The entire gathering sat in shock as Richard's mother, shaking with anger, marched across to where her husband stood at the lectern.

'Caroline, please...' Arthur Lewis tried to calm her but to no avail. Grace could see that the woman was too riled up.

Most of the congregation were steadfastly staring at their shoes, and the minister was making desperate eye contact with Arthur as if to ask 'What do we do now?'

Finally Nathan stood and approached his mother. 'Mama, come and sit down...' he said, as he tried to gently lead her back to her seat.

Caroline shook him off angrily. 'No, Nathan. I know you all think I'm going crazy, but I'm not. Richard was my child, and I would know if he died, I just know I would. We have no body. There's no proof whatsoever. He's just missing. This' – she gestured about the church at the congregation – 'is premature.'

Sarah, also on her feet now, took her mother's elbow and showed less restraint than her brother. 'Mother, sit down, you're making a scene,' she said through gritted teeth.

'I don't care, Sarah. I don't believe my child is dead. I just don't believe it...' Caroline looked more animated than Grace had seen her, and judging by the reactions of everyone present in the church, it was entirely out of character. 'I would know,' Caroline continued. 'I would feel it...'

At this, Grace saw a look of fury cross Sarah's face as something in her snapped.

'Just sit down and shut up, Mother, will you please? Richard might have been your son, but you were never a mother to him. All you ever did was criticise him and throw cold water on his dreams. You think you're so connected to him that you'd know if he died? You overestimate your relationship...'

Caroline's face turned pale, and she stared at her daughter as if she'd been physically struck.

Arthur pushed himself between the two. 'Ladies,' he murmured, 'we're all going to take our seats now.' Then he turned to the gathered crowd. 'I'm sorry about this, folks. It's a very difficult time for our family, and as you can see, we're all a bit overwrought by it all.'

He motioned to Sarah to sit down, which she did, still glowering at her mother. He and Nathan then led a trembling Caroline back to her seat. But as she reached the front pew, Caroline stopped and fixed her gaze on Grace. 'You don't believe Richard's dead either, do you, Grace?'

Caroline's voice was soft and calm, but her words chilled Grace's heart. The whole scene felt dreamlike. The eyes of the gathered crowd on her, the photograph of Richard on a gilt stand beside the altar, everyone – his parents and siblings, neighbours, friends, Esme, Charlie, Mrs McHale – all waiting for her to say something.

Caroline leant forward towards her. 'I know you don't believe it, Grace. You loved him and he loved you. You know he isn't dead. Please, Grace, tell them...tell them that my boy isn't dead.'

Arthur gave a gentle pull on Caroline's arm. 'Please, my dear,' he said, 'let's sit down now.' But he threw a quizzical look at Grace as he spoke.

Caroline shook her head. 'Tell them, Grace,' she insisted. 'Please... tell them.'

Grace stared at her, the blood thundering in her ears. What did Caroline want from her? Did she want Grace to admit that maybe she, like Caroline, just couldn't face the terrible truth – that Richard was gone? That she knew what it was like to lose a beloved husband and this just felt...different? That the connection, that tantalising thread linking her soul to Richard's, still felt strong and alive? But how could she say all those things when she was so unsure? Indeed, what right did she have to believe that she and Caroline were any different to all the people in the world who had lost their loved ones through this terrible war, with no hope whatsoever of their return? And yet...

'I can't tell you that,' she said, her voice barely audible. 'Not for certain. All I know is that I want him to come back to me. Soon. And I know if he can, he will.'

Caroline's face lit up with a broad triumphant smile at Grace's words. 'There,' she said to her husband. 'You see.'

Then, to everyone's astonishment, including Grace's, she returned demurely to her seat as though nothing had happened at all.

CHAPTER 22

*G*race tried not to squirm. It was two days after the memorial service, and Caroline Lewis had invited her to lunch at the beautiful Marshall House on Broughton Street in the city.

She and Mrs Lewis were driven to the hotel by a coloured man who worked in the Lewis's gardens – Grace didn't know his name as he was never introduced to her. On the way there, Richard's mother explained how this hotel had been used as a Union hospital under the governance of General Sherman during the Civil War.

Grace wasn't sure what sort of reaction she was supposed to have to this information. Nothing in Mrs Lewis's demeanour suggested an appropriate response. All she could remember was Richard telling her that the Civil War wasn't over yet in the USA, despite what people might say. The division between the North and the South was still very much in evidence. Grace could see that with her own eyes as she witnessed the segregation in Savannah that was so different to what she'd seen in New York. In the end she decided noncommittal interest was the best way to handle it.

They pulled up beside an enormous building with an iron veranda that stretched one hundred and twenty feet along the front of the hotel, making it an imposing structure.

Caroline Lewis was rail-thin, dressed in a black tailored dress and coat despite the sweltering heat and a birdcage hat with a net that covered her eyes. Her shoes had heels so high, Grace wondered how she stayed upright. 'The hotel was called the Gilbert Hotel after the last owner, George Gilbert. He sold it two years ago to a tycoon from Jacksonville – Arthur knows him well. But everyone here still calls it the Marshall House,' she said.

Grace just smiled.

As they entered the lobby of the hotel, Grace was directed by Caroline to admire an oil painting of a woman with dark hair and old-fashioned dress, who Grace guessed must have been in her forties.

'That's Mary Marshall,' Caroline declared. 'She was a very prominent Savannah figure. She was born on the last year of the American Revolution and died at the age of ninety-three during the last days of the Reconstruction of the South. She had relatives on both sides of the Civil War.'

Grace was apparently supposed to infer some meaning from this based on the tone of her would-have-been mother-in-law's voice, but, again, she wasn't sure what that might be.

If she was honest, that morning over breakfast when Caroline Lewis had asked if Grace would join her for lunch, Grace had been taken aback. Sarah had an appointment with a friend of Jacob's, and Arthur was taking Charlie and Mrs McHale back out to the yacht club to see his pride and joy, the *Arabella*. They were going to sail around the bay, but Richard's mother disliked boats and declined to join them.

Grace had felt there was no polite way to refuse the lunch invitation. That said, the idea of spending any time alone with the terrifying Mrs Lewis was not something she relished.

The two women were shown into an opulent dining room and to a table by the window.

'Can I get you ladies a drink to begin with?' drawled a polished-looking waiter, middle-aged, with a smile playing around his lips.

Richard, Grace now realised, only had a slight Southern accent. She had thought it was strong, but now that she was here in Savannah, she found it wasn't at all. She found she loved the melodic drawl of the South; she found it enthralling, especially when she spoke with Esme. Caroline's accent was Southern as well, but more refined. And Arthur's was different again; he'd explained, with a chuckle, that he was originally a Texan and that was a 'whole other ball of wax'.

He and Charlie discussed the cowboy films and how true to real life they were. It fascinated Grace to see how the two men got along; an Irish-speaking postman from Knocknashee and a millionaire financier from Texas had more in common than she could ever have imagined. She pictured herself and Richard smiling fondly at how the two men bonded so easily.

Thankfully, neither Mrs McHale nor Charlie had mentioned the Caroline Lewis memorial affair to Grace, although she had seen both of them throw her sad looks over the past days, and both had, at different times, patted and squeezed her hand in earnest sympathy.

Mrs McHale was enjoying her time in Savannah immensely, in between bouts of grief for Richard. She was so fond of him, she explained, and having no children of her own, she had taken him to her heart in a profound way. She might be no blood relation, but she loved him.

Arthur Lewis had had a photo of Richard printed and framed several times for anyone who wanted one. It was one taken the day Sarah and Jacob got married, and Richard looked so handsome, his head thrown back laughing. Grace took one copy, and so did Sarah, but when Arthur gave a copy to Mrs McHale, she was overcome. Grace wished she had a photo of her and Richard together; they'd even had Eloise's camera with them that day when they exposed the canon but had never taken one of themselves. It was one of her many regrets.

They would all return to New York the day after tomorrow, and Grace and Charlie would catch the boat directly after that. Then it was home to Knocknashee, and despite Grace's bravado at the memorial, the painful fact of a life without Richard Lewis in it. Even now, it was hard to have it sink in.

'We'll have some iced tea,' Caroline said, without consulting Grace.

'So, Grace, how have you found Savannah?' she asked as the waiter left to fetch their drinks. 'Is it as Richard described?'

'Yes. Well, yes and no, because we didn't talk much about the city itself. He mentioned some places – the yacht club where we had dinner last night and the Crystal Beer Parlor...'

Mrs Lewis pulled a face. 'Why my children frequent such establishments is beyond me, but they do.'

'He told me about the squares, and River Street, and about St Simons Island and Tybee, and they are so lovely. Savannah's a beautiful city, Mrs Lewis, and I'm so grateful to you and Mr Lewis for inviting me.'

'You're welcome.' No word of 'of course you should be here, you were my son's fiancée' or 'it was nothing' or anything like that. She had done Grace a favour and Grace knew it.

Grace racked her brain as to why this woman wanted time alone with her. The two had barely spoken since Caroline's distressing outburst at the memorial service, which still made Grace wince to think about. But apart from that, she'd had a lovely time with Richard's family. Arthur had even flown her and Sarah to Warm Springs in his private airplane so Grace could bathe in the waters there. They were said to have therapeutic properties and were even frequented by the president for his polio. It had been a beautiful day, but so sad for her. It was here that Richard had planned to take her all those years ago, until Agnes got the stroke the night before she was to sail. To be here now, without him, was heartbreaking, although she knew he would want her to be there nonetheless. She had sobbed in the hot pool at the thought, and thankfully, Sarah had just let her cry.

'Did you enjoy Warm Springs?' Caroline Lewis unwrapped a starched napkin and placed it on her lap.

'Very much. Richard had planned to take me there in 1938, but I couldn't come that time because my sister became unwell and I had to care for her.'

'Did he indeed?' Mrs Lewis's face was enigmatic. Was she doubting the veracity of Grace's story? Or was she being sarcastic? It was impossible to tell.

'Tell me about Ireland,' the woman demanded. Certainly more of a command than a chatty enquiry.

Grace swallowed and steeled herself. She was not going to allow this woman to belittle her, not after everything. 'Well, I live in a village called Knocknashee. It's on the end of the Dingle Peninsula, a finger of land jutting into the Atlantic on Ireland's southwest coast. It's small, and we all speak Irish there –'

'Gaelic?' Mrs Lewis interjected.

'Well, we don't call it that, but yes.'

'And yet you can speak English as well?'

Grace heard the condescension in the woman's tone and ignored it. 'We all can. We just choose not to.'

'And how did you envisage life with Richard? Did you two plan to live there or here or somewhere else?'

Grace thought for a moment. 'We hadn't decided, but I know Richard would have been happy anywhere so long as we were together. As would I.' She knew it sounded defiant but didn't care.

'Did Richard tell you about Miranda Logan?'

'He did.'

'She was at the memorial.'

'Yes, I believe she was.'

Caroline was surveying Grace with that shrewd look of hers; it made Grace wonder what on earth was coming next.

'Miranda and Richard were at the point of engagement, you know, but he refused to go to the bank and she broke it off. I think she regrets it now, but…' Caroline Lewis shrugged as the waiter arrived with the jug of iced tea, pieces of lemon and ice floating on the top. He poured two crystal tumblers. Grace took a sip. She'd had cold tea before in New York when she visited with Declan, and she wasn't sure she liked it. The idea of serving tea cold would be incredible to her friends and neighbours, but she didn't comment.

'Now then, ladies, what can I get you to eat?' the waiter with the mischievous eyes and pointed beard asked.

'Oh, let me see… I'll have a shrimp salad and a glass of Sancerre. Grace?'

Grace perused the menu. She had no idea what lots of the items were, but she remembered Richard saying he would take her to try fried chicken, fried okra and collard greens, so she would have that in his honour. She couldn't see it on the menu, but she asked the man. 'I've never been to Georgia before, but my fiancé was from here.' She swallowed hard before her next sentence. 'He was…killed in the war… just recently. He always said I should try fried chicken and fried okra and collard greens sometime. Do you have that?'

The man's face was a picture of kindness. 'Well, ma'am, I sure think we can arrange that for you. No chef worth his salt round these parts would admit he can't fix that, even if it's not on the menu.'

'Thank you,' Grace said, handing him back the menu.

Caroline Lewis eyed her, and Grace felt that something had subtly changed between them. 'You're not how I imagined,' the older woman said candidly.

Grace just smiled; there really was no response to that.

'I honestly wondered what he was thinking in being with you. And when I saw you… Well, you are pretty, of course, but he could have had any number of pretty girls here…including Miranda Logan.'

Grace felt herself redden. She hoped Caroline Lewis would read it for what it was – annoyance, not embarrassment. But Richard's mother didn't seem to care.

'But now I see it.' She sighed. 'You have the same…defiance…as Richard.'

'I'm not sure I'd say I was defiant –'

'I mean it in a complimentary way, my dear. Women need to be defiant, otherwise we get trampled on.'

'Perhaps you're right,' Grace replied, taking a sip of the iced tea, which was refreshing if a little odd tasting.

'Richard didn't confide in me, so I don't know the full story, but I understand you and he formed a friendship when you threw a bottle with a note in it into the ocean in Ireland and it washed up here?'

'Yes, that's right. I think it was your old dog Doodle that actually found the bottle, and Esme gave it to Richard. So, yes, that's how we met, as it were. He wrote back and well…in the last five years, we've written over a hundred letters to each other.'

'And yet you married another man, and he had an entanglement with an English girl?'

The way she said 'entanglement' made it sound sordid or trivial. Grace didn't like it. 'Richard was in a relationship with a woman called Pippa Wills, and I was married to Declan McKenna, Charlie's son. Declan was killed in an accident, and Richard and Pippa broke up.'

The older woman's brow furrowed. 'And yet you two had feelings for each other for the last five years?'

Grace hated that she had to defend her and Richard's relationship to this woman, who'd been so cold to her son all this time. 'It was complicated. But we got there in the end,' she said, hoping it would shut down this uncomfortable conversation.

There was an awkward moment of silence as their food arrived.

Once the curious waiter was gone, Caroline began again. 'I assume he told you about me? About how we didn't exactly see eye to eye?'

Grace inhaled. The truth was the only way. 'He did.'

The older woman nodded, and to Grace's astonishment, her eyes seemed bright with tears. Caroline opened her mouth, but no sound came out. Instead, she dabbed her perfectly coloured lips with the snow-white napkin, and Grace could see she was trying to compose her thoughts.

'I'm sorry about what happened,' Caroline said at last. 'At the memorial service. I was a fool. And I involved you in my foolishness. For that I am truly sorry.'

Grace could see from the woman's face that her apology was sincere, but she didn't know what to say in response. 'Thank you.' It was all she could think of.

'I did not want to believe…' Caroline dabbed her lips again nervously, and Grace could see the older woman was struggling to keep herself together. 'I did not want to believe that my child was… dead.' The words came out in a harrowed murmur, sending a shiver up Grace's spine. For the first time, she was seeing this woman for who she was – Richard's mother.

'I think he thought I didn't love him,' Caroline whispered at last. 'He wrote to me, at the same time as he wrote to us all. It was as if he knew something bad would happen...' She opened her black patent leather handbag with the gold clasp and extracted an envelope. With a pang, Grace recognised Richard's handwriting.

Mrs Lewis pushed the envelope towards her. 'Read it, please.'

Grace did as she was asked and extracted the single sheet from the thin blue envelope. It was well worn on the creases – from many readings, she guessed. She read the short note.

Dear Mother,

Today I am going on a special assignment, and I just wanted to write and tell you that I wish you well. I hope you will try to understand that Daddy was only supporting Sarah and me. He didn't make us go to war; we were going either way. I would have been a terrible banker, and Miranda and I were not a good match. I have told you already about Grace. She's a very special person, and I'm very lucky to have her.

I would urge you to accept Sarah and Jacob. He's a good man, and they love each other. And if anything happens to him, she will need love and support. And if this war has taught me anything, it's that love is important. In fact, it might be the only important thing. Daddy still loves you, and making him choose between you and us was a stupid thing to do, you know it was, but I'm glad you were able to find a way back. Well done on going to the wedding—it's a hard thing to admit you were wrong. Forgive, move on, and be happy. We all deserve a bit of happiness.

All the best,

Your son, Richard

'It's a hard thing to realise your son hated you and now there's no hope of redemption.' The words dropped like stones.

'He didn't hate you,' Grace said, folding the letter and returning it to its owner.

'Oh, we both know he did,' Caroline said bluntly. She shrugged as Grace looked at her in surprise. 'And he died thinking I didn't love him.'

'He didn't. In fact, we spoke about it.'

The silence hung heavily between the two women, Grace no longer on the back foot.

'What did he say?' Caroline asked eventually, and Grace could see how difficult it was for this normally guarded woman to be so vulnerable.

'He said that he admired how you went to Sarah's wedding, how it was hard for you to back down but he was happy for both you and Sarah that you did. Richard said that you wanted the best for them all, even if your version of what that might be was different to theirs. He told me that he knew his father loved you and that he was happy you were both able to find a way to continue your marriage.' This last part was a bit of a white lie, because Richard had told his father that if he wasn't sure, then he should seek happiness elsewhere, but Grace felt that it would not be helpful to add that now.

Caroline listened intently but was silent when Grace finished. She picked at her shrimp salad for a time, then put down her cutlery and looked Grace straight in the eye. 'I did love him, you know. It was just we... Well, it just wasn't the done thing... I hardly ever saw my mother – the help raised me and my sisters. And Richard and Esme were so close. She is naturally more...I don't know...' Caroline waved her hand, knowing perfectly well the word she was looking for was 'maternal' but not able to say it. 'He was taken from me when he was born and given to Esme. It wasn't the way we did things, holding infants and such. Not women of my class. I tried in the early years, but she was so much better at it. He always wanted her, not me, and I don't blame him. She had songs and cookies and cuddles, and all I had were manners and rules...'

Grace's heart went out to this woman. She had none of the tools to be a mother, despite her fancy house and all of her money. The bonds Grace had seen in her life between mothers and their children were nurtured from birth, and to have your baby given to someone else must have been so hard.

But she knew Caroline wouldn't appreciate sympathy, so she just said, 'The reason people liked Richard so much, one of the many reasons, was because he was warm and polite and respectful. He could talk to anyone, from a child to a president – he adopted the same easy manner – and that didn't come out of nowhere. He was raised to be confident but not cocky. Nobody was above or below him – he met everyone as an individual.'

His mother nodded sadly. 'I wish I could tell him…have just one more minute…' She tried to compose herself. Grace could tell displays of emotion like this were entirely out of character for her.

'He knows.' Grace reached over and placed her hand on Caroline's. 'I believe he knows. He's always known. Your approval is – was – important to him.'

She caught a glimpse of hope in Caroline Lewis's eyes, which then disappeared as quickly as it had come. 'Sarah…' she said. 'I have a chance with her, but I just don't know how. I'm trying to help her rebuild her life, but that's the wrong thing… Everything I say and do infuriates her.'

'Just have patience.' Grace paused. 'Do you want some advice?'

Caroline Lewis looked bemused. 'I need it, even if I don't want it. Go ahead.'

'Acknowledge her relationship with Jacob, encourage her to talk about him, ask about him. She feels like you just want to sweep him under the rug, forget it ever happened, but she can't forget. No more than I can. And I know you're trying to help, but Sarah is like Richard – they will do things their way – so maybe stop trying to manage her and just let her grieve.'

'I was going to…' Caroline flushed. 'Well, I arranged for two trees to be planted in the garden at St Simons, and I had two plaques made – one for Richard and another for Jacob, although I didn't say anything. The trees are planted, but I have the plaques. I'm not sure they would want…' She looked so uncomfortable, Grace felt for her. And Caroline was right about Sarah; she could be prickly, especially around her mother.

'I think Sarah would like that,' Grace said. 'Could we all go there tomorrow maybe to put the plaques down? Before we have to leave? I would love to see the house on the island where Richard spent his summers.'

'Well, perhaps if you suggested it…'

Grace realised then that the cool, austere persona that Caroline Lewis exuded was just that – a front. Underneath, she was a vulnerable woman who had no idea how to relate to her own family.

'Of course I will,' Grace said with a smile, and the relief on Richard's mother's face spoke volumes.

CHAPTER 23

SOMEWHERE SOUTH OF STRASBOURG

It was dark and he'd been asleep for hours, but he couldn't say what time it was. The guard opened the cell door and gestured to Richard to get up and walk out past him. It had been two weeks since Gabriel's visit, and nothing had happened.

No more interrogations, no more beatings, and the food was edible – just about. He'd been given a clean set of clothes yesterday, the first change he'd had in weeks. The door had opened, and a guard gave him a bundle of clean clothes, a basin of water, a tiny cake of soap and a razor. He'd washed and shaved and then dressed in the clean shirt, trousers, underwear, socks and shoes.

His French was improving now that he was mixing with the general population of the prison, and he'd managed to ask a few questions. Nobody had ever heard of Gabriel and didn't recognise him by any description. Richard figured he must be somehow connected to the Germans; there was no way he would have been allowed in otherwise, and there had to be some link between the cessation of beatings and interrogation and the man's strange arrival.

He'd gone over all he could remember of the strange conversation, the vagueness of it all. Who was he? What did he want? Why had he come? Round and round the questions went in his head, but no answers ever presented themselves.

'Walk.' The one-word instruction came as he was escorted along the stone corridor, passing other cells and the gate to the exercise yard, and down through a part of the prison he barely remembered seeing before. He had only a vague memory of arriving here; the last time he saw Jacob was when they were shoved out of the back of the lorry.

They clearly hadn't fallen for the Spanish story. Jacob being a Jew would make him less than human as far as these Nazis were concerned. He missed his friend in ways he couldn't articulate, but he could not allow himself to dwell on the fact that Jacob was gone and he was entirely alone. One step at a time, one hour, one minute – that was all he had to do. If he did that, he might, just might, get to see Grace again.

The guard was behind him as he walked on. At the end of the corridor was a huge medieval door; there was nowhere to turn left or right. He stopped.

Before he had time to register what was happening, the door opened from the other side and swung towards him. He stepped out and saw that it led to a town square. Without any further discussion, the door shut behind him.

The night was sultry and humid, the air heavily scented with some fragrant flower he thought might be lilac. The square was deserted and completely silent but for the sound of crickets. On the far side of a dried-out village green was an official-looking building with the scarlet and white flag of Nazi Germany, emblazoned with a menacing black swastika, hanging limply in the still night.

Richard swallowed to fight a growing sense of panic. He had nothing. No money, no map and no plan. Worst of all, no Jacob. What was he supposed to do now? He was an enemy alien in occupied France, with no resources or connections. The Germans had released him for a reason he couldn't fathom, but for how long? He didn't even know where he was. The Ducrot farm had been outside Strasbourg, he remembered, but where was he now?

He walked along the wall of the prison, hugging the grey stone as he did so, trying to be inconspicuous. As he approached the corner, he was startled by the flash of a light up ahead. Should he go towards it? Should he hide? This was ridiculous; he needed time to think. Could he find Alfie? How would he ever begin to do that? He could hardly just walk into a café or a bar and ask if anyone knew him, the most wanted man in this area. No, that wasn't an option. How far was he from the farm they'd been captured near? Should he try to go back there? He couldn't. Not without money, food or a map. And the Ducrots had been overrun by Germans last time he saw them; he was sure they wouldn't have the welcome mat out, even in the unlikely event they had survived the raid.

Getting out of the town and into the countryside seemed like the most sensible thing to do, at least until he figured out his next move. His heart was thumping in his chest, and sweat ran between his shoulders, whether from heat or fear, he didn't know. Probably both.

Did Gabriel have something to do with this? And if so, while he was grateful, what good was it to release him if he had no resources?

He crept along the wall that formed the northern boundary of the old prison when there was that flashlight again, up ahead. Then a figure appeared, slight and short.

'Come,' the person hissed.

Richard couldn't make out if the person was male or female. It might be a trap. But why? He'd been captured and released, so why would someone want to set him up now? He forced his thoughts to be logical. His instinct said to trust this person, the voice, mainly because he had not one single other option.

He rushed forward and found himself pulled into a gap in the wall and down into a tunnel.

'Follow me.' The man – Richard realised now it was a slight man in his sixties – mercifully spoke at least some English, though heavily accented. 'Don't make a sound.'

Richard did as he was told, trying to focus on keeping up and ignoring the ominous scurrying and loud squeaking around them. The tunnels seemed to go on and on, with junctions and cross tunnels every few hundred yards. The only light was the flashlight the man used intermittently; Richard found he was running mainly in the pitch-black.

Eventually they came to what looked like a medieval portcullis, a metal grid, which the man pulled up with surprising ease. Richard followed him through into a stone circular room, and there, to his astonishment, was Gabriel.

The other man moved away down a tributary tunnel and disappeared into the darkness.

'So you made it?' Gabriel lit a candle, and the small room was illuminated in its eerie glow. The well-cut suit had been replaced by a workman's shirt and trousers, but even in that peasant outfit, he looked better groomed than anyone Richard had seen in quite a while. His fair hair was brushed off his face and held in place with oil, and his bright-blue eyes danced with mischief, as if this was just some schoolboy prank.

'Well, wherever here is, I guess I did.' Richard looked around.

'You're in the fortified town of Belfort, in northeastern France. Or to be more precise, you are under it. It's been a defensive town since the Middle Ages. The first castle to be built here, the grounds of which have been your latest accommodation, was built in 1226. It's been modernised over the years, of course, new walls added and so on. This complex series of tunnels underneath it have also been improved and added to, so it's withstood many sieges.'

'OK, but what am I doing here?'

Gabriel carried on as if Richard hadn't spoken at all. 'After the last war, when the fortifications here proved more than useless, several more forts, under the guidance of the *genius* Marshal Pétain' – Gabriel grinned, the sarcasm dripping through his words; Pétain was seen by most French as a traitor to his country – 'were added to extend the eastern part of the Maginot Line defences along the line of the Rhine River.'

Richard had no idea why he was getting this lecture, but his saviour seemed determined to carry on, so he let him.

'This *region fortifiée de* Belfort was under the command of the Eighth Army in 1940, but then... Well, you know what happened.' Gabriel shrugged as if the capitulation and occupation of France were a mere trifle.

'Actually' – his eyes lit up – 'this is something you might be interested in. There is a lion, a huge sculpture of a lion up on the citadel, right above us here, and it was the work of Bartholdi, the same sculptor who did your Statue of Liberty, the lady you Americans love so much.'

Once again Richard found himself nonplussed in this man's presence. What the hell was he talking about? He was in some kind of a cave trying to figure out what he was doing here, and this guy was going on like they were on a summer picnic to a local beauty spot. It was bizarre.

'So now what?' he asked, not caring if it sounded rude or ungrateful.

'Now, my dear Monsieur Lewis from Savannah, Georgia, we try to get you out of France and over the border to Switzerland, where you will be free.'

Richard exhaled. So Gabriel was going to help him escape. But why? What did he want in return? He didn't strike Richard as the altruistic sort. 'And what do you want from me?' he asked bluntly.

Gabriel smiled angelically – as if butter wouldn't melt, as Esme might say.

'Nothing. I am just going to do you a good turn and hope that somehow this comes back to me. Do you know the Hindu idea of karma, Mr Lewis?'

'I've heard of it.' He didn't trust this man, no matter how friendly he seemed. Gabriel was probably around his own age, but there was something almost superior about him, as if he was speaking tongue-in-cheek, laughing at an inside joke that only he knew.

'Then you will know it is a philosophy that refers to the universal principle of cause and effect, where actions, thoughts, intentions lead to consequences in the future. Good karma follows me, because I try to do good things.' He took a gold cigarette case, inlaid with mother-of-pearl, from his pocket and extracted a cigarette, offering Richard one. Richard shook his head.

'Very wise, Mr Lewis. Terrible habit, but in these times...' Gabriel shrugged and sighed before putting the cigarette in his mouth and lighting it from the flame of the candle. In the flash of light, the man's face was illuminated, and Richard realised once more just how young he was. Probably not even Richard's own age, and yet he held his life in the balance.

'So you're helping me out of the goodness of your heart?' he asked, not believing it for one second.

'Well, not exactly. I owe a favour. Someone helped me, and now I am paying it back.'

'Who?' he asked, intrigued.

'Doesn't matter. It's between me and them. Now, Anton here is going to drive you. He'll get you as close to the border as he can, but obviously enough, our occupiers are getting very jumpy these days, trigger-happy. They are exhausted – we all are. So we'll do our best.'

He walked around Richard, examining him as if he were a horse he was thinking of buying. 'Good... Some muscle wastage, but you will be strong enough, I think.'

'How far is the border?'

'Twenty-five kilometres or so, but that distance is not really the issue.'

Richard began doing the calculation from metric to imperial in his head. 'I could walk sixteen miles...'

'You'd be shot after one,' Gabriel said matter-of-factly. 'You were released because I was owed a favour, but there it ends. You have no sanctuary here. If they pick you up again, all bets are off, as they say.' He exhaled the last puff of his cigarette and crushed the butt with the heel of his shoe. 'No, you need to go much further south, along the border, but the only place we stand any chance of getting you across is at Archamps, two hundred and fifty kilometres south of here.'

'And there's nowhere closer?' Richard asked in dismay, but the look Gabriel gave him silenced him. The tone when the other man replied sounded bored at Richard's petulance.

'Contrary to what you might believe, Switzerland has set very high hurdles for legal entry to their country. They want to keep the numbers low and really only will admit those they see as being valuable, those with familial ties to Switzerland or the very wealthy.'

He thought about interjecting that his family was wealthy, but that wouldn't help at this point, he knew.

'Up to Christmas of last year, it was easier – children under sixteen and those due to be drafted to work in Germany could hope to be given exile. But nothing like that is allowed now. So illegal entry over the mountains is the best we can hope for. But the Jura are difficult to traverse – if I can get you that far, and that's a big if.'

'OK, well…I guess we try. If you tell me the plan, I can see if –'

'Oh, be under no illusion, Mr Lewis.' Gabriel's voice was whip-sharp now, all trace of the avuncular charm gone. 'It is me and my associates who are taking the risk here. There is no "we" in this. You will do precisely as you are told, with no debate, no discussion. Is that clear?'

Richard knew this was the moment that would decide his fate. Any dissention, however slight, might be the difference between him ever seeing Grace again and not. 'Clear,' he replied. 'And thank you.'

Gabriel regarded him for a long time, his gaze locked with Richard's. 'You are welcome.'

Anton, the slight man in his sixties, reappeared to lead him on through more tunnels and, eventually, out through a gate where a car was waiting.

The journey in the false compartment between the back seat and the trunk of the car was the most uncomfortable of Richard's life. He was too tall and too large, and he had to fight feelings of panic as he squeezed himself into the impossibly tiny space. The false wall of the trunk was right against his face, and he couldn't move an inch.

Anton was alone and spoke not one word to him. The car drove and stopped, turned and, at one point, screeched to a halt and Richard had absolutely no idea what was happening. He tried at the beginning to keep some kind of time count going, but it proved impossible.

There was air circulating; he told himself that over and over. He would not suffocate however much it felt like he might. Every muscle, tendon and sinew of his body screamed in protest for the first few hours, or at least that was how it felt. Then he went numb, and he wondered if he was in fact paralysed. If this was what it felt like, he decided he would rather die. He was parched with thirst and his head pounded, but on and on the car drove. He assumed it was light now – *it must be* – but there was no way of knowing.

Then abruptly the car stopped. He may have slept; he didn't know. He wondered if it was a checkpoint, and the thought of being recaptured filled him with dread. Although at this point he would be happy to get out of this prison, whatever the circumstances.

The trunk was opened and the board concealing him removed. Strong hands pulled him out. He was in such pain, he screamed, and the men around him hissed for him to stay silent. He was in a barn or a shed of some kind, and dawn was streaking across the sky, visible through the large open door.

Three men and Anton, all speaking in rapid French, so fast Richard couldn't understand a word of what they were saying, gestured that he should drink some water they offered from a tin mug. He chugged it back and promptly vomited. His head spun and he fell to his knees, retching.

Before he had time to compose himself, strong arms pulled him to his feet, and to his horror, he saw where they were leading him. At the back of the barn was a flatbed truck on which was a rough coffin.

'You go in. I close. *Hépatite.*' One of them, a middle-aged man with a flame-red beard but brown hair, then turned from him and went back to conversing with his comrades in more unintelligible French.

Hepatitis. Did they think he had hepatitis? Did he? Were they going to tell any passing patrol that he'd died of hepatitis? This was insane. He couldn't get into a coffin, he just couldn't.

He was about to object when another man appeared at his elbow with a cloth soaked in liquid. He was manhandled to the coffin and laid in it. He was too weak to object, his body in such pain, and he succumbed. The cloth was put to his face, and he knew no more.

CHAPTER 24

SAVANNAH, GEORGIA

Arthur Lewis sat opposite Grace in his wood-panelled study an hour before they were due to depart. The room smelled like him, of leather and shaving soap and money.

'Thank you, Mr Lewis,' she began.

He cut across her. 'Grace, I keep telling you. Arthur, please.'

She blushed; despite his kindness he still intimidated her a little. 'Thank you, Arthur, for everything,' she said sincerely.

'It was a pleasure, Grace, and you're family now, so you call on me any time. I mean it. And I wanted to thank you too. That day we had yesterday with the plaques arranged by my wife was so meaningful – I don't know how, but I feel like you had a hand in that.'

'No,' she said truthfully. 'Mrs Lewis arranged it all.'

He raised a sceptical eyebrow but didn't pursue it. 'And having you here was good for Sarah too. I'm worried about her. She sure as blazes doesn't want to stay here, and I'm scared half to death she'll want to go back to London, or worse, and I can't bear to lose another child. The way she is these days, I'd be afraid she won't take any care.

There's a saying where I'm from – "You're gonna need to be tough if you're gonna be stupid." I think Sarah is plenty tough, but some of her decisions might be, if not stupid, at least reckless.'

'She's grieving,' Grace said simply.

He nodded. 'I know. I'm trying to be...look, I wasn't raised up on soft talk and the likes, but I can see she's broken but you have a way with us...When you had lunch with my wife, she told me how kind you were. So I'm grateful. She and Sarah...well, they don't exactly rub along together.'

Grace knew that was an understatement.

Sarah wasn't going to stay here. Jacob's friend David and his fiancée, Rachel, were both serving in the forces, and Sarah had mentioned she might apply to train as a medic or an ambulance driver or something. This had been within Arthur's earshot when Sarah had invited David to the house, and the thought filled him with dread.

'I don't know what to do, and this is not a sensation I'm familiar with, Grace.' He smiled, and once again Grace could see where Richard got his good looks and charm. If she was honest, being around Arthur Lewis these past days had been painful for her at times. It had been difficult not to keep seeing Richard as he might have been had he had the chance to grow older. Tears pricked her eyes each time she had to tell herself that, like so many other young men of his generation, he would now never have that chance. Caroline Lewis was right – it was easier this way, to accept he was gone; no good would come of giving into that tiny pinprick of hope that still jabbed at her stubborn heart.

'Will we see you here again?' Arthur inquired gently. He came out from behind his desk and stood before her. 'You're always welcome here, Grace. I hope you know that.'

'I don't know, Mr Lew – Arthur. To come to America once in a lifetime is so unusual for anyone from Knocknashee, and I've been twice. I feel so lucky to have had the opportunity.' She looked up at the man who would have been her father-in-law, and for a fleeting second saw not Arthur but Richard, and her eyes filled with tears.

'Aw, come here...' Arthur opened his arms wide, and she allowed herself to be enveloped in a hug. 'Richard said you were special, and he was right. Imagine that you consider yourself lucky, after all you've been through, all you've endured, when so many people have had none of your adversity to face and all they do is moan about how dang tough it all is.'

He kissed the top of her head as she clung to him, sobbing. 'You come on back here, girl, do you hear me? I know you might not feel much like it now, and everywhere is a reminder of all you've lost, but in time, being here, in his place, with us, I think it might give you a bit of comfort.'

'We'll have to win the war first.' She half laughed.

'Oh, don't you worry about that, Grace, not for one second. 'Cause that nasty little runt Hitler don't know what fury he's unleashed now, but by God, he's gonna find out, and he'll regret the day he ever started this war.'

'I hope so, because there's been enough sadness.' She wiped her eyes with her handkerchief.

'Ain't that the truth.' Arthur sighed. 'OK, Clay is ready to go when you are, if you're sure you don't want me to fly you back to New York. I feel bad sending you by train, especially now that you're upset.'

Sarah had told Grace that Arthur had a big merger of two of his companies on his plate this week, and the last thing Grace wanted to do was take him from his work. Besides, if she was honest, she found the flight terrifying and was much happier to travel by train.

'Honestly it will be nice to see more of the country as we travel back. And Charlie and Mrs McHale will keep me company.' She stood back from him. 'I'll be fine.'

He placed his big hands on her shoulders. 'You ever need anything – anything at all – or you feel like a break, or you want to start a new life here, you name it, I'll make it happen, y'hear?'

She nodded, swallowing the lump in her throat.

He walked her out to the drawing room where Sarah and Mrs McHale were deep in conversation discussing Canon Rafferty and the other adopted babies she'd discovered. It had been a topic Sarah found fascinating, and Mrs McHale was so outraged by the man's actions, she was happy to share as much as she knew. Grace could sense this was something Sarah had a plan about.

'So this little girl who lost her parents is in the orphanage system, but she could well have family back in Ireland?' Sarah was trying to understand Mrs McHale's storytelling, which was interspersed with lots of side details that had nothing to do with the original story.

'That's right, poor little pet. And God knows how many more there were. I asked Father Dempsey, and he gave me as much information as he had. He's not great, you know. Cancer. The poor man. And my friend Bridget Hanley, she had the same. Well, she's more of an acquaintance than a friend, to tell you the truth – she can be very cutting. She said I should do something about my chilblains, and I thought she had a nerve to comment on my noughts and crosses on my legs, considering hers aren't exactly fit for doing the can-can either, but how and ever, she went very yellow around the eyes, she did, and the skin too. But she got a cream from the doctor then, and he said it would improve it, but it didn't. She looked like a fried egg, the poor woman. Anyway, Father Dempsey's livid with that Rafferty yoke, but he's still an ordained priest at the end of the day, and they don't speak out of turn. But really and truly, he was a nasty piece of work and no mistake.'

'And do you think Father Dempsey would speak to me?' Sarah asked.

'Why would you want him to?' Mrs McHale looked surprised.

'I think I'd like to investigate this. Find out more about these children and just make sure they are all right. I enjoyed digging around for the facts of a story when I was working with the boys in London. And' – Sarah sighed – 'I don't know, I think it would give me something to do, and I might be able to do some good?'

Grace caught Arthur's eye. This was exactly what Sarah needed: a project. It was a much better prospect for Sarah than going into the forces; she was still too fragile and heartbroken for that. Perhaps in time but not yet.

'I think that's a marvellous idea,' Grace said. 'And you're right – it might do some good.'

Sarah nodded. 'I think I will then. There might even be a story in it. Kirky syndicated a lot of our human-interest stories from the refugees in London, like families reunited and that kind of thing...' She glanced at Grace as Charlie and Richard's mother walked past the window. They were deep in conversation, and Grace wondered what they were talking about.

'I would never write anything without permission obviously...' Sarah was quick to add.

'I know, of course you wouldn't,' Grace reassured her.

'But there are so many people lost in the world now, so many children who will never see their families again. It might be nice to deliver some happy endings at least.'

'It would. Look how well it's worked out with Charlie and the Maheadys. I think it would be a wonderful project.'

As she spoke, Caroline and Charlie came back inside. 'What does Sarah want to do?' Caroline asked, and Grace hoped her imperious tone wouldn't set off another argument between mother and daughter.

'I'm going to work on a story for the paper, maybe go to New York for research. And then maybe even to Ireland, depending on what I uncover.'

There was no asking for permission, Grace noticed. Sarah just said she was doing it and that was that.

'For the *Capital*?' Caroline was trying to keep her voice light and interested, and Grace felt a wave of sympathy for her. She really was trying, but she just had no skill at it. For all their money and power and fancy houses, Grace realised, being brought up in a loving home, surrounded by decent people who were kind and funny and considerate, taught you all you needed in life. Of course Richard had grown up around this kind of wealth, she admitted that, but he was different. He had his brother and his sister and his father; though it was hard to reconcile the sweet, considerate man Arthur was now with the cold, distant father Richard had described from his childhood.

Richard had never mentioned his grandparents, but she had asked Sarah about them yesterday when they were alone, as they sipped iced tea on the terrace at St Simons. Sarah said her maternal grandfather was a Confederate to his fingertips, a scary booming man with a huge moustache, still fighting the Civil War, and with no time whatsoever for women or children. His wife, their grandmother, was ice cold. Sarah said she remembered biting her nail one time when she was only four, and her grandmother had the help dip all her fingers in hot sauce, which burnt her tongue when she next put a finger to her lips. The woman sounded horrific, Grace thought. No wonder Caroline was like she was, raised by a mother like that.

'Yes,' Sarah lied. She hadn't pitched the idea to Kirky yet.

'On what subject?' Caroline asked.

Sarah was vague. 'Oh, just a human-interest story. Kirky says people like to hear something cheerful in the midst of all the carnage. We did quite a few of them in London, families reunited, daring escapes, dogs found after weeks, that kind of thing.'

While it seemed that Sarah was never going to confide in her mother, at least she wasn't eating the head off her, so that was progress.

'I was going to suggest you invite Jacob's friend David to dinner again next week. I think you mentioned that David's parents have died and his fiancée was serving overseas, so he might enjoy a home-cooked meal. I'm sure Esme could impress him.' Caroline tried to smile, though it looked more like a grimace.

Sarah caught a look from her father and softened a little. 'Thank you, Mother. That would be nice.'

Caroline was rewarded for making an effort by her husband putting his hand on her shoulder and giving it a gentle squeeze. It was the first time Grace had ever seen them touch.

'Find out what day he's free and what he likes to eat, and we'll arrange it.' Caroline glanced at Sarah, and Grace could see she was trying hard not to wince at her daughter's outfit. Sarah was dressed today in a pair of khaki trousers – men's, Grace suspected – and a white shirt. Or at least it had once been white. On her feet were a pair of canvas shoes with woven soles that she told Grace were called espadrilles. She got them from a Spanish woman in exchange for

Sarah's winter boots in London last winter. Her hair was wavy and messy and hung around her face; Grace wondered if she ever brushed it at all.

Charlie stepped forward then. 'Thank you very much for your hospitality, Arthur and Caroline. I'll never forget it. And I know we're not of the same religion, but Richard will always be remembered in our prayers in Knocknashee.' Charlie shook Arthur's hand warmly, and the American clutched Charlie's arm as he did so, the affection on such a short acquaintance evident. To Grace's surprise, Charlie then hugged Caroline, who clung to him.

Mrs McHale clasped Caroline's hands. 'I'll pray for your lovely boy every night of my life. He was such a wonderful young man, and a credit to the pair of you. You should be so proud of him, and I'm so grateful to you for inviting me to your lovely home. I was never down here before in my life, and it was such a treat. Aggie Richardson went to South Carolina once, and glory be to God and all the saints, we never heard the end of it. And 'twas all to fight over a pearl necklace that Aggie thought was coming to her but went to her sister Judy instead – you never heard such ructions.' Mrs McHale chuckled as she went off on one of her tangents. 'Aggie is gone to God now, and didn't Judy wear the pearls to the funeral? That woman is a pure solid scourge, to be fair. On and on she went about the pearls, 'twas like being pecked to death by a duck. Anyway, it was a wonderful trip, to get to know Richard's family and see where he grew up. 'Twas a good day for me the day Richard Lewis came to St Patrick's, and I'll miss him more than any words could ever say. And I know we were no relations, but when the other women would be talking about their sons or grandsons who were fighting, I would tell them about my Richard, and it felt like I had someone I loved there too, someone to worry about, and knit for and...' her voice broke huskily with the emotion of it all, 'I'll have the bishop say a special Mass for him.'

She was enveloped in a bear hug from Arthur, and even Caroline managed a smile through her tears. Mrs McHale might as well have been a creature in a zoo for all the sense she made to Richard's mother, with her speech peppered with Catholicisms and her rambling way of talking, but even Caroline could see that Mrs McHale loved her son.

Grace slipped away for a moment as they said their goodbyes and Clay loaded the car with their bags.

Esme was in the kitchen peeling vegetables as Grace knocked gently.

'Oh, Miss Grace, was there something you needed?' The woman looked startled, and Grace saw her eyes were bright with tears.

'Just to say goodbye. We're leaving now.'

Grace found it very disconcerting to see such a divided society, and she had noticed that Esme always stayed in the kitchen. She still didn't quite understand how to behave here, but she couldn't leave without saying goodbye. Esme worked for the Lewis family and had raised their children. She was held in high regard by Richard's father, and treated as a servant and nothing more by his mother, but there was a subtlety to it that an outsider didn't fully appreciate. Grace knew that she probably should not be here in the kitchen, but she didn't know why. Esme looked on edge, and the last thing Grace wanted was to make her feel uncomfortable.

Esme wiped her hands on a towel and turned, her movement slow because of her bulk and also her rheumatism. The poor woman was so grief-stricken, it was painful to see. Grace hoped she wasn't doing or saying the wrong thing. She'd been waited on by Esme, of course, since she'd been here, but they'd never spoken face to face before.

'Richard spoke about you so often. I'm so very sorry for your loss,' Grace said.

The woman didn't speak for a moment, her kind, dark eyes fixed on Grace. Her curly grey hair was swept back from her face, and when she moved towards Grace, her legs were stiff. The hand that took Grace's was calloused from years of hard work. 'He told me about you too, that you were fixin' to get married?'

'That's right, we were,' she said, her eyes filling with tears. 'I just wanted to say goodbye and thank you…'

'Oh, child…'

It was the most natural thing in the world to allow herself to be enveloped in the arms of Esme Carter, who loved Richard as if he were her own son.

'You take care of yourself now, Miss Grace. You're a lovely young woman, and I know my Richard wouldn't want you to be sad forever. So you grieve for as long as you need to, but then you go and live your life, you hear me?'

Grace could only nod. Tears stung her eyes as Esme rocked her in her arms. Then she heard herself say, 'Sometimes I think if I'd never met him, or encouraged him, he'd still be here and safe and...' She'd finally expressed the thought that had been lingering in her mind since she'd arrived here.

Esme released her from the embrace but kept her hands on Grace's shoulders, her brown eyes kind. 'Your heart is breaking now, child, and that's OK. It's how it should be. But you know this – that boy would never have got up the guts to do what he done, leave the bank and leave this city and that girl Miranda Logan, if it wasn't for you. *You* did that, *you* gave him the courage. And 'cause you did, even though he's gone too soon, he *lived* his life. And he done it the way he wanted to, having adventures and doing some good for folks. So, he wouldn't change a thing, I know it.'

'He loved you,' Grace managed.

Esme smiled, her white teeth in contrast to her dark skin. 'And I sure loved him' – she leant in and whispered into Grace's ear – 'like my own child.'

'Do you have any children – of your own, I mean?'

Esme shook her head. 'I had a baby girl, Louisa, but she got scarlet fever when she was only three years old. Mrs Lewis paid for the good doctor to come tend to her, and we even took her to the hospital. Richard's daddy drove us in his car. But there wasn't nothing to be done.'

'I'm so sorry, Esme.'

Esme dropped her hands from Grace's shoulders and said,

'She's with Richard now. He was the same age as Louisa. They used to play together sometimes.' Grace didn't need Esme to tell her they only played together when his mother was out of the house.

'She is, God rest her.' Grace reached out her hand, and Esme took it in her calloused ones.

'You live your life, Miss Grace. He'd want that for you.'

'Can I write to you sometimes?'

'Sure you can. Write to my home, though. Not here.' Esme took a pencil and scribbled her address on a piece of paper, handing it to Grace. 'And someday, with the Lord's help, you'll send me a wedding picture, and maybe even a baby on your knee, and that will make this old lady smile.'

Grace knew that would never happen, but now was not the time to say so. 'Goodbye, Esme,' she said, her voice cracking and the lump in her throat making her swallow to try to stem the flow of tears. .

'You take good care, Miss Grace. You got yourself another special angel looking after you now.'

She walked back to the hallway, wiping her eyes as she went. So many angels watching over her was not the comfort people thought it was. Why could she not have her parents, Declan or Richard here in the flesh?

'Goodbye, my dear.' Arthur hugged her and led her to the car, where Caroline stood.

'Goodbye, Grace,' Richard's mother said. 'It was wonderful to meet you. I can see why my son thought so highly of you.' She proffered her hand, but on a whim, Grace embraced her as Charlie had done. To her relief, the woman hugged her back.

'Goodbye, Mrs Lewis, take care,' she whispered into her ear.

'Thank you, my dear,' she murmured. 'I mean it. Thank you – for everything.'

CHAPTER 25

NEW YORK CITY

The journey back to New York was uneventful as the train chugged past miles and miles of farmland. The train conductor explained that, to the west of the Carolinas, there were mountains – the Appalachian, the Blue Ridge and the Smoky ranges – and to the east was the coastal plain stretching to the Atlantic coast. However, the train went through the middle of the states, a region he called the Piedmont, which was made up of rolling hills and valleys.

It was an incredible eight-hundred-mile trip, so they stopped in Richmond, Virginia, overnight and stayed at a hotel Arthur Lewis's secretary had booked for them. He'd insisted they travel first class on the train as well, so they were waited on hand and foot.

Seeing the people on the streets of the handsome city of Richmond, they realised not all Americans lived as the Lewis family did. There was old money there certainly, some beautiful homes and signs of wealth and privilege, but there were also signs of poverty everywhere. And a distinct lack of men. Old people, women and children populated the city, as so many young men had joined up.

The following morning, back on the train, the three travellers settled into their comfortable seats once more.

'How I'll go back to cycling up the Geata Bán hill in the lashings of rain after this treatment, I don't know.' Charlie chuckled as the liveried waiter offered them morning coffee or iced tea with a plate of delicate pastries, while outside the large picture window beside them, the countryside rolled gently by.

'I know, Charlie. We'll never be able to go back to the way we were,' Mrs McHale replied, helping herself to a cream puff and allowing the waiter to pour her a cup of coffee.

They left Virginia, with its tobacco farms, then Maryland, Delaware, New Jersey, places Grace had heard about but never in a million years thought she would ever see.

'George Washington was from Virginia, Mount Vernon. I wonder if we passed near it?' Grace mused as the landscape served as a moving picture. This land was forged from blood and determination, and she thought about how Richard often mentioned that British people seemed to have forgotten that America had to be wrestled from the grip of King George III and therefore knew a thing or two about colonialism.

'I don't know,' Charlie said. 'A man in the hotel last night said it was in Fairfax County, Virginia. If we had more time, it would be something to go and see his house, wouldn't it?'

'It would, indeed,' Mrs McHale agreed. 'I've lived here since I was a girl. Imagine that. But I've travelled more this week than in all those years. I should have done more, I suppose, but I never had much money, and sure, I suppose I always felt like I'd be going home someday.'

'Will you now, do you think?' Grace asked. 'My offer is open-ended.'

'Ah, you're very good, and I will think about it. I haven't gone back in years, and sure there's nobody belonging to me there any more. I never had children myself – we couldn't for some reason. And Des, my late husband, said it was all right, we'd be grand just the two of us, when I'd be sad over it. But when he died, then...' Mrs McHale's voice faded, and Grace knew exactly what she felt. The old lady gazed out the window, her eyes bright; clearly she didn't want to talk about this any more.

Charlie sensed it and changed the subject. 'I sent a telegram to Joey and Sylvia saying we sail at six o'clock but we should arrive to the city in the early afternoon, so maybe we could meet up. I know I said my goodbyes to Lily before we came down to Savannah, but the idea of being in the same city as her and not seeing her... Was that all right, do you think, Grace?' Charlie looked uncertain.

'I'm sure it will be fine, Charlie, and if they can get in to meet us, then I'm confident they will. Lily will definitely want to see you again – she hangs on every word you say.'

'She's a lucky girl, no doubt about it. I just hope the rest of them fared as well.' Mrs McHale wiped some cream from her lip, now recovered and having helped herself to another cream bun.

'Well, if Sarah Lewis has anything to do with it, we'll soon find out. Her father is relieved she's got this project now, so it's a good thing all around. He was terrified she'd join the forces or go back to London.' Grace sipped her tea. She would never really get used to iced tea and would always prefer it hot.

'She might have luck over here, but I can't see her getting anywhere if she goes back to Ireland,' Charlie said, the sadness of the years still in his voice. 'I can tell her from bitter experience, they guard that information very carefully and close ranks if you try to find out anything. I tried for years and years to find Declan and Siobhán, as you know, but got nowhere.'

'But maybe now that the canon is wherever he is, there might be a bit more opportunity to get someone to talk,' Grace suggested, though she agreed with Charlie. 'Sarah doesn't know who she's dealing with. We could ask Father Iggy or even the bishop to help.' But she knew how ridiculous that suggestion sounded.

'God bless your innocence, Grace,' Charlie said. 'But she hasn't a hope, and that's the truth. She can try, of course, and I'm happy to help her, especially if it saves some other poor person what I endured over the years, but it won't come to anything.'

'Our bishop in New York heard about it. Well, I told him is how. Nora d'Furio marched right up to the palace to demand he do something about the hard seats in St Joseph's – she's a martyr to the piles, and the seats were killing her. She made deputations to the parish priest, but sure he never sits on a church pew, so he sent her away. But she wasn't letting it go. Nora is from Longford, married to an Italian plumber called Marco, and she gives him a dog's life. But anyway, says I, if it's good enough for Nora to march up to His Eminence complaining about her sore arse, 'tis good enough for me for something much more important. But he didn't seem to want to get involved, said it sounded more like an issue on the Irish end of things. He's all right, I suppose, this new bishop, but he's ambitious. He's got his eye on a post in Rome, I'd say, and he won't want anything sordid like this blotting his copybook,' Mrs McHale declared sagely.

'His brother went to Rome before him. His mother married twice. Her first husband was red rotten useless, knew as much about a day's work as a pig does about a bank holiday, so he got the high road, and then she married another fella, the bishop's father, and he was a pure solid workaholic. Died falling off a wall, the poor man. But it was the wall of a Jewish nursing home, and nobody knew what he was doing up there in the first place – sure he was a fisherman, and not a Jew either. But anyway, he has an older brother...well, a half-brother...' And on she went. Grace and Charlie were only half listening, not that the old lady ever noticed. She was happy to ramble on uninterrupted with yet another very complicated tale with endless conversational meandering about people her companions had never met and never would, and which bore no relation to the original story.

The three dozed and ate and read their books, and eventually the train pulled into Penn Station on 7th Avenue at midday. To their delight, all four Maheadys were on the platform – Ivy was with them this time as well. As Charlie alighted, carrying his own, Grace's and Mrs McHale's bags, Lily ran to him. He dropped the bags and embraced her in a hug.

'I'm so happy, but I feel like I just met you and now I have to let you go again,' Lily said in her usual forthright way.

'I know, *a chroí*, but we are in touch now and we'll write. Maybe you'd come over for a visit when the war is over. I could send you the fare?'

'I could come now?' Lily looked up at him hopefully. 'I asked my folks, and they said it was OK if you agreed. I'm on summer vacation now, and I checked with the ship and they said they could take me, and I have saved the fare. I was going to go to Rhode Island with my friends, but I'd rather go to Ireland.'

Charlie looked at Joey and Sylvia. 'You don't mind?'

'We didn't get much choice. She's a stubborn girl, this one, and she got the idea in her head after you guys left to go south – she's been plotting ever since.' Joey smiled indulgently at his daughter. 'She's eighteen, so technically she doesn't need our permission.'

'I wouldn't take her if I thought you were unhappy about it, though,' Charlie was quick to interject.

'We're happy for her to go, Charlie,' Sylvia said, although Grace could see the sadness in her eyes. 'She's never been away from us before, but she'll be going off to college in the fall anyway. She even got a passport this week. A teacher at her school is married to someone in the government, so she got it extra quick. She's all set, if you're happy to have her.'

'Sylvia, Joey, I…' Charlie was speechless.

'Can I come, Charlie?' Lily asked. 'Just for a few weeks? I need to be back at the end of August for enrollment.'

'How will we get you passage back? Could you do that on your own?'

Grace knew Charlie would love nothing as much as taking Lily to Knocknashee, but these were dangerous and uncertain times, and undertaking an ocean voyage as a family was dangerous enough. For a girl on her own, it would be nerve-racking.

'We talked about it,' Lily explained. 'I went down with Dad to the maritime office yesterday and explained what I wanted to do. The guy there said I would be able to get passage back if I was flexible with dates, but it would be expensive. I'd have to have a single cabin to myself, and I'm not allowed to mix with the men or anything. But I have enough saved up. I think I do, anyway.' Lily now looked a little unsure. 'But maybe now isn't a good time? I could, you know...wait until after the war, if that would be better? I probably sprung this on you, Charlie, and I guess you'd have to talk to your wife and –'

'Come here to me now, you.' Charlie put his arm around his daughter as the people on the platform rushed around. Everyone was in such a hurry in New York; it was quite jarring, Grace found, after the slow, relaxed pace of life in Savannah.

'If you want to come to Knocknashee with us now, then I'm over the moon to take you. Dymphna and the children will be so excited too. But I'll warn you, Lily. We only have a small house, and we don't have much money. But we'd love to have you, really love it.'

'Right, that's settled then.' Joey put his arm around Lily. 'How about we take these people for a pizza, a proper Italian pizza in Little Italy?'

Ivy spoke for the first time. 'Yes, let's go to Lombardi's on Spring Street.'

'I'll let you at it – pizza and me don't get along.' Mrs McHale chortled. 'Sits in my stomach like a rock, it does. I wouldn't be right for days.'

'Oh, we can go someplace else...' Joey Maheady was anxious to include her.

'Not at all, I need to get home anyhow.' She gave Charlie and Grace a quick squeeze each. 'Thank you both very much for including me, and letting me say goodbye to Richard – I'll never forget you for it. I'll write, Grace, and I'll think about your very kind offer of a little holiday when the war is over. And Sarah said she might come up to see me in a few weeks to do a bit of digging, so we'll keep you posted.' There were hugs, and Grace found herself welling up again; she was like a leaky tap these days.

With that, Mrs McHale trundled off, a small, stout figure battling through the crowds and taking no prisoners. The old Irish lady and seasoned New Yorker had strategic use of the elbows well rehearsed.

'Will you be all right without your sister for a few weeks?' Grace asked shy thirteen-year-old Ivy as they walked out of the station.

'Yeah, I'll miss her, but don't tell her that.' Ivy grinned.

'Seriously, though, how are you about all of this?' Grace asked as Lily linked Charlie's arm and led the procession.

'I'm OK. I think we kinda knew anyway. We talked about it a lot, and me and Lily are real close. I don't care that she's not blood related to me. It felt a bit weird at first, having it confirmed, but nothing changed, so I'm fine with it. And it's good she's so excited, and Charlie seems like a nice guy.'

Grace admired her confidence and the articulate way she expressed the complex set of circumstances that had just turned her family upside down. The Mahedys were good parents that was clear, both Lily and Ivy had turned out so well. 'He is, and he's very anxious not to cause any upset to your family.'

'Nah, we're good.' Ivy smiled as they turned a corner. 'And I get the bedroom to myself for the rest of the summer.'

Lily said something to her, and she went to join her sister up ahead.

They would drive to the restaurant, it was a few blocks away; Grace had had no idea what a block might be until it was explained to her. Her leg ached as they walked to the car. She really needed someone to lean on, but Charlie had her bag and his own. Sylvia and Joey were walking along arm in arm, and Grace didn't want to interrupt that; she knew that however much they were putting on a brave face, this must be very hard for them. Ivy and Lily were deep in conversation, but Lily had linked Charlie as they progressed down the street, so Grace walked on alone.

It struck her that this was how it would be from now on. Everyone had someone, except her. On that busy New York street, with cars and people and noise and sirens, Grace had never felt so lonely and alone.

CHAPTER 26

NEAR THE TOWN OF BELLEFONTAINE, FRANCE

The gentle hill to his right became a steep climb. Richard shielded his eyes as he tried to make sense of his surroundings. Anton, the man who had brought him this far, had presumably also driven him in the coffin. Mercifully, Richard had no recollection of the journey – the thought still gave him shivers – and he'd woken up on this deserted part of the narrow mountain road. To his right was a mountain peak; possibly he was near the Alps? The Jura? He'd never been there before, but this looked like pictures he'd seen. The mountain flowers grew in pretty abundance all around him, and the air was clear and clean. If he wasn't feeling the worst he'd ever felt, he might have enjoyed being here.

Anton's English was almost nonexistent, and Richard could hardly remember his own name, let alone any French. His head was pounding, and he was parched with thirst. His limbs felt like jelly; even standing up tested his strength.

Anton pointed in the direction of the mountain. *'La Suisse.'*

Richard just stared, his vision blurry.

'*La...*' the man jabbed with his finger to the mountains again – '*La Suisse. La... Nord-est. Comprends? Nord-est.*'

Richard managed to nod that he understood. Switzerland was to the North West.

Anton pushed a knapsack into Richard's arms and got back in the van. Without another word, he drove away.

The sun was warm and beat down on his head. Richard needed to find some shade and a drink, and then perhaps he could figure out what on earth he was to do next.

He walked up the road that was really more of a gravel path, and at the next bend there were the ruins of a shed. He crossed towards it and walked through what was once the door, though the timber had long since rotted off the hinges. Inside smelled damp and a little cooler, the floor covered in grass and stones, but on one side of the twelve-foot-square structure were the remains of a roof. Richard sat down under it, resting his head against the cool shed wall, grateful for the respite from the heat. From the empty water trough and bits of wool lying around, he decided this was a shelter for mountain sheep.

He opened the knapsack and found a bottle of water, as well as an apple and some cheese wrapped in greased paper and a round loaf of country bread. There was also a military-issue compass, which would be useful. And he discovered a pistol, wrapped in a dark rag. There were six bullets in the chamber. *All right. This is something. I can do this.*

He would need to go northeast. That's what Anton said. Where was he headed, though? Was he north of Strasbourg? Or south of it? It must be south if he was being told to go northeast. It depended on where he was. There were no signs left in France, and anyway his geography was atrocious, so even if he saw a placename, there was not a snowball's chance in hell he'd know where he was. Anton had said to go over the mountain in a northeasterly direction, so he would go up until he could come down the other side and hope for the best. His stomach was churning like he might vomit any minute – but he drank the water. He knew he should ration it, but he was so thirsty, he couldn't help drinking it all down in one go. As the cool liquid hit his insides, he felt better, and in the minutes that followed, as he just sat there, his head against the rock with his eyes closed, he began to feel a bit more human.

He looked down. He'd been given strong boots and socks, as well as trousers and a shirt, so at least he could try to get over the mountain properly clad. And it was summertime, so the ice and snow had melted on all of the range but for the very top, which he prayed was not where he needed to go.

Gabriel had mentioned German patrols at the border crossing points, but surely this place was far enough away from civilisation to mean he was safe from arrest again. A great weariness came over him. Had he the strength to do this again? On his own this time? Without Jacob?

When he'd been a boy in Savannah, he'd read adventure books about guys going on daring missions and escaping terrible foes, and he recalled, as he sat then on the porch of the summer cottage on St Simons, feeling disgruntled that his life was never going to allow for anything like that to ever happen to him. Yet here he was. And it was nothing like the adventures described in his books. It was terrifying, painful, and he felt nauseous with the stress of it all.

He supposed he had better start his journey, though he had no map, or even an indication of how far or how high he needed to go to get to Switzerland. He did as he always did in moments of despair. He brought her face to his mind. Her beautiful smile, her green eyes flecked with amber, her copper curls. He saw her in his mind's eye; he heard her voice. *Come home to me, Richard, please come home. You can do this. I know you can. Please, Richard.*

He would get back to her. Or die trying.

He ate some of his bread and cheese and felt the energy return to his body. He thought the chloroform must be the reason he felt so dreadful, so he hoped it would wear off soon.

He stood up. He had no idea how far he needed to go, but this was his only hope of getting out of here. His legs felt a bit stronger, though the prospect of a mountain climb over the Alps was so daunting, he decided not to think about it. One step at a time. Anton said Switzerland was on the other side of the mountain, so he would just start walking.

He hoisted the knapsack on his back and was just about to emerge from the shed when he heard a motor. Quickly, his heart pounding, he retreated to the corner of the structure once more. A missing stone served as a window, and he held his breath as a German patrol vehicle drove by. There were two soldiers in it, the driver smoking a cigarette, his shirt sleeves rolled up, chatting amiably to his companion, who had a rifle trained out the passenger window.

To his horror they stopped about five yards before the shed. There was no way to hide himself. The stone structure was completely empty, and the only exit was the open doorway that would put him right in their sights. He could hear them talking; he had no idea what they were saying, but it sounded good-natured.

The driver got out of the jeep; the other man stayed where he was. The driver walked in the direction of the shed. Was this it? Captured again? Surely not.

Then he heard loud urinating against the wall of the shed.

The man finished his business, did up his fly, jogged back to the jeep, turned the key and drove off. Richard barely exhaled until the sound of the motor was fully gone. He needed to get off the road as fast as possible, as the likelihood of running into a foot patrol was less, and if it was one or two, he might be able to shoot them.

The thought gave him pause. Was that who he was now? Someone who could take lives? If it meant he could get back to Grace, then, yes, it was. He prayed he didn't have to, but if he needed to, he would.

He secured the knapsack on his back and ran as quickly as his legs would allow across the gravel road, up a slight grassy incline and through a gate, presumably placed there by the sheep farmer.

Up and up he walked on the grassy hill, the ground hard and rutted under his feet. There had been no rain for weeks. Soon his shirt was soaked in sweat and his muscles ached in protest at the exercise after being restricted for so long.

He refused to stop; he was still too exposed. A car driving on the road far below him could still see him, and he needed to be out of sight. On and on he walked, forcing his mind to remember words to songs or poems from school, anything to not think about his body's agony.

All day long he walked. A mountain stream, barely a trickle now, slaked his thirst. The longing to lie down and just rest on its banks was so hard to resist, but he drove himself on, ever higher. Hour after weary hour, he climbed. The sun began to set, and Richard stopped to watch it. He had been moving for what must have been hours. He was no longer visible from the road, and all around him were rocky and snowy peaks. If anything, the mountain in front of him looked higher than it had from down on the road. He took out the compass; he was still on a northeast course.

The landscape here was less verdant and lush, more rocks and craggy edges. Small hardy alpine flowers grew in the grikes and cracks of the rocks, and as the sun set over the Alps, illuminating the whole place as far as he could see in a blazing orange sunset, Richard wondered if he'd ever seen a sight so beautiful. This might be what Grace's heaven looked like: warm, welcoming and so exquisite. He hoped that some day he would be able to tell her about it, maybe even take her here.

He heard her gentle teasing. *Oh definitely, Richard, mountain climbing is something polio survivors excel at...* Well, maybe she couldn't climb, but he could take her in a car, up as far as the road went, and they could have a picnic, and they could lie on a blanket, and he would kiss her and...

The thoughts of this future romantic date spurred him on. He would walk until it was dark and then try to settle someplace. It might get cold overnight this high up; he didn't know. Georgia was flat, and so he had very little experience with mountains. Grace might know more about it, but really there were just hills around Knocknashee. She told him the tallest mountain in Ireland was not far away, near the town of Killarney, and it was over three thousand feet high. But these peaks were multiples of that, he was sure.

Once darkness fell and the sunset gave way to inky night, he decided to rest. He had hoped there would be a hut or another sheep shed or something to offer at least the illusion of shelter, but there wasn't. He settled beside a large flat rock, leaning himself against it. He had no jacket or anything to cover himself with, and the knapsack was flimsy, but it would have to do as a pillow.

He took out some more of the bread and cheese. He'd filled his canteen back at the stream. He was so hungry, he was tempted to eat all the remaining bread but decided that would be foolish. There was nothing he could forage up here, so he would have to make his food last. The top of the mountain seemed so far away, and he still had to come down the other side, so he would have to conserve what little nourishment he had. Maybe Anton thought this was all he would need, and so maybe he was nearly at the pass where he could begin to descend the other side? The idea was a comforting one for a second, but logic told him that was not likely. Food was so scarce in France now, even in the rural areas. The Germans took everything for themselves, so it was more likely that this was all they could spare.

He chewed slowly, washing the bread and cheese down with the water, before putting the knapsack behind his head and closing his eyes. Despite his bone-weariness, he was reluctant to shut his eyes and relax; he felt exposed and vulnerable, though he'd not seen a trace of human activity for hours.

There's nobody here, he told himself. *Just sleep. One day closer to getting back to Grace.*

CHAPTER 27

Near the Swiss–French Border, Jura Mountains

A CHILD, a skinny, wiry boy of about ten or twelve – it was hard to tell when everyone was so thin – herding his goats high in the mountains, had taken him in. Richard wasn't sure he understood the boy correctly, because the dialect the child spoke was not like any French he knew, but after climbing the mountain, following a northeasterly course the whole time, and finally descending the other side, he had been glad to meet anyone.

The boy had taken him to his home, where his mother was alone. She was so careworn and weary of life high in the Alps, she could have been any age between thirty and sixty. But she was kind and didn't rebuke her boy for bringing a stranger into their midst. The boy explained using words and gestures that the Germans did patrol, even all the way up here, and Richard had to be careful. The woman gave him some soup and a piece of bread and gestured that he should rest on the only bed in the house until it was dark, that he would be safe. She left him alone with the boy.

The house was just one room and sparsely decorated, just a bed and a table and two chairs, a pot over an open fire and a shelf with a few utensils.

The boy had shown him his prized possession: a battered copy of *The Sword in the Stone* by T. H. White. It was, of course, in English, so Richard couldn't see how the child could read it, but the boy was so proud of it, and he kept asking Richard to *lire...lire*.

In the best French he could muster, Richard tried to tell the boy the story of Wart, the boy who would become King Arthur, and the wizard Merlin.

'*Il retira l'épée de la pierre. Et alors, ils surent qu'il était le vrai roi,*' Richard managed, sure that his French left a lot to be desired, but the boy hung on every word. The realisation that the story was about how Wart was able to pull the sword from the stone, which showed he was the true king, made the boy clap in delight.

'*Comment t'appel tu?*' Richard asked with a grin.

'Luc,' the boy replied. '*Mon père est anglais.*'

That explained the book. The boy's father was an Englishman. '*Óu est-il maintenant?*'

The boy pointed to the sky and pretended to fly a plane. '*Il tue des Nazis.*'

Richard wondered how on earth an RAF man managed to father a child ten years ago up here, but he knew that was a mystery that would never be solved. He just hoped the man would survive killing Nazis and that Luc would get his father back.

'*Tu es anglais?*' Luc asked.

Richard shook his head. '*Non, je suis Amèricain.*'

'*Non!*' The boy seemed astonished and pleased. 'Joe Lewis?' he said, miming a boxer.

Richard laughed. '*Oui,* Joe Lewis *est Amèricain aussi.*'

Luc seemed thrilled to have a real American in his home, but he could see Richard was wiped out. He gave him a blanket and a pillow to put on the bed.

'*Tu te reposes, je veillerai,*' he said quietly.

Richard didn't need to be asked twice and gratefully took him up on his offer to keep watch while he slept.

It seemed like mere minutes later that Luc shook him awake. It was pitch-dark outside. The boy's mother was sleeping on the floor, and Richard felt a pang of guilt. He would never knowingly put a woman out of her bed.

'Shh.' Luc put his finger to his lips. *'Allons-y.'*

He gestured to Richard to follow him, and out into the dark night they went. They walked over shaley ground with sparse vegetation. They passed the herd of goats, who bleated loudly at the sight of their young master, but he ignored them. The colours of the flowers were barely visible, but Richard could smell their heady scent, the heat of the night releasing their oils. He didn't know the names of any of them, but they sure were pretty.

They crossed over a shallow stream, merrily gurgling its way over the time-smoothened rocks, and crossed a lush grassy meadow. One of the surprises of the mountains was every so often there was a perfectly fertile piece of land.

Luc pointed to a stony precipice just beyond the field, where a herd of animals – maybe deer, Richard thought – bounded gracefully up vertiginous slopes.

'*Chamois*,' the boy explained, and Richard remembered something from school about these goat-antelope-type creatures that inhabited mountain areas and were so dexterous at climbing.

'*Sauvages?*'

The boy nodded to confirm they were indeed wild.

On and on they walked. Richard feared the dawn would break and he would be out here exposed again and liable to be picked up. But Luc just continued on.

Then, with almost no warning, the boy raised his hand for Richard to stop. He put his finger to his lips and glanced left and right. There was no sign of another living soul, but Richard did as he was told. Then Luc gestured to Richard to lie down, which he did. They were in a thicket of undergrowth just under the brow of a hill, and Richard wondered why they were stopping. After a moment, Luc ran forward about fifteen yards up the remainder of the hill, crouching low. Hand-signalling to Richard to stay down, the boy stood and peeped over the brow of the hill, waited for what felt to Richard like an eternity but was probably only ten minutes, then beckoned him forward.

Richard sidled up to him as the pink dawn streaked across the sky. His heart lurched as Luc pointed down the grassy field on the other side of the hill, at the bottom of which was a thicket and beyond that a ribbon of narrow road. But about two hundred yards to the right was a border post, manned by soldiers in German uniforms.

'*Tu dois courir. Traverse ce champ et franchis le grillage en bas. Le trou dans la cloture se trouve derrière cet arbre.*' Luc pointed to a large tree beside the road. '*Tu seras alors en Suisse. Rends-toi à la patrouille Suisse,*' the boy hissed urgently.

He was telling Richard he should run for it now – down the hill, across the road and through a wire fence at the bottom that had a gap behind a tree. And that would be it. This was the border. He would be in Switzerland. He'd have made it. All he had to do was surrender to the Swiss police and he would see Grace again. Except that he would almost certainly be seen by the Germans and shot on sight.

'*Attendre une voiture, puis courir.*'

Wait for a car. *All right.* That made sense. Wait for the border guards to be distracted and then run like the devil was after him. *Sure.* He could do this. His heart pounded in his chest, sweat trickling between his shoulder blades.

Luc left then, shaking Richard's hand like he was a grown man and not a kid forced to do adult things long before he should have to. This was not the first time Luc had seen someone over this mountain, and Richard knew it would probably not be the last. He also knew what the Germans did to anyone helping the enemy. He offered a prayer to protect Luc and his mother.

The road below was quiet, and the voices of the two young Germans carried on the thin air. He had his pistol too, that was always an option, but he didn't trust himself as a shot. Richard had never been interested in guns, even when his father would go hunting when he was a child; guns held no appeal for him. Besides, the guards were just kids, with mothers and sweethearts – why should he end their lives and cause misery to their loved ones?

Because they'd kill you without giving it a second thought. He heard Jacob's voice as if his friend were beside him.

Jacob was right, of course. Richard took the pistol from his pack and held it in his hand, cocked. He left the knapsack there. It was empty now, and he didn't need anything slowing him down. Luckily his basic training before taking the flight that crash-landed him in occupied France included weapons, so he knew how to fire the weapon, if not exactly on target, then at least in the direction of the target.

He lay there, watching the two in the sentry box. They were at ease, joking and laughing with each other, smoking. They were in their early twenties at most. Would they be the reason he died? Two kids from rural Germany? Surely not.

He lay there for almost an hour, the sun rising higher and higher in the sky, before he heard the distant rumble of an engine. This was it. His chance. He clambered up the grassy slope again and glanced to the left. There it was. A delivery truck of some kind, civilian, not military, which was good. They might just wave a miliary vehicle through, but they'd have to stop a civilian.

Could he get down and across the road in the time it would take? He'd have to try.

The truck passed below him and slowed to a halt at the instruction of the two soldiers. This was it. Both of them were busy, one speaking to the driver, the other walking around the back of the truck.

Richard inhaled, stood and ran down the hill. He ran until his lungs burnt and his limbs screamed for mercy, but on and on he ran. The field was so much longer than he'd imagined it to be. He didn't dare look to his right; he was focused on the tree Luc had pointed out. The hilly field levelled out, and he was within twenty yards of the road. There was no hedge or barrier; the field gave way to the ribbon of gravel. His pulse was pounding, the blood pumping like a repetitive thud in his head. Then he heard it. The shout. He'd been spotted. The next sound was a gunshot, but still he refused to stop or look to his right as the firing cracked the air. He was still moving, with no pain. He wouldn't stop. *Keep running!*

He stumbled as the grass became road but righted himself. The soldiers were bellowing now, and several more rounds were fired, but still he was unhurt. They ran towards him, boots rattling on the hard stone road, gaining on him, but he was almost to the tree. Luc was right, the gap was there. He dove behind the tree, pulled the wire fence aside and scrambled inside it. The exposed wire ripped his shirt and scratched the skin on his chest. Still more shouting, more gunshots. A piercing pain. *No. No!* He was hit. He was bleeding, he knew. His lower left leg was in agony, but he pressed on.

He turned and shot back with his pistol, the sweat in his eyes making it impossible to see. He wiped his brow with his sleeve and fired again. A scream, then another volley of shots was returned. The engine of the truck revved. He shot the last of his six bullets over his shoulder as he dragged his wounded leg deeper into Swiss territory. The terrain on the other side was a thicket of hedge, so he buried himself inside it, thorns and briars having no effect on him. He was out of sight. The gunshots coming from behind stopped; he heard no more voices. Had he shot one of them? Both of them? He had no idea.

He couldn't afford to wait. He was over the border, but the Germans were only yards away, if they were still alive. He pressed on and on, scrambling through the undergrowth, a trail of blood in his wake. But he kept moving. He was in Switzerland.

CHAPTER 28

KNOCKNASHEE, COUNTY KERRY

'I can't believe you've now been to America twice, you lucky duck. I'd love to get a chance to go there. Go anywhere, come to think of it.' Tilly was in a grump because Eloise was back in Dublin. The summer holidays were nearing their end, and the Swiss woman had to get back to the language school to prepare her classes.

'What's stopping you?' Grace asked as they lay on the flat rock on the beach, their usual spot. Odile was running in and out of the water with two of Marion and Colm's children. Poor Marion needed an operation on her knee, so the children were being farmed out to various relatives. Colm's three sisters had taken one or two each, and the two little ones had come to Knocknashee on their holidays. Odile was delighted to have the cousins to keep her company.

'Oh, just no money, Odile, my arthritic mother, a farm – you know, a few minor little issues like that.' Tilly sighed.

'Well, I'd mind Odile, and your mother would be grand if you went on a holiday. Didn't she manage fine when you were in jail?' Grace chuckled. Tilly's arrest and incarceration had become a joke between them. When they were girls, they feared that nothing interesting would ever happen to them in Knocknashee, but so far their lives had been no end of drama. 'And the Collins brothers would be only thrilled to mind the farm. They're mad for work, and if you saved a bit instead of hareing up to Dublin every chance you get, you could get the money together to go.'

'Oooh, listen to Mrs Sensible. I'm not the one just back from swanning around America on an all-expenses-paid trip.' Tilly blushed and her hand flew to her mouth, as she realised her gaffe. 'Ah, I'm sorry, Grace, that was so insensitive. I know you went for Richard's memorial. I was only messing, I didn't mean –'

'It's all right. I did sound a bit prim and proper.' Grace nudged her friend playfully. 'I know it's not easy for you.'

'Eloise and I met a woman recently. She was American, over here on some government business to do with the war, she couldn't say more. And she was telling us about a bar in San Francisco called Mona's 440 Club that's for women.' Tilly's eyes lit up. 'The staff dress like men, and they have performers and everything, and all the clients are women... Can you imagine it?'

'Having been to America *twice*' – Grace emphasised the last word with a grin – 'I can. It's an incredible place where people can do what they want, as far as I could see, anyway. Well, in New York I got that impression, but less so in Savannah where Richard was from. That place is like here. Not in the look of it or anything, but more like the feel of it. Like people had to behave a certain way and doing things outside of that wasn't really allowed.'

'What were they like? His parents? Really.'

Grace had told everyone who'd gathered in her house the night she got home – Maurice and Patricia, Tilly, Mary, Nancy, Eleanor and the girls – all about her adventure, but this was the first time she'd had a chance to talk to Tilly alone.

'It was strange, honestly. Sad. And odd. I knew he was wealthy, but I had no idea how wealthy. His father has a private airplane. And the house... Oh, Tilly, you should see it. It's like a mansion. And everyone has staff – they call them the "help", and they are all coloured people.

The white people are nice, really polite and friendly, but they are so privileged, and yet they complain about how hard life is now the war is dragging on. But I never saw such abundance.'

'Was the father nice or was he kind of forbidding? I imagine him as a bit intimidating.'

'I think he could be very scary if he was your business adversary, but he's sweet. It was really hard because he looks so like Richard...' Her voice was husky with emotion as she pictured Arthur Lewis in her mind's eye. 'I kept thinking that's how Richard would have looked when he was older. Being there in his place, with his people... The lady who looks after the family, Esme – she raised Richard and his sister and brother – she was heartbroken, just devastated.

'I suppose having plenty of money kind of insulates people from the everyday hardships the rest of us deal with all the time, so the big blows come harder on them or something. Richard said that his father never really spent time with him when he was young, and I think Arthur regrets that now very much. But he was so welcoming and kind to us. I was glad I went – it made it real or something.'

Tilly reached over and patted Grace's shoulder. 'I can imagine it must have been so hard. And what was the mother like? She and Richard were daggers drawn, weren't they?'

Grace sighed. 'They definitely clashed, and he found her cold and unreachable, but I kind of changed my mind about her. She was aloof when we arrived, perfectly polite and all of that, but icy. But then we went for a lunch to this frightfully posh place, and she admitted she had no relationship with her son and she was so sad about it.' She gazed out to sea, thinking about Caroline Lewis. 'It's hard to explain, Til. These babies of white, wealthy people are handed over to these coloured ladies to raise. The mothers get no opportunity to bond with their child. Changing nappies and feeding and bathing, all the things mothers do for their babies, are done by the help. So the white women don't learn. Then the children go to school and the chance to bond is gone. I felt sorry for her, even though she's loaded and has clothes and jewels and everything so fancy. She wants to be close to her children, but she doesn't know how to – she never learnt.'

'And yet she still fights with her daughter all day every day?' Tilly was fascinated.

Grace laughed. 'They'd clash regardless, like chalk and cheese. Sarah is her own woman, and nothing whatsoever like her mother or anyone else down there. Before the war, she and Jacob were part of a group of sort of bohemian people. I think you would have blended in far easier than I could have. She had reconnected with one of them, a friend of Jacob's called David. He's the one that encouraged her to go and live her life on her own terms.'

'A new beau already?' The comings and goings of the glamorous Lewis family were a source of great interest to her friend.

'No, no, not at all. He has a fiancée already. No, just a friend. But it's been good for her to be around people who remembered Jacob.' Tears filled Grace's eyes. 'Sarah felt about Jacob the way I felt about Richard, the way I still do.'

She sat up, and Tilly placed her hand on her back, letting her cry.

'I can't believe he's gone, Til. I just can't. We wasted so much time, and now there's no hope. I don't think I can bear it...'

All the strength she'd mustered for the visit to America, all the energy she'd put into helping Charlie be reunited with Lily, all the effort to be polite and understanding and helpful to the Lewises and Mrs McHale, and even Sarah, evaporated. All that was left was naked raw grief, so profound she thought her heart might break. She allowed Tilly to take her in her arms, and she howled and sobbed until she was so spent, she could hardly manage the walk home.

Tilly must have said something to Maurice and Patricia, because they left her alone. Grace went upstairs and got into her bed, though it was only five in the evening, and she took her box of letters, bursting now because it also contained all of her letters to Richard that Sarah had brought with her from London. Like her, he'd kept every single one.

She took out his letters and held them to her face, as if by placing something he touched against her skin would somehow bring him closer. She knew it was stupid, but it was all she had. Sarah had Jacob's old shirt, and when Declan died, Grace had snuggled up in bed with his jumper. She had things from her parents, little keepsakes and mementoes, but all she had of Richard were his letters. Their lifeline, the way they communicated, opening their hearts and minds to each other over five years.

She had hoped the memorial service would give her some peace, and in a way, it had. Seeing his name on the plaque beside the tree his mother had arranged had really had a profound effect.

Richard H. Lewis 1918–1943

She had not known his middle name was Harold. It was after his uncle and grandfather, it seemed. He'd never told her that. There was so much of him she didn't know, and now she never would.

She drifted off to sleep and had a vague sense of someone creeping into the room, the rattle of crockery, but she didn't open her eyes. She wasn't hungry and she didn't want company. Whoever it was – Patricia probably – shut the curtains and withdrew. Grace drifted back into sleep.

'Shush, Grace, shush. It's all right. It's just a dream, love. It's just a bad dream. You're safe. You're all right...'

It was dark when she came around, her face against the soft pyjama jacket of her brother.

'What... I...I...don't know...' Her nerve endings were jangling as she tried to force herself awake.

The dream had been horrible. Richard's body had been hanging from a tree. When she was in Savannah, Sarah had shown her a terrible picture of a man who had been lynched in the South years ago. She explained the history of segregation, and Jim Crow laws, and Grace had been horrified. Caroline Lewis had walked in on the conversation and cut Sarah off, saying, 'Guests don't need to hear any of that. Really, Sarah, must you always be so controversial?'

But somehow in her dream the coloured man became Richard, and Germans were below him, laughing and sticking sharp knives – like bayonets on the ends of their rifles – into his feet. He was dead, but he could still feel, and she screamed and tried to make them stop, but they couldn't hear her...

She heard Maurice's voice again, soothing her. 'It was just a dream, Grace. Wake up, love. It's all right…'

She allowed her brother to sit her up, and slowly she came back to the present. Richard wasn't being tortured; he was dead. That was better. But how could someone you love being dead be the best option?

'I dreamt he was on a tree, hanging…' She tried to match her voice to her brain, but it was difficult. The horrifying images of lynchings Sarah had mentioned had lodged in her brain but in her dream it was Richard being hung from a tree.

'He's gone, love. He's in heaven with Declan and Mammy and Daddy and Agnes, and all the people belonging to him, and his best friend…' Maurice rubbed her hair gently. 'Nobody can hurt him now, Grace, he's safe.'

Her hysterical tears gave way to quiet sobs.

'Will we go down for a cup of cocoa? Mrs O'Donoghue gave us a bit extra this week. She got an unexpected delivery and was unusually generous with it.' He gave her a wry smile. The stinginess of the local grocer was legendary, but for some reason, she had a soft spot for Maurice. Biddy had always been a gossip, but there had been a kindness to her too, but in recent years she'd become much more bitter, Grace wondered why. Maybe it was because her husband was a terrible flirt, and a philanderer if rumours were to be believed, embarrassing her constantly by looking at other women, so maybe she wanted some revenge and she could see Maurice was a handsome man. Patricia had noted with a laugh how whenever he went for the groceries, they ended up with more than when she went, so she let him do the shopping.

Grace allowed him to help her downstairs. The house was quiet. Her screaming must have woken Patricia, Cáit and Molly, because once he sat her in a chair in the kitchen, he bounded back upstairs. She could hear him tell them everything was all right and to go back to sleep.

She was still dressed; she'd fallen asleep in her clothes. And as she sat at the kitchen table, she shivered. The clock on the mantel said it was just after three o'clock in the morning. Maurice returned and put a saucepan of milk on the gas ring, then got a crocheted blanket from the sitting room and put it around her shoulders.

She smiled. 'Thanks. And sorry for waking everyone.'

'Ah, it's grand. Don't worry. Poor old Cáit was getting desperate nightmares too on our way here. There was a child fell off the boat. It was overcrowded and people were clinging on. The parents were hysterical, and it was bedlam, but there was nothing to be done. I don't think any of us will forget it.'

'That must have been horrible!' The haunting image crowded her brain. How could the world be so cruel? Was this madness ever going to end, or was humanity just faced with loss after loss, death by a thousand cuts, until not a home or family in the whole world was left without someone to mourn?

'It was,' Maurice said as he stirred the cocoa powder into the hot milk. 'People tried, and the poor child's father had to be held back from jumping in, but the ship was gaining speed and he would have died undoubtedly if he'd gone after her. His wife and other children needed him. But what a horrific thing it was to see.'

'Do you ever just get tired, Maurice?' she asked as he handed her a steaming cup of cocoa.

'Of what?'

'All of it,' she said as he sat opposite her at the kitchen table. 'I try to be cheerful, honestly I do. I try to be thankful for what I have, and I am thankful, but sometimes I just wonder, what is it all for? If God is supposed to love us, why does he make it so hard for us? If I had a child, I'd try to make things easy for them. Like, you don't want the girls to have to face tragedy and hardship, and if you could, you'd make sure they were spared that pain. But it's like God is only happy when he's causing havoc.'

'I'm not sure God is behind this. There's a nasty little ferret over in Germany that we have to thank for all of this, him and his henchmen.' Maurice took a sip of his cocoa, closing his eyes in pleasure at the rare sweet treat.

'Yes, but who made him? We're told God made the world and

everything and everyone in it, so he bears the responsibility then in that case, doesn't he?'

Her brother smiled. 'It's a bit early in the morning for a theological debate, Grace.'

'Do you still believe it?' She asked the question that had been playing on her mind since he'd turned up. 'As much as you did when you were a priest? Or...?' Maurice and Patricia went to Mass every Sunday, took the girls there and conformed to all that was required. He was very friendly with Father Iggy, and they spent a lot of time together. But something about him made Grace question whether he was truly a believer or just going through the motions.

He put his cup down and steepled his fingers, tapping them gently, something she'd noticed he did when he was thinking about something.

Long seconds passed.

'Do you want the long or the short version?' he said at last.

'The long, please,' she replied, settling back in the chair.

'When I was a priest, I was so angry, so bitter at the life that had been thrust upon me, I kind of dismissed it all. Nobody knew, of course – I'm a good actor. But inside, I was dead. I hated the life and knew I was in the wrong place.'

Grace sipped her cocoa and let him talk.

'So when I decided to leave – something I should have done years earlier, by the way – it was like a weight was lifted off me. I didn't know then that there was a chance of being reunited with Patricia, but I knew I had to stop living a lie. I thought it was all codswallop, to be frank.'

She smiled. Her brother had the same engaging way of speaking that their father had. He'd been a much beloved schoolmaster and could hold a classroom of children in the palm of his hand with a story.

'I think I was about three weeks from being formally released from my vows, and to be fair, the bishop put me on light duties, sick calls and administration, that sort of thing. This night, I was called on to go and see a parishioner who was very sick. An old Filipino man, who had lived his life following the traditional pagan religion. This system of believing in deities and spirits connected to nature and the supernatural was practised by his ancestors. He had spent most of his life in a very rural place up in the mountains.'

'But I thought Catholicism was the main religion there?' Grace asked, intrigued.

'It is. The Spanish colonisers of the sixteenth century made sure of that, but it kind of went hand in hand with the old traditional ways – a bit like here. The Catholics are clever that way,' Maurice explained. 'They don't make people abandon all their indigenous beliefs – they just kind of layer their system on top. So while they believe in Catholic doctrine, they also believe very strongly in anitos, the ancestral spirits, those belonging to them that have gone before, who act as kind of intermediaries between the living and the divine. Nature is very important too, with spirits associated with trees and rivers and animals.'

'Did you believe more in that kind of thing?' she asked. Priests going to the missions and going kind of rogue, becoming more pagan than Christian, was not unheard of.

He sighed and ran a hand over his stubbly chin. 'I didn't know what I believed, apart from knowing in my heart that I had to get out of the priesthood. I was kind of blinded to everything else, honestly. Anyway, I went to see this old man. He'd been baptised and all the rest, as well as the traditional rituals and ceremonies. He laughed about how he'd covered all eventualities.' Maurice chuckled at the memory. 'I really liked him. He was great fun.'

He looked at Grace. 'Do you know what *bahala na* means?'

'No, I've no idea,' she replied.

'It's the Filipino central value, I suppose. It roughly translates to "whatever will happen will happen." They believe strongly in fate, and that the dead and spirits influence our lives in ways we can't see or imagine.'

'All right, so no free will?' She liked learning from him; it was nice to think about something other than her own woes for a while.

'Yes, in a way. They don't believe that things happen by chance, or that we influence things as much as we think we do.'

Maurice took another sip of his cocoa. 'This man always spoke about his Lola, his grandmother. His mother died young, and his grandmother reared him. He was in his eighties, of course, by this stage, and the grandmother was dead years and years. By the time I arrived, the man was hours from death. He hadn't been conscious for a day or two by then, hadn't eaten or drank anything for a long time. His family were there, and they stepped out of the room for me to give him the Sacrament of Extreme Unction. I was getting ready to do it – I'd brought the oils I needed – when he opened his eyes and began talking. Not the monosyllabic groans of the previous weeks, but full sentences, and he was so animated and excited. It was hard to make out the words, but he was bright and content, and his eyes were fixed on the corner of the room. He was talking to someone, and he was laughing...' He paused. 'But obviously there was nobody there. I just watched and waited and let him babble away. After a little while, he smiled, the loveliest smile, and lay back and relaxed, but his eyes were open. I put my hands on him, anointed him with the oil and prayed over him. He was not remotely agitated or distressed, but he was awake, and he was more full of life than he'd been for week and weeks.'

'And then what happened?'

'He went on that way for a while, then he fell asleep. I waited with his family, as I had nothing else to do and I was interested by now in what would happen. An hour or so later, he woke again, looked over my shoulder, said something like, "Lola, Lola." He raised his hands... and he took his last breath.'

'And what do you think that was?'

'I think... Look, nobody knows for sure what the truth is, but that night, that man was talking to someone. I think his grandmother came for him.'

'I hope Richard comes for me when my time comes, and Mammy and Daddy, and Declan, and even Agnes. It would be nice to think that will happen.'

'They will, Grace. I believe they will.'

CHAPTER 29

KNOCKNASHEE, COUNTY KERRY

LATE JULY 1943

*D*ear Grace,
How are you doing? I imagine it must be a relief to get back to beautiful Knocknashee after the craziness of our country. I find New York exhilarating, I must say. It's so vibrant and everyone is too busy rushing around to care much what anyone else does. Unlike Savannah, where the activities of the neighbors are a daily obsession. It feels to me like a glasshouse from which there is no escape.

I love Georgia, it will always be my home, but it suffocates me. Daddy sent me a clipping from the paper today saying Georgia was the first state in the Union to lower the voting age from twenty-one to eighteen. I think he's trying to do a sales pitch on me to make me want to come home, and I will, someday, but not now.

Thank you for getting behind my plan to research the babies the canon stole. It was only a nebulous idea when I mentioned it in Savannah, but it's really getting under my skin, so I came to NYC to see Mrs McHale. I'm happy here in the Big Apple doing my investigation.

I know Richard used to call Mrs McHale Miss Marple, and she really is. She is such a sweet lady, and I think she's lonely too, so she's helping me any way she can. And her stories are one of the few things that make me laugh these days. Today she told me about some guy who was an ophthalmologist, and despite that qualification, he almost drowned anyway. Then she carried on with no explanation as to why an eye doctor was less likely to face a watery death than anyone else. I know better now than to ask. But she does make me giggle.

We went to visit Father Noel Dempsey yesterday. He's got cancer and is in the hospital. He doesn't look well at all, but he said he was not going to protect or defend his fellow priests anymore and so he told me all he knew. As far as he was aware, at the time of Lily's adoption, she was the only one, but it came to light later that there were at least four children sent over here by Rafferty. Possibly more.

One is a girl, two years younger than Lily, so she's sixteen now and is the child of the man Mrs McHale had dealings with a while ago, the man who was going to tell the story of the canon extorting money from him but was talked out of it by his wife since the adoption wasn't done through legal channels. I contacted him and promised him complete anonymity if he spoke to me. He said he would, so I'm meeting him next week.

The child Mrs McHale found out about here in New York is named Carrie Dwyer. Her parents were killed in a traffic accident, and she was made a ward of the state of New York. She's younger than the other girl, so the canon was doing this for a long time after he took Charlie's children.

She's twelve years old. Mrs McHale is on the case looking for a baptismal record for her to see if we can find out anything about her birth mother that way. Not surprisingly the official channels are proving less than helpful, but I met a woman at the Graham School—the new name for the Orphan Asylum Society—who was very helpful.

This is the oldest orphanage in New York City. It was set up by Eliza Hamilton, the widow of one of our founding fathers, Alexander Hamilton.

The woman there, Lydia Benson, was most helpful, and they would love it if some family could be found for Carrie.

I went to see Carrie a few days ago, and Grace, she would break your heart. She is such a sad kid. Her parents were wonderful by the sounds of it, so at least there's that. They told her she was adopted from Ireland, that her mother had been a young girl with no husband so couldn't keep her, and a kind priest said that he could take her and she would be loved by the Dwyers in Rochester, New York.

She didn't know anything else, and she asked me if there was any way I could find her real mom. Carrie said that she knew her mother was young when Carrie was born, but that she keeps thinking maybe her mother would be able to take care of her now. I swore to her that I would do all I could to find her, and I will. It was so hard to leave her. She has no aunts or uncles that she's close to. Her adoptive mother was from Kentucky originally, and Carrie doesn't remember her mom ever going there for a visit or anyone from there coming to see them, so we assume they weren't close or something happened—who knows? The father was also an only child, and his parents are long dead. She knew her grandfather a little bit, an Irish immigrant, but her grandmother died before she was born.

I had thought I would write a piece for Kirky on this, and I still might. But having met Carrie, Grace, I really want to find her mother. She might not be able or interested in taking care of her daughter now, but I have to try. In this world where chaos and destruction are at every turn, it feels like something I could do. It's just one kid, I know, but she's a life and she deserves to be loved, and I really want to help her. The only way I can think of to do that is to track down the Canon, much easier said than done I know, but I have to try. He's at the centre of all of this, and he knows things.

I hope things are OK with you. I miss Jacob so much that sometimes I lie to myself and say he's just away on an assignment, because I can't breathe thinking I'll never see him again. I don't have any sense of him, and I thought I would. Do you feel Richard around you? People say that you do feel something, a sense of those we love who are gone, but I sure do not.

Love, Sarah

Grace put the letter down as Cáit popped her head around the sitting room door. The sun was shining and the long summer holidays were in their closing weeks, so the children were all making the most of the fine weather and spending their days on the strand.

'Tilly is here, Auntie Grace,' Cáit said in perfect Irish. Maurice had not been exaggerating when he said they were fluent, and it was a source of wonder to her that he made sure his children could converse in the language of a country he never imagined them setting foot in. Life was very strange sometimes.

'Thanks, Cáit. Are you and Molly going to the strand?'

The little girl nodded. 'Mammy says we have to sweep the bedrooms and change all the beds and then we can go. There's great drying today, so she wants to get everything out on the line while it's sunny.'

Grace smiled. Her sister-in-law was a great mother. She adored the girls, but everyone in the family pulled their weight. Having them here, far from being an intrusion, was actually keeping her sane. It was impossible to be too miserable around her nieces, who were such sweet, funny girls.

'You are brilliant,' she said, going to get her purse. She took out a penny and handed it to the girl. 'Now there's a halfpenny each to get an ice cream in Bríd's on the way.'

'Ah, you don't have to give us your money, Auntie Grace. You're giving us enough already.' Cáit was reluctant to take it. She knew her parents were most anxious that they pay their way and not be a burden on Grace, but Grace liked treating them. The Department of Education were continuing to pay her, which was amazing. Father Iggy had written as the chairman of the board, explaining the tragic circumstances, and said Grace just needed some time to recover. Maurice had taken over teaching her class until the end of term, under Eleanor's guidance, and she would go back to her job in a few weeks at the start of the school year. That idea was both a comfort and a source of pain. Life could never go on as before, not now.

The idea that Charlie would never again deliver a letter to her from Richard cut like a knife. Normally there would be a bundle for the school, and if there was one from him, she'd put it in her pocket to savour that evening after dinner. That would never happen again.

Maurice had spent the summer labouring for various farmers and doing a few runs with fishermen to bring in the mackerel. With meat being severely rationed, there was great demand for fish in the towns, and the fishermen were taking advantage of it. ''Tis an ill wind that doesn't blow someone good,' as her father used to say.

'Not at all. It's only a little ice cream, and if your auntie can't treat you now and again, what's the point of life at all?' Grace smiled at her niece. She'd grown into a strong, lithe girl since she'd arrived and was thriving. Her dark-brown hair had a lovely sheen, and her skin was turning golden under the Irish summer sun. Her nose was freckled, and her green eyes were the same shade as Grace's own.

'Thanks, Auntie Grace. Molly will be delighted. We saw one of the tourists with an ice cream in a wafer yesterday, and our mouths were watering. Mammy says we can't waste any money until Daddy starts his new job, but then we'll go to Killarney, and she says we can get a new dress and shoes for Christmas.' Her eyes danced with delight at the thought. Everything they wore was a hand-me-down from someone in the village, and while people were kind, money was scarce. Besides, there was little to buy, with or without coupons.

Maurice had been given a job teaching maths and science in the boys' seminary and secondary school in Dingle starting in September, so it was a great relief to him that they'd be able to pay their way properly from then on. Maurice was far more worried about that than Grace was.

'Only us,' Tilly called, pushing the door open. Odile hurtled across the room into Grace's arms.

'Aintín Grace! Look, I hurted my knee.' Odile was nothing if not dramatic. She showed Grace the miniscule cut on her pudgy little knee with a look of tremendous misery on her cute little face.

Her dark-brown hair was in two pigtails, and at just over three, she was a ball of mischief who loved to be the centre of attention. She was dressed in a faded pink frock that had seen many, many owners in the village, and on her feet were brown buckled leather sandals.

'Oh no!' Grace responded, aghast. 'What happened?'

'I was getting over the gate after feeding the sheep and I scraped it.' Her bottom lip stuck out dramatically.

'You poor thing, that looks fierce sore altogether.' Grace winked at Tilly and Cáit. They both knew what Odile was up to.

'A bull's eye would make it better,' the child suggested in a pained voice.

'Do you think so?' Grace asked her sincerely.

Odile nodded, her dark eyes wide.

'Well, maybe I better look in the special box so. Are you sure a spoon of medicine wouldn't work better?' Grace stifled a grin.

'No, only bull's eyes work for cuts,' Odile answered, brooking no argument.

Grace went to the sideboard where she kept a brown paper bag of the round black and white sweets and handed one to Odile, who popped it in her mouth with a beaming smile.

'Better already?' Grace asked.

The child nodded enthusiastically, and Tilly rubbed her head.

'We had to come straightaway after getting such a terrible injury, didn't we, Odile?'

The little girl nodded again as Cáit took her by the hand to take her upstairs to play with her and Molly. Odile was devoted to the older girls and followed them everywhere like a little duckling.

'Tea?' Grace offered her friend.

'Have you anything nice to go with it?' Tilly had a real sweet tooth and missed cakes and sweets more than anyone else Grace knew.

'Alas no. No sugar to be got, even with the ration book, so no baking.' She sighed. 'I could offer you a slice of bread with a suggestion of jam?'

Tilly laughed. 'A suggestion of jam' was one of Charlie's sayings. The only jam was blackberry, made last autumn, and the berries were yet to ripen for this year, so everyone was on the dregs. 'It'll do, I suppose,' she grumbled as she and Grace went to the kitchen.

Patricia was washing sheets in the sink and wringing them out with her hands. Tilly helped by twisting one end, with Patricia holding the other, to get as much water out as possible.

'Thanks. Tilly, you're as strong as a horse. Fair play to you,' Patricia said.

'Farming does that to you.' Tilly flexed her impressive biceps with a grin.

'Will we have tea, Patricia?' Grace asked. 'I'll make it while you hang the sheets.'

'Cushy job for the teacher while we do the donkey work, I suppose?' Tilly teased her.

'Oh, I'm far too delicate for that kind of thing,' she joked, filling the kettle.

While the sheets billowed on the line in the back yard, the three of them sat down to tea and a thin slice of bread with half a teaspoon of jam each. They could hear the gales of laughter coming from the girls upstairs.

'So what's the news, Til?' Grace asked as she sipped the weak tea. One teaspoon per pot was all they could allow.

'Nothing really. Eloise was at a photography exhibition last week, and she wrote to tell me that she met someone who told her that the American government has banned anyone from taking photos, or even doing paintings or sketches, anywhere on the Atlantic coast. Anyone caught is going to be barred from going to the coast and could even be charged with a crime. It's all part of the defence of the East Coast of the United States apparently.'

'They should bring that in here too,' Grace said. 'I know Eloise was blamed for taking pictures and all of that, but if nobody was allowed to do it, then there would be no fear of the information falling in the wrong hands.'

'Good luck with monitoring the thousands of miles of Irish coast, though,' Patricia said.

'God,' Tilly groaned, 'I wish this was over, I really do. I'm so sick of it all. Nothing nice to eat, no petrol, no nice clothes, no shoes…'

'Millions dead,' Grace added pointedly.

'Sorry, yes, of course. I know that, Grace. I didn't mean…' her friend flushed.

'No, I'm sorry. I'm in terrible form these days.' Grace pinched the bridge of her nose and exhaled, immediately contrite. 'I know, we're all sick to the back teeth of it. Apparently, there's going to need to be a major drive to get all the beets harvested this year. We've no cane sugar any more, so beets are all we have. But they were saying in the paper it was going to be close to impossible to get enough workers to harvest the 230,000 acres.'

'I'd volunteer if it meant we could get a bit of cake or a bar of chocolate. I'm going mad thinking of sweets.'

'Oh, I forgot, this might cheer you up.' Grace went to the sitting room again and took a book off the shelf. She returned and handed it to Tilly.

'Oh, Grace, thanks.' Tilly beamed, delighted with her gift. 'It's Kate O'Brien's new book. You're so good.'

'I got it in Cork when I stayed with the Warringtons overnight on our way back from America. I was telling Lily all about her, and she spotted it in Liam Russell's shop there, so I got it for you.'

Tilly had met the great Irish writer in Dublin with Eloise, who moved in the same circles, and had been so impressed by her. She read the title. *'The Last of Summer.* I can't wait to read it. You're a dote, thanks.'

'You're welcome.' She smiled, glad to make her friend happy.

Tilly yawned expansively. 'Sorry, I was awake all night. Mam had a nightmare about Alfie, and nothing could console her.'

She knew better than to soothe her friend. Alfie O'Hare could well be dead. They'd not heard anything for ages, and opposing the Germans in France was dangerous work. Mary had a kind of gift; she had uncanny intuition about things and was renowned on the peninsula as a *Bean Feasa*, a wise woman. She knew about herbs and plants and the old ways, and if she said something was going to happen, it invariably did.

Grace placed her hand on Tilly's as her friend's eyes filled with tears. 'He might be all right,' she said tentatively, not knowing what else to say.

'Maybe, but you know Mam. She's rarely wrong, but she's not sure herself what the dream meant. She dreamt he was walking down a dangerous road alone. She said the image was so vivid, so real, that it woke her, but she's been out of her mind with worry for so long now, it could well be her imagination playing tricks on her.'

'My brother Alfie is in France. He and his girlfriend are fighting the Germans over there, kind of covertly, we think,' Tilly explained to Patricia. 'Richard had a contact, a mutual acquaintance, who spent some time in London, so we got a little bit of information that way. But now...' She didn't need to finish the sentence.

'They're Odile's parents?' Patricia asked.

Before Grace could intervene, Tilly said, 'It's all right, I trust you. We tell people Odile is Alfie's and that he and Constance are married so there's no question about her Irish citizenship, but she's actually the child of Paul and Bernadette Dreyfus. Bernadette is Constance's older sister. Paul was a Jew – the Germans shot him in 1940 – and nobody's heard a word about Bernadette in years. We hope, of course, that she's still alive and might see Odile again some day, but we just don't know.'

Patricia sighed. 'Don't worry I won't breathe a word. She's a lucky little girl to have you. It's all so hard, isn't it? So many of our friends back in the Philippines too are distraught, not knowing what's happened to people. My heart goes out to you. You must be worried sick about your brother – and poor little Odile's mother too.'

Tilly nodded. 'Alfie was always getting involved politically. He was in Spain fighting Franco with the International Brigades before he went to Paris, but I always thought he'd be all right. He's kind of invincible, you know? But Mam having that weird dream has really rattled me. She's eerie how she knows things, so...'

'We can just wait and hope,' Grace said, knowing how useless her words were. 'At least you still have hope.'

Tilly nodded. 'So, any other news?' She was clearly anxious to change the subject.

'I got a letter from Sarah this morning,' Grace said.

'Ah, really?' Her friend's eyes lit up. She liked Sarah. They were kind of kindred spirits.

'Apparently she has some ideas about how to get information

about the canon. I think she's on a wild goose chase, but she's determined to track him down and extract information from him, it seems. She and Mrs McHale are in New York together. So we're all about New York these days.'

'How's Lily getting on? Is it strange for Charlie not to call her Siobhán?'

'Fine, I think. And her name is Lily now, so he's just happy to have her back in his life.'

'It must be very strange for Dymphna, having a complete stranger turn up on your doorstep like that and she being your husband's daughter. I'm not sure how I'd react, if it were me.'

Grace caught Patricia's eye. They'd heard some stories from Cáit and Molly recently, so she wasn't sure that everything in the McKenna household was going as well as either Charlie, or Lily herself, had anticipated when they had decided Lily should come to Ireland with Charlie after their New York trip.

'She seems like a nice girl, from the little I've seen of her,' Tilly added. 'And my mother says she is the spitting image of poor Maggie McKenna. But it must be a big shock for her coming from a place like New York to our little village of Knocknashee.'

Grace agreed, ' I'm sure, but Lily is a lovely girl. And she's happy to see where Charlie and Maggie come from and meet the rest of the family,'

'It's a strange situation, you have to admit.'

'Yes, it is, really. But at least most of our neighbours have accepted her as Charlie's long-lost daughter, so that's something. I know Charlie was worried about that.'

'It was hardly the child's fault she was adopted,' Tilly said. 'That was down to that auld divil Rafferty. And by the sound of it, Sarah and Mrs McHale are hot on his tail, so he'd better watch out.'

Grace exhaled, 'It couldn't happen to a nicer man,' and her friend grinned.

Patricia was pairing freshly washed socks at the same time as having her tea. 'I hear there's a whiff of romance in the air for young Lily also.'

'Really? Who with?' Tilly's eyebrows shot up, this was news.

'Fiachra O'Flynn.'

'Oh,' Tilly said. 'I thought he was courting Evelyn O'Sullivan this past year?'

Grace adjusted the framed photo of her parents on the windowsill, so it caught the light. 'He was, but Fiachra broke it off with Evelyn since Lily arrived. Apparently he's going around like a sick calf, according to his mother. I met Eileen outside the post office. She says Lily is all he can talk about. It's Lily said that and Lily thinks this. The rest of the family are giving him an awful slagging over it.'

'Ah, Fiachra is a dote. And he's turning into a fine-looking lad. He was desperate skinny, remember? But he's after filling out, and that mop of red hair has been calmed down a bit with oil, I notice.'

All the O'Flynn children had various shades of red hair, from dark auburn like Eileen to the strawberry blond of their father.

Tilly shifted in her seat, crossing her long slender legs. 'They'd make a handsome couple.'

'Depends on who you ask,' Patricia remarked wryly. 'I don't think Evelyn O'Sullivan is too pleased about it.'

'I can't imagine she is,' Tilly admitted. 'Does Charlie know about this romantic entanglement?'

Grace felt sorry for poor old Fiachra. 'I doubt it. Poor Fiachra is his apprentice, so not just his neck but his job is on the line if Charlie finds out.'

'He should tell him. Better than Charlie finding out any other way. And you know this place, a secret is something you tell one person at a time. Best be up front and tell him,' Tilly drained her cup.

'I agree, but Fiachra's scared of his life of Charlie. I've no idea why.'

Patricia grimaced at a loud thump from upstairs but since there was no accompanying scream she carried on, 'Well, Lily will have to go home soon anyway, won't she? She's going to university, imagine that?'

'She is. She's booked on a passage on the last day of August. So still a few weeks to go yet.'

'It will be an awful wrench for Charlie to let her go.' Patricia finished her cup of tea and took the cup to the sink to wash.

'It will,' Grace conceded, 'but he's so grateful to the Maheadys for allowing it, and now that they are in contact, I feel like they'll see each other more.'

'I just had an idea.' Tilly's eyes lit up. 'Why don't we throw a party, a going-away party for Lily. God knows, we could use something to cheer us up. A Lúnasa party.'

'The feast of Lúnasa is the first of August, you goose,' Grace said.

'Well, let's make it the end.' Tilly dismissed her objection with a wave of her hand. 'Sure, who's going to report us? To the god Lugh, for not celebrating his feast properly? We could build a big bonfire down on the strand and have music and dancing. Eloise would definitely come down for it. Maybe even Marion and Colm and the kids. We could invite the Warringtons from Cork. It would cheer us all up.'

Grace didn't really want to be cheered up, but she could see how much Tilly liked the idea, and giving Lily a nice send-off was thoughtful. Besides, Tilly was right – there wasn't much to celebrate these days. The war was on the turn, they said, but nowhere near over yet, and even if it was, Richard was still dead.

'What do you think, Grace, will we do it?'

'Let's.' She smiled at her friend. 'We'll have to give everyone plenty of notice to try to get some grub, maybe even a few cakes and sandwiches. Everyone will bring something.'

'And I might happen to have a small operation going up at the farm…' Tilly winked.

Grace rolled her eyes. Scotch O'Hare, Tilly's late father, was known for miles around as a producer of poitín, the illegal spirit made from potatoes, and the still was in working order to this day. Sergeant Keane knew about it and turned a blind eye so long as Tilly dropped a few bottles to the station every Christmas.

'I had that once. I thought I'd die the next day,' Patricia said, wiping the cups and placing them back on the dresser.

'Ah, that's because it wasn't expertly made with loving care and generations of expertise.' Tilly examined her fingernails nonchalantly.

'Remember when we were kids and Denis Ahern dared Alfie to put poitín in the altar wine bottle?' Grace giggled at the memory.

'And the canon spat it across the altar and was so savage afterwards, nobody went near him for a week?' Tilly howled with laughter. 'Mammy murdered him, but Daddy was only laughing.'

Patricia smiled. 'He sounds like quite a character, your brother.'

'He's that all right,' Tilly said, with a heartbreaking sadness in her voice. 'I just pray he still is.'

CHAPTER 30

BERN, SWITZERLAND

A man spoke as Richard entered the room. 'So, Mr Lewis, you made it?'

The man was dressed in an impeccably tailored suit and had a neatly cut head of silver hair. He wore wire-rimmed round glasses and held a smoking pipe in his mouth. His eyes were kind in his handsome face as he smiled across the large teak desk. Hearing his American accent caused Richard to exhale in relief.

He was on the third floor of a large house on a square in Bern. 'Herrengasse 23' was all that was written on the brass plaque beside the six-foot wide oak door. The house looked identical to the others around it: vaulted ceilings, marble staircases, large mahogany doors off parquet-floored corridors. The whole place smelled of beeswax and cologne. He'd been brought here by car from a hospital where he'd been recuperating for well over a month. He'd been going out of his mind in the single room, guarded by a man who refused to speak to him. Doctors visited, but no matter how often he asked about being discharged he was ignored. The food was fine, and he was comfortable, but he so badly needed to get out, and it had felt like he was a prisoner.

Three days ago, he demanded that he be brought to the American consul, he was able to walk now and he'd recovered enough. He'd been sure they'd just ignore it like they did all other requests for discharge or even a way to contact the outside world, but to his surprise this morning someone came and said he could go, a car was waiting. The chauffeur never said a word about where he was going or what was happening. He seemed not to speak English.

Richard's leg was bandaged beneath his trousers, but he felt OK. It was sore but he didn't care. He just needed to get out of here.

'I did, just about,' Richard answered.

'And the Swiss authorities thought taking you here was the best course of action?'

'Well, yes, I guess so. I was arrested when I crossed the border, and then taken to a hospital. I was shot in the leg as I got out of France, but luckily the bullet wasn't embedded – so I just needed some stitches and some blood.'

'The Jerries weren't the only ones doing the shooting, though?'

Richard had been debriefed by an American officer in the hospital, who must have reported to this man, whoever he was. 'Er, yes, well…I don't know if I hit anyone, but I did fire some shots, yes.'

The man exhaled, and Richard couldn't guess if this information was something he approved of or didn't. 'It's healing now? Your leg?'

'Yes, thank you. They were very kind.'

The man looked at a file on his desk. 'You did well. Dr Paul Niehans is much sought-after.'

'I'm grateful, and if there's a bill to be paid, I'm happy to –'

'No, it's all right. We will take care of it. Now, what to do with you next is the question.'

'Well, if I could make contact with my family, then –'

The man raised his hand. 'Let me stop you right there and explain something.'

Reassuring as it was to speak to a fellow American, Richard didn't like the other man's condescending tone; he felt like he was in the principal's office. But he had no choice but to abide by what he said. He was under the protection but also the governance of the American consulate to Switzerland, which was what this place must be, and this man held all the cards. He was under no illusion about his options.

The man lifted a typed sheet, which Richard assumed was a report on him. As he read he winced and his brow furrowed. 'For some reason you've landed on my desk, so I guess you're my problem now. But the extent to which I can help you is limited. All traffic in and out of Switzerland – and I mean every single scintilla of communication – is overheard and reported to Berlin, Moscow, Washington, London and Paris. This place is a rat's nest.' He wrinkled his nose distastefully. 'So it's not simply a matter of sending a telegram to the folks back home. Where is home, by the way?'

'Savannah, Georgia. My father is Arthur Lewis of Lewis Holdings.' He hated slipping that in, but anything he could use that would help at this stage was fair game.

Did the man react? He wasn't sure. He had the ultimate poker face.

'So, Mr Lewis of Savannah, Georgia. First, let's call you…let's see… What was your mother's maiden name?'

Richard had to think. 'Anderson.'

'Fine, you won't forget that. And a favourite uncle, or your grandfather?'

'Harold.' He recalled his godfather, who disgraced the family by going to live with a married woman. Richard had been given Harold as a middle name before the scandal broke.

'Ok, Harry Anderson you are for now.' The man made a note on a sheet of paper. 'I'll get you some credentials in that name.'

'I don't think that's necessary. I –'

'It is.' Clearly Richard was merely a pawn here and would be doing exactly as he was told. He finished scribbling on the page and looked up. 'And while I can't go into specifics, let me elucidate in general terms. We are maintaining a very delicate balance here. The Swiss authorities are insisting on preserving their neutrality, so we must be very, very careful not to do anything to upset them. And the news that an American just wandered in here and is being welcomed over the Swiss border, having shot German soldiers in his efforts to escape, is not the kind of thing we want to have in our conversations with our hosts. We will need them in the near future if the war goes our way, so like it or not, we've got to play by their rules.'

Richard wanted to object but kept his mouth shut.

'Germany uses the Swiss railways to transport weapons and' – the man waved his hand – 'other ill-gotten gains. The Swiss banks issue reichsmarks and offer secure banking for the Germans. In return, Herr Hitler doesn't overrun this little country.' He gave a wry smile. 'The Swiss will tell you it's because of their defences – the Great Redoubt, as it's called – but that's only half the story. Now FDR and Churchill are none too pleased with the Swiss because they see it as collaboration, but that's a matter of opinion. And they've accidentally' – he made quotation marks with his fingers – 'dropped some bombs to show their displeasure. Of course it was all explained away as a navigational error, but nobody here believes that. And perception is reality, Mr Lewis. The Swiss say they are a neutral country going about their business. They shoot down enemy planes in their airspace, be they Allied or German, thus proving their neutrality as far as they're concerned.'

Richard tried to take this all in. And not for the first time, he realised that the realpolitik of what was happening was very far removed from the government-approved newspaper headlines.

'So' – the man sucked on his pipe and exhaled a plume of pungent smoke – 'with Allied and Axis planes in the sky over this place, and the Swiss trying to stop them, things are on a hair trigger. On top of that, the Allies are taking advantage of this situation by using Swiss airspace as a safer route on their bombing runs to and from Germany. And also as a preferred distress landing spot, rather than inside German territory, when things go belly up, which is infuriating the Führer.' He smiled at his joke. 'Switzerland is on a diplomatic knife edge. They are trying to hold their own while also not antagonising or appeasing either side too much. By rights, you should be interned, but since technically you are not military personnel, you can probably roam free if you keep a low profile and do as you're told.'

'Thank you,' Richard heard himself say, but what he felt resembled frustration far more than gratitude.

'Look, son, I know this is tough.' The man's voice softened a bit. 'But tempers are frayed and feelings are running high, and our hosts are not exactly thrilled with us right now. I know it feels important to get you out, and to you it is, but the whole world is going up in flames and things are at a critical stage. We just sent a group of B-24s to take out the oil refineries in Romania, the major supplier of German fuel, and we lost over five hundred airmen and over fifty planes. Patton is making the headlines for all the wrong reasons – that jerk is hitting soldiers in the hospital for not being tough enough or something. We're stretched on every front, and we can't blink, not now. So you see, son, every day, every single day, we're trying to fight fires and win this damned war so we can *all* go home.'

He fixed Richard with a steely gaze. 'I know you want to get out, and you want to let people back home know you're OK. I understand that, but it is just not possible right this minute for the reasons I outlined. Something like this could be just the catalyst to escalate an already fraught situation, and nobody wants that. I need your word that you'll just do as we say and stay out of trouble. Don't communicate with anyone above a superficial level and don't tell anyone anything. Keep all conversations light. Be wary of anyone asking questions, and don't ask any yourself. You told the debriefing sergeant that you're a journalist, so that's gonna be tough, but resist. Am I clear?'

'Clear,' Richard said reluctantly.

'Good. Now the best thing you can do, Mr Lewis, is just blend in. You'll find plenty of people here to buddy up with. Of course, I'll try to get you out, but it will take time, and it might not even be possible. So for now, just keep your head down, stay out of everyone's way, and

I'll be in touch.' His tone brooked no argument. Richard was being dismissed.

'But Mr... –'

'Dulles. Allen Dulles.' He introduced himself.

'Mr Dulles...' Richard knew he had no choice but play it his way, but how was he to do that? 'I don't have any resources, nowhere to stay or money or...' Richard felt about twelve years old saying this, but it was true. He literally had what he stood in.

The man stood up and smiled. He opened a desk drawer, extracted a roll of Swiss francs and handed them to Richard. 'Pay me back when you get home.' He placed a hand on Richard's back as he ushered him out. 'Go down to the first floor, ask for a guy named Steven Kempler – he's one of my aides. He'll help you get settled. Tell him I said to take you to Mont JeanClare tonight. You'll enjoy it. Get to meet people, settle in – you might be here for a while.'

Before Richard had time to ask anything further, he was outside in the corridor, and the door shut behind him. He should have asked if Dulles knew Gabriel, who he was or if he had any role in getting him here, but he had no opportunity.

The roll of banknotes was thick, so he assumed he was going to be all right, financially at least. He could find a place to stay and get some other clothes, so that was something. He'd follow instructions and just be glad to be alive. There was a gravitas to the man under the avuncular exterior. And besides, he didn't want to be the cause of anything worse happening.

Feeling slightly more optimistic, he put the money in the pocket of his trousers, a pair that was three inches too short and that had been donated to him, along with the shirt, shoes, socks and underwear he was wearing, by the hospital staff.

On the first floor there were several doors identical to those on the third floor, and he knocked on one. Nobody answered, so he went to the next. A small woman, middle-aged and bespectacled, opened it and peered out at him.

'Yes?' she said in what he realised to his relief was an American accent.

'Sorry to disturb you, ma'am, but I'm looking for Steven Kempler, please?'

'Last door on the left.' She pointed and shut the door.

He went where she directed and knocked. A man was talking inside – Richard assumed on the phone because he could only make out one voice. Then he heard, 'Come in.'

He pushed the door and found inside a man around his own age, tall and skinny with fair hair that refused to lie flat despite liberal use of hair oil. He had freckles and dimples and reminded Richard of a character from one of the comic books he'd read as a kid.

'Steven Kempler?'

'Harry Anderson?'

Both men laughed as they spoke simultaneously.

'Come in, come in...' Steven was warm and welcoming and had an infectious smile. 'The boss told me to babysit you. You just got here, huh?' His accent was Midwest, with long o's and flat a's, possibly Minnesota.

'I did.'

'Where you from, Harry?'

'Georgia. But I've been living in London since the start of the war.'

'Nice. You're a journalist, right?' Steven offered Richard a cigarette, which he declined.

'That's right. Look, I'm sorry to be a burden, I just don't...'

Steven lit a cigarette and then patted his breast pocket. 'It's OK, buddy. Glad to have someone my own age to knock around with. There's a party tonight at a big house down in Montreux – everyone is going.' He looked Richard up and down. 'But we got to get you a monkey suit – black tie only – but that won't be a problem.'

Richard stared at him, surprised. Switzerland was like another world. Here it seemed there was plenty of money, and the deprivations that were biting ever harder in the rest of Europe appeared to be having no impact here at all.

Steven eyed him shrewdly. 'I dunno who you are, Harry, but you must be a big deal. Most other guys don't get the gold standard treatment, but you're to be taken care of, it seems. So let's get crackin'.'

Steven patted his breast pocket again, thought for a second, grabbed a bunch of keys from his desk and then said, 'OK, let's go.'

'We can just buy that stuff?' Richard asked as they started down the stairs.

'You betcha. There's a men's store just around the corner from here,' Steven said as he ran down the last flight of stairs and out into the street. Richard's leg injury meant keeping up with Steven was a challenge, and the guy just kept talking. He seemed to do everything at double speed.

They entered a very upmarket store, where a man in impeccable morning dress approached. To Richard's astonishment, Steven swapped to what sounded like perfectly fluent German and told the shop assistant what they needed, and within fifteen minutes, Richard had been measured and an entire wardrobe, including a black-tie suit, flannel trousers, a few shirts, socks, underwear, pyjamas, shoes, a sleeveless pullover and a sports coat were all purchased.

Then Steven said something about a valise, and the man went into the back and emerged with a brown leather suitcase, into which all of Richard's purchases were placed. Even a shaving kit, a comb and some toiletries were added, although Richard had no say whatsoever in any of it.

Richard then handed over what felt like an extortionate number of Swiss francs from the roll Dulles had given him for his various purchases. A quick count in the changing room meant he knew Dulles had given him around a thousand Swiss francs, which, by a rough calculation, was about five hundred dollars.

They drove at great speed to Montreux, around a hundred miles away, stopping for gas and food on the way. As they drove, Richard heard Steven's life story.

His maternal grandmother was from Strasbourg, his grandfather Austrian, and his paternal grandparents were Dutch. All four old people lived with his family. He was the eldest of six, two girls and four boys, and from St Paul, Minnesota, and when he was at school, it was discovered he had a knack for languages.

'For me, it was just normal, you know. Grootje and Grootvater, my

Dutch grandparents, spoke Dutch but also Flemish, and Bubbe and Zeyde, the other grandparents, spoke German and French. So there were lots of languages in our house. I never thought it was strange until we went to school and I realised most people could only speak one.'

He laughed, and they narrowly missed a pony and cart as Steven careened around them without ever reducing his speed. Richard clung to the passenger door, fearing for his life. The landscape went from flat farmland to soaring snow-covered peaks, and around each corner, each vista was like a postcard. How Jacob would have loved to photograph this, he thought, with a deep pang of loneliness.

His new friend prattled on. 'Uff da, I go there to school, y'know, and everyone is like, woah…what's he doing? What're you saying? But anyway, we had a teacher, and he really pushed me to apply for the foreign service. So I did and here I am. Being Jewish through my mom, I'm sure glad to get to do whatever we can to crush Hitler. What about you? How'd you get here?'

'It's a long story,' Richard said, looking out the window, thinking about Grace.

'It's a long ride. C'mon, you putz. I told you my story…' Steven thumped him playfully on the shoulder, one hand on the wheel, without ever slowing down. 'I know the boss told you to be cagey, but he didn't mean me.'

'Well, I work for the *Capital* newspaper in New York…' he began. Then he remembered Dulles's warning – keep it light, no more information than was necessary. 'I was on a reconnaissance mission, hoping to write about the reality of the bombing missions, when we were shot down. My colleague and friend was killed, and I got here.'

Steven nodded. 'That bastard Hitler and his Nazis sure are gonna get what's coming to them…too late for so many folks, I know. But nothing can stop the fires unleashed against him now.' The young man's eyes blazed with intensity of purpose.

'So what do you do here? Or are you not allowed to say?' Richard asked.

Steven shrugged. 'I work for Allen Dulles. He's the United States government representative here. I can't really say more, but we keep our fingers in several pies. And let me tell you, Switzerland has all the pies. Everyone is here, Germans, Austrians, the Swiss of course, French, resisters, communists, Russians, Americans, mercenaries willing to work for whoever pays the highest price – you name it, we got it. And nobody is who they seem. Remember that and you'll be OK.'

Richard had no idea what he meant. 'Even you?' he asked.

Steven just turned, narrowly missing a woman pushing a pram on the narrow road, and winked.

'What are they all doing here?' Richard asked.

'Looking out for number one mostly, don'tcha know?' Steven lit another cigarette.

'How do you mean?' Whatever Steven was telling him, there was more to the story; his reporter nose sensed it.

'Well, put it this way. Everybody thinks they know how this war is gonna go, right? And depending on who you are, then there's a preferred way for it all to pan out and a not-ideal way. Everyone here is using every connection they have to make sure they and their assets are protected, regardless of the outcome of the war. Ain't no poor here. Well, maybe the native Swiss, although I don't think so. But certainly none of the foreigners. Everyone here is a person of influence in some way, or has something to offer, or... Well, you'll see for yourself. As I said, head down, mouth shut, eyes and ears open and you'll be OK.'

Richard was reminded of the cryptic conversation he'd had with Gabriel back in the prison in France. It sounded like this. Friendly, but the meaning opaque. This war had made everyone speak in riddles.

'Do you know a man, around my age, could be French but maybe not, called Gabriel?' he enquired.

Steven's brow wrinkled as he thought. Then he shook his head. 'Don't think I ever came across a Gabriel. Couldn't swear to it. We meet a lot of people. But no Gabriel off the top of my head. Why?'

'No reason, really. He helped me get out of France, and I don't know why. Maybe I was just in the right place at the right time.'

'You bet.' Steven grinned.

The conversation went from baseball to films to things they missed from back home. All fairly innocuous, nothing noteworthy.

As they finally arrived at the heartbreakingly beautiful town of Montreux, Steven said expansively, 'Welcome to the Swiss Riviera.'

The Alps peaked all around, snowy-topped, while Lake Geneva glittered azure in the late-summer heat. Mansions of all different architectural styles were dotted along the lakeshore, and right on the shore, its ancient walls being lapped gently by the lake, was a castle right out of a fairy tale.

'What's that?' Richard asked.

'Chillon Castle, thirteenth century,' Steven said as he manoeuvred the car into a space barely big enough outside a fancy-looking hotel. The flower-strewn lakeshore was busy, with people strolling, many eating ice cream; it was hard to believe there was a war on.

Vineyards dominated the steep terraces in the foothills of the mountains above the picture-perfect town. And over to the right was an incredible building, enormous, that overlooked the lake with the mountains behind it. It was in the Belle Époque style, stately, with elegant proportions and long windows to maximise the beautiful views.

'What's that?'

Steven got out of the car, taking their bags from the trunk. 'That was the most famous hotel in Europe, maybe even the world – the Montreux Palace. The crowned heads of Europe, movie stars, musicians, aristocrats and the richest people on the planet have all come and gone here, but not so much tourism these days, so it's being used as a hospital. Pity. It would have been nice to stay there.' He shrugged.

Richard couldn't take his eyes off the incredible building. It was at least seven storeys tall, with over twenty balconies across the front of each level.

'How old is it?' he asked as they stood and admired it.

'Mid-1850s, I think, the original hotel. Then it was taken over by two Swiss businessmen, who did a huge renovation on it, extending it up and to the sides and behind as well. There is the Salon de Musique, the Grand Hall and several ballrooms. When it opened, it had central heating, electricity, private bathrooms, hot and cold running water – all of which were incredible for the time. Some of the finest homes in Europe didn't have the luxury they had there. They even have their own theatre for shows or movies, tennis on the lawn, a skating rink… You name it, they got it.'

'And now it's a hospital?' He was incredulous that such a magnificent building would be used for such a purpose.

'Sure is, needs must.' Steven shrugged again. 'OK, let's get checked in here.'

He pointed to a pretty little hotel on the lakeshore. Huge whiskey barrels cut in half were being used as planters outside it, and a profusion of coloured flowers spilled over the sides. It was painted gleaming white, with black Tudor-style leaded windows, and looked like another building from a fairy tale. He would have to bring Grace here. 'We'll stay for a few days, I think. I have some people I need to see at the party tonight, and there are a few guys knocking around who we're interested in. So…'

He bounded up the five steps, and Richard followed him into the dark wood-panelled lobby. Two rooms were procured, and Steven handed Richard his bag. 'See you down here at six o'clock – in black tie – for the party, OK?'

Steven was gone before Richard had time to ask anything, but he wondered what he was doing here. Why was he being put up in hotels and taken to parties? He had absolutely no interest whatsoever in socialising here in Switzerland, but he knew that Dulles was trying to get him out, or he said he was at any rate, and that he had to sit tight and wait. He might as well be babysat by Steven, he supposed. But it was all very strange.

He noticed there was a barber shop down the street, so he walked down and got a badly needed haircut and shave. For the first time in months, he felt and looked like himself again. As he strolled up the street back to the hotel, the pleasure boats bobbed on Lake Geneva as if there was nothing whatsoever wrong in the world, and it struck him that he was going to survive. Steven was right – the war was turning. Surely it could only go in the Allies' favour now, with Russia's might brought to bear on the Eastern Front, and Britain and the US on the west and south? But he recalled Dulles's sum-up and realised that it was far from over. He would give anything to get a message to Grace, but his best chance of getting out of here was to do what Dulles said. And Steven had been told to babysit him – in other words, watch him, he was sure – so he'd just have to put up with it.

CHAPTER 31

MONTREUX, SWITZERLAND, AUGUST 1943

The party was a huge affair judging by the number of cars approaching the magnificent house overlooking the lake. Mont JeanClare was an old convent bought in the thirties by a wealthy banker named Gerhardt Gruber and completely renovated, according to Steven, who was driving them up a corkscrew hill from the lakeshore to the house nestled in the foothills of Rochers de Naye, the seven-thousand-foot-high peak.

'Gruber is the beating heart of Switzerland,' Steven explained. 'Nothing happens here without his nod. He controls everything, even up to the government, and he is a slippery snake. Despite being the hosts and the toast of Swiss society, he and his wife are feared more than liked. They are self-serving. Dulles thinks he's ideologically more of a Nazi than anything else, profiting at every hand's turn. But they run with the hares and hunt with the hounds, and to be on the wrong side of them is not good, not good at all.' He shook his head. Richard wondered what that meant.

'Don't worry.' Steven changed back to his upbeat self once more.

'Everyone is going to play nice, on the surface at least. Even in Switzerland some luxury goods can't be sourced, but these guys always come good, so I hope you're hungry. Last time there was a pig on a spit, as well as that damned fondue.' Steven's expression told Richard all he needed to know about his new friend's attitude to Swiss cuisine. 'I sure miss my mama's hot dish. I write and tell her all the time how I dream of it. Noodles, a can of mushroom soup, loads of pork... Man, you'd lick the plate clean, don'tcha know. What do you miss? Your mama's cooking?'

Richard smiled as the vertiginous drop down the mountain to his right made him once again grip the door handle in fear for his safety. 'My mother can't boil an egg, but Esme, the lady who helps in our house, oh, she can cook. She makes fried chicken with this crispy coating – I don't know how she does it. I never asked – although I should ask her one day. And collard greens and cornbread and peach cobbler...' His mouth watered at the thought.

Steven laughed. 'You sure sound Southern when you talk about food, peach caaahbler, caawhrn bread...'

Richard laughed at his good-natured teasing. His accent was far less Southern than Esme's or most other folks from Georgia, and he'd tempered it even further in England, but he liked that he still sounded like himself. So much of who he was, was gone.

They were crawling in a line of traffic with a very flash sports car ahead and a limousine behind. There was no shortage of fuel here, it would seem – not for the rich, anyway. It was one of the things he'd admired about England, how the wealthy and the poor bore the deprivations equally. Everyone survived on the ration, and to live ostentatiously, even if you had the means, was not socially acceptable at all. He smiled at the memory of a titled lady who volunteered at the refugee centre with Sarah, telling his sister how to make a pie with suet and parsnips that you had to steam for ages apparently. It had sounded so revolting that Sarah had blanched, and Lady whatever-her-name-was reprimanded her. 'We must all make do, my dear, and it's actually quite palatable if you serve it with Worcestershire sauce.' It had become a running joke in their apartment that they'd taken to calling a 'flat', to say in haughty tones at their meagre and often tasteless food, 'It's actually quite palatable with Worcestershire sauce.'

Eventually they were approached by uniformed groundsmen, who allowed them to alight, explaining they would see to the car for them. Steven seemed fine with that, so they got out and walked down a gravel driveway lined with shrubs and flowers to a large limestone house. From a terrace to the side jazz music wafted over the surrounding manicured gardens. Gathered in their finery, at least a hundred people, ladies in floor-length gowns, men in black tie, socialised. Immaculately dressed waiters circled with drinks on silver trays borne aloft. A cocktail bar had been set up inside the main foyer, with a dizzying array of alcohol, and a handsome young man in a gleaming white shirt was mixing drinks to order.

As they pushed through the crowds, Steven greeted people here and there. Richard followed, a head taller than his Minnesotan comrade, and drew several interested glances. They joined a group of young Americans, and he was introduced as Harry Anderson to a charming if a little coquettish young lady from Delaware and her friend, a more surly girl from North Dakota, who barely nodded at him. They were typists at the embassy, they told him. There was a burly guy from Kansas who seemed very quiet, and two handsome tanned Californian engineers. Both had gleaming white teeth and looked well cared for. The three men didn't elaborate as to their role, and Richard remembered Dulles's instructions – don't answer or ask any questions.

Steven seemed relaxed around them as the conversation moved to baseball.

'Looks like the Cardinals and the Yankees are going to dominate again,' one of the Californians said.

'Yeah, I think the Cardinals will take the National League and the Yankees the American. Cardinals took it last year, so the Yankees ain't going to take that lying down this year,' his buddy surmised.

'You like baseball, Harry?' Steven asked.

He nodded. 'I follow the Detroit Tigers. We finished fifth last year, but I have faith in Del Baker.'

'A Southern boy into baseball? I thought you all played football down there?' the girl simpered.

'We sure do, but I like baseball.'

'Looks like the Senators' long stream of mediocrity is set to continue, so no glory for us...' Steven grumbled, helping himself to two coupes of champagne from a passing waiter and handing one to Richard.

It seemed to Richard that everyone had had the same conversation with Dulles, as the progress of the war was not mentioned even once. It was baseball, and then they moved on to movies and music. The band was wonderful, now playing some Glenn Miller tunes, and one of the girls – he couldn't remember their names – asked Richard if he'd like to dance.

Before he had a chance to answer – he definitely didn't want to dance with her – everyone's eyes went to the stage where a small, glamorous woman had joined the band. She walked regally up to the microphone, her black sequinned evening gown skimming over her waif-thin figure, her ash-blond hair in an elegant chignon. Diamonds glittered at her throat and ears, and a gold watch hung on her thin wrist.

'Our hostess...Madame Ghislaine Gruber,' Steven whispered in Richard's ear before the woman spoke. All eyes were on her as the conversation trickled away.

'*Mesdames et Messieurs, meine Damen und Herren. Bienvenue et Willkommen.* You're all so very welcome to Mont JeanClare, and Gerhardt and I are very happy to see so many familiar faces, and of course, some new ones too. Dinner is a buffet and will be served in the grand salon in an hour. So in the meantime, mingle, have a drink and enjoy the music. Tomorrow afternoon we hike Dent de Jaman. A picnic and entertainment will be provided, so if you don't have what you need and would like to join, please see Hans on Avenue des Alpes – he will ensure you are equipped.'

The girl from North Dakota said something, but Richard blocked her out. His mouth was dry. *It can't be.*

He crossed the room through small groups of people talking and laughing to where the elegant woman was being helped down off the stage. She was surrounded the moment she was on the same level as everyone else, but Richard moved ever closer. *No.* He was wrong, surely.

Within seconds he was standing before her, towering over her. She looked up at him, and their eyes met. A second, a flash, a fleeting moment of recognition. Then a barely perceptible shake of her head – a warning, a pleading? He just stood there as some man thanked her for the lovely party. She smiled and moved away. Richard followed her out of the room and down a corridor where the crowd was thinner.

She turned left down another corridor, this one mainly populated by waiters, and by the noises coming from the cavernous room at the end, he guessed it was the kitchen.

She slipped in through a doorway, and he glanced behind him to make sure nobody was watching before following her. As he did, the door shut behind him. It was a stone wine cellar, about fifteen feet square. They were alone.

'I didn't believe it was you,' he managed.

'It's not what you think.'

'I don't know what to think. You live here, like this, with a man that –'

She put her hand up. 'We can't talk here. Meet me tomorrow at the ski chalet halfway down on the red slope of Dent de Jaman, at 6 p.m. I'll explain everything.'

Then, without another word of explanation, or giving Richard a chance to ask any more questions, Bernadette Dreyfus walked out the door.

CHAPTER 32

KNOCKNASHEE, CO KERRY

The idea of a Lúnasa party to say goodbye to Lily before everyone went back to school had gripped Knocknashee. In the dreary never-ending war, where rationing was getting tighter and tighter, when so many young men and women had gone over to England to join up, when more and more Irish families were getting the news they'd dreaded from the moment their child walked out the door, people were glad to have something cheerful to focus on.

There was baking going on in every house, everyone determined to bring their fair share for the feast. Bríd had mysteriously got a larger than usual sugar ration, and the aroma of her famous caramel pervaded the entire village, making everyone's mouths water at the thought of her legendary toffee apples.

Tilly and Mary had devised a way to make ice cream up at the farm, sweetening it with honey from the hive on the land, and they were experimenting with different flavours. Only Tilly was brave enough to tackle the beehive. She looked a sight as she did so, covered up in a suit made of old net curtains full of holes that had hung in the window of the Worth house, donated by Eleanor, under which she wore a large picture hat that Peggy Donnelly had finally admitted was a mistake of a purchase and nobody from Knocknashee would ever wear it.

Carroll's butchers suggested that they make extra batches of sausages that could be cooked on sticks in the fire, and of course there were spuds wrapped in tinfoil to be cooked in the embers around the fire.

The local boys and girls had spent weeks gathering timber and anything flammable from their homes and surrounding farms and land to build the bonfire, and Grace feared at how high the pile was getting. She'd have Charlie and some of the other men go down to make sure it was secure and wouldn't cause any injuries once it was lit on the beach. The bonfire wasn't for another ten days, but the fuel gathering had become somewhat of a competition among the boys, each trying to outdo the other.

Fiddles and banjos, accordions and tin whistles, in any house that had them, were being tuned up and dusted off, and the O'Connor boys supervised the creation of a platform for the dancing.

The excitement was palpable everywhere, and for everyone, except, it seemed, the McKenna household. Dymphna McKenna was unusually absent from the party preparations, and Grace noticed that Kate wasn't spending as much time with Cáit and Molly as she had done in the past. In fact Grace was nearly certain the little girl was avoiding her. She made a note to herself to ask Charlie about it the next time she saw him.

Lucky for Cáit and Molly, they didn't have to wait until Christmas for their new dresses. Maurice had declared that for the Lúnasa celebrations, the Fitzgerald girls would be decked out in the finest of garments and there was going to be no more about it. Tilly had expanded her herd considerably in the last year – she was now milking twenty cows and had ten beef cattle too – and Maurice did a lot of work for her, so he had saved up some money to treat them.

Patricia was getting a new dress too, though she'd tried to argue that the one she had was fine.

'The one you have, my darling wife, is falling off you because you've gone so slim. And I can't even tell what colour it once was because it's been washed that often. I know you never want anything, but please, let me for once treat my wife and my daughters to something nice. Please?'

Grace had felt a rush of love for her brother, but also a pang of pain; nobody would ever do something like that for her again.

As if reading her thoughts, Maurice turned to her. 'Grace, you must come too. Everyone will get a new dress. Tilly got a great price for the calves at the mart, and she gave me a nice bonus, because she said if I hadn't done all those nights up at the farm over the winter months when the herd were calving, we'd have lost a few, so she insisted on splitting the profits with me. I told her there was no need as she paid me a fair wage, but she wasn't for turning, so I have it to spare. And I'll be getting a proper wage once I start in the secondary school next month. So please, let's do it.'

'You're very kind, Maurice, but I have a dress I love that I'm going to wear. It's one Richard used to admire on me, so I'm going to wear that. And I'm actually going up to Tilly's later. She's asked me to mind Odile for an hour or two, and I said yes.'

'Are you sure?' Patricia asked as she scraped the last of the porridge out of the pot and put it on Molly's plate. The child was still woefully thin, and they were all trying to feed her up. 'We could go a different day?'

Grace was touched by how kind her family were, always anxious to include her in everything, but they needed a day to themselves and she was happy to let them go.

'Not at all.' She went to her purse and extracted two shiny shillings. Then she addressed her little nieces as she gave them one each. 'I want you to go off, have a great day, buy beautiful dresses. And when you're finished shopping, I want you to go to the Lobster Pot for fish and chips for your tea. And no arguing from Mammy and Daddy. Fish and chips and an ice cream for afters before you get the bus home.'

Maurice began to object. 'Grace, there's no need –'

'This is between me and my nieces, if you don't mind.' She mock-glared at her brother, which made Cáit and Molly giggle. 'It's nothing to do with you.'

'Thanks, Aintín Grace,' they chorused, hardly able to believe their luck.

'Will we bring you something back,' Molly asked, 'to make you smile? I don't like it when you're sad.'

Grace forced the tears back; she could not be like this miserable old spinster aunt on the brink of tears all the time. These poor little girls had seen enough in their short lives. 'I was very sad, but I'm mostly all right now. Do you know what would make me have a big, big smile?' She forced a big beam onto her face.

'What?' her nieces chorused enthusiastically, and she was so touched at how much they wanted to make her feel better.

'A ribbon for my hair. A red ribbon that will match my dress to stop my mad head of curls falling all over my face for the Lúnasa party.' She laughed. 'Would you bring me a ribbon?'

The girls looked to their mother to make sure they weren't making promises they couldn't keep. And Patricia nodded with a smile.

'We will, Aintín Grace. We'll get the nicest one in the whole shop,' Cáit declared.

'Well, we'll be the belles of the ball in that case. Now off you go so you don't miss the bus.' She shooed them out the door.

No sooner were they gone when Charlie arrived with a letter for her. The postman looked somewhat harried, Grace thought, as he entered the kitchen. She propped the letter behind the clock to read later. It had American stamps but handwriting she didn't recognise.

'Is everything all right with you, Charlie?' she asked. 'You look a bit frazzled, if the truth be told.'

He sighed and plonked himself down at her kitchen table. 'The telegram machine is on the blink, we don't know if it's something wrong with our machine or if it's a problem with the Posts and Telegraphs. And as usual, no information. It's dead as a duck anyway and poor Nancy is demented trying to fix it. No hope though.'

'I'll make a cup of tea, so,' she said, and she filled the kettle with water and placed it on the stove to heat. 'Is that all? You seem, I don't know....'

He sighed again. 'Poor Lily,' he said at last. 'She's finding it hard here, Grace. Harder than I think any of us thought it would be.'

She suspected that Dymphna could have told Charlie it would not be all plain sailing for Lily in Knocknashee – nor for the rest of them. But she hadn't been asked her opinion in the matter before Charlie agreed that Lily could come back with them from New York.

'Is Dymphna all right?' she asked.

Charlie shook his head. 'We had an argument,' he replied glumly. 'A bad one.'

'Over Lily?'

He nodded and told Grace what had happened. He'd just come back from his round and sat down at the kitchen table to read the paper. Dymphna was in the kitchen making bread.

'Are you still taking Paudie fishing this afternoon?' she'd asked. Something in her tone caused Charlie to look up from the paper.

'Is everything all right, love? You seem a bit –'

'I'm fine. Are you taking him? He's been going on about it all morning, apparently the mackerel are in.'

'I will,' he replied. 'I said I would. Lily wants to come too, so we can all go. She's never gone fishing before, which struck me as strange considering they live by the sea. But Joey wasn't interested in it, so she never went, she said. She'd be nervous of gutting the fish, but I told her she'd get used to it.' He chuckled.

He returned to the paper, but the set of her shoulders as she kneaded the dough told him she was seething. She was a patient and kind woman, but she could be fiery when riled, and something was annoying her, he was sure of it. The way she added flour and buttermilk to the bowl, her jaw set, focusing hard, made him wary.

He put the paper down again. 'What's wrong, Dymphna? Because something is wrong. I'm not thick.'

'Nothing, I told you.' She added more flour to the sticky mixture in the mixing bowl on the table in front of her.

'Well, if you won't tell me, I'm not going to try to guess. I'm not a mind reader. So let me know when you want to talk to me.' He knew he sounded petulant, but he was tired of the constant tension in the house.

'You know perfectly well, Charlie, so don't pretend you don't,' she muttered.

'I don't, actually. For God's sake, Dymphna, can't we just have a conversation and get whatever this is out in the air?' He was exasperated now. Séamus was cutting his back teeth and was awake most of the night screaming, so they were all exhausted into the bargain. Lily had not endeared herself to his wife by groaning loudly in frustration at the baby in the middle of the night. She was also sharing Kate's room, which was tiny, and Lily's big suitcase blocked the door, which drove Kate mad, but there was nowhere else to put it.

'All right, since you don't seem to be able to see what's under your nose. This isn't working.'

'What isn't working?' He tried to keep his voice neutral.

'This. Lily here,' Dymphna said, her fury barely contained.

'Why not?'

'Because she doesn't fit in, Charlie. She's come over here with an image in her mind of what Ireland would be like, all leprechauns and castles and magic, when the reality is it's a poor place, with little respite from hard work and harsh weather, the war grinding on and making everything even more scarce than normal. She doesn't know us, and we don't know her. It doesn't help either that she doesn't speak Irish, and our English isn't that great, so we can't even talk to her properly.'

Charlie didn't want to hear any of this, but Dymphna was determined that he would. 'Kate is sick of her. She takes up all the room in the bedroom. She refuses to learn any Irish, and she wants you to herself all the time and makes Paudie and Kate, and even little Séamus, feel like they are in the way.' She turned the bread out onto the floured board and began pounding it. 'And she treats me like I'm the staff.

'You landed her in here on top of us when we don't have room for her, and she's upsetting everyone. I don't know what you – or she –

thought was going to happen, but it's not fair, Charlie. We barely have enough to go around, and she eats like a horse, and now to top it all, Eilis O'Sullivan, Kate's best friend, isn't talking to her because her sister Evelyn is heartbroken over the eejit Fiachra O'Flynn who broke it off with her to moon around after Lily.'

'What?' Charlie grimaced, this was new to him clearly.

'Well and you might look bewildered. Honestly, all you can think about is the happiness of your precious daughter, when her arrival has caused nothing but trouble for the rest of us.'

'Ah, Dymphna, that's not fair...'

'Fair? You want to talk about fair?' She rounded on him, her eyes glittering. She had a temper. It was seldom seen, but when it did show, it was best to run for cover.

'Yes, I do. Lily is my daughter, love, I can't just abandon her. She wanted to come. She wanted to meet you all. And I know it's a tight squeeze in here and things are scarce, but we'll manage, and it means a lot to me to have her here. This is her home too –'

'Ah, do you hear yourself?' Dymphna thundered at him. 'This is not her home! This is *our* home. And Paudie and Kate feel so left out. You have no time for them or for me since she turned up.'

'She's my daughter, Dymphna, my child, what do you expect?' Charlie couldn't believe his wife was being so unreasonable.

'And we're not?' A sad little voice piped up from the doorway, and Charlie spun around to see Kate standing there.

'Ah, Kate, love. It's not that, but –'

'I hate her, Charlie.' Tears flowed down Kate's cheeks. 'I wish you'd never found her. I thought you loved us like your own, but it wasn't true.'

Charlie gaped in astonishment as a sobbing Kate stormed out of the house and headed up the street. 'She'll be all right, Dymphna, won't she?' he asked tentatively.

But his wife simply glowered at him and shoved the bread tins into the oven with more force than was strictly necessary.

'Oh, for God's sake...' Charlie pulled on his post office jacket and left to follow Kate.

'Oh, Charlie, I'm so sorry,' Grace said, when he had finished his tale of woe. 'But Kate is all right, is she?'

Charlie nodded. 'I found her at the O'Sullivan house. She'd calmed down, but I left her there. She wanted to stay with Eilis. I think she didn't want to go home in case Lily was there.'

'She'll get over it,' Grace said kindly.

'I know she will, but I wish it had never happened. None of this is what I wanted. For them or Lily. And I know Lily's not happy either. But I just don't know how to make it better for any of them.' He looked over at Grace dolefully. 'You couldn't help me, Gracie, could you?'

'What do you want me to do?'

'Talk to Lily, maybe? See if there's anything we can do?'

'Don't you think it might be better if you talk to her?'

'Maybe,' he said sadly, 'but I don't think she'll listen any more than Kate will just now.'

She sighed. 'All right, Charlie. I will talk to Lily as soon as I can, but you need to talk to Kate and sort it out with Dymphna. Promise me you'll do that.'

He nodded, looking relieved. 'I promise, Gracie. And thank you. You're a great girl.'

CHAPTER 33

That afternoon Grace kept her promise to Charlie and went looking for Lily. She found the girl down by the beach, watching Charlie and the other men making the bonfire safe by taking several of the high things off it, much to the disappointment of the Knocknashee boys.

Lily stood a distance away from the group, near the flat rock where Tilly and Grace had their special spot, and Grace felt a pang of sympathy for her. The young woman had wanted this so badly, and it was a shame that it had not worked out exactly the way she imagined it. But that was life for you, Grace thought with a sigh. After all, her own life had hardly gone to plan either.

Lily smiled at Grace as she approached and nodded as Grace asked if she could join her.

'It's amazing to think they are doing all this for me,' Lily said, pointing at the activity down by the bonfire site. 'They're all so very kind. And I'm not sure I'm worth it.'

'They're doing it for themselves as well,' Grace replied. 'And you are worth it. You are a reason for all of us in Knocknashee to celebrate.'

The girl smiled again, her eyes welling with tears. 'It's very kind of you to say that, Grace, but I'm not sure Dymphna and the others would agree with you.'

'It's a strange situation, Lily, for all of you. And we'd no right to expect it to go without some upset to someone, did we?'

Lily nodded. 'Mom and Dad did try to warn me, but I wouldn't listen.'

'They are wonderful people, and they love you very much. But sometimes we have to find these things out for ourselves.'

'I guess I thought it would be easier,' the young woman murmured. 'I thought I would just fit in without any problems. But I didn't count on everything being so different here. Not bad or awful,' she added hastily. 'I don't think that at all. But …different. I guess I thought it would be like a magic kingdom from a fairy tale, with ruined castles and ancient forts from six thousand years ago. And it doesn't help that I can't understand a word of Irish. I'm trying, but I'm not very good at it, I'm afraid.'

'How are you feeling about going home?'

'I'm kinda looking forward to it. But also kinda sad about leaving, despite everything.'

'We'll really miss you,' Grace said. 'But you'll come again now you know where we are, won't you?'

'Do you think I should?'

'Oh, definitely. There are people here who love you dearly. And others who would love you dearly, given a proper chance. You have to understand, Lily, these are not normal times. Things are very scarce and everyone is a bit fed up, which is making us all grumpier than we normally are. But you just need to be patient and give people a chance.'

Lily looked a little sheepish.

'And I don't mean just a certain young postman,' Grace continued. 'You know that, don't you?'

The girl nodded. 'I wasn't really fair to Dymphna,' she said after a pause. 'Or Kate, to be honest.' She turned to Grace, her eyes wet with tears again. 'I thought they didn't like me, and so I wasn't very nice back. I get that it's hard for them. The house is so little, and I guess we in America don't understand what rationing really means. We grumble when we can't get stuff we love, but nobody there is going hungry, not like here. But I'll try harder now, and maybe they'll forgive me.'

Grace linked the girl's arm and gave her a smile. 'I'm sure they will, Lily. And I know they will be glad to see you when you come back. Although I don't think Sylvia and Joey will be over the moon to hear you've a boyfriend here, will they?'

'I might not have mentioned it to them.' Lily made a face. 'They're terrified I'm gonna want to stay as it is.'

'Ah, they're just dying to get you home. They miss you terribly, I'm sure.'

'And I miss them. And Ivy. And I'm excited for college, but a part of me is finding it tough to go.'

'Well, Knocknashee isn't going anywhere. It'll be here when you are ready to come back to us.'

Lily smiled and nodded. 'Fiachra took me to see – I'm going to say this wrong – a *fulacht fiadh* yesterday, and we went down into the souterrain. He knows all about this kind of thing. It was amazing.'

'Out on the peninsula? That was a long cycle.'

'I know. I had to borrow Dymphna's bike, and I'm walking like a cowboy today, but it was wonderful to see it.'

Grace could imagine the excitement at going down into the underground tunnels under a Stone Age ring fort, the feeling of being all alone in a world so ancient.

'The *fulacht fiadh* was amazing. When I saw the pit lined with stones, I didn't know what it was, but Fiachra explained how it would fill with water and then they'd light a fire beside it and put rocks in the fire to get hot. Then they'd roll them into the big pit of water, and it became a way to cook a whole deer.' Lily shook her head. 'This place. It's incredible.'

Grace laughed. 'There you go now. And your Irish isn't as bad as you think it is.'

'Oh, it's not good, really, but I know *fiadh* is deer, and I can say a few simple things. But I was wondering...' She blushed. 'How do you say "I love you and I'm going to miss you" in Irish?'

'You'd say, *mo grá thú, is fada liom uaim thú.*'

Lily tried it a few times, Grace correcting her pronunciation. She said it slowly and phonetically – *muh graw hoo, iss, fahdah lum ooh-im hoo* – and Lily repeated the phrase over and over.

'You have it,' Grace declared, once Lily was saying it correctly.

'Thanks, Grace, and not just for this,' the girl replied. 'I wanted to say thank you so much for all you did. I would never have met Charlie, or known Declan, or known anything about my family here if you hadn't made it happen. I'm so grateful.'

'Ah, Lily, it was my pleasure. Charlie has been a kind of father figure to me for a long time, and Declan...well, you know Declan and I married, and I loved him very much. He was so relieved when we found you. It had haunted him, worrying about what might have happened to you. So finding you safe and well and loved by your family was all he needed.'

Lily's eyes filled with tears again. 'I wish we'd had more time. I wish I'd known when he was there that he was my brother.'

Grace put her arms around her. 'I know, Lily, but he knew you were his sister, and he loved meeting you. And every time you wrote to him, it lifted his heart. And Charlie's. Of course Declan should be here. It seems unfair somehow for you to be here when he isn't, but life isn't fair, love. I wish it was, but it isn't.'

'You know,' the girl said through her tears, 'sometimes I see Charlie looking at me and I see the sadness there. I think seeing me makes him think of Maggie. At least when I've gone back, I won't be a constant reminder of all he lost.'

'No, Lily, you're wrong there.' She put her hands on the young woman's shoulders and looked deeply into her eyes. 'He never ever forgot Maggie or Declan, so you couldn't remind him, but he sees his precious daughter when he sees you, and that has made him the most content man on earth. I didn't know Charlie well when Maggie was alive – I was just a child. But I've seen him all these years. He wore his loss like a coat – he never took it off. Until now. Finally he's free to live without the heavy burden of grief. Having you back in his life has done that. So don't ever think seeing you makes him sad – quite the opposite, in fact. He was sad for so long, and now he's not.'

A wistful look crept over Lily's face as she turned and stared out over the Atlantic Ocean in front of them. 'I'm missing my parents, and Ivy, of course,' she said, 'but it's strange. I also feel like I belong here, like this is where I'm supposed to be.'

'That's a natural thing to feel, Lily, because on some level, this is where you belong. But you also belong in Rockaway Beach. Because of how your life has turned out, you're going to now face a future of having two places to call home. You'll be glad to return to each place while being sad to leave the other. That's just how it will be for you from now on. If you accept that, it will make it easier to manage.'

Lily looked at her as if considering asking something.

Grace smiled. 'Go ahead, ask away.'

The girl looked awkward but hesitated only a second before speaking. 'Is this how you face life, Grace? Just accepting things are the way they are? Like the polio, or your parents dying, or your sister? Charlie told me a bit about her. Or Declan dying and then Richard? Is just coming to accept it the way you coped?'

She considered the question for a moment. Was that how she survived, by just passively accepting all that had happened? Probably. She could do nothing to change it, so maybe that was what she did; she'd never really thought about it until now. 'I'm not really sure to be honest, Lily, but perhaps it is. I try to live in the here and now. The past is gone. We can't do anything to change it, and it only exists in our minds, in our memories. And the future, well, that's a mystery. So right now, this minute, I'm all right. I'm sitting here chatting with you, and while a part of me will never accept Richard's death…' She paused. She wanted to be honest, but she would never relegate the loss of Declan to something less than that of Richard; it was different but not less. 'Or Declan's, I have no option but to keep on living.' She smiled at the younger girl, feeling like a very old woman, though she was only twenty-three years old.

'We have to play the cards we're dealt, Lily, that's just how it is.

And this is the hand you got, so play it. Go home to your parents and your sister, and get your education, and do wonderful things, and when you can, come back to visit us. Write and keep in touch. But you can't live permanently in either world is the truth. Because your future is' – she waved her hand – 'out there somewhere. Your destiny, whatever it is, has yet to reveal itself.'

They stood in silence for a moment, the words hanging in the air between them. Then Lily smiled and linked Grace's arm. 'Thank you, Grace,' she said again. 'Thank you for everything.'

* * *

THAT EVENING GRACE sat in her bedroom and read the letter that had arrived that morning. It had been posted ages ago but everything was so slow because of the war, and the telegram machine was still not working. It was from Mrs McHale, explaining how she and Sarah were still trying to find the other two children and also trying to find family for the orphaned girl. Mrs McHale's descriptions – she wrote exactly as she spoke – were long, winding sentences that stopped abruptly or went down rabbit holes of other stories that had no connection to the original thought.

We had a terrible thing happen last weekend at our local parish here, Grace. There were five deaths in the nursing home beside the church on the same day, all of them well into their nineties to be fair, so no big tragedy there, and one of them, Tessie Dirk, was a huge woman, between you and me and the wall, so lifting her was going to test them. But anyway, poor Father Pucillo had to do five funerals at the same time on account of him going into hospital on the Tuesday to get his bunions seen to. His father too was a martyr to the bunions, and his aunt died of corns, I heard, but I don't know if that's true. She had chilblains too, I think. Anyway, he had to do them all because Father O'Leary is gone home on account of his mother saying she's sick. She isn't, in my eye, she's as fit as a trout – she just wants to show off her son the priest to the neighbours. But Father O'Leary is a tender-hearted poor eejit, so when Mama calls, he runs. Well, Grace, the church was packed out the door, and the undertakers, well, 'twas the son – old Mr Gregson is excellent, but his son Wilbur is an awful yoke, very impatient with the grieving. He told one of our widowed parishioners here that her crying was making his myalgia worse. He's a draft-dodger too, flat feet apparently. His feet look fine to me, though God forgive me, 'tis his face he should be worrying about, looks like it was on fire and someone put it out with a skillet. Maybe if they sent him to face Hitler, it might be just the job. Wilbur Gregson would frighten the dogs, the state of him.

Anyway, they didn't bring enough things to put all five coffins on – they have kind of wheeled stands here. But anyway, he only had four, so there was no place to put the fifth coffin. 'Twas out in the hearse and they didn't know what to do.

Mr Lane, the sacristan, very good-looking except he broke his nose walking into a lamppost two years ago, so his nose is kind of crooked since, had an idea. There were some chairs at the back of the porch that the women use during the flower-arranging committee meetings, and so he goes up onto the altar before Mass started and asked the crowd for three chairs for the coffin. But he's from Long Island, and he can be hard to understand at times. Well, if he did anyway, didn't some bucko down the back yell out, 'Hip, hip...' and sure everyone had to answer 'hurray'. The dead got three cheers instead of three chairs. It was all very unseemly, but sure we couldn't help but laugh, so poor Father Pucillo came out onto the altar to the congregation in stitches laughing.

Grace found herself laughing too, and heaven knew, she needed the laugh. But it soon turned to tears as she realised she could never tell Richard about this story, or about anything else ever again.

CHAPTER 34

MONTREUX, SWITZERLAND

Richard was silent for the rest of the evening, finding it hard to make small talk when all he could do was think about the fact that Odile's mother, the Parisian who had made him so many meals in her little apartment in Paris, with her husband Paul and her new baby, was now Madame Gerhardt Gruber, at best the wife and indeed a willing accomplice of an unscrupulous man, profiting off the misery of others.

On the car ride back down the mountain after the party, he tried questioning Steven. 'She's a piece of work, the wife there, isn't she?' He tried to sound nonchalant.

'She sure is, buddy. People say she's the one wearing the pants, but I don't know. They're both in it. Rumour has it that if you want art, jewels, anything stolen from the wealthy Jews of Europe, then the Grubers can sell it to you. For the right price.'

Steven drove as fast down the mountain as he'd come up it, but at least it was pitch-dark so Richard couldn't see the near-certain death drops. 'They can get Nazis the papers they need to go to South America, so that when this is all over, they can get out of Europe rather than face the music for what they've done. Genuine ones too. They say Gruber has influence with the Argentinian government. Selling weapons, moving gold – you name it, the Grubers are in it up to their necks.'

'If they're so blatantly profiteering from misery and handling stolen goods, how come they're so popular?' he asked.

'Because they throw great parties, and you know the old saying, "Keep your friends close and your enemies closer." This is a neutral country, don't forget. We have no jurisdiction here, we're just guests.' Steven pulled up outside the hotel. 'So will we hike tomorrow?'

'Sure, a hike is just what I'd like…' He grimaced, taking in the towering peaks all around them.

'You'll be fine. It's easyish. The picnic is first, then the hike, and afterward everyone retires to Gigi's, the cocktail bar and nightclub on the lakeshore. The après-hike is worth it.' Steven laughed. 'This weekend is the social highlight of the year down here. The Gruber weekend. There will be a formal dinner at Mont JeanClare tomorrow evening. Us riffraff don't get to go to that. High-ranking Nazis, American businessmen, French winemakers, Russian oligarchs, they're on the guest list, but we're mere minnows in the pecking order, so we're excluded. But to be honest, the hike and the cocktails after are more fun anyway.'

'Then we go back to Bern?' Richard hoped that was the case. The closer he was to Dulles, the quicker he might be getting out. He would meet Bernadette, hear whatever she had to say, though he couldn't think of anything that would redeem her in his eyes, and get out of here as soon as possible.

'Yes, probably tomorrow. You can stay with me. I have a three-bed flat to myself, so there's plenty of room.'

'Thanks, Steven, hopefully it won't be for long.'

'Don't hold your breath, buddy. And be grateful you're not in Wauwilermoos, 'cause that ain't no picnic, don'tcha know?'

'What's that?'

'A Swiss internment camp. Anyone downed or seeking asylum or escapees are being put there. It's near Lucerne, but it's not fun. I don't mean to come over all authoritarian, but Dulles is giving you a chance. I don't know why – you must have connections or something. I don't want to know. But he doesn't do second chances, and he has no patience for insubordination. He's fair, but he runs a very tight ship. So if I was you, I'd do as I was told, you know?'

He nodded. 'Message received loud and clear. On my best behaviour.'

'Just stick with me and don't get yourself into anything. Read some books, take some naps. He'll get you out when he can. But as I said, it might take some time. See you for breakfast. Oh, and by the way, Darcy from Delaware asked that I bring you.'

'I have a fiancée,' Richard said. He needed to put a stop to that right away. 'So she's barking up the wrong tree with me.'

'Oh, yeah, you said. She must be something pretty special, 'cause that Darcy's a cutie-pie. I've been trying my luck there for months.' Steven gave a mournful sigh. 'But this good-lookin' stranger rides into town and eclipses the sun.'

'Shut up, Steven,' he replied with a chuckle. 'You were doing fine, and doesn't that girl with Darcy like you – what's her name? She seemed to be hanging on every word you said.'

'Uff da, Joyce?' Steven said without enthusiasm. 'Uh-uh, not for me. She's got a face that would turn milk and a personality to match. Tonight she said she didn't know why everyone raved about how beautiful Switzerland is, that there are parts of North Dakota even better...' He winked. 'Now I'm a patriot, I love my country, and I'm sure there are great folks in flat, barren, windswept North Dakota, but it's more beautiful than Switzerland? Come on.'

Richard smiled, imagining just such a sentiment from the sour Joyce.

He left Steven in the lobby and went back to his room, kicking off his shoes and taking off his evening clothes. It was warm, so he lay on the bed in his underwear.

This was all so surreal. Was he dreaming? Was that it? He was here in possibly the most beautiful place on the planet, but he couldn't tell

Grace or his father or anyone that he was still alive. But he could go to parties as a man named Harry Anderson. He trusted Dulles was trying to get him out, and Steven was probably under strict instructions not to let the newcomer out of his sight. Did Dulles know his father? Was that why he was being taken care of? Or was this something to do with Gabriel? Kirky? Did Dulles send him to Mont JeanClare knowing he'd recognise Bernadette? How could he have? He felt like Alice going through the looking glass. Nothing made any sense.

All he wanted was to get back to Grace.

But he would have to be patient.

Bernadette. She was now Madame Gruber and a cold-blooded parasite getting obscenely rich off the profits of human suffering on a scale not seen in centuries. How could that warm, bubbly woman, adoring mother to baby Odile, become that? What was she going to say to him tomorrow? Assuming he could find a hut or shed or whatever it was halfway down the red slope. After all he'd endured so far, he could probably do it somehow.

His mind went to Tilly and Odile, and Alfie and Constance. Alfie would put a bullet in Bernadette and her new husband without a second's hesitation. They were the epitome of all he hated. Had the war made her into the monster she now was? When the war was over, assuming she wasn't shot for her activities, would she want little Odile here? That sweet little girl who spoke Irish, could she be ripped from Tilly and all she knew and loved to be brought to Switzerland? To a mother who was capable of such evil?

He tossed and turned for hours, so many thoughts crowding his brain. Eventually he must have dozed off because he woke to the sound of Steven knocking on his door. 'Come on, Georgia boy, time to get up!'

Richard got out of bed and padded across the deep-pile wool carpet. The room was decorated with gleaming hardwood furniture, a full-length gilt swivel mirror and large bay windows overlooking the flower-trimmed lake. He'd never closed the curtains last night. There was not a breath of wind, so the snowy peaks of the Eiger and the Jungfrau were reflected in the glass-topped lake.

He opened the door to find Steven dressed for a day on the mountain, carrying two bags.

'A wool sweater, a thermal underlayer, because believe it or not, it gets cold up there, even this time of year.' He thrust the bag at Richard.

'Have you had breakfast?' Richard asked as he dressed.

'You bet. Five hours ago. It's almost two in the afternoon.' Steven opened the windows and went out onto the little stone balcony, where he lit a cigarette. 'I was going to wake you, but I reckon it's been a rough few months for you, so I let you sleep. I had work to do anyway. Unlike you, I'm not really on vacation.'

Richard knew better than to ask what the nature of the work was.

'We can get you a pastry and a coffee on the way. Come on.'

Once again he found himself in Steven's car, driving at breakneck speed up the corkscrew hills, switchback turns coming one after the other as the pines soared on one side and the lake got smaller below in the distance. Higher and higher they went, until they came to a flat piece of ground where people were gathered.

'The picnic is set up on the veranda over there,' Steven said with a grin, pointing to an elaborate chalet with a huge deck all around it. He waved to the people from the night before, who were now sipping beers and accompanied by three additional girls. He parked the car and crossed the road to join them, Richard following behind.

Staff of Mont JeanClare milled around, providing assistance and glasses of schnapps, lemonade, beer or champagne to anyone who wanted a drink before setting out. It seemed the Grubers owned this place too.

He estimated there were thirty or forty people here, mostly young but some middle-aged. The older dowager ladies and distinguished gentlemen of the night before must have thought this pursuit too strenuous. Of Bernadette or her husband there was no sign.

The picnic went on and on and Richard wondered when, if ever, the hike was going to happen. But gradually people started peeling off the veranda to stroll up the hill behind them. Steven explained they waited until late afternoon to walk because it was too hot beforehand, then took off to do something he didn't explain.

His new friend appeared at his elbow an hour later. 'Harry, I'm sorry, buddy, but I've got to pop back into town. Duty calls. But why don't you take the hike. It's sure pretty up there, and it only takes an hour. Two at the most, if you stop to smell the flowers. I'll see you at Gigi's later. Someone will give you a ride back to town.' He'd been gone for most of the picnic, but Richard had made small talk with a variety of people. Harry Anderson was no more unusual than anyone else here, so his presence didn't seem to cause any suspicion.

It was a stroke of luck, actually, because now he didn't need to find a way to shake Steven off to meet Bernadette.

The route was well marked, and the trip would have been pleasant if the circumstances were not so peculiar. He couldn't imagine how the conversation would go. Something told him it wouldn't be just a friendly chat.

The guys were too busy flirting with the new girls – local Swiss, who had just finished attending some fancy school run by nuns and were dying for a bit of fun – to take any notice of him, so he wandered off on his own. The red slope was the walking trail in the summer, he'd learnt, so he assumed the chalet was somewhere on the route. The crowd had thinned out into small groups of two or three people.

He saw the guy from Kansas, who was now with a middle-aged woman, and gave him a wave, which was returned with a nod. He wondered what his story was.

If everything was bugged, as Dulles hinted it was, then the outdoors was probably the only safe place to talk. The words Dulles had said to him, *nothing is as it seems here*, were making more and more sense.

He deliberately slowed his pace. It was just coming up to five in the afternoon, and Bernadette had said six o'clock, but he didn't know how far away the rendezvous was or if it was on the route or off it.

Groups were walking in pairs and foursomes, but they were all strangers to him. He strolled on, trying to look inconspicuous, and as he came over the brow of a hill, he saw a wooden house on the horizon. Was that the place? He hoped so. He should be right on time if that was the right spot. How would he get in there, though? There were hikers before and behind him; he'd surely be noticed if he struck off the trail to the chalet. Though nobody would probably care, he remembered Steven's warning – *Don't do or say anything to draw attention.*

Either side of the trail, there was a grassy verge of about twenty feet or so before it gave way to forest. He glanced behind as a man a bit older than himself ducked to the nearby trees to answer the call of nature. That's what he'd do. Slip off the trail as if to get a bit of privacy, stick to the trees for cover and approach the hut from the northern side where the forest looked much denser.

A group of three women, deep in conversation in French, gave him a smile and a greeting as they passed. Behind him were two men; he had no idea what language they were speaking, but they seemed engaged with the topic they were discussing so he wasn't worried they were watching him. Why would anyone be watching him anyway? Dulles and Steven had made him jumpy.

He followed the plan, walked for another hundred yards and then ducked off to the left, noticing that the men behind him glanced in his direction. Once he got to the trees, he dropped his backpack and made to open his trousers, his back to the path. They looked away and walked on. Once he was sure they were well gone, and before another cluster of people gained on them, he took the chance to retreat into the trees and, within a moment or two, was deep in the forested foothills. He carried on upwards, the going a bit more difficult without the benefit of a path, but it was safer this way. Thirty minutes of steady climbing, and his back was wet with perspiration. He wished he'd brought some water. As he climbed a ridge, he could see the back of the chalet to his right. All he had to do was drop down behind it and go in.

The little house had a small yard at the rear, with boulders along the edge, presumably to hold back snowdrifts in the winter. He watched for a while, wondering if anyone was in there. There was no vehicle, or even a cart or carriage. There didn't appear to be any sign of life. The cabin was more substantial than he'd first thought; there were at least five rooms and plumbing – he saw the pipework at the back – and two open fires because there were two chimneys. It was roofed in dark slate, and the walls were made of a kind of shiplap board, painted teal with pale-blue trim. It was like most things here – so romantic. He could imagine being here with Grace when it snowed, the fire blazing in the hearth and nobody to disturb them.

He dismissed such a fanciful notion. He was here to do a job – to find out what Bernadette had to say for herself – and leave.

He stood behind the house, in the shelter of the trees, and watched. It was ten to six. He'd wait until six and then go in. If there was nobody there, well then, that was that. He'd go back to Bern and wait for his orders to leave. He realised he'd more or less made up his mind about Bernadette anyway; what could she possibly say to exonerate herself?

Part of him didn't want to meet her, didn't want to hear her pathetic excuses. He thought of Alfie and Constance and all they'd endured, fighting fascists and bigots and those who would change the world order with their hate-filled ideology. He thought of Odile, happy in Knocknashee, loved so much by Tilly and Mary and all the community there. Would he tell Bernadette where her daughter was? Did she deserve to know? If he told her and she came and took Odile, bringing her back to this life, luxury funded by cruelty, surely that wouldn't be in the child's best interests? No, he decided as the sun sank lower over the mountain, he wouldn't tell her. He knew where Bernadette was now, and he could tell Tilly all about her and what and who she was; then it was Tilly's call to make.

At six he scrambled down the steep slope behind the house, jumped off a boulder into the small yard and approached the back door. As he raised his hand to knock, it opened, and there she stood. Bernadette Dreyfus, now Ghislaine Gruber.

CHAPTER 35

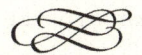

He followed her wordlessly through a small back hallway to a central room with a large fireplace and some comfortable-looking but deliberately mismatched furniture. Bohemian chic was probably what the designers would call it, and it was all designed and planned, nothing to chance.

'Drink?' she offered, speaking for the first time. She seemed nervous, not the self-assured woman who'd addressed the crowd last night.

'Water, please,' he answered, and accepted the glass she handed him, having poured it from a crystal decanter on the sideboard.

'Please sit,' she said.

Richard took the seat on one side of the fireplace; she took the other. She was dressed simply in a white shift dress with a square neck, her blond hair in a ponytail. The only indications that she was wealthy were the diamond studs in her ears and the enormous diamond and gold wedding rings on her left hand. She looked exhausted, dark circles under her eyes, and her face was drawn. She'd been not exactly plump when he knew her back in 1940 but certainly curvy, but now she was angular and waif-like.

'What's going on here, Bernadette?' he asked eventually.

'Richard, please, all I ask is that you hear me out, all right?'

He sighed and nodded.

'I know how this looks, bad, I'm sure, but this is not what you think.' Her accent was still French, about the only thing that remained of the woman she was.

'So you said. So what is it?'

'When I escaped from Paris...well, when Constance, Alfie and I escaped, hours before the Nazis arrived to our flat, we were separated in the melée. Paris was in chaos. I fled to the Bois de Boulogne, hoping we could be reunited there, but it was impossible. I hid. I lived outside. There are several abandoned places there, and a week or so after I lost Constance and Alfie, I was hiding in a house, in the home of some family who'd fled, hiding beneath the floorboards, when I was discovered and arrested.'

Richard hung on every word. So far he had no reason to believe she was lying.

She twisted the fabric of her dress anxiously in her fingers. 'I was put on a train and sent to Ravensbrück, a camp for women. It was hell. Worse than hell. Overcrowded, no food, punishments, work... I can't describe it. The commandant was Max Koegel, who had spent some time in Switzerland as a young man and had become friendly with Gerhardt Gruber.'

She faltered, then steeled herself to continue. 'I got a job working in the commandant's house, in the kitchen, as a scullery maid at first but then as a cook. I was a good cook, if you remember.' She didn't smile.

Richard nodded. He did remember – boeuf bourguignon with roast potatoes, coq au vin with crusty French bread, all washed down with red wine. 'Go on,' he urged.

'Well, Gruber was even then making trips to Germany, buying confiscated items from high-ranking Nazi officers, but it soon became apparent that small jewels were being smuggled to the camps, confiscated on arrival of course, so the commandant did a nice trade in selling them. Gruber was a buyer.'

'So that's how you met him?' he asked, not sure he was ready to hear a story of love and rescue in the circumstances.

'Yes, he took an interest in me. We would talk. He would visit the kitchens after the meal, and we talked some more. He gave me extra food, a pair of shoes one time. Koegel had no idea who I was. I had no papers and so I said I was Cecille Marchant from Paris, a cook. They knew I'd had a child. I had stretch marks on my stomach and when I was arrested, I was still producing milk, but I said my child died. There were so many of us women, Polish, Dutch, French, Belgian. They didn't care. I could work, I could cook, and the commandant liked my food. He was well travelled and liked French food.'

'So what happened?'

'One time when Gruber came to do a deal on yet more jewels, I served dinner as usual, and afterwards both Koegel and Gruber came down to the kitchen. I was terrified of Koegel. His eyes were dead – he was a monster. I stood there with my head down as he said, "Go now, with Herr Gruber, this minute. You were never here, we never met."

'Gruber took my hand and led me out of the kitchen, up the steps and out to his waiting car. He told me to climb into the trunk, and I was so scared, I just did it. Koegel would shoot a woman as quickly as look at her. He starved people to death just because he could. There was enough food there – I saw the stores with my own eyes – but he wouldn't distribute it.'

Richard sat and listened. The sunlight coming through the window turned a buttery yellow and orange as the sun began to set.

'We drove, I didn't know where, I don't know for how long – hours, I think. And then we stopped. The trunk of the car opened, and Gruber helped me out. He led me into a house. It was empty, a nice house in the countryside. He brought me to a bedroom where there were clothes and a bathroom. He told me to wash and dress and meet him downstairs.'

Birds outside were singing and chirping as the sun set, which was completely at odds with the story he was hearing.

'I had been at the camp for six or seven months by then. I was so thin, but I dressed and washed and did as he told me. When I went downstairs, he had made an omelette and some bread, and he gave me a small glass of wine to drink. I was not used to food. I'd only had thin soup and black bread for months, but I ate it, and though I felt a bit queasy, it stayed down.'

'What did he want?' He dreaded the answer.

Bernadette shut her eyes for a moment. 'He wanted redemption, to feel he wasn't a bad man, to do a good thing to salve his conscience. To be able to call what he did "just business", because under it all, he was decent. He must be if he rescued me, right? He told me that he bought me. Along with diamonds and rubies and sapphires, stolen from the women, he bought me – like a slave.'

'Did he ask who you really were?'

She shook her head. 'He asked me if I was a Jewess. I said I wasn't, and he said, "That's all right then." He slipped these rings on my finger and said from now on, I was his wife, my name was Ghislaine Gruber, we met in Berlin. I'm French but was visiting friends in Berlin, we fell in love, and we got married. We moved back to Switzerland. He's Swiss, and now we live like this.' Bernadette opened her hands to incorporate all of their surroundings.

Silence hung between them.

'Are you not going to ask about Odile?' he said at last.

She gave a small sad smile. 'She's better off, wherever she is.'

'And you can just live like this, profiting on the misery of others?' He tried to contain his outrage, but it was hard.

'I'm not finished,' she said quietly.

'Go on.' He sighed, not sure how much more he wanted to hear. He felt for her, of course he did; that camp sounded horrible, and he didn't blame her for allowing herself to be liberated. Of course she should have, but did she have to carry on with this life?

'Paul was a Jew, as you know, but he was also a communist. We all were. Before anything else, we were communists. Once I was here, I thought I might be able to help somehow, to do something, to progress the war effort. Gerhardt was gone a lot. He trusted me completely, and I had time to make connections and meet people.' She stood then, licked her lips to moisten them, smoothed her dress over her slim hips and went on. 'Switzerland is a melting pot, every side and faction, the idealists, the greedy, the altruists, the communists, the resisters, the self-servers – every type and breed of person is here now. I became the perfect hostess. Money was no object, so we have the best of everything. Gerhardt was happy. It meant more contacts for him, more money to be made. Our events became the most sought-after invitation in the country, possibly in Europe.

'I met a man called Henri Laballe, not his real name, and he was working for Russian intelligence. Over months, we discovered a common outlook, and he recruited me as an agent for the Kremlin. At last I was able to do something concrete to help. Russia was doing wonderful things on the Eastern Front, and with more accurate intelligence on what the Nazis planned to do next, they could strike harder and deeper at Hitler's war machine, thus ending this war.'

Richard was nonplussed. This conversation was taking a turn he could never have anticipated. 'So you're telling me you're a Russian spy?' he hissed incredulously. 'And you expect me to believe that?'

'I do,' she said simply, 'because it's true.'

'And where do you get this so-called intelligence that you can pass to Moscow?' He didn't know what to believe.

'From the most accurate of all sources. The Nazis themselves.' She smiled.

'What? I'm confused...'

'Many of the Germans who come here, high-ranking military men and influential men of business, want this over now. They think Hitler is a madman. One of my associates has links to a German communist called Beppo Römer, who vowed to assassinate Hitler after the Night of the Long Knives. He failed but has tried since...' She sighed and took a mother-of-pearl cigarette case from the mantel, extracted a cigarette and lit it. She offered Richard one, but he declined.

'So they pass information to me, which is sent to Moscow and informs the decision-making there.'

'And nobody knows you do this?'

'No.' She shook her head. 'Well, that's not strictly true. Some do, a select few. But generally, no.'

'And your husband?'

'Totally in the dark, would never suspect even for a second. I claim to find politics boring and too hard to understand. I talk about fashion and food and gossip. He thinks I'm a pretty but featherheaded woman. But I ply these Germans with drink and feed them and loosen their tongues as well as their belts, and they –'

Richard jumped as the room door opened.

'Sing like canaries,' said the man Richard knew as Gabriel.

'Don't worry, Mr Lewis. Mrs Gruber works with me too, but our friends in the Kremlin don't like to share, even though we're supposed to be on the same side, so we keep that under our hats.'

'I don't understand any of this,' Richard admitted.

'I'm sure you don't. Most of the time, neither do I, but suffice to say, Mrs Gruber is the best asset we have.'

'And why are you telling me this?' he asked. 'Why did you help me?'

Gabriel looked exactly as he had that night in the French prison. He was dressed in a light-coloured suit with a clean white shirt and polished shoes. He helped himself to a drink from the sideboard.

'I owed Mrs Gruber here a favour. Her husband and I are in a similar line of work, but unlike him, the items I deal in are sold and bartered and used to bring about the defeat of the Nazis. The goosesteppers love me, think I'm one of them, but I almost had my cover blown recently, and Ghislaine here got me out of a very sticky situation. Used her influence, shall we say, vouched for me as a true believer of the dreams of the Führer, even got old Gerhardt to sing my fascist praises too, so the top brass believed it and I was off the hook. I said if she ever needed anything, just to ask. You were the favour. You saved her child – she owed you.' Gabriel sat down on a sofa and crossed his legs.

'I'm still confused. How did you know I was even here?' His head was spinning.

The man rose again and left the room, while Bernadette said nothing.

'Bernadette, please, I don't know what's going on...'

'Just wait,' she said with a smile.

What was going to happen? Were they going to shoot him now? Was that how this would end? Why would they, though? Because he knew who they were? But that wouldn't make any sense. They were on the right side, if they were to be believed. They were on the same side as him.

'Tell me, damn you.' He stood, sick of this game. 'How did you know I was in prison in France?'

The smile that lit up her face reminded him of the old Bernadette – there she was.

'I told them,' a voice from behind him said.

CHAPTER 36

Richard spun around. He opened his mouth but no sound came out. How could this be?

'They said you were dead...' was all he managed as Jacob Nunez crossed the room and embraced him.

His eyes welled with tears. 'I thought you were dead,' he managed, his voice choked as he placed his hands on his friend's shoulders.

'I'm not. I'm OK. We made it, Richard. It's OK, pal...'

'But how?' This was added to the other million questions buzzing around his brain.

'Alfie could only get one of us out. Even then, it was tricky, bribes and what have you. It was the toughest jailbreak he ever had to do, but he reckoned best get the Jew out, because you stood a better chance of making it than I did. Using up every favour he had, and exerting pressure everywhere, eventually he got me over the border, told me to find Ghislaine here, said I'd recognise her.'

Richard turned back to Bernadette. 'So Alfie knows you're here, knows what you're doing?' His heart thumped so loudly in his chest, he could hardly hear.

'Yes. We all work together. He and Constance and I, just as we always did.'

'But you give information to the Russians as well?'

She nodded. 'And the Americans. Anyone who wants to defeat Germany.'

'And the Russians are all right with that?'

A glance passed between her and Gabriel. 'Not exactly.'

'So are you in danger?' he asked, and she let out a peal of laughter at the question.

'Every minute of every day, but yes, right now, I'm in danger. The Kremlin suspects me of being a double agent. They don't really have any evidence, but our Russian friends don't need much in the way of actual proof. If I can't convince them I'm not, then...' She shrugged.

'Can't you get away?'

She shook her head. 'No, that's not an option for me. I'm a French citizen, married to a Swiss collaborator. The Allies can't save someone like me. I'm the enemy, remember? Besides, it is taking all the resources they have to save you two. But I am happy to say Mr Dulles has had Steven working on it night and day. Two famous American journalists don't need to be here. You need to be over there, telling people the truth, getting them to send us what we need – more money, more men, more guns, more tanks, more planes, more of everything. We can do it, I know we can, but we need more help.' Her eyes burnt with intensity. 'There's a small flat field further up the mountain. You two are being picked up tonight, so it's time to start out – it's a long climb.'

'So Steven knows about all of this?' Richard asked.

'He does,' Bernadette said. 'His job was to take care of you, reunite you with Jacob here and arrange the plane. He's a good man. We love him.'

Richard recalled the chatty Minnesotan, unable to believe he had such hidden depths, but clearly he had. 'And what about you, and Gabriel and Alfie? We can't just leave you here, especially if you are in trouble with the Russians...'

She crossed the room, taking Richard's hands in hers as Jacob left with Gabriel to get his bag. 'My dear Richard, I will always remember you bouncing my Odile on your lap. How she loved you from the start. Even as a tiny baby, she saw your kind heart.' She put her hand on his face. 'We must all play the cards we are dealt, and these are mine. No matter what happens, Odile lives, because of you. Jacob told me all about Tilly and Grace and Mrs O'Hare, and Knocknashee, where she speaks Irish and is full of fun. Paul and I will be forever in your debt. She has a loving home, a safe, peaceful country to grow up in, and that gives me so much comfort. I can't tell you how much.'

'But what will happen to you?'

She shrugged again, but her eyes were bright with tears. 'Who knows? If the Russians suspect me, they'll either deport me to Moscow for questioning or they'll end me. If my husband thinks I betrayed him, then he might do it. Or if the Germans I've been plying with brandy to whisper in my ear find out who I really am, they will come up with something unpleasant, I'm sure. But none of that matters. Victory is all that matters. Nothing less will do. People die in the pursuit of victory, so many millions already, the fight of good over evil, and if I have to die, then so be it.' She reached up and kissed his cheek. 'Be happy, my darling Richard. Go and marry your Irish girl and kiss my precious daughter and tell her that her *maman* never stopped loving her. And that her papa and I will watch over her forever from the stars.'

Richard was too choked up to say anything, but he pulled Bernadette into an embrace, and she clung to him.

Gabriel and Jacob walked back into the room, Jacob with a camera bag over his shoulder and a warm jacket, despite the heat of the evening. Gabriel threw a similar one to Richard. 'Those Lysanders are freezing once you get any altitude, so you'll need these.'

Gabriel gazed out at the darkening sky..

'Alors, *mes amies*, now we must part. Perhaps we will meet again, perhaps not, but thank you for all you have done, and keep up the good work.' He shook Jacob's hand and then Richard's.

'I'm taking you to the plane,' Bernadette said. 'You won't find it on your own, and we can't miss this. It is not an opportunity that comes every day.' She disappeared behind a bookcase to change into men's trousers and walking boots, then reappeared, pulling a sweater over her head.

'Don't you have a big dinner tonight?' Richard asked, remembering Steven's explanation.

'Yes. I've told my staff to tell my husband I am gone to bed with a headache and women's problems – that will be enough to keep him away. I never do it, but I told him this morning I was having some gynaecological problems and I was seeing the doctor, so he won't be concerned. Besides, this is a men's dinner really. I was only there to meet and greet. I would be dismissed then.' She beckoned them to follow her. 'Let's go.'

As they climbed, Jacob filled Richard in on how Alfie got him out. It sounded hair-raising, and Jacob was so full of admiration for all that the Resistance were achieving. Even that brief glimpse had shown him the power of even a small number of agitators to disrupt things for the Germans. He'd also seen Constance, who he said was looking well, despite a long scar running from her eye to her ear that was created when, under interrogation, a Nazi threatened to cut out her eye if she didn't talk. She didn't.

The small flat field high in the mountains was almost a perfect square. It was fully dark now, and someone had lit candles in jars along what was going to be a makeshift runway.

'The plane can be on the ground no longer than a minute or two. There is really only room for one person comfortably with the pilot in the cockpit, but you will have to squeeze in. Richard, you are bigger, so go in the back. Jacob, sit in front of him between his legs. It will be horrible, cold and cramped, but, please God, you will make it safely.'

As they heard the distant hum of an engine, they looked to the western sky. The plane was coming in to land.

A figure ran across the field to join them. 'Holy buckets, I was scared you weren't going to make it...' Steven panted as he came up beside them.

'Thank you for this, for everything, Steven, it's –'

'You're welcome, Richard.' Steven winked. Steven had known his real name all along. 'Now get the hell outta here, yeah?' He pointed to the Lysander that had just touched down.

Richard ran towards the plane, Jacob, Bernadette and Steven behind. He climbed the ladder; there was no time for more goodbyes. Bernadette was right, it was so cramped, but he did his best to tuck himself in. He glanced out, waiting for Jacob to join him, but Jacob hadn't moved.

'Jacob!' Richard shouted through the hatch, but it was too late. Jacob slammed the door shut, and within seconds, the plane was taxiing down the bumpy grass. Richard manoeuvred himself in the cramped space just enough to see his friend standing beside Steven in the field, giving him a salute.

Then, with an ache in his heart, the realisation dawned. Jacob Nunez had never had any intention of getting on this plane. His best friend was finally getting to do what he'd always wanted – fight this war.

CHAPTER 37

KNOCKNASHEE, COUNTY KERRY

31ST OF AUGUST 1943

The day of the Lúnasa party, the village buzzed with excitement. Grace's house was a busy hive of activity. Lily was being taught how to make scones by Dymphna, while Lizzie Warrington chatted in the sitting room with Nancy O'Flaherty.

The Worth girls were looking after Odile, Kate, Paudie, Cáit, Molly and Séamus by having a very raucous game of hide-and-seek all over the house, thirteen-month-old Séamus being carried on Paudie's shoulders and screeching with delight.

'The sooner we get everyone down to the beach, the better. I can hardly hear myself think!' Charlie yelled over the din the children were making. He and the O'Connors were carrying chairs down for the older and less agile members of the community.

Grace laughed. 'I told them that we won't be lighting the fire until seven, and its only half past five yet.'

Hugh and Lizzie Warrington had come to stay, and Hugh was currently up in the parochial house tending to poor Father Lehane, who had stood on a nail earlier and had driven it up through his foot. Dr Ryan was delivering a baby out near Ballyferriter. Father Iggy had come running looking for help. Medical emergencies were not his strong suit, so he let the Warringtons go to the poor curate, and he stayed in GHQ – as Grace's house was being called – wrapping spuds in tinfoil for baking in the embers.

Having heard about the big party in a letter from Grace – he wrote faithfully every two weeks – Arthur Lewis had sent an enormous box of rockets, which they discovered were fireworks, and an even bigger box of sweets and treats for the children. They could hardly believe their eyes when they saw the tea-chest-sized box of goodies.

Sensibly, Grace said they would be rationed, not all gobbled at once, but each child got to pick three things from the box of unrecognisable delights. The children of Knocknashee deliberated for hours and hours over Hershey bars and Boston Baked Beans, which were chocolate-covered peanuts, Wrigley's chewing gum, something called Goobers, Whoppers, Tootsie Rolls, Cracker Jacks, Cherry Mashes, Rocky Roads and so many other things they'd never even heard of before.

'Whatever you do, keep these fireworks under your eye all the time, will you, Charlie. If they get their hands on them, I can't imagine...' Grace said in exasperation, trying to avoid Molly, who scrambled under the kitchen table as Grace extracted two apple tarts from the oven.

'Pádraig Ó Sé is in charge of them. He's so sparky himself, it should be no bother to him. He told Sergeant Keane not to go reporting that the Germans were bombing us now when the fireworks go off at midnight.' Charlie chuckled.

'Has Tilly the trestle tables set up, do you think? We could start bringing some stuff down – we're running out of space here.' Grace wiped her brow with her sleeve.

'She has. Herself and Eloise spent the whole day at it. The place looks wonderful. The tables are all decked out with every tablecloth in the village – well back from the inferno – and the seats are all set up. The platform for dancing has been extended. A delegation of girls came to young Seán O'Connor to tell him that the one he built wasn't nearly big enough, so like every sensible man since the dawn of time, he did as he was told and made it half as big again.'

'And Murty has set up some horseshoe-throwing games, a tug-of-war and a high jump, so the young guys can show off for the girls,' Lily interjected.

'I met Eleanor up the street – she was beaming,' Father Iggy said. 'Douglas got some leave, and he arrived this morning. And Bobby the Bus told me yesterday that he's only driving as far as Knocknashee tonight because he's staying here for the festivities, so woe betide anyone wanting to go further out the peninsula.' He chuckled. 'He asked could he have a bed in the parochial house.'

'He did not!' Grace exclaimed. 'The cheek of that fella. You know he'll be stotious drunk, don't you? He's heard of Tilly's little industry up at the farm, so that's what he's after.'

'Ah sure, Grace, didn't our Lord himself turn the water into wine for the wedding feast of Cana, and times have been so tough for everyone, 'twon't do any harm for people to let their hair down for once.' Father Iggy was generous as always.

'I suppose you're right, but don't say I didn't warn you when Bobby the Bus is singing his head off in the small hours and you can't get a wink of sleep.'

The priest chuckled again. 'Sure, don't I intend to be out dancing myself till all the clocks.' He winked and grinned at Grace. 'Myself and Father Lehane had a lovely quickstep worked out, but I think he might have trod on the nail on purpose to get out of it.'

'I haven't danced in years,' Patricia said as she buttered a loaf of bread for sandwiches. 'Maurice and I used to love going dancing.'

Grace was incredulous. 'Maurice is a dancer?'

'Oh, he is. Wait till you see him in action, very light on his feet for a big man,' Patricia said proudly.

Grace laughed. 'Well, that's something I'm looking forward to seeing.'

'Do you like dancing, Grace?' Lily asked.

Grace shot her a look that made her laugh as well. 'Oh, didn't you know? They call me Twinkle Toes.'

'Just because you've polio doesn't mean you shouldn't dance, though, should it?' Patricia insisted.

'Well, if I'm asked up, I'll give it a go. Is that fair enough?' She shook some precious icing sugar over the golden pastry.

Dymphna smiled. 'Oh, I don't doubt you'll be asked, Miss Fitz.'

Eventually the time came, and every man woman and child in the village and surrounds headed for the beach.

Betty and Tomásin Meaghar were playing the fiddle and concertina, and a few enthusiastic early dancers were already on the platform. Tilly was manning the drinks stall; tea and blackcurrant cordial were the official drinks, but the barrel of poitín was in full view. The sergeant turned a blind eye, and everyone was grateful. Tilly would make sure nobody got too messy. Fred Corrigan the grave digger and Tomás Kinneally who had yet to give up his hopes of Tilly, were doing their best to flirt with her and Eloise, and Grace smiled. Even if Tilly and Eloise were interested in men, she doubted toothless Fred or the incorrigible Tomás would have had any luck. But still, God loves a trier.

Grace was wearing her red dress, and true to their promise, her nieces had brought her a red ribbon from their shopping trip that she used to tie her curls back from her face.

She settled into a seat and prepared to watch her friends and neighbours have a great night. The food was being gobbled up. People were not hungry here, but they really missed sweet things and treats, and the children were almost dizzy on the sugar in the American candy.

A few more musicians joined the Meaghars, a banjo player and an accordion, and as the night wore on, the dancing became less energetic and more swaying and romantic. There was no sign of Bobby the bus, maybe the bus had broken down again, it was a temperamental old jalopy. This was probably a good thing because the longer Bobby the Bus could be kept from the barrel of poitín, the better.

The sun sank below the horizon as Tilly and then Eloise came to join her. Janie O'Shea was singing – she had a beautiful voice – and couples risked dancing a bit closer now that the darkness had fallen. Miah Danny Gurteen, the local matchmaker, had his eye firmly on all the courting couples – more likely, his eye on making a few bob from the match if it was suitable and he could take the credit for it.

'They look sweet, don't they?' Tilly nodded towards the dance floor as the fire crackled and warmed the briny air. The smell of smoke and sausages, the voices of children playing games in the dunes, the clear voice of Janie O'Shea singing 'She Moved through the Fair' all had an enchanting effect.

Odile was tiring, so she was happy to snuggle up with Tilly beside Grace. Mary joined them and put her shawl over the child, who was now half-asleep, before going to help herself to a nip of poitín.

Eleanor was dancing, her head on Douglas's shoulder. Maurice and Patricia swayed together, his chin resting on her head. And Charlie and Dymphna, and even Hugh and Lizzie, had taken to the makeshift dancefloor. Lily and Fiachra clung to each other like drowning people. That separation was going to be a wrench, Grace thought. Everyone smiled indulgently at the young love.

Eloise got up to take a cup of tea and a slice of cake to Father Lehane, who was sitting with his injured foot up on a bale of hay, and Mary was chatting with Nancy. Grace saw Tilly's eyes follow the willowy figure of Eloise.

'I wish you two could have a clinger,' Grace said quietly to Tilly.

Tilly smiled sadly. 'I do too, but could you imagine? Poor Father Iggy would have to start giving Extreme Unction to those who'd die of shock.'

'I know this is hard, Grace, but you're doing great,' Tilly murmured.

'I'm trying, Til, that's all I can do.'

Janie finished her song and called on Eleanor Worth, who everyone called Knocknashee's answer to Vera Lynn. All eyes went to her as she left Douglas and went to stand beside the band.

Some of the musicians were children in the school, so they knew the tune. They played the opening bars, and then Eleanor sang in her sweet alto.

'We'll meet again, don't know where, don't know when, but I know we'll meet again some sunny day. Keep shining through, just like you always do, till the blue skies drive the dark clouds all away...'

Everyone joined in, even though the song was in English.

'And won't you please say hello to the folks that I know...'

At first nobody noticed the two figures walking across the dark strand. But just before the second chorus, there was a loud cry from Lizzie, and the audience hushed. Eleanor stopped singing, and Tilly gripped Grace's hand tightly.

'Oh my God...' she cried. 'Grace! Grace!'

Puzzled, Grace looked around to see what on earth had happened to make the song die on everyone's lips. The two figures were nearer now, and Grace could see it was Bobby the Bus, and a taller man...

The tall figure ran across the last few yards of sand until he stood before her. 'Grace...' he gasped as stood in front of her. 'Oh, Grace.'

She felt arms behind her, raising her to a standing position, every eye in the village on them now.

'Richard?' was all she could manage before bursting into tears and falling into his arms.

CHAPTER 38

Grace and Richard sat holding hands in the sitting room the following day as Tilly pulled up in the pony and trap. Neither of them had been to bed yet because there was so much to say, so many questions to be answered. Richard told her that he'd telegrammed her and his father the moment he was back in England. Because Nancy's machine was still broken, it had never arrived but he didn't know that.

He said he'd have to go home to see his family soon, but for now he didn't want to let Grace out of his sight. He'd also telegrammed Sarah in New York to say Jacob was alive but still in Switzerland.

The party had broken up after Richard's arrival – it was almost midnight anyway – and everyone walked home, astonished at the turn of events.

All through the night, they sat on the sofa in the sitting room as he told Grace the incredible tale of his escape from France. It sounded to her like something from a novel or a film, but it had actually happened. Richard supposed that Steven must have been in on Jacob's plan to remain and would no doubt be in big trouble...or maybe not. They couldn't bear to be apart so they fell asleep where they sat, a crocheted blanket pulled over them.

They woke at dawn and began talking again, there was so much to say.

Then they washed and dressed and Grace could barely allow him out of her sight to shave.

'So, how is Lazarus today?' Tilly said with a grin as she entered the kitchen the next morning. Last night, in the excitement of Richard's return from the dead, Pádraig Ó Sé – of course – had started calling him Lazarus.

A freshly shaved Richard grinned. 'Remarkably well, all things considered, Miss O'Hare. With full thanks to your brother,' he added seriously.

Tilly smiled. 'Alfie's a menace, but he's a good, decent menace when all is said and done.'

'One of the best. One of the very best.'

'So...' Tilly hesitated, and Grace knew how hard this must be for her. She had heard about Bernadette briefly the previous evening but didn't know the full story.

'Why didn't she come with you?' Tilly blurted out. 'Did she not want to see Odile? Did she not want to save herself?'

'Oh, she did, but she wouldn't.'

'I don't understand.'

Richard indicated for her to sit down. Tilly did so, and Richard spent the next half hour or so explaining Bernadette's situation, while Grace made and served a simple breakfast of scrambled eggs and tea and soda bread.

'I thought long and hard about it,' he told Tilly. 'I couldn't understand myself at first why she would not take the opportunity to flee. But I think I get it now. She knows Odile is safe with you and Mary, and she wants to keep it that way. But it's more than that. She's like Alfie and Jacob in that respect. She's focusing on achieving total victory and destroying Hitler and the Nazis, because only by ensuring their destruction can her little Odile be truly safe. She knows that if she left, her absence might alert the Nazis and the Russians to others who are doing the same good work and endanger them. So she has chosen to stay. That's the calibre of woman Odile's mother is.'

Tilly listened carefully to what Richard told her. Finally, she sighed. 'Bernadette Dreyfus, or whatever she is calling herself now, is a very courageous woman.'

'Yes,' Richard said. 'She is. She is as brave and committed as any of the others working for the result we all want – Alfie, Jacob, Gabriel – and we will owe them all a debt of gratitude when this is over.'

'Odile can be proud of her mother, her parents,' Tilly said, her voice choking with emotion. 'I am sure she will be very happy to meet her after all this is over.'

Richard nodded. 'Yes, I am sure she will. But in the meantime, she will be safe and loved by you and Mary and Eloise, and that's just as important.'

'Yes,' Tilly murmured. 'Yes, it is.'

Tilly left soon afterwards, still visibly upset at what she had heard.

'I didn't mean to distress her,' Richard told Grace.

She squeezed his arm. 'You didn't. She's just torn. She wants Bernadette to live and for Odile to know her mother, but she also doesn't want to lose Odile.'

'I can understand that,' he said, and looking at his earnest face as he spoke, Grace thought she couldn't possibly love him any more than she already did.

She smiled up at him. 'Come on,' she said. 'Let's go.'

He assumed they were going out, but she took his hand and led him back into the sitting room.

Maurice and Patricia had taken the girls down to the beach to begin the clear-up after the big party, knowing that Grace and Richard needed the house today, and it had been like a train station for the last while with everyone coming and going.

He led her to the empty fireplace, his bulk seeming to fill the room, and put his arms around her waist. He dipped his head then and kissed her, softly and gently at first but with growing ardour, as time seemed to stand still and all that existed in the world was the two of them. They'd kissed last night, but not like this.

Eventually, too soon, they drew apart.

'That is what kept me going, the thought of holding you in my arms and kissing you like that,' he said, his voice husky.

'Are you really here? I'm not dreaming? Are you sure?'.

'Not dreaming,' he confirmed.

'You must go home, I know that. You have to see your parents before you do anything else. But I hate the thought of letting you out of my sight again. With our track record...' She gave a rueful chuckle and rested her head on his chest.

'I'll get back as quick as I can, I promise.' He whispered. 'Nothing can separate us Grace, not really. I just wish I had my letters, they were in the flat in London but when Sarah left she was too distraught to think of them and now...well, someone else lives there I guess.'

'One minute.' She left the room and went up to her bedroom, reached into her bedside locker and extracted the box Charlie had given her all those years ago, when the first letter from America arrived. Then she brought it downstairs.

'You have mine too?' Richard rifled thought the tightly packed letters his face incredulous.

Grace nodded. 'When Sarah came to tell me, she came all the way in person. That was so kind of her. She brought your letters with her. I put them with my own, and for the longest time, I couldn't even look at the box, let alone the letters. It hurt too much. And then, I started and I couldn't stop reading them.' She spoke now without looking at him.

'And I felt guilty as well, because even though I grieved for Declan when he died, and I was devastated, it wasn't like when I lost you. Or thought I had. The pain...it was almost more than I could bear. I felt some days like I didn't want to go on. A world without you in it wasn't worth staying in for me.'

They sat on the sofa again and Richard put his arm around her shoulders, letting her talk.

'Everyone was kind, they tried their best. And your parents – they were so generous and open-hearted. Your father especially, but your mother too. They were so welcoming. But it all felt like a dream, or it was happening underwater or something. It was like I was watching myself in a film, trying to comfort Esme, seeing Miranda Logan in tears, poor Sarah as bereft as I was, and your mother trying to help but making it worse and worse with every suggestion she made. I couldn't even look at your brother, you're so like him. He was lovely to me. They all were, but…being there in your place, with your people, but without you…'

The tears that had trickled on and off through the night now flowed in earnest.

He drew her closer and she could feel the beat of his heart through his shirt. She put her hand on his chest, the steady thud reassuring her that this was real, he was alive, his heart was beating, and she could once again look forward to a future with him.

'I can't imagine,' he said, his deep voice rumbling in his chest. 'When I was picked up in Switzerland, all I wanted to do was contact you, let you know I was all right, but that wasn't possible.'

'Oh, Richard…'

She kissed him then, her hand on his face. He traced the Claddagh ring he had given her as an engagement ring with his finger.

'You didn't take it off?' he asked gently.

'No. I never planned to, either.'

'You still don't want a diamond?'

Grace held her two hands out before her. On her right-hand ring finger she wore the engagement and wedding rings Declan had given her, and on her left, the gold Claddagh with an emerald for the heart that Richard had proposed with. 'I don't. This one is perfect, and it will be even more perfect with a wedding ring under it.'

'The sooner, the better.' He chuckled. 'Because it's taking every shred of restraint I have not to make love to you. You know that, don't you?'

She laughed. 'We've waited this long – another small while won't kill us.'

He groaned. 'It actually might, you know… Kill me, I mean…'

'It will be worth waiting for on our wedding night, Richard…at long last.' She ran her hand over his chest, feeling the muscles ripple. He was thinner than she remembered him, but his body had been through so much, it wasn't surprising.

'I know it will. You're everything to me Grace, absolutely everything.' He sighed. 'Thinking of you is the only way I survived.'

'I never stopped thinking about you either.' Grace said, 'Even when you were dead, I just couldn't get it through my head, I couldn't think of you as gone. In my mind you were always alive.' She sat up, 'Your mother too, she didn't believe you were gone.'

Richard paused for a second before speaking and she settled back on his chest.

'You know, when I was in prison, and they would take me out and question me every day, I was so battered from the beatings, everything hurt.'

When he spoke she could hear the distress in his voice at bringing to mind that time and her heart ached at the idea of him being hurt, but she was grateful he could tell her. 'And afterwards, I would be thrown back into my cell, and all I could do was lie there. I was bloodied and bruised and reduced to the most basic essence of myself. I would compose letters to you in my head. Because they controlled where I was, what I ate and drank. They wouldn't let me wash. They controlled my body, they tried to break me, tried to get me to give Alfie up – which I couldn't have done even if I wanted to, because I had no more idea where he was than they did…'

His breathing became ragged with the horror of reliving those awful days and weeks. 'But I knew that for as long as they had no control of my mind, I could survive and get back to you. I kept telling myself that. So, no matter what they did to me, I would just picture your face. Your beautiful smile, wearing a red dress, your green and amber eyes shining. And at night, alone in that dank cell, I would write to you, tell you all about what was happening, how I was bearing up, ask you questions about life here. Sometimes I'd tell you about Savannah, like when I was a kid, or when I was at school, stupid stuff that doesn't matter really. But you were my lifeline. You connected me to my life outside of those four damp walls.'

'Did you ever fear you wouldn't get back?' she whispered.

'So often. There were so many times when it could have gone badly. But somehow I just knew I'd make it back to you, Grace. You and me. It's taken so long, and so many bumps and twists and turns that, at times, it seemed hopeless, but we are destined to be together. I didn't used to believe in stuff like that, but now I know. The day you put that letter in that bottle, our course was set. We sure went in a circuitous route to get here, but let me tell you this...'

He gently raised her face off his chest and gazed down into her face. 'I love you, Grace Fitzgerald, and I swear to you now that I will never ever let you go again. Till death us do part. Deal?'

Grace felt the tears spill down her face. 'Deal,' she replied.

The End

* * *

I SINCERELY HOPE you enjoyed this book, the final instalment of this series, The Last Post is available now for preorder and will be published in December 2025.

Here's what to expect:

The Last Post - the final book in the Knocknashee Series

As the dark clouds of war finally begin to break, Grace Fitzgerald and Richard Lewis glimpse the possibility of a future together after years of turmoil. Their hard-won love has withstood so much already.

Now, as the Allies launch their final assault on the European continent—determined to rid the world of Nazi terror at whatever cost—Grace must say goodbye once again. Richard has a dual mission: to witness and report on the invasion that will decide the world's fate, and to fulfil a promise to find someone who vanished without a trace.

But in Richard's absence, Grace faces her own reckoning. Drawn back to an old adversary, she must fight one final battle. Will their love survive not just the war, but the ghosts of their past?

BY JEAN GRAINGER

* * *

IF YOU WOULD LIKE to hear from me about new books or just my general musings on life, feel free to join my reader's club - just pop over to www.jeangrainger.com - it's 100% free and always will be and I'll send you a free ebook novel as a welcome gift.

ABOUT THE AUTHOR

Jean Grainger is a USA Today bestselling Irish author. She writes historical and contemporary Irish fiction and her work has very flatteringly been compared to the late great Maeve Binchy.

She lives in a stone cottage in Cork with her lovely husband Diarmuid and the youngest two of her four children. The older two come home for a break when adulting gets too exhausting. There are a variety of animals there too, all led by two cute but clueless micro-dogs called Scrappy and Scoobi.

ALSO BY BY JEAN GRAINGER

The Tour Series

The Tour

Safe at the Edge of the World

The Story of Grenville King

The Homecoming of Bubbles O'Leary

Finding Billie Romano

Kayla's Trick

The Carmel Sheehan Story

Letters of Freedom

The Future's Not Ours To See

What Will Be

The Robinswood Story

What Once Was True

Return To Robinswood

Trials and Tribulations

The Star and the Shamrock Series

The Star and the Shamrock

The Emerald Horizon

The Hard Way Home

The World Starts Anew

The Queenstown Series

Last Port of Call

The West's Awake

The Harp and the Rose

Roaring Liberty

Standalone Books

So Much Owed

Shadow of a Century

Under Heaven's Shining Stars

Catriona's War

Sisters of the Southern Cross

The Kilteegan Bridge Series

The Trouble with Secrets

What Divides Us

More Harm Than Good

When Irish Eyes Are Lying

A Silent Understanding

The Mags Munroe Story

The Existential Worries of Mags Munroe

Growing Wild in the Shade

Each to their Own

Closer Than You Think

Chance your Arm

The Aisling Series

For All The World

A Beautiful Ferocity

Rivers of Wrath

The Gem of Ireland's Crown

The Knocknashee Series

Lilac Ink

Yesterday's Paper

History's Pages

Sincerely, Grace

Folded Corners

Allied Flames

The Last Post

Made in the USA
Las Vegas, NV
29 October 2025